D0338531

"Is this the way these bargains are normally sealed? Or do you require a sampling first?"

A sampling? His imagination took flight, but he reined it back in.

"In such circumstances I trust you to know your business and you trust me to know mine."

Marietta Greentree considered this. "Well," she said, "I know my business, but perhaps an entire night is too long for you, Max."

The minx was questioning his credentials as a lover! He gave an angry laugh. "I am not an inexperienced boy, I'll have you know."

"I do think I should test the truth of your claims."

"Very well," he said, a determined glint in his eye. "You asked for it."

Max reached out and took her hand in his. Slowly, watching her closely, he lifted her hand as if it were a succulent dish, then bowed his head to inspect it. With infinite care, he sucked her fingertips, one after the other.

He heard her catch her breath. "I . . . what are you doing?"

"Sampling you," he said.

From behind them came the rustle of silk skirts.

"Lord Roseby," a woman's voice called out. "What are you doing with my daughter?"

Other **AVON ROMANCES**

SARA BENNETT

RULES OF PASSION

AVON BOOKS

An Imprint of HarperCollinsPublishers

This is a work of fiction. Names, characters, places, and incidents are products of the author's imagination or are used fictitiously and are not to be construed as real. Any resemblance to actual events, locales, organizations, or persons, living or dead, is entirely coincidental.

AVON BOOKS
An Imprint of HarperCollins*Publishers*
10 East 53rd Street
New York, New York 10022-5299

First Avon Books paperback printing: October 2005

Avon Trademark Reg. U.S. Pat. Off. and in Other Countries, Marca Registrada, Hecho en U.S.A.
HarperCollins® is a registered trademark of HarperCollins Publishers Inc.

Printed in the U.S.A.

10 9 8 7 6 5 4 3 2

Prologue

Somewhere in the North of England
1841

Marietta Greentree opened swollen eyelids and peered miserably across the small, cluttered room. Her bag lay on the floor, clothing spilling from it. Among the froth of undergarments was the fine silk nightgown she had thought to wear on her wedding night. Her gaze slid away, found the light that trickled through a narrow window. There were sounds drifting up from the stableyard. Grooms, servants, employees who worked and lived at the inn—the voices of those going about their daily routine. Everything normal.

Except for Marietta, whose life could never be the same again.

Gerard Jones, the man she had believed she loved, the man she had trusted, the man who had persuaded her to run off with him to Gretna Green, was

1

gone. He had left her here, in an impoverished inn on the road to the Scottish border.

Her mother, Lady Greentree, had warned her, her sister Francesca had warned her, but she hadn't listened. His unsuitability in their eyes had only made him the more appealing to her—in her youth and romantic idealism, she had been certain that she knew best. They just didn't understand, she told herself. This was love as she had always dreamed it to be! So when Lady Greentree refused to allow the banns to be called, Marietta thought her heart was broken and made the desperate decision to agree to run away with him. He loved her, and she loved him— surely that was all that mattered? She told herself that when her family realized how happy they were together, they would see their mistake and all would be forgiven.

Stupid, stupid, stupid! Marietta groaned and covered her face with the pillow.

Gerard hadn't loved her at all. He had wanted her body, or perhaps not even that. Perhaps he was the sort of character who found his enjoyment in destroying a young girl's heart and reputation. He was the sort of cad who had been secretly laughing at her all the time as he lured her into his trap. And she was too silly to know it.

And yet . . . was being warm and loving and trusting so silly? Marietta had been in love with love for as long as she could remember, and Gerard had seemed a natural progression. She had fallen in love with him, or had she? Was she simply in love with the idea of being in love with him? She had imagined herself Isolde to his Tristan, Genevieve to his Lancelot.

Her heart was numb. She squirmed with the knowledge that she had been putty in his hands—naïve putty, but putty all the same. Gerard had come to her room last night, pleading to be allowed to make her his in truth—that was what he had said, "mine in truth," just like a melodrama. Indeed, as he kissed her and wrapped his arms about her, she had felt as if the entire moment was slightly unreal. Delightful, yes, but dreamlike.

Briefly she had heard a serious voice, a little like her mother's, telling her that what Gerard was saying sounded suspiciously like flummery. But then he was kissing her and saying he loved her and only her, and . . . Her mind skipped forward, finding the scene all too humiliating. In her favor, she had protested a little—a very little—but she was young and inexperienced and Gerard was neither. In fact he had not been the gentle and caring lover she had imagined he would be—she had felt nothing in his arms beyond the creeping onset of doubt and dismay. She had simply wanted it to be over.

With burning cheeks she remembered how Gerard had risen from the bed, afterwards. Anxiously, she had said something about their wedding, about how she hoped her mother would forgive her—already deep in her heart the golden image of the make-believe Gerard was beginning to tarnish.

He had laughed at her. "Wedding?" he said. He began to taunt her, informing her in a smug voice that he had never intended to *marry* her. He had heard that she was the natural daughter of Aphrodite, a famous London courtesan, and he had wanted to sample her firsthand. And really, dear me, he'd had better.

At first she had been too shocked to take it in. She

tried to smile. He must be joking her, she told herself, he must be playing a cruel prank. But he kept on, and slowly, surely, the horrible truth had sunk into her brain.

Suddenly Marietta felt as if she was looking back upon herself from a distance, as if at a complete stranger whose pitiable actions were seriously flawed. When Gerard had closed the door behind him, abandoning her to her fate, he had taken more from her than her reputation. He had stolen something innocent and sweet and trusting, and Marietta doubted it would ever return. She did not want it to return. She swore that she would never place herself in such a vulnerable position again.

With a wince, aching in mind and heart and body, Marietta sat up. She gazed bleakly about her. It was done. They had spent the night together in the same inn. In the same *room*.

That was bad, very bad.

And yet . . . Marietta sat up straighter, something of her old spark returning. She was a long way from Greentree Manor—this inn was well beyond the sphere of her family or those they knew. Had anyone seen her arrive with Gerard? She did not think so. Perhaps she could escape Gerard's cruel trap after all, at least that would be a small victory over him.

Melancholy lifted as new hope surged through her. The situation could be salvaged. No one but she and Gerard knew the truth, and he was long gone. She doubted he would show his face again—he was too cowardly for that. Perhaps, just perhaps, if she could make her way home incognito, no one would be the wiser. She would beg the forgiveness of her family, allow Mr. Jardine, her mother's secretary and family friend, to make up some clever story to account for her short absence. No one need ever know that Lady Greentree's second daughter had fallen into the clutches of Gerard Jones . . .

The chamber door opened and a tall dark shadow stood there. The face was starkly familiar, and the mean little eyes were gleeful. With sinking heart Marietta recognized Lady Greentree's former estate manager, Rawlings. Her mother had sacked him years ago, and he had always resented her for it. What shocking bad luck had brought him to this place at this moment?

"Miss Marietta Greentree!" he crowed. "I thought it was you last night when I saw you climbing the stairs, and then this morning when I heard one of the maids say a young lady had been left high and dry . . . Aye, I see you're surprised to see me. I warned her ladyship many years ago that she was bringing trouble on herself when she took you and your sisters into her home. I was right."

His smug self-satisfaction was plain to see—he hadn't even knocked in his eagerness to discredit her. But Marietta knew all depended upon winning him to her side, and she swallowed what pride she had left.

"You won't . . . won't tell anyone?" she managed, despising herself for the pleading note in her voice.

" 'Course not," he said, "wouldn't dream of it."

She knew at once he had no intention of keeping quiet. She should have saved her breath. In a day everyone in the district would know her misfortune, in a week everyone in the county, in a month it would even have trickled down to London.

Marietta Greentree was well and truly ruined.

Chapter 1

Vauxhall Gardens, London
1845

The gas-filled balloon bobbed sluggishly in the breeze, as if seeking to escape its tethers, reaching toward the distant blue sky. The wicker basket, fastened to the balloon by an iron band and cords, appeared smaller than she remembered, while the crowd gathering to watch the ascent appeared larger.

Marietta wasn't afraid.

No, not at all. She was exhilarated!

She had been planning this outing all week, ever since she had come to Vauxhall Gardens with Mr. Jardine, and for the first time seen a balloon ascent over London. Her breath had caught in sheer wonder and she had begged Mr. Jardine to allow her to pay her money and become a passenger. But he had refused even to contemplate it.

"What would your mother, Lady Greentree, say if

6

I allowed you to do something so dangerous?"

"She would understand that fear has no place in our new world of science and discovery."

"That's all very well, Miss Marietta, but it doesn't alter my decision. You're a single young lady and it would not be proper—"

"*Psht!*" It was a sound she had heard Aphrodite make—Aphrodite the famous courtesan and her real mother. "What does that matter? My reputation is already in tatters, you know that as well as I. If it wasn't ruined long ago by being one of Aphrodite's daughters, then it was certainly ruined by Gerard Jones."

"Your sister Vivianna doesn't believe that for a moment—"

"Then she is deluding herself, Mr. Jardine. Vivianna believes she can make everyone better, but she can't repair me. I am ruined and there is no chance I will ever make a good marriage. I have resigned myself to it. Going up in a gas balloon can make no possible difference to that plain fact."

"Whether or not that is so, I won't let you put your life in danger in one of those . . . those contraptions, Miss Marietta!"

However Marietta was not the sort of girl to be easily thwarted when she had made up her mind about something. At home in Yorkshire, at Greentree Manor, she and her sisters had been allowed a great deal of freedom—to her own cost, unfortunately— and although Marietta knew that things were different in London, she could not see the point of being fettered. Especially when it could make no possible difference to her prospects of finding a suitor, which were already nil.

Vivianna was lucky, she had Oliver, and she had love, but Marietta had destroyed her chances of emulating her sister when she had tried to run off with Gerard Jones. She had wept long and hard when they brought her back to Greentree Manor, not so much for Gerard, whom by then she had realized was a lying rogue, but for her own lack of foresight. Time had resigned her to her fate as the "scandalous Greentree sister"—no matter how interested a man was in her, he soon faded away when he learned of her past. She may wish it was otherwise, that love conquered all, but she was no longer such an innocent as she had been. Love did not conquer all, in fact love was more often than not the crux of the problem.

However all was not lost. She may never live a cozy life as Lord Somebody's wife, but she still had a life to live. Why shouldn't she experience everything it had to offer, and without the fear of exposing her vulnerable heart once more? Marietta had a plan, and she hoped, very soon, to put it into practice.

At the Vauxhall Gardens, she had waited until Mr. Jardine became interested in one of the displays, and then given him the slip, claiming she had dropped her glove and must return for it. "I'll only be a moment," she'd promised. "You go on and I'll catch you up." She'd hurried back to the balloon to have a word with the ticket seller. A ticket tucked safely into her drawstring bag, Marietta had returned to her companion.

Now she recalled what the ticket seller had said. "It's at your own risk, miss. As long as you realize that."

"I do," she had replied firmly.

"Then be here same time next week, and if the

weather permits, you can go up with Mr. Keith."

"Mr. Keith?"

"The aeronaught, miss. Don't you listen to them what says Mr. Green's the best aeronaught in England—I'd leifer go up with Mr. Keith any day!" The lad had said it with a smile.

People, Marietta found, usually did smile at her. Perhaps it had something to do with her petite stature, or her bouncing blond curls, or her open face and big blue eyes. Outwardly she was transparently honest in the joy she gained from life, and people gravitated towards her because of it.

Until they discovered she was ruined, she reminded herself bitterly—then they were quick to avoid her.

"Such people aren't worth knowing," her sister Francesca had said in an attempt to make her feel better. "Your true friends will never desert you."

Francesca was younger than Marietta by only a year, but in appearance and character they were very different: Francesca tall and dark; Marietta small and fair. Francesca was intense and serious, whereas Marietta was, outwardly at least, all light and laughter. But they were close despite all that, and she wished that Francesca had agreed to leave her moors behind and come to London. Her sister had a way of comforting her—of making the truth seem not so bad.

The balloon awaited her, and this time she wasn't about to be left behind on the ground, oh no. This time she'd be up there, in the sky, looking down.

Marietta hurried forward, and the crowd parted for her. The aeronaught, a man of about forty with graying dark hair and lush side-whiskers, was making some last-moment adjustments. He looked up, distracted by the crowd's murmur, and the lad who had sold her the ticket leaned closer and murmured something in his ear. The aeronaught's face underwent a transformation and suddenly he was all smiles.

"Ah, Miss Greentree! How do you do? I'm Ian Keith. We're almost ready to take off. Please, come aboard." He had a slight cockney accent, as though he had risen in the world.

Appropriate, Marietta thought, seeing he was an aeronaught. She smiled back, eager to be aboard, and it was only as she reached to take his gloved hand that she realized there was another passenger already in the wicker basket. He had been partially hidden in the shadow thrown by the balloon towering above them, but now she looked up and saw him clearly. A man. A stranger. And not a friendly-looking one.

Marietta allowed herself to observe him frankly, not for a moment considering it might be more polite to lower her gaze. The Greentree sisters had been brought up to believe a woman should say what she believed and act accordingly, that she should face life head on and never shy away from it. Her experience with Gerard may have dented her confidence, but it was far from destroyed.

Unsmiling, he returned her gaze.

The stranger was certainly very handsome, with hair of a deep mahogany brown and eyes of a similar color. He was dressed in a dark green jacket and buff trousers, and although there was the appearance of a gentleman about him it seemed slightly shabby, as if his valet had forgotten to give him a good polish. A neglected stranger, Marietta thought. A brooding and solitary man with secrets, who was not inclined to laugh and enjoy himself as she fully intended to do.

Marietta found herself wishing he wasn't going up in the balloon with her. His presence threatened to spoil her enjoyment on this, her first adventure since she had made the journey to London from Yorkshire. At least she wouldn't have to make polite conversation with him—he looked as dismayed to see her as she was to see him—and polite conversation meant exchanging the broader details of one's life, and inevitably that led to who she was, and whose daughter she was, and then suddenly the person she was speaking to would find something urgent to do.

The man raised his eyebrows, and Marietta realized she was still staring at him. His mouth quirked, and she discovered that he could smile after all. "Perhaps you'd better get into the basket," he said, in a deep, aristocratic voice that didn't go at all with his shabby look. "If you don't want to be left behind."

There were some steps set against the woven wicker to enable passengers to climb inside. Marietta negotiated them with difficulty. She was hardly in the forefront of fashion—indeed, she was at least two years behind and she hadn't had time yet to visit the London shops—but she had dressed in what she thought was a suitable outfit for a balloon ride. Now the blue wool dress and its modest two petticoats seemed cumbersome. The fashion was changing, skirts were becoming more rigid and hems longer. Marietta preferred the less fussy styles, too many flounces made her curvaceous shape appear even more curvaceous. But today even her Amazone bodice, plain and tightly buttoned to the neck and wrists, felt awkward, while the long ends of her scarf mantella were threatening to strangle her, and her velvet bonnet had been tipped to the side by her exertions.

As she climbed over the edge of the basket, she was just congratulating herself on her nimbleness when the toe of her elastic-sided boot caught. She stumbled and would have landed flat on her face if the stranger had not reached out and caught her.

Her breath whooshed out as she fell against him, his hard, masculine body a bulwark against hers. For a moment she could not think—her mind went completely blank. *Shock*, whispered a voice in her head. *You aren't used to being this close to a man.* But it was more than that. Her senses were overloaded with information: the clean male scent of him, the dark shadow on his jaw above her, the heat of his palm on her back. Marietta found herself a little shaky just from being there, which was ridiculous enough in an untouched spinster, but for a ruined woman . . . !

The thought sent her instantly to the furthermost corner of the basket.

"Thank you," she said, an afterthought.

Politely, he bowed his head; his eyes never left hers, and there was no smile in them. Nothing to tell her that what she had just felt had been experienced by him, too. Indeed the look he gave her made Marietta think he was also wishing her miles away.

"Perfect," she muttered under her breath. "I am about to ascend in a balloon with a man in a mood."

Mr. Keith had finished his preparations. He climbed into the basket with them, swinging his legs over the side with practiced ease. The basket was big enough for five, but it seemed only Marietta and her companion were to be passengers today. "Are you ready?" the aeronaught asked, but it was obvious he did not expect a negative answer. Marietta sat down and clung to the side and nodded vigorously.

"Get on with it, Ian," the stranger said in a deep, impatient voice. He sat down and crossed his long legs.

"Dear me, Max." Mr. Keith shook his head as if he found the other man beyond his comprehension, and then he called out to his helpers. The balloon was cast off without fuss, ballast was thrown out, and they began to rise, quite quickly, into the London sky.

"Oh!" Marietta gasped.

The ground was rapidly slipping away from her. The crowd—their faces lifted—was growing smaller and smaller. There was a strange silence, almost like a dream, as they rose higher. Below her lay Vauxhall Gardens, and then the Thames, and beyond that the bustle of London, with its pall of smoke, stretching away as far as she could see. The Houses of Parliament and St. Paul's dome were visible, looking awfully small, and the green squares and parks stood out among the lines of streets and the boxes that were houses.

"You haven't been introduced." Mr. Keith spoke above the soft underlying roar of the city below them.

Reluctantly Marietta lifted her eyes from the Thames as the breeze tugged the balloon along.

Mr. Keith smiled at her as if he understood her sense of dislocation. "Miss Greentree, this is my friend, Max. Max, this is Miss Greentree."

"How do you do," Max said in a disinterested voice. He gave her a brief glance that was more indifferent than unfriendly, before turning once more to gaze down over the city spread beneath them.

Marietta shrugged off his behavior, and returned to her own perusal of the Thames, a glittering silver snake broken up by bands of bridges, with ships at anchor and steamboats like wind-up toys. Soon they were moving towards Richmond, sailing over fields and hills, leaving behind the smoke of London and its pointed spires.

"Are you enjoying yourself, Miss Greentree?"

Marietta beamed at Mr. Keith. "It is even more wonderful than I imagined, sir."

"Not anxious about heights then?"

"Oh no, not at all!"

He grinned at her, the lines about his eyes deepening. "I am glad. My friend here didn't want to come. I insisted—when I knew you were the only one making the ascent today I thought he would be company for us. Now I wish I'd told him to stay home. He's like a rain cloud in the corner there, threatening to spoil our fun."

Marietta giggled, and then bit her lip when Max shot her a hard look from narrowed dark eyes.

"Perhaps I am not in the mood to enjoy myself," he said in a low voice. "Perhaps circumstances won't allow me to."

Marietta gave him one of her unflinching stares. "But can't you forget your troubles for now?" she demanded, not pretending she didn't understand him. "Look down there. How can you not feel amazed by such a sight? How can your own concerns not seem insignificant, Mr. . . . . eh . . . . ?"

"Max," he said shortly. "And I am amazed. I'm just not in the mood to show it."

Marietta laughed at him because he was so absurd.

She noticed a gleam in his dark eyes. He *did* look like a rain cloud, just as Mr. Keith had said. Or maybe he was more like a thunder cloud—a rather dangerous one. Perhaps it was not such a good idea to tease him, and yet Marietta suddenly and unexpectedly yearned to turn that frown into a smile.

"Haven't you heard of Max?" Mr. Keith said, lowering his voice. "He's the scandal of the moment. He has been turned out of his boyhood home by his cousin. Perhaps now you can sympathize a little with his unhappy mood, Miss Greentree, even if you can't condone it."

"Turned out of his home? No, I have not heard of him. I am only lately arrived in London. How could his cousin do that, Mr. Keith?"

"Well," he considered his words. "This cousin has produced proof that Max is not his father's legal heir. In short, that Max's father is not his father after all."

Marietta's shocked gaze slid to Max.

"Now," Mr. Keith continued on, "we could say 'Poor Max,' and feel very sorry for him, or we could look at the situation from a different angle. We could say that Max has been a prisoner of his upbringing, and now he has a chance to begin again. Start afresh."

"I know what you're doing, Ian," Max said, giving his friend a narrowed look.

"Put aside your woes, Max. Life goes on."

"You do not have as much to lose as I."

"Think of your past as a shackle to be thrown off, Max. Just imagine how much lighter and freer you will be without it."

"Lighter and freer to do what?"

But he sounded resigned, as though Mr. Keith's attempts to cheer him up were something to be borne for the sake of their friendship.

"Max," Mr. Keith said reprovingly, "Miss Greentree is probably the only lovely young lady in London who is ignorant of your situation. You should make the most of the moment, my friend."

"Thank you, Ian," Max said gravely, and turned his face away so that only his profile showed against the pale blue sky. Handsome, wounded, brooding—the words were descriptive of the perfect Byronic hero. If she was Francesca, she would paint a picture of him standing grimly alone on the moors, or write a poem in honor of his moody good looks. But she was not dark and dramatic Francesca; she was generous and impulsive Marietta. And despite her decision not to bother with him, her mind was already seeking for ways in which to tackle the fates and make his life better.

"Mr. Keith," she said quietly, turning again to the aeronaught. "Has Max anything left at all? Of course," with a glance at Max, "you do not need to tell me if it is personal."

"But everyone knows, Miss Greentree. And yes, Max has a few odds and ends remaining." There was a dry note in Mr. Keith's voice that Marietta did not understand but she let it pass. "The thing is, Max loves his boyhood home, and of course he now has to deal with the shame of his birth, and the despoiling of his mother's memory in the eyes of the world. He's feeling a little lost."

"It seems cruel and unnecessary of his father to let everyone know. Such a scandal is normally hushed up. In my own family my uncle has gone to great lengths to hide the slightest whiff of disgrace." That was true enough, Uncle William Tremaine had been appalled when he learned of Gerard Jones and how gleefully the London gossips had taken to the story. He hadn't spoken to her since, but she had heard that he'd declared her "her mother's daughter well and truly."

Marietta edged closer to Max, and he looked at her as if he would much rather she stayed away. But Marietta didn't let that stop her, and in a moment she was sitting beside him in the basket, her arm bumping against him as a stronger gust shook them. He stared down with that haughty lift of his eyebrows, but she had never been easily intimidated and she wasn't now. Clearly Max was in need of some good advice, and Marietta knew she was just the person to give it.

"Can your *real* father help you?" she asked him candidly. "Perhaps he is not even aware yet that he has been blessed with a son."

Max gave a nasty laugh. "Perhaps he took to his heels and left my mother with no choice but to marry another man to cover her shame."

Marietta sighed. "I am so sorry . . . Max. I am in a similar situation myself, you know, so I understand a little of what you must feel. I do not know who my father is either."

Max stared at her as if he had wandered into a nightmare and could not find his way out. Marietta felt her face color. She hadn't meant to tell him that, and her words *had* sounded odd, but she had been trying to comfort him. And anyway it was the truth; she didn't know who her father was. Her mother, the courtesan Aphrodite, knew, but she hadn't spoken of it, and besides, Marietta wasn't sure she wanted to meet him. More than likely her father would want to avoid her, just like everyone else.

"I think," Max said at last, in a weary voice, "that you are trying to be kind. I beg you not to be. I do not want your kindness. Despite what Ian believes, I just want to be left alone."

"To wallow in your bad fortune?" Marietta asked, and had the satisfaction of seeing that angry sparkle return to his eyes. "Max, don't you know that we make our own fortune, good and bad? That is what I intend to do—"

The wind had been growing stronger, and now there was a violent gust. Beneath them treetops swayed, and a herd of cows mooed and tried to flee from the balloon. Mr. Keith had been going about the important work of controlling his balloon, but Marietta had been aware of him listening to their conversation with interest. Now he glanced at her and nodded his head, as if keen to egg her on. But Marietta had said all she had to say. If Max wanted to revel in his bad fortune, then she was content to let him.

There was another sharp gust—the basket swayed. "I'm going to start our descent," Mr. Keith said. "The wind is stronger than I anticipated, so be warned: our landing may not be a gentle one."

Max frowned at him, and Marietta sensed the unspoken anxiety in their exchanged looks. She swallowed, and peering over the side, knew she had no desire to tumble to earth from this height.

"You must brace yourself, Miss Greentree." Mr. Keith was brisk. "The basket may well fall over when we land, but if you hang on tightly you will not be cast out of it. Max?"

Marietta turned blindly toward her brooding companion and saw him nod. Whatever Mr. Keith had asked of his friend had been agreed upon. And then they were descending, and rather quickly.

The silk flapped overhead, and the basket swayed alarmingly. The wind was even stronger down here, and the aeronaught cast a worried glance at the farmer's field below—what had looked green and softly undulating now appeared less and less inviting. Marietta gave a cry as the basket struck ground and bumped roughly once and then again. They were dragged along, bouncing, as the quickly emptying envelope flapped wildly. And then they began to tip over.

A strong arm clamped about Marietta's waist, anchoring her, and her face was pressed into a broad chest. She was enveloped, swallowed up by her companion. And safe. Despite the seemingly endless journey along the ground, Marietta felt remarkably safe in the shelter of Max's arms.

That was why she clung to him, she told herself later, her nose deep in the folds of his necktie above the buttons of his waistcoat, her head full of the clean, masculine scent of him. A particularly nasty bump flung her upwards but he hung on to her, swearing under his breath, calling out to Mr. Keith to "Get on with it!"

And then, at last, they came to a standstill. They were down, and the cacophony of sound gave way to an eerie silence. Marietta lay still, aware of the large body beneath hers, of each breath gently lifting and lowering her. She raised her head and looked about, her fair hair tangled and falling down, her bonnet nowhere to be seen.

The basket was on its side in the farmer's field, its contents scattered, and the silk envelope flapping gently. A horse was standing some paces away, tail twitching, keeping a suspicious eye on them. And then Mr. Keith was on the move, checking his equipment, frowning as he worked.

And Max . . .

Max was lying on his back, looking up at her, an expression of long suffering on his handsome face. Just at that moment, a thick strand of her hair slipped out of its pins and tumbled across his cheek and into his eye. He sighed as if he'd just about had as much as he could take.

Marietta felt the heat suffuse her face—the man was *insufferable.* "Excuse me," she said in the chilliest tone she could manage in the circumstances, and proceeded to clamber off him. It was awkward, and her skirts and petticoats seemed to have become tangled up with his long legs. She folded her knees up, the better to crawl, but she had hardly begun when he grabbed her against him, cursing, and rolled to one side with her still clasped in his arms. With a gasp, she wound her arms about his neck and held on, his hair like rough curled silk against her fingers.

"Careful, Miss Greentree, I may need to father a son and heir one day." His voice, with its slight mocking drawl, tickled her ear. "But then again, who would want my child?" he added, and she realized the mockery was for himself.

"Oh, Max, I'm sure someone would!" she said, before she could consider her words. "Not me, of course, I-I am not . . . but *someone* . . ."

Her clumsy attempts to make him feel better touched him. He smiled. A slow smile that lifted the corners of his unhappy mouth and made his brooding face come alive with humor.

"Perhaps we won't make an heir just yet," he said, and began to untwine her arms from his neck and untangle her skirts from his legs. He eased himself out of the basket and pulled her after him. He held her briefly, his hands on her waist, allowing her to catch her balance, but as even that made her oddly breathless, she was relieved when he finally stepped away.

"Thank you," she said with stiff politeness. "I am grateful."

"You're not hurt?" He ducked his head to see into her face, he being so much taller than she. Close up, his eyes weren't quite so dark, and there was a little scar on his chin.

She made herself look away. "I'm perfectly all right, thank you."

Evidently he believed her. He turned to Mr. Keith. "You've made better landings, Ian."

"And worse ones, Max." Mr. Keith didn't even look up from what he was doing. "Don't be ungrateful. You're in one piece, aren't you?"

Max grunted, then took a few steps away and gave a bone-jarring stretch.

Marietta stood and watched—she could not seem to help it. The pull of his big body—and he was big, she could attest to that—the fluid movement of his muscles and sinews, the purely sensual enjoyment on his face as he tested himself. Marietta decided there was something very attractive about Max, but at the same time she was aware of wanting to remove herself as far from him as possible.

"Miss Greentree, you are unhurt?" Mr. Keith had finally remembered there was something other than his balloon that might be broken.

"Yes, thank you. Max . . . kept me safe."

Mr. Keith's mouth twitched. "I thought he might," he said evenly.

Max stopped in mid-stretch, turning to glare at him over one broad shoulder. "I'm not a nursemaid, Ian."

Stung, Marietta straightened to her full height— and still had to tilt her head back to meet his eyes. "For your information, sir, I am well past the age when I need a nursemaid."

Max sneered—or at least Marietta, who had never seen a sneer before but had read about them in books, thought that's what he did. "Are you? You look a mere child to me."

Again she felt her cheeks flush red. A *child*? It was a long time since Marietta had felt like a child. Some people mistook her petite stature and vivacious manner for immaturity but they were mistaken. She was a grown woman with a mind of her own and a particularly strong will.

"Most of my friends already have their own households, and *nursemaids* for their children," Marietta replied in what was for her a subdued tone.

"But not you, Miss Marietta?" Mr. Keith smiled, attempting to lighten the atmosphere.

"No." Marietta smiled back, but her gaze slanted sideways toward Max. "I have no plans to marry. Ever."

Max made a sound like a snort. "In my experience all women want to marry," he said, as if he were an expert. "What else would they do *but* marry?"

"Yes, you're right," she said dryly. "What else can they do? Respectable society and those who command it have made it impossible for a woman to survive without the shelter of a husband. But I am . . . different, and I have no intention of being told how to live my own life. I am going to do something else."

Max had the gall to lift his eyebrows, his smile supercilious. "I see. Perhaps you are going on safari to Africa, Miss Greentree. Or taking a climbing trip in the Highlands. Or setting up a shelter for orphans where they are taught to play the piano, as one eccentric lady has done."

Did he mean Vivianna? Her elder sister had begun the Shelter for Poor Orphans some years ago. "I believe that life should be savored to the fullest," she said, glaring back at him. "And I mean to taste it, every single drop."

It was true, in a way the ruination of her reputation had set her free to explore other pathways. There was a certain freedom in knowing you couldn't make things much worse than they were already.

Something flickered in his dark eyes—as if she had struck a chord in him. "Perhaps you would like a partner in your adventures," he said, and his voice was no longer supercilious. "I am available." He laughed, and it was hardly bitter at all. "I have nothing else to do but sit and feel sorry for myself, as you so rightly pointed out. Let's go adventuring, Miss Greentree."

Marietta wasn't certain what she would have said. *Yes* trembled on her lips, but that was impossible.

She had no intention of falling in love, not with Max and not with anyone, and the adventures she was planning were not the sort he would be able to afford—not any longer. Because for some time now Marietta had made her mind up that she was going to be a courtesan, just like her mother.

It was the only way in which she could have that life she craved, that full and satisfying life, without exposing her damaged heart. And her tattered reputation would be of no importance if she was a courtesan, in fact it might be a bonus. She had thought it over, and really, it was the only way she could move forward. Of course, it would not be easy. There was her family to convince—and Marietta did not pretend they would be pleased with her choice of career—and she did not want to hurt them more than she had already. But neither did she want to languish in the shadows for the rest of her life. She was young and alive, and it was time to begin to celebrate that fact.

Luckily, she did not have to explain all of that to Max, because they were interrupted.

"Hello there!" It was the farmer, peering over the fence. "Do you folk need any help?"

Soon afterwards they had loaded themselves into his cart and were jolting their way back to London. Marietta had been given the place of honor on the seat beside the farmer, while the two men sat in the tray at the back. She could hear them passing comment, but she did not join in the conversation. She felt shaken from the landing, but more than that.

She felt shaken by Max.

Yes, he made her angry. Yes, he was moody, and it

wasn't fair that he was so physically attractive. When he had held her in his arms, her body pressed to his, she had felt . . . well, it frightened her, because the last time she had felt like that it had ended in disaster. Marietta sympathized with his predicament, of course she did, but they were strangers, and soon they would go their own ways and live their own lives.

She found comfort in the fact that she would never see him again.

When they reached the outskirts of London, Mr. Keith found Marietta a hackney cab to take her home. She glanced at Max as she climbed inside. He was looking at her, but his smile was gone, and it occurred to her that soon he would have forgotten she existed. With a little shrug, she ignored him too, and turned her face for home.

"It was no accident Miss Greentree being with us, was it, Ian?"

Ian Keith glanced at Max, taking in his obvious bad humor.

"The truth, if you please," Max added, his dark eyebrows drawing down at the corners to mimic the shape of his mouth.

Ian sighed. "I don't know why you're complaining. Any other man would have been more than happy to while away a few hours in the company of so sweet a girl. I thought . . . I *hoped* she would drive away your dark mood."

"Did you? I suppose she did have a certain naïve charm. If I were ten years younger—"

"Max you're twenty-nine!"

"I feel like one hundred and twenty-nine. I've seen

girls like that before, Ian. Too many of them." He sounded pompous and he knew it, but it seemed important to convince Ian that he had no interest in Miss Greentree. Because if he couldn't convince Ian, how on earth was he going to convince himself?

"I take it you're not hanging out for a wife then?" Ian said curiously. "Not that I'm suggesting Miss Greentree is the woman to share the nuptials with you, but I have wondered."

"If I want a woman in my bed I'll go to Aphrodite's and find one there, and as for the rest . . . My servants cook my meals and launder my clothes, and I have you for a friend." The drawl was back in his voice, to show he didn't care. "A wife would be an added burden, especially now, when I have no future."

Ian shook his head. "It isn't the end of the world, Max. Even if you can't persuade your father to change his mind, or break your cousin's hold on your inheritance, you still have a lot to be grateful for. Remember, you have your mother's estate in Cornwall, and your house in London. Admit it, you're hardly destitute, Max!"

Max's expression grew bleak. "You have a very simplistic view of the world, my friend. My mother left me property in Cornwall, it's true, but the house is falling down. And the house in London isn't mine, it's part of the Valland estate and it belongs to Harold now. My father has sent his man of business to tell me to leave by the end of the month, but I don't know if I can wait that long. You see I can't pay my servants or my household bills. Although my cousin Harold has been generous, I cannot . . . I do not expect him to support me."

"Why not?" Ian asked coldly. "He's taken what is yours, hasn't he?"

Max's handsome face turned grim. "It isn't Harold's fault this has happened. I don't blame my father either, not really. I've never seen him as hurt and angry as he was the night he read out my mother's letter."

Ian did not dispute him, although his expression said he would like to.

"And then there is my name," Max went on quietly. "I can no longer call myself Lord Roseby—I am plain Max Valland. And although my mother may be dead, her reputation as a caring and generous woman, an honest and respectable woman, is in jeopardy. Vicious gossip follows me wherever I go. I am the scandal of the moment, and I do not like it."

"You think it's true then, that your father—?"

"Is not my father? That he married her all unsuspecting, believing the child she was carrying was his own? I have seen the proof with my own eyes—my mother's letter of admission—I must believe it."

"So who *is* your father, Max?"

"I don't know."

"Not even an inkling?" Ian asked softly.

Max hesitated and then he said, "No," firmly. Ian knew there was no point in trying to force Max to confide in anyone, that was not Max's way. Max would tell only when and if he wanted to; when the burden was finally too heavy and he had to lay some part of it down. Ian had often thought that a wife was exactly what Max needed, a strong woman to confide in and stand at his side, someone to love him whatever name he bore. But then that, he supposed, was the wish of most men, and most men never had it realized.

Max might not be an easy man, and at the moment he was a troubled man, but he had many good points. Ian only wished that Miss Greentree of the big blue eyes and irrepressible smile had had the chance to see some of them.

Chapter 2

***

The sounds and sights within Vivianna's bedchamber were almost more than Marietta could
bear. She did not like to see her sister in pain. Who
would have thought it would be quite so exhausting
to bring a baby into the world? Even one as anticipated and loved as Vivianna and Oliver's baby.

Marietta wasn't supposed to be in the room, she
knew that, but in the confusion no one had had the
time or energy to send her out. Besides, Oliver was
here, too, and he wasn't supposed to be! A father, the
doctors had informed him roundly, should be at his
club awaiting the news in the presence of his friends,
or else downstairs with a glass of brandy, pacing the
carpet. Certainly not up in his wife's bedchamber
holding her hand.

Just then Vivianna gave one last cry of effort, and
suddenly it was over. The baby was born.

"A boy!" declared the doctor with obvious relief,
and the baby was taken off to be sponged and

wrapped in the same shawl used by Montegomery babies for hundreds of years. Evidently this didn't suit Oliver and Vivianna's son, because when he was presented to the proud parents he was howling loud enough to wake the whole of Berkley Square.

Gazing at Oliver across their son's red, angry little face, Vivianna gave him a beaming smile. "You're not the last of the Montegomeries now," she said, her voice husky from exhaustion. Then, tears filling her hazel eyes, "Oh, Oliver . . ."

Oliver drew them both gently into his arms, and closed his own eyes, burying his face in her hair. In the bedchamber people moved about them, tidying up, murmuring words of congratulation, but Oliver and Vivianna and their son were in a little island all their own.

Watching them, Marietta felt the burn of tears in her own eyes—a mixture of sorrow and joy and even a touch of envy. For this would never be her life. She was destined for something very different, and if her hopes became reality then it would be a life to savor and to look back on with a smile of satisfaction. But she would never have what Vivianna had right now. The heart of one man.

She had come to London to be of help to her sister during her confinement, and to assist her afterwards with household matters. Lady Greentree was to have come herself, and in fact had been ready to do so, until she had an unfortunate accident. Two weeks ago, she tripped and fell down some stairs, and wrenched her ankle. Although the ankle was not broken, she was unable to walk, and a journey by coach to London had been out of the question. Even if she had been able to travel, of what possible use could she be, hobbling about? So she had handed the task over to Marietta, a little reluctantly to be sure—Lady Greentree did not like letting her second daughter out of her sight, not since Gerard Jones, and London was a long way from her watchful gaze. Marietta, with strict instructions as to what she could and couldn't do, and with Mr. Jardine as her companion, came to take her mama's place at Berkley Square.

Vivianna was very glad to see her.

"Oh Marietta, thank you for coming to be with me. I have missed you so!" It was nice, Marietta had thought, to be appreciated, even if she knew her sister was a little overwrought because of her condition. And she intended to do her duty, of course she did! But now she was finally in London, Marietta also meant to make the most of it. She had plans of her own, and one of them had been the ascent in the gas balloon. The other . . . Well, that was something both Vivianna and Lady Greentree had expressly forbidden.

Marietta planned to visit Aphrodite at her home, the famous Aphrodite's Club. And she planned to ask Aphrodite for her help.

"You are not to go there under any circumstances," Vivianna, knowing Marietta's adventurous and impulsive nature, had spoken to her on the matter. "Are you listening to me, Marietta? Mama has forbidden it, and if Uncle William Tremaine were to hear of it . . ." She shuddered at the image of Lady Greentree's brother discovering yet another scandal in the family. "He already considers you beyond redemption. You should concentrate on showing him how good and obedient you can be."

"When did you begin to care what Uncle William

said and thought?" she asked her sister, trying not to be hurt by her words. "Besides I *am* beyond redemption."

"Nonsense! There are gentlemen here in London who have never heard of your . . . your misfortune. Oliver says he can find several who will be very interested in offering for you."

Marietta bit her lip to stop herself from saying what she thought about that. Vivianna probably believed she was doing her sister a good turn—as the eldest she had always tried to look after them, ever since they were kidnapped from Aphrodite as children and later abandoned on Lady Greentree's estate, where she had found them and taken them in. But the idea that Marietta would need Oliver's help and persuasion to find herself a husband—probably some old man with lecherous eyes—made her feel ill. She was twenty-one now and the scandal had set her well and truly on the shelf. She had no intention of allowing Vivianna to boss her about just to avoid Uncle William's displeasure. Particularly when she knew that same older sister had visited Aphrodite's Club, incognito, when she was of a similar age.

Marietta took one more look at Vivianna and Oliver, admired their new son, and slipped out of the bedchamber. Mr. Jardine was waiting at the head of the stairs, his blue eyes anxious, his graying hair standing on end as though he had been running his hands through it.

"A son," she said, with a smile to set his mind at ease. "And everyone is very well."

His face sagged in relief. Mr. Jardine had been with the Greentree family for so long that they always thought of him as one of them. He had come to

Greentree Manor shortly after Lady Greentree's soldier husband, Edward, had died in India, and Marietta and her two sisters had been found abandoned in a cottage upon the estate. At the time Rawlings was their estate manager, but he had proved unsatisfactory and Lady Greentree had let him go—only for him to bob up in that inn and ruin Marietta's life.

Mr. Jardine was a mature gentleman of medium height and build, and handsome. His skin had been darkened by the years he had spent in the West Indies.

"Lady Greentree will be so pleased," he said now, and it was clear from his expression that he was imagining her joy when she heard about her grandson.

Such a wish to please an employer might be due to friendship or gratitude or loyalty, but Marietta knew differently. It had been obvious to her for many years that Mr. Jardine loved Lady Greentree. Unfortunately his love went unrequited, for although Amy Greentree was clearly fond of her secretary, she was still mourning her husband, and perhaps she always would be. It did seem to be a pity that she could not put aside his memory for just long enough to allow herself to brush the past from her eyes. If she could once see Mr. Jardine clearly, without the veil of her bereavement, Marietta was certain she would love him, too.

Marietta left Mr. Jardine and slipped down the stairs. News of the new Montegomery heir had already spread, and servants with beaming faces had gathered in the entrance hall. Soon congratulations would begin arriving at the town house, and with them would come Lady Marsh, Oliver's wealthy aunt. Mr. Jardine would send a message posthaste to Lady Greentree and Francesca, and Marietta would follow that with a letter of her own. A notice would be placed in the more important newspapers, and that would bring more congratulations. Queen Victoria herself would send a gift, for Oliver was a favorite of hers, and Prince Albert would attach a personal note, because Vivianna was a favorite of his.

But there was someone else, someone Marietta considered more important than Her Majesty. Someone who should be told the news as soon as possible, and with Vivianna so completely absorbed in her brand-new family, that important person might be otherwise forgotten until tomorrow.

A grandmother deserved to be informed face-to-face.

Marietta hurried off to find Lil, her sister's maid. Lil could keep an eye on Vivianna while she slipped out to tell Aphrodite the good news.

And it has nothing to do with my wish to visit Aphrodite's Club and my plans to be a courtesan. Nothing whatsoever . . .

But Marietta was fibbing to herself, and she knew it. Visiting Aphrodite's Club was not a whim, it was an important step toward her future. Everything depended upon Aphrodite's reaction to her request for patronage—for if she was going to be a courtesan, she wanted only the best advice.

"Do you think you should go off to that place, miss?" Lil said. "I don't know if Lady Montegomery would approve."

"Lady Montegomery's approval is neither here nor there," Marietta retorted.

Lil opened her mouth as if to argue, and then took note of the stubborn tilt of Marietta's chin, and closed it again. The Greentree sisters were all alike, she thought wryly to herself. When they wanted their own way there was just no stopping them.

Aphrodite's Club had a somber elegance that gave little clue to its real purpose, thought Marietta as the hansom cab set her down. She had never seen her mother's club before, but she had read of such places and steeled herself for a certain amount of gaudiness. This was more like a private school for young ladies!

Marietta lifted the hem of her skirts above her slippers to climb the stairs towards the white portico that framed the entrance. Apart from tossing on her emerald velvet cloak, Marietta had not changed her clothing from the red and green shot silk dress she had worn all day. Changing would have meant delay, and the news she carried seemed too important to wait. Besides, this might be her only chance to speak to Aphrodite privately, and Marietta meant to take it.

The doorknocker brought a man in a red military style jacket to the door, his thick graying hair neatly combed, his gray eyes quizzical in his rugged face. This was Aphrodite's faithful Dobson—Marietta knew him instantly from Vivianna's description. And just as her sister had said, he looked as if he had been involved in a great many fistfights over the years.

"What can I do for you, miss?" he asked sternly, in the accent of the London streets. "Do you know where you are? Maybe you're lost, is that it?"

Marietta smiled. "No, I am not lost, Dobson. I am Miss Marietta Greentree, and I have come to see Aphrodite."

Dobson's eyes gleamed with intelligence behind

his rough mask; his mouth did not smile but it looked as though it wanted to. "She's in the salon at the moment, Miss Marietta."

"Oh, is she?" Marietta's curious gaze flicked past him. "I came to tell her good news, Dobson. Vivianna and Oliver have had a son, and I thought Aphrodite would want to know immediately."

Now Dobson did smile. "Why, that's wonderful news! Aphrodite will want to know all right. You wait here, miss, and I'll go and fetch her."

And he dashed off.

Marietta stood alone in the vestibule. Really, she hadn't expected a bordello to look so . . . so ordinary. Nothing exciting appeared to be going on, or if it was, then it was all happening behind tightly closed doors. She could hear music and talk and laughter from the salon, but even so there was nothing here that was different from any other large, fashionable, London establishment.

Almost a disappointment, Marietta admitted to herself.

A curving staircase rose up to a gallery circled by a black and gold balustrade. There were boudoirs up there, she supposed. Perhaps they were gaudy, perhaps they were occupied. Marietta sighed. Alone on her chair in the vestibule she felt very removed from it all, just as she had felt removed from life for the past four years.

The doorknocker rattled.

Marietta stared at the closed portal. The knocker sounded again, louder this time, and she shifted nervously. Elsewhere, apart from the faint laughter and music, the house was silent. No footsteps hurrying closer, no Dobson returning. Perhaps whoever it was would simply go away . . . The knocker sounded again, impatient that no one had answered.

There is no one here, she wanted to shout. *Only me.*

The knocker clattered furiously.

Agitated, Marietta reminded herself that this was her mother's house. Although it was not considered proper for a young lady of Marietta's social status to open a door—especially the door to a disorderly house—the person on the other side could not possibly know who she really was.

Marietta gave a quick glance down at herself, and then removed her cloak. Her red and green shot silk skirt was creased but reasonable, the square collar and matching cuffs were clean if a little limp. She patted her hair, and found that the soft curls were still in place.

The knocker rattled again, one last furious attempt to rouse Dobson, and then she heard steps, beginning to move away. Perhaps it was an important guest? Someone Aphrodite would be upset about losing?

Marietta hurried over and flung open the door.

A tall man in a top hat had descended the stairs, and was already moving toward the street—evidently leaving in frustration.

Marietta called out, "Sir? Please!"

He stopped and turned to look at her over his shoulder. The gaslight from the street was bright and against it he was nothing but a dark shadow—a tall shadow with broad shoulders.

"I am sorry you had to wait. Come in. Let me . . . eh . . ." What did one say to welcome a gentleman into Aphrodite's? "Let me make you comfortable, sir."

He went still for a moment, as if considering her

proposal, and then he began to retrace his steps toward her. The lamp in the hall shone out through the door, a pool of light fell low onto the ground. It illuminated his shoes first, showing the dark shine of the leather, and then the legs of his black trousers. He wore a black buttoned coat, tailored to fit his broad chest and shoulders, while his white shirt looked to be of the finest linen. Above his black necktie his jaw was strong and square and cleanly shaven, and there was a little scar on his chin. Odd. Almost familiar. In fact, everything about him was strangely familiar. His nose was straight and aristocratic, and his lips were narrow, without the hint of a smile, while his eyes . . .

His eyes were mahogany brown, and they were watching her beneath lowered black brows with startled disapproval.

"Miss Greentree?"

Marietta gasped. "Max!"

"What are *you* doing here?" he demanded, and now he was close enough to her that she had to look up into his gaze.

"I had a message for Aphrodite," she said and knew it sounded stupid. Then, as her mind began to free itself from the shock of seeing him, "You've come to visit one of her protégés, haven't you?"

Max stared at her, and his brows drew down even more. "Miss Greentree, I really don't think that's a question you should be asking me." He drawled the words out in the sort of patronizing manner she loathed.

"Why not?" she said, just to irritate him further.

"It is inappropriate," he retorted. And then, as if he had just realized exactly *how* inappropriate the situation was, Max's mouth closed hard. His brown eyes narrowed, and his gaze dropped to her breasts, and then down to her narrow waist beneath which her skirts belled out.

He's viewing the merchandise!

At that moment Marietta wanted to slap him. Hard.

As if Max himself had just realized what he was doing, his gaze shot back to hers. To her surprise, a flush warmed his tanned cheeks, and his frown grew even blacker than before.

"Do you *live* here, Miss Greentree?" he asked her in that disapproving manner that instantly caused her hackles to rise even more than they had already. What right did he have to question her reasons for being here?

Marietta fixed him with one of her clear, unflinching looks. "I don't think that is any of your business, Max."

Max was attempting to find his way through his confusion. The direct and discomforting Miss Greentree was certainly the last person he had ever expected to see standing framed in the doorway of Aphrodite's Club. She had been an annoying and yet interesting interlude in Ian's balloon, with her pert conversation and big blue eyes that seemed to be looking right inside him. She was sweet, yes, pretty, undoubtedly, but—he had told himself firmly—not worth a second glance when you had been to as many social engagements and been match-made as many times as Max.

And now here she stood, those blue eyes blazing and her kissable pink mouth determined, upon the threshold of the most famous bordello in London. It was very disconcerting for a man who considered himself a reasonable judge of character. He would never have picked her out as one of Aphrodite's protégés—she lacked the experienced eyes. Now suddenly she wasn't the woman he had believed her to be, and he felt his interest captured in a way it had not been captured for a long time. Miss Greentree, the sweet innocent with the eccentric conversation, had now become Miss Greentree, the mysterious lady of the night.

A fascinating and intriguing combination.

The memory of holding her in his arms during the balloon landing tripped blithely into his mind, and brought with it a surge of sensations. He remembered her soft curves, bountiful for such a petite woman, as she lay atop him, and the sweet fragrance of her hair as it fell loose about his face. The way her long dark lashes had framed her big blue eyes, as she gazed at him in startled trepidation. And yet she'd been courageous in their moment of danger. He wouldn't have let anything happen to her, of course, but she couldn't know that. Yet she hadn't shrieked or fallen into hysterics. There was a toughness beneath the fragile exterior, a hint at hidden depths that intrigued him.

Miss Greentree was certainly an unusual woman.

Max realized that she was staring back at him, warily, watchfully. And no wonder. They were standing very close, and the scent of her, the look of her, was heating his blood. He had come here tonight on a whim, for some distraction, to try and forget his troubles. For one night at least, it would be pleasant to have a woman in his arms who made no mention of the scandal his life had become, who would pretend he was just an ordinary gentleman—a *desirable* gentleman and not one to avoid at all costs.

Miss Greentree might be irritating and pert, but suddenly Max knew that he wanted her—with a deep and primeval urge. She was here to sell her services, whatever he had previously believed to the contrary, and he was here to buy them. Why was he hesitating?

Max wasn't a man to make snap decisions, far from it, but he made one now.

"Miss Greentree, are you free for this evening?"

"This evening?" Marietta goggled at him. *Did* he mean, *could* he mean . . . ? But of course he meant what she thought he meant! He was about to proposition her—she felt light-headed with a combination of shock and triumph.

Max's jaw had tightened. "No, I've changed my mind."

He didn't want her after all! Marietta gave a sigh of relief, and ignored the little jolt of chagrin. "Well, I didn't like to embarrass you, Max, but I'm only here—"

"I've changed my mind about the evening," he went on, talking over her attempts at an explanation. "I want you for the entire night."

The entire night!

"Oh," she gasped, her mind suddenly blank. "I don't know . . . That's very . . . *flattering*, Max. I hope . . . Maybe the evening would be more sensible. I mean, what if I was no good at . . . at *it*, and you had to ask for your money back. Awfully embarrassing for us both. Although I'm sure it's something you get better at, with . . . with practice. Although my own is limited and . . . and . . ."

He laughed as if he didn't particularly want to but he just couldn't help it. "Miss Greentree—"

"Marietta. My name is Marietta."

"Marietta. Enchanting." He gave her a small perfunctory bow. "To answer your question, I think that the physical attraction between two people depends on a great many things and none of them are easily—"

"Well I think one glance is often enough."

Of course she had decided views on this, as with everything. She was looking at him as if she expected him to argue, so he did.

"Nonsense," Max said mildly.

Her pretty mouth quirked. So she liked to be at odds with him, did she? She was one of those women who preferred to be at loggerheads than to be in agreement? In a world where politeness was all important, the thought of arguing with Marietta Greentree was oddly attractive to Max. Since he had lost his social standing and become embroiled in scandal he had discovered that being polite was often just an excuse not to express one's true feelings. Being impolite could actually be extremely liberating.

"Do you feel a physical attraction for me, Max?"

"You're direct, aren't you?" he retorted. "Yes, Marietta, I do feel a physical attraction for you."

She smiled at him as if she was delighted with his answer.

He felt like smiling back.

Despite his present circumstances, Max had been born a gentleman. A gentleman was taught to revere gentlewomen as precious objects that must never be sullied by a man's basest desires. Gentlewomen were destined to be wives, pure and perfect, raised upon the pedestal of Victorian womanhood. But

Max was a man, too, and he needed to release those base desires. When he did so it was with the sort of women who inhabited Aphrodite's Club, not gentlewomen, never gentlewomen.

But Miss Greentree confused him. On one hand she was a pure vision of womanhood, and on the other hand she was the sort of woman he felt he could happily and unrestrainedly take to his bed. The best of both worlds, in fact.

"I must say I am surprised, Max, and flattered. An entire night. Is that the way these bargains are normally sealed? A simple yes or no on my part? Or do you require a sampling first?"

A sampling? His imagination took flight, but he reined it back in. "In such circumstances I trust you to know your business and you trust me to know mine."

Marietta Greentree thought about this. "Well, I know *my* business, but perhaps an entire night is too long for you, Max."

The pert minx was questioning his credentials as a lover! He gave an angry laugh. "I am not an inexperienced boy, I'll have you know."

She widened her eyes as if she was impressed, but it was all show.

"Are you goading me, Miss Greentree?"

"Not at all, Max, but I do think I should test the truth of your claims."

I'm flirting with him! I must be out of my mind, Marietta thought, and yet she couldn't seem to stop herself. She didn't want to. *If I'm going to be a courtesan then I must practice, and Max seems so perfect . . .* She wasn't afraid of him, she realized with surprise. Perhaps it was because of the balloon ride, when he had protected her during the rough landing, but she felt as if Max would always keep her safe, whatever she said and did. It gave her a remarkable sense of freedom in her dealings with him.

"Very well," he said, a determined glint in his eye, "you asked for it."

Max reached out and took her hand in his. Slowly, watching her closely, he pressed his palm to hers and measured the length of her fingers against his. He noticed that her skin was fine and soft, a lady's hand, and her nails were buffed to a rosy pink. Slowly, he lifted her hand as if it were some succulent dish, then bowed his head to inspect it until, with infinite care, he sucked her fingertips, one after the other.

He heard her catch her breath, the sound echoing about them in the vestibule. "I . . . what are you doing?"

"Sampling you." He smiled and her eyes went slightly out of focus. Perhaps she was not as knowing as she pretended. He turned her palm this way and that, as if to read the lines that crossed it, and then he ran his finger lightly over the fleshy pad beneath her thumb. Marietta's was especially pronounced.

Gently, Max blew warm breath upon that mound, and then he closed his mouth over her and bit her, very lightly, his teeth scraping her skin.

Marietta shuddered and gave a gasp. "What are you doing now?" she whispered, as if she were shocked and intrigued, both at the same time.

"*This* is your Mount of Venus," he said, running his thumb over the fleshy pad again, his face very close to hers. Her pupils were large and dark as if they would swallow the blue, and her lips were a little apart, as if every word he spoke, every movement he made, was of tremendous importance to her. As if she hadn't been in this situation many times before.

"My Mount of Venus?"

"It is a sign of the depth of your womanly passion." He ran his thumb over her flesh again, caressingly, back and forth, and watched the effect it had on her. He couldn't help a triumphant smile.

But she saw it, and her eyes narrowed. "And what does it say about me?" she demanded tartly.

"It tells me, Marietta, that you are a very passionate woman indeed," he said, his voice soft and deep and seductive.

She didn't seem to know what to say to that, and he took the opportunity to draw her closer, until they nearly touched, but not quite. He felt her trembling, and knew she was anticipating his next move. Good. His mouth hovered above hers, ready to taste, ready to take. How long since he had felt this degree of desire? His body was alive with need, almost out of control.

"The entire night won't be long enough for what I want to do to you . . . Marietta," Max said. And he meant every word.

"Lord Roseby, what *are* you doing with my daughter?"

They froze. From behind them came the rustle of Aphrodite's black silk skirts, and from behind her came the sturdy tread of Dobson's boots. Marietta withdrew her hand from Max's, closing her fingers hard over the tingling in her palm, and trying not to notice the suddenly blank look of shock in his brown eyes.

"Lord Roseby?" she repeated, rather shocked herself. "You told me your name was Max!"

"And I thought you were one of Aphrodite's protégés," he said, anger and frustration growing in his face and voice. "You have deceived me, Miss Greentree."

"I am . . . well, I'm Aphrodite's daughter. One of her daughters. There are three of us."

"I am a gentleman, and I do not take advantage of a lady unless she is experienced in these matters. Do you know how close you came to being compromised?"

He seemed very upset about something.

"I . . . don't care about that," she said quickly. "I am already ruined, Max."

He blinked at her. "I don't believe it," he said quietly. "You seem to have an aversion to telling me the truth, Miss Greentree."

But Marietta gave a little shrug. "Why didn't you tell me you were Lord Roseby?"

"Because I am no longer Lord Roseby," Max's voice was suddenly both hard and bitter. "I lost the right to call myself by that name when my father declared me a bastard." He turned swiftly to Aphrodite and bowed. "Good evening, Madame. My apologies if I have offended."

The door closed behind him.

Aphrodite came and took Marietta's hand, her fingers firm and cool where Max's had been so strong and hot. "Whatever has been happening here, Marietta? Dobson says that Vivianna has had a little boy."

Memory returned and Marietta smiled—for a moment Max had wiped everything else from her mind. "Oh yes, she has! A dear little boy. I came to tell you. You must see him, at once."

Aphrodite's face lit up, and then, just as suddenly, it dulled into the cool aloofness that was her shield. "I cannot," she said. "It would not be proper for me to be there among Lord Montegomery's friends and family. I would embarrass Vivianna."

Marietta laughed in disbelief. "I don't think so!"

Aphrodite smiled wryly. "No, well perhaps Vivianna would not be embarrassed, but . . . I would feel . . . awkward. I will come to Berkley Square a little later. Thank you for taking the time to call and tell me the wonderful news, Marietta. It was good of you to think of me."

"*Good* of me?" Marietta retorted. "Of course I thought of you! Aphrodite, you are a grandmamma now."

Aphrodite turned her dark gaze on Dobson, who was standing so solidly behind her. "*Mon dieu,*" she whispered, "I had not thought of that."

He cast up his eyes. "It had to happen one day," he said. "Makes no difference, does it? You're still my beautiful girl."

Aphrodite laughed, pleased. Marietta watched the by-play between them. Clearly there was far more to the relationship of Aphrodite and Dobson than mistress and servant, but she didn't have time to consider it, not now.

"May I wait for you, Aphrodite?" she pleaded. "I promise I won't speak to any more gentlemen, and I'll stay out of the way until you're ready." The journey to Berkley Square would be the ideal time to broach Aphrodite with her plans for the future.

The courtesan's eyes narrowed suspiciously. "You will not flirt with men like Lord Roseby?"

"Of course not," she said innocently. "What an idea! I don't like Lord Roseby very much, anyway."

Aphrodite smiled. "He wasn't very happy with you, was he, Marietta? You made him feel foolish, and gentlemen do not enjoy feeling like fools."

"Why did he feel like that? Because he thought I was one of your protégés? That was his own fault. He didn't ask me, he just presumed."

Aphrodite shrugged noncommittally. "That and other reasons." She glanced at Dobson, and some unspoken communication passed between them. "Very well, you may wait. Dobson, show my daughter into the smaller sitting room. And see that she stays there."

Dismissed, Marietta followed Dobson to one of the doors leading into the vestibule. In a voice as artless as she could manage, she said, "Dobson, what is the scandal about Lord Roseby? Is he really a . . . a . . ."

"A bastard?" Dobson said with a matter-of-factness that was refreshing. "That's what they say, miss. His father disinherited him, and as the estate and the title aren't entailed, there was nothing he could do about it. Lord Roseby's mother had been dead only a short while when his father came out and declared that Max had never been his son. Put it in all the newspapers and everything, refusing to allow the boy any further claim upon him, and acknowledging Max's cousin, Harold, as the new heir."

Marietta was genuinely shocked. "How cruel!"

"Maybe Lord Roseby's Mama should have thought of that before she cuckolded the old man,"

Dobson retorted unsympathetically. "Now, you go in there, miss, and don't you stir a whisker until Aphrodite comes for you. Got that?"

"Yes, Dobson," Marietta replied meekly.

His mouth twitched as he closed the door.

Marietta settled down before the fire in the sitting room, and gazed into the flames. It seemed unfair that Max had been made to suffer for something that was not his fault. Such a misfortune was similar enough to her own situation to ensure her sympathy. She, too, had been looked down upon and socially ostracized by people who did not know her at all, just because of the circumstances of her birth. Why couldn't it be as Vivianna was always saying it should be: that children ought to be loved for themselves and not reviled for the actions of their parents?

Sometimes life just wasn't fair.

Chapter 3

Max, Lord Roseby, would probably have agreed with her. Or maybe not. He was not presently inclined to agree with anything Marietta Greentree said. She was a confounded nuisance, not least because she had the bluest eyes he had ever seen and the most dazzling smile. He wanted to watch her face, especially when she was lying in his arms.

Well, *that* wasn't going to happen now.

Max had been dreaming of an hour or two's relaxation with one of Aphrodite's more accomplished protégés, and instead he was left feeling tense and frustrated and more than a little foolish. He had wanted her. *Her*, Marietta, Aphrodite's daughter.

He couldn't have made a worse choice.

Despite her parentage, the girl was obviously an innocent playing with fire—he didn't for a moment believe her claims that she was ruined—and that was the worst kind of complication for Max. As if he didn't have enough problems, he would be accused

50

of tampering with a virgin. He could hear the gossips now ... "Well, he wasn't really a gentleman, was he, what can one expect?" Or, "He's taken up with a drab's daughter. Like will find like."

Was Marietta really Aphrodite's daughter?

Max swung his cane and strolled along the street. Now he set his mind to it, he recalled that there had been some scandal a few years ago. Something about the daughters of the famous courtesan being stolen as children and being found again when they were grown. The thing had been hushed up, though. He would have to ask around for the details, refresh his memory—Harold would be the obvious choice—Harold knew everything about everyone. Except that Harold was now, supposedly, his enemy. Harold, who had supplanted him as the heir to his father's title, Duke of Barwon, and the sprawling Valland House in Surrey, where both Max and Harold had grown up. Not to mention the old man's fortune.

"Ill-gotten gains," Max muttered to himself. The old man had inherited the title when he was hardly more than a child, but the money had all been frittered away by his gambling addicted family. He had set off to the West Indies and made his own fortune, although there had always been a bit of a smell about the whole thing. Max had asked, but his father would never discuss it. "Money is money," he'd say testily, "who cares where it's come from?"

True enough, money was money, and it was money Max needed to keep himself afloat.

He would have to sell his mother's house in Cornwall. The thought was a bleak one. Blackwood had been in her family since medieval times, but he could not see how he could hold on to it and remain in

London. Unless he left London altogether—why not, it was too painful here anyway, with so many reminders of his old life. Then he could retire to the isolation of Cornwall and live as a recluse.

The image suited his mood exactly, even though he knew it was awfully indulgent. And he'd probably get bored doing nothing but brooding. Max sighed.

"Perhaps something can be done," Harold had said awkwardly, last time they met. "You know how rotten this makes me feel, old chap. Don't do anything rash. I won't let you go under."

"I can't rely on you for the rest of my life, Harold."

"I wouldn't blame you if you hated me, old boy."

"It's not your fault," Max said, and it was true. It wasn't Harold's fault. Max's mother had evidently been carrying him when she wed his father, and now the truth had come out. Max was disinherited, and as the eldest male issue of the duke's brother, Harold was legally the next in line.

A tragic tale, yes, but then again Harold was not to blame. Just as Max wasn't to blame. One day he had been Lord Roseby, heir to a dukedom and an estate in Surrey and a fortune in funds—the world had been at his feet. And the next . . . Everything, his prospects, his position in polite society, had disintegrated like ashes in the wind.

The deed had been done at Valland House, during a family supper to celebrate the new year. They had been chatting and laughing, his stepsister Susannah had been playing the piano, and then his father had risen to his feet and cleared his throat. He always made a toast at these gatherings, paying homage to the dying year and looking forward to the one to come. But this time he had not raised his glass, instead he had reached into his pocket and taken out a letter and begun to read. The letter had been written by the duchess some years ago, and Max did not want to believe that she ever expected it to be found and spoken aloud.

That letter had destroyed his life.

He hadn't been able to remain in the room. His father hadn't even looked at him as Max got to his feet and walked out, through the doorway and into the freezing night. He had walked in circles in the garden for hours, until Susannah and Harold found him and brought him in. But he had been numb, unable to speak or weep or rage. That had come later.

Max sighed, pushing aside the bad memories, and remembering instead Marietta's soft hand in his. If he closed his eyes he could recall the scent of her hair, and the sight of her blue eyes staring up at him so boldly. Even now, standing still in the laneway, he felt his body tensing at the thought of her naked in his arms.

Blast it, he *had* been looking forward to spending the entire night with Marietta Greentree!

The blow came out of nowhere. A crashing thud to his temple. Max saw lights and then darkness washed over him. And then nothing at all.

Marietta's head was nodding. It had been a very long day—Vivianna had begun her labor well before dawn and everyone had been in such a state of anxious anticipation they hadn't been able to rest. Now, seated here in Aphrodite's warm and comfortable parlor, she found herself slipping into sleep.

She was remembering the first time she met Aphrodite, at Greentree Manor, shortly after Vivianna married Oliver . . .

* * *

Beyond the windows in the drawing room the sun shone fitfully. Ominous clouds jostled on the horizon, where the moors rose bleakly to meet them. But here in the sitting room the fire was crackling in the fireplace and the lamps were lit, and the occupants were awaiting their visitor.

"It is such a long journey, and she did not arrive until very late last night," Lady Greentree said calmly, making another stitch in her embroidery. "I know you haven't seen her for fourteen years, my dear. Since you and your sisters were taken from her by the baby farmer Mrs. Slater. You may find it a little strange at first, but believe me when I tell you your mother is very eager to reestablish her relationship with you, as far as that will be possible . . . ."

"Oh, but where is she!" cried Marietta, jumping to her feet and all but dancing in her impatience. "I cannot bear to wait another moment!"

Francesca rolled her eyes, but Marietta wasn't deceived—her younger sister was rigid with nerves.

Just then the door opened and the woman they had all been anxiously awaiting entered the room.

Aphrodite stood for a heartbeat. Perhaps it was a habit learned in her younger days, when being noticed was so essential to making her living, or perhaps she was just overwhelmed by the moment. In her black silks and diamonds she was magnificent, a creature from a dark fairytale, and Marietta longed to be just like her.

"Marietta, Francesca, come and meet your mother," Lady Greentree sounded as tranquil as usual, but even she had an edge of strain to her smile. Lady Greentree had been their "mother" since Marietta was two years old, and now she must give way to another. But it was ac-

cepted by all, including Aphrodite, that nothing in their lives would change—all the courtesan was asking for was to be acknowledged by her daughters.

Suddenly shy now, Marietta moved toward Aphrodite. "Ma'am," she said, and curtseyed.

Aphrodite held out her hands, and took those of Marietta warmly in her own. "Marietta, you are grown so beautiful! But then you were always a pretty child."

"Ma'am." Francesca stood well back, not as inclined as Marietta to welcome her mother.

"Francesca, my baby. It has been so long . . ."

But Francesca did not come forward, glancing sideways to the door and clearly wishing herself elsewhere. Marietta felt no such trepidation. As she looked into the face of the famous courtesan she saw that there were tears in her eyes. Tears, because she had found her daughters again! As much as she loved Lady Greentree, this woman was her mother, and suddenly Marietta knew she wanted to be just like her.

In her sleep Marietta smiled. Had she really been so young? The image of herself then seemed as far removed from her present self as the moon. Gradually her memories gave way to dreams. She was floating high above London. Only this time she didn't have a gas balloon to support her. She was riding in a carriage pulled by four horses, and the horses had wings. This was unlikely enough, but even more bizarre was the fact that she was seated beside Max, Lord Roseby, and he was sucking on her fingers. "We're going to Mount Venus," he said, "you'll like it there."

Marietta was enjoying this unusual but rather nice

fantasy, when a sound catapulted her back to her chair in the parlor. There were voices in the vestibule, and they were getting louder. And then a shout, and footsteps, running. Startled, Marietta sat up, quickly returning to full wakefulness. She left her comfortable chair and hurried towards the door.

Dobson had told her not to leave the room, but Marietta didn't think his instructions would apply in the case of an emergency. And, she thought, as she opened the door and her eyes widened at the sight that confronted her, an emergency was just what was happening.

Dobson was kneeling on the marble floor, supporting a man's upper torso against his red-coated chest with one arm, while he pressed a large cloth to the wound on the man's head with the other. There was blood, lots of blood. A servant was standing, her face very white, holding more cloths, while another was clutching a wiry boy by the arm. The door to the street was wide open and cold air blew in, bringing with it the wet smell of a spring shower.

Marietta went to the door and shut it. Then she came and stooped over the injured man, intending to ask Dobson if there was anything she could do to help. She froze. The leather shoes, the fine dark trousers, the buttoned jacket now dirtied and torn. They were all familiar.

It was Max!

She seemed to turn icy and then hot. The room shimmered briefly before it righted itself. The man in Dobson's arms was Max! His face, beneath the bloodied cloth, was pallid, his hair matted. Marietta's hand hovered, and then she snatched it back, for suddenly she did not dare to touch him.

"What happened?" she whispered.

"This errand boy here found him in the lane," Dobson said without looking up from his task. "He came and got me."

Only a short time ago Max had been holding her hand in his, his mouth against her skin, his dark eyes promising her all sorts of things. And now he was lying, hurt, unconscious.

"Was he in an accident? A fight?" she said.

Dobson reached for a clean cloth, and Marietta saw the gash on Max's temple bleeding sluggishly, and shivered. "Weren't no accident, and he's not been robbed. And take a look at his hands," he suggested. "That's the way to tell if a man's been in a stoush."

Tentatively Marietta touched one of Max's large hands where it lay, fingers curled, on the floor beside her. He felt cold, and instinctively she tried to warm his flesh with hers.

"Are his knuckles bruised?" Dobson asked.

She turned his hand, inspecting the long fingers with their square, capable-looking nails. "No."

"Then he wasn't in a fight. I reckon he was set upon while he was walking, and knocked down with no warning."

"Who could have done such a brutal thing?"

"Could have been any number of coves."

"Let me go," the boy suddenly whined. "I done you a good turn, ain't I? I need to get back to the bonesetters. There'll be gen'lemen wantin' fares."

"Bonesetters?" Marietta said.

"Hackney coaches," Dobson explained.

"Oh."

Dobson looked at the boy, his face grim. "You didn't see nothing?"

"Not a thing," the boy said quickly, meeting his eyes. "Just the gen'leman, lyin' on the ground. I recognized him, from fetching him a bonesetter a couple o' times before. Knew he'd come from the club."

Dobson nodded. "You did a good deed. Good deeds are rewarded, remember that." He glanced at the servant who still held the errand boy. "Take him to Madame and tell her I said he was to have a crown."

The servant's eyes popped. "A crown, Mr. Dobson!"

"Yes. He's saved a life tonight. I reckon he deserves a crown."

The boy crowed as he was led off.

"Any sign of the leech yet?" This to the servant with the cloths.

"Not yet, Mr. Dobson."

"Right then, we'd better get the gen'leman upstairs and into a bed. No point in leaving him down here in the cold."

"What can I do?" Marietta asked instantly.

Dobson turned to her with warm gray eyes. "What are you like at bandaging, Miss Marietta? I've done some of that on the battlefield in me time, but I don't have a woman's gentle touch, if you get my meaning."

"I-I'm certain I can manage," Marietta said, because he seemed to expect it of her.

"Goodo. Then follow me."

With the help of a burly footman, Max was carried upstairs and into a bedroom at the far end of the gallery. The room was neat and clean and plainly decorated. There was nothing suggestive in the cream quilt or the pale chintz curtains or the white porcelain jug and bowl—not at all what Marietta had expected from a house of ill repute.

Was that another flutter of disappointment she felt? Had she really expected it to be so shocking?

While the servant lit a fire, Max's boots were removed by Dobson and the footman, and Marietta was sent for warm water and more cloths. By the time she returned Max had been put to bed. She set about gently cleaning the wound on his head—beginning at his temple where the gash ran up into his hair and the thick curls were stiff and matted with dried blood. She hadn't realized before how curly his hair was, or how long—it hung in dark twists over his brow and kissed his nape. It seemed a shame she had to cut some of it to get at the wound.

Someone had used a great deal of force to strike Max—maybe they had even hoped to kill him rather than just incapacitate him. When Marietta suggested this to Dobson, he replied that some men didn't care who they hurt. His coolness about the matter made her think he had known many such men.

"I hope the doctor comes soon," Marietta said. "The bleeding has stopped, and the wound is clean, but I don't know what I should do next. It is quite deep, and I think it will need to be held together, to allow it to heal properly."

"He needs sewing up," Dobson replied, casting his expert eye over her efforts. "Best if we let the leech do that, miss."

Relieved Marietta agreed. "Will it leave a scar, do you think?" she said, speaking her thoughts aloud. "Lord Roseby is a handsome man and it would be a pity to spoil his looks."

Dobson raised an eyebrow at her.

She felt her color rising and her voice took on a justifying note. "I'm thinking of Lord Roseby, of course."

"Of course. I doubt it'll scar if the job's done proper. Besides, some women like a man with a scar or two. Shows he's been out in the world a bit."

Marietta tried to imagine Max with a scar, apart from the one he already had on his chin, which was barely noticeable. She touched his hair, gently brushing it away from the wound. He made no sound. Although his chest was rising and falling quite normally he was dreadfully pale; his lashes lay like dark crescents upon his cheeks. He didn't look like the man in the balloon, or the Max who had made her quiver as he inspected her palm. He looked helpless and vulnerable and dangerously appealing.

Downstairs the doorknocker was violently manipulated, and voices and footsteps on the stairs followed soon after. The doctor appeared in the doorway, looking as if he had been dragged out of bed only moments before. He barely seemed to notice Dobson or herself, his gaze fastening at once upon Max as he moved forward to examine his patient.

"Hmm, nasty," he commented, prodding the wound with a force that made Marietta wince. "Whoever did this wasn't just trying to put him to sleep."

Marietta, observing over his shoulder, hated to think that such desperate people lived in such close proximity to Aphrodite's home. The doctor glanced around, seeking whomever was in charge, and Dobson cleared his throat.

"I'll sew the wound," the doctor said. "It will be easier while he is unconscious. The gentleman seems to be breathing evenly, but a blow to the head like that can cause damage to the brain. Bruising and swelling, even bleeding inside the skull."

"Should we make arrangements to take Lord Roseby home?" Dobson asked.

"No, no, best to leave him where he is for now," the doctor spoke authoritatively. "My advice would be as little disturbance as possible. Let him sleep and, if he wakes, give him water or broth, if he can take either. Someone must keep a watch on him; he should not be left on his own."

The stitching was an unpleasant business. Marietta was given the task of holding Max's head still, her palms gentle but firm on either side of his face. He didn't struggle—he was beyond it—and apart from an occasional wrinkle of his brow it was as if he was oblivious to the doctor's probing. It wasn't until the wound was sewn, and the doctor put on a fresh bandage, that his eyes flickered and opened.

"Miss Greentree?" Max looked up at Marietta, clearly puzzled, before his gaze slid to the doctor.

"Sir? Can you hear me, sir?" the doctor held his attention.

"Of course I can hear you. You're shouting," Max said grumpily. And then, trying to sit up, "What's going on?" But the slight movement drew a low, agonized groan from him, and a cry of, "Dear God, my head!"

"You were hit, sir. Nothing to worry about. Close your eyes now and rest. That's it."

Max didn't need to be told twice. He had already shut his eyes and appeared to have fallen asleep, or lost consciousness. The doctor was pleased with even that brief, lucid moment, however.

"He'll be right as rain," he announced with jovial certainty. "I'll come and see him in the morning, but I don't expect there to be any complications now." He caught Marietta's wide-eyed glance and smiled reassuringly, "Oh, he'll be sore, miss, don't doubt it, but he'll live to make his nurse's life a misery, you mark my words. I've seen forthright gentlemen like him before, and they don't like to be incapacitated."

After a few more stern instructions, the doctor and Dobson left the room, and Marietta was alone with Max.

He didn't wake again, or move. Watching him in silence, she decided that he looked even more like a Byronic hero than before, if that were possible. Although Marietta had never been much of an admirer of the wild antics of the late Lord Byron—Victorian society considered him shocking—Francesca was besotted with him. *So romantic, so tragic!* As she looked upon the stricken Lord Roseby, for the first time Marietta could understand Francesca's addiction.

It was an amazing thing, to find oneself attracted to a man one didn't know. The jolt of recognition, the tingling in her bones, frightened her and Marietta had no intention of allowing it to go further. She had enjoyed flirting with Max earlier, and she felt sorry for him now, but there must be no more to it than that. Max would recover and go his own way, and she would go hers.

Aphrodite arrived in due course. She had a worry line etched upon her normally smooth brow, and Marietta noticed that her eyes were tired. "You must go home at once, Marietta," she said. "I should never have let you stay so long. I will sit with Lord Roseby."

Marietta looked again at Aphrodite's weary face. "No. You go to Vivianna. I don't mind staying—I want to. I know Lord Roseby, remember? If he were to wake in pain and confusion . . . Well, it will not be such a shock if he sees me rather than some stranger."

Aphrodite gave her a look that was a mixture of amusement, irritation and doubt. "I am sure Lady Greentree would be very cross with me if I let you stay here with a man you hardly know. It is not the done thing, Marietta."

"Mama would be cross if I did *not* stay," Marietta corrected her politely. "She brought me up to always be kind and helpful to injured creatures, no matter who or what they are."

Aphrodite gave a little snort of laughter. "Very good, Marietta! You are accomplished at getting your own way, I see."

"Honestly, Aphrodite, I will be perfectly all right. It is my duty to stay. Please, I feel as if it is partly my fault. If I hadn't made him cross he would never have strode off in such high dudgeon. He'd still be here, enjoying himself." She did feel responsible for Max, and not just because his leaving had been her fault. It was as if she already knew him well enough to worry about his welfare.

Aphrodite sighed and shook her head. "*Very* good at getting your own way," she murmured. Then, with a little shrug, "Very well. The doctor has told me he may be thirsty when he wakes, so I will have some water brought up for him. And there will be broth kept warm downstairs, in case he needs that later on. As for you . . . one of the servants will bring you tea and sandwiches, Marietta, *mon petit puce*."

Startled, Marietta blinked. Did Aphrodite just call her a little flea?

But Aphrodite's thoughts had moved on from such mundane considerations as broth and tea. "You will think me very hard-hearted, and you must believe I do care about what has been done to Lord Roseby, but I am wondering at the moment whether this will be good for my business. How do you think it looks when the customers of Aphrodite's Club are knocked down upon leaving? As pleasant as these surroundings are, they may well think twice about calling if they are risking their lives."

Marietta did not believe Aphrodite was hard-hearted at all—as a businesswoman her concern was valid. "Perhaps no one will know."

"I think it is already too late. The servants know, and the doctor, and the errand boy who found him. They will all talk to their friends. And what if the monster who did this to Lord Roseby does it again, to another gentleman? No, no, this is not at all a good thing."

Marietta hadn't thought of that. "Do you think it will happen again?"

"I do not know, *mon petit puce*. But we must ask ourselves this: Was it a random attack or was it aimed at Lord Roseby in particular? He is involved in a scandal of the blackest kind. His father has disowned him, his life is ruined. Perhaps there is someone out there who is not satisfied with him being merely ruined; perhaps they want him dead."

Marietta opened her mouth and closed it again. Max, dead? She felt dizzy with dread at the picture forming in her mind. It was odd, because she was not even certain that she liked him. He had sunk himself in gloom at his own misfortune, and yet he had related with her sense of adventure. When she had questioned his abilities as a lover, he had proved he was quite capable of making her heart thump and her flesh quiver. He had held her hand in his and sucked her fingertips, and gazed meaningfully into her eyes, and just before Aphrodite had interrupted them, he had been going to kiss her. And she would have let him; she had been looking forward to it.

Aphrodite was observing her, and Marietta had the uncomfortable feeling that her mother had read every thought that flitted across her face. The courtesan must be adept at understanding gestures and expressions—unlocking her clients' secrets was one of the tools of her profession.

This seemed like the moment to talk of her own hopes and ambitions.

"May I speak to you, Aphrodite?"

"Of course!"

Marietta doubted Max could hear them, but she still felt awkward expressing her most private thoughts in front of him. She opened the door and stepped outside into the gallery. With a puzzled smile, her mother followed.

"Do you remember when you came to Greentree Manor, and we were reunited?" Marietta began cautiously.

"Of course I remember! To be with my two youngest daughters again after so long . . . I will never forget."

"And do you know what I thought when I saw you, Aphrodite?"

Aphrodite shook her head, clearly puzzled. "No, Marietta, what was it you thought?"

"You were so different, so exciting. Greentree Manor had not seen anything as exotic as you since a circus leopard escaped onto the moors and it took twenty men to recapture it." Marietta took a breath, realizing she was becoming a little melodramatic and Aphrodite was hiding a smile. "I always intended to fall wildly in love, like Vivianna. I suppose that was why I was so foolish as to run away with Gerard Jones, despite all the good advice I had to the contrary. I was a silly little romantic, in love with the idea of love. I know better now. I know that my destiny lies in becoming a courtesan, like you, and I want you to help me attain my goal."

Aphrodite's smile faded and she went still, seeming to withdraw into herself. Marietta waited, not knowing what to expect, but hoping that her mother would understand what she was asking. That she might even be proud that one of her daughters wanted to follow in her silk-slippered footsteps.

But as impatient as she was, the waiting grew too much for her. "Aphrodite, what are you thinking?"

The courtesan fixed Marietta with her dark gaze. "I am thinking that this is nothing but another romantic dream, *mon petit puce.* The life of a courtesan is not romantic. To survive in her world, to thrive in her world, a courtesan needs to be practical and clever and cold-hearted, just as I was a moment ago, when I wondered whether the attack on poor Lord Roseby would be bad for business. There is nothing of romance in it, or if there is, then it is very fleeting and must be . . . suppressed. You see, Marietta, romance is love and a woman cannot be a courtesan and love only one man. Many prosperous careers have been destroyed through falling in love."

Marietta could not help but ask, "Have you ever fallen in love with just one man, Aphrodite?"

Her mother smiled, and there was something about that smile that reminded Marietta of Vivianna when she looked at Oliver. "Ah yes, I have loved, and it was love that finally led me to end my career."

Marietta wanted to ask more, but the need to discuss her own plans had greater urgency.

"How can I make you understand? I don't care about love anymore. I have ruined myself for love, and I have had my fill of it. I do not mean ever to put myself into a man's power again, or to place my trust in his keeping."

"You want to remain in control of your own destiny," Aphrodite said softly. "You want to protect your heart. I understand that."

"Yes!" she answered with relief. "And if I did not take this path, then what else would I do, Aphrodite? Stay at home and dream of what might have been? Allow Uncle William to lecture me on my scandalous behavior? I cannot, I *will* not. I want to live my life as fully as I can."

Aphrodite smiled. "Is there no other choice between these two extremes?"

"I cannot see it."

The courtesan sighed. "Being my daughter has destroyed all your chances of happiness. I see it now, and it is all my fault."

"No!"

"*Oui, oui,* it is. Because I was selfish and wanted children of my own. That is so, Marietta."

"How can Gerard be your fault? I was young and silly, and I let myself be swept away by him. He was a clever cad, but if I had been wiser, more cautious, I would have seen through him. No, I ruined myself. It is my fault and mine alone, and I accept that, just as I accept that I will never allow myself to love and trust a man again. But I do not intend to let any of those things spoil my life. I want to *live*, Madame, surely there is nothing wrong with that?"

Aphrodite sighed. "Marietta, you cannot just wish for a thing and have it happen to you. A courtesan does more than smile and take a gentleman's coat and hat. You know this."

She stepped closer. "Of course I do. I know what men want, and I'm sure I have some aptitude—I am your daughter, after all. I do not pretend I am very experienced in these matters. But I think I can learn, I want to learn. That is why I have come to you."

Aphrodite cast up her eyes, but she was smiling.

"Do you see now why I think I would make a very good courtesan, madame? I am not looking for romance, I am very practical, and my reputation is already in tatters."

Now Aphrodite laughed aloud, but sobered as quickly. "You say these things, but you do not really know—"

"That is why I want you to teach me!"

The courtesan's dark gaze slid over her, before returning to her face. She was reading her, judging her sincerity, and suddenly it was extremely important that Aphrodite take her seriously.

"Aphrodite, please," she sounded as desperate as she felt. "I don't know what else to do but ask you again to help me."

"Hush, child, listen to me for just one moment. Have you truly considered what it is you *are* asking of me? You will be stepping well outside the boundaries of polite society. You think you are beyond them now, but you are not. Being a courtesan is to be a woman apart. *Is* that what you want? Have you truly understood what this decision will mean in five, ten, twenty years time?"

The way Aphrodite put it did make the consequences of her decision sound daunting, but Marietta was not a coward. She had chosen her direction and would not turn back so easily—besides what were her alternatives? Allow Oliver to find some willing victim to wed her despite her ruined reputation? Live at Berkley Square as a spinster aunt for the remainder of her days? The choice of courtesan was exciting and a little frightening in comparison because it was so unconventional, but it was one she was eager to embrace.

Of course, there was her family to consider and the effect upon them. Marietta was aware that people would call her selfish, and that there would be gossip, but she had thought long and hard on the matter and she did not see that the situation could be much worse than it already was—she was the ruined sister already. Her family might suffer privately from her actions, yes, but that did not mean the rest of the world needed to know. She would change her name, her identity—Marietta would vanish from sight and Madame Coeur would be born—that was the name she had chosen for herself. In time her family would accept her decision and see that it was right for her—Marietta truly believed that.

"There would be compensations, surely?" she said at last.

"Oh yes, there are compensations." Aphrodite tapped her chin with one elegant finger. "May I suggest something to you, *mon petit puce*? Before you make up your mind irrevocably, I want you to have a . . . a, what do they call it, a trial! Not a trial in a court, I do not mean that. I want you to try out the life of a courtesan, and see if it is what you really want."

"But I know I—" Marietta began impatiently.

"Yes, yes, you think you know. But the reality of living such a life is quite different to the imagining of it. And when I say to try it out, I am not saying you should wander about Aphrodite's Club peeping into doorways. No, you should work with a flesh and blood man. Someone who is willing to take part in your game, but who knows it is a temporary affair, and that if you change your mind he has no power over you whatsoever."

Marietta trembled, feeling the excitement building inside her. "I won't change my mind. It is what I want above all things."

"I almost believe you."

"*Almost* . . . ." Marietta felt frustrated. Why wouldn't Aphrodite believe her? Why couldn't she accept that Marietta was completely sincere in her desire?

"No, no, listen to me, *mon petit puce*. If you do as I tell you, and if, once the game is over, you still want to pursue the life of a courtesan, then I promise I will help you. I will give my time and experience to you, completely!"

"I don't understand," Marietta said carefully. "You want me to practice at being a courtesan but you also want me to have the option of changing my mind if I don't like it? How can I do that? Once I have burnt my bridges, then surely I can never go back to being Miss Marietta Greentree?"

"No, you cannot. But I have an idea. You will choose one man upon whom to practice. You will play the courtesan with him, learning how to think and use your senses, and at the same time he will teach you what it is to feel desire and to mold that desire for your own purposes. So you will both gain something from your liaison, and neither will go away unhappy, whatever the final outcome."

"I don't want to fall in love—" Marietta began uneasily.

"I did not say that you would love him, *mon petit puce*. I said you would *desire* him. A courtesan must desire, she must learn to show the man she is with that she desires, make him feel as if he is everything to her, the best of lovers. You see?"

"Yes, I see." Marietta thought a moment, some of her excitement fading beneath a new apprehension. "But who would agree to such a thing? I don't know any man who would be willing to be used like that and then say nothing if I changed my mind—which I won't!"

Aphrodite gave her a little smile, and reached out to open the bedroom door. Inside, Max lay unmoving upon the bed, his dark curls tumbling over the white bandage, his profile pale and handsome.

And even before she spoke, Marietta knew what she was going to say.

Chapter 4

"**M**ax? You want me to use Max? Oh no, you cannot mean—"

"But why not Max? He is embroiled in a terrible scandal so if he decides to tell the world your secrets then no one will listen to a word he says. But he will not tell because he is a gentleman, and a desirable one, with a great deal of experience. He can teach you much, and you can use your new skills upon him. He is perfect for the role."

Aphrodite wanted her to use Max in her courtesan training. She wanted Max to teach her about desire. She wanted Marietta to practice seduction and the use of her senses on *Max* . . .

"Good heavens," she whispered.

"He is a good choice, Marietta. I would not suggest him if I thought he would be any danger to you."

"But . . . he wanted to buy me for an entire night's pleasure!"

72

"An entire night, eh?" Aphrodite smiled wickedly. "That was when he made the mistake of thinking you were one of my protégés. As soon as he realized his error he became the perfect gentleman once more. *That* was why he was so upset with you, my innocent Marietta. Lord Roseby had set his heart upon having 'connection' with you, but he is far too much of an English gentleman to seduce what he thinks is an innocent girl of your class and breeding. He is the perfect man for your little game, *oui*?"

"Oh." Was that why he had been so cross—like a little boy who has been given a shilling and finds the sweets shops are all closed? Because he had wanted her and he believed she was out of his reach.

Aphrodite was twisting a gold mesh bangle upon her slim wrist. "So, do you think you can persuade his lordship to say yes?"

"I am not sure," Marietta said pensively. She took a breath. "I beg your pardon, Aphrodite, but even if he does want my body, I cannot believe he would agree to play such a role."

Aphrodite chuckled. "He is hurt and you are caring for him. Max is a gentleman and he will feel he owes you a favor, Marietta. Make use of that. And as for him not agreeing to play such a part . . . Doesn't that make it an even greater test of your skills? It will be a challenge, and I think that is what you need. I want you to show me you are serious in your endeavor."

"But—"

Aphrodite grew formidable. "No buts, listen to me now. In this game there will be rules you must abide by and there will be tasks you must accomplish. I will set you a task, and when you have completed it, then I will set you another, and so it will go. When the game is over, if you have completed all your tasks to my satisfaction, without breaking the rules, then I promise that I will help you in whatever way you wish."

The thought of Aphrodite's unconditional help made her giddy. But Marietta was a practical girl, and she asked, "What will my first task be?"

"Ah, he must kiss you—"

"But that is simple!"

"Yes, but you must ask him to show you *how* to kiss."

Marietta's cheeks flushed pink. There was something very risqué in such an idea, and yet she said, "I know how to kiss. Gerard kissed me."

"*Psht*! Who was this Gerard? He was a nobody. Max Valland is a duke's son, Marietta, who has been on the town for many years and has had a great many women. Believe me, he knows how to kiss."

Marietta found that she had to actually take a deep breath, in order to think clearly. "When you say that Max and I will have a temporary affair, do you mean we will . . . do you mean it will be physical?"

Aphrodite looked at her carefully. "It will be whatever you wish, Marietta. Do not frighten yourself yet with what may or may not happen. Let things develop and wait and see, *oui*? Each affair has its own pace, its own beginning and its own end. First you must get Max to agree, and that may well prove the most difficult part of all."

But if what Aphrodite said was true, and Max desired her body, then surely that would be to her advantage? His wanting her would help her to win him over. Therefore it would not be as difficult as she feared, and Aphrodite would *have* to keep her promise.

"Very well," she said quickly. "I will do it."

"Then it is a bargain."

"Thank you for—"

But Aphrodite motioned her to silence, and her voice was brisk once more. "We will talk about it again. I will make sure that Vivianna knows you are staying tonight. Remember to ask Dobson or the servants if there is anything you need. The club will be open and busy until dawn, so do not fear you are disturbing them."

"Thank you."

Aphrodite left, and Marietta slipped back inside the bedroom with Max. She stood close to the bed, so that she could look down at him. Suddenly this stranger had taken on a new and fascinating appeal. He was going to help her attain her wishes—somehow she must persuade him to agree, whether he wanted to or not.

Max lay very still beneath the bedclothes. Dobson had stripped him of his clothing after he sent Marietta from the room, and Marietta didn't know whether he was completely naked or not, but she could see his bare shoulders and throat. Smooth skin curved over the muscles of his upper arms, and his throat was broad and strong, while on his chest, just before the bedclothes cut off her view, there were some wisps of dark hair.

She barely remembered Gerard Jones without his clothes on and what she did remember made her shudder. There had been a great deal of haste; perhaps Gerard had realized Marietta was having serious doubts and might balk at the final hurdle. Had she enjoyed it? No, she hadn't. She had lost her virginity and her reputation for very little, really. If a girl was ruined, then shouldn't she at least savor it?

Marietta hovered over Max. The doctor had done a good job when he sewed the wound and bandaged it, and apart from some of the blood that still matted strands of his hair, Max looked clean and comfortable. His whiskers were beginning to show dark against his pale skin, and when she ran her fingertip over his jaw, it felt slightly prickly and rough. Is this what she would do, if she really was a courtesan out to seduce him? Touch him like this?

It was surprisingly easy—a tremble of excitement started deep in her belly, spreading outwards. Her fingers seemed to move of their own accord, exploring the firm flesh of his chin and jaw, running very lightly over his thin upper lip and the more sensual lower one. She immediately imagined those lips on hers. She touched his eyelids, gently, and brushed her fingertips through the thick curls of his hair. Yes, seducing Max Valland would be an enjoyable experience. But . . .

With a sigh she drew her hand away.

But that was because Max was asleep and could not frown at her or give her one of his haughty ducal looks. Things would be totally different when he was awake and himself again.

If, that is, he ever was.

Marietta sobered abruptly. This was neither the time nor the place to play at being a courtesan. Max was hurt, and despite the doctor's optimism, may be seriously so. And she was his nurse. Tempting as it was, it would not be fair to take advantage of him in his unconscious state.

Marietta sank back into her chair and prepared to keep vigil.

Aphrodite was readying herself to go to Berkley Square, a smile hovering at the corners of her mouth as she remembered her conversation with her second daughter. Marietta believed her task to be an easy one, but Aphrodite knew differently. Max, Lord Roseby, would put up a fight, and although in the end Marietta would probably get her way, the journey would be an interesting one.

As for Marietta, Aphrodite was not certain that she really knew just what she was asking. It was true that she had caused herself a great deal of grief by falling under the spell of the scoundrel Gerard Jones, but setting herself forever beyond her comfortable and familiar world might not be the best answer. Lady Greentree would be saddened and disappointed when she discovered Marietta's ambitions—as liberal as that lady was, Aphrodite could not imagine her applauding her daughter's choice of profession. Still, if Marietta truly wanted to be a courtesan, then what could Aphrodite do but help her to achieve her aim?

Aphrodite smiled again and tapped her finger against her cheek. Well, she could see that Marietta found such a life not to her taste after all. There were alternatives to saying no, which had been Aphrodite's first response, and as she was very much aware that Marietta was not a girl to give up easily, she had not wanted her daughter to feel desperate. Who knew what she might do, if she were pushed into a corner? Better if she believed that Aphrodite was helping her, as she was, just not in the manner Marietta was expecting.

"What amuses you?"

"My daughter, Jemmy. She's very clever, don't you think?"

"She's a minx, my love."

Aphrodite brushed his rough cheek with her fingertip. "I was a minx, too, and it did not harm me."

"It caused us both a lot of grief."

Her breath caught. "Oh Jemmy, I wish—"

But Jemmy Dobson hushed her and took her in his arms. "I didn't mean to stir up bad memories. Go and see your grandson. I'll watch the club for you, and keep an eye on your minx of a daughter."

Aphrodite buried her face in his coat. "She wants to be a courtesan," she sighed.

Dobson chuckled in surprise. "Does she now? Well, she's your daughter, isn't she? She'll follow her own head and her own heart. Just keep her out of too much trouble, my love, and all will be well. It was with Vivianna."

"Yes, you're right. Vivianna turned out well." Aphrodite nodded, and drew away to put the finishing touches to her outfit. "There, what do you think? Will I bring shame upon the house of Montegomery?"

Jemmy smiled, his hard gray eyes full of love. "You are a jewel, Aphrodite, beyond price."

It was close to dawn when Max woke at last. Marietta, who had been dozing off and on as she kept watch from her chair, heard him murmuring, and the swish and slide of the bedclothes as he moved restlessly beneath them.

She jumped up, her legs leaden with weariness, her head dizzy, and stumbled to the side of the bed.

He was shifting about but in an aimless sort of way, as if he didn't know where he was. Marietta put a hand on his shoulder and felt hot, bare skin. "Hush," she said gently, leaning closer. "You're safe, Max. You were hurt, but you're safe now."

The sound of her voice seemed to agitate him more and he tried to sit up. The quilt slipped to his waist, and Marietta saw that he was indeed naked. Broad chested, his tawny skin dusted with dark hair, his stomach flat and hard. She pressed her palms against his shoulders to try and push him back down again, but the feel of him, the heat of him, confused her. Even as her voice murmured reassurance, her mind was focused on something else.

For instance, that he looked and felt so completely different from her, and those differences were fascinating. He had flat aureoles, slightly darker than his chest, and when she accidentally brushed over them his nipples turned tighter and harder. She wanted to do it again. She wanted to lean down and put her mouth to his skin and see what it tasted like. The unfamiliar thoughts shocked her into the realization that once again she was allowing the courtesan to overpower the nurse.

"Please, Max. Back to bed," she begged, as much for her own sake as his.

But she wasn't strong enough to force Max back into the bed, and neither was he paying attention to her coaxing. Now he swung one leg over the side of the mattress, taking her by surprise. Marietta's eyes widened as they traveled the length of that bare leg, hard with muscle. Luckily the bedclothes had tangled around his hips, otherwise Marietta would have seen far more of Max than he would want her to, she was sure. Although, she thought, as she continued to struggle with him, it wouldn't be long before the covers were tugged free. Her gaze skittered away from the dark hair low on his belly.

"Max!" Her voice high and panicked. "Stop it right now!"

He seemed to hear her at last. He stopped pushing against her and his brown eyes opened and fixed on hers. His hair was standing on end, and he looked rumpled and flushed. And Marietta's stomach fluttered in a way it never had before. Nerves, or was it . . . could it be the desire that Aphrodite was just speaking about?

"Wha'?" He blinked at her. " 'Etta?"

"Yes, it's Marietta," she said it as if she were in charge of the situation. "Now go back to bed. You're tired and you need your rest. You can't possibly get up yet. Back to bed, Max, and back to sleep."

He stared at her for a while—as though it took that long for her words to find their way down a long tunnel and into his brain—and then, abruptly, he lay down.

There was only one problem.

Max's leg was still hanging outside the bedclothes. With a groan, Marietta wrapped her hands around his knee, struggling to lift his leg. She tugged but could barely move it. She reached down to his foot and pulled at that, but he simply arched his toes, as though they were ticklish. The sound of the bed creaking made her look up to find his brown eyes only inches from her own. Max had raised his head from the pillows, and he was clearly puzzled by her actions.

"Miss Greentree? What *are* you doing?" he said, surprisingly lucid.

Marietta released his foot and jumped back as if she had been bitten. "You were restless. I was trying to . . . to . . ."

"You were playing with my toes." Giving her one of his haughtiest frowns, Max proceeded to draw his leg modestly under the bedclothes. Then his head fell back against the pillows, his eyes shut, and the frown turned into a grimace.

Tentatively Marietta reached out and pulled the covering up over his chest—removing temptation—and tucked him in securely. But he wasn't asleep.

"Water," he whispered.

She reached for the jug the servant had brought last night, and poured some water into a glass. She supported his head against her shoulder, aware of the heat of his skin even through her layers of clothing. She held the glass to his lips, carefully tipping a little at a time between them. Max swallowed greedily, but after a moment he seemed to have had enough, and turned his face away. Gently she lowered him back onto the pillows, and smoothed his wild curls.

The doctor would be coming this morning, and she was relieved to know it. Max was too hot, surely? A fever was to be expected, but how did she know what was acceptable and what was excessive?

" 'Etta."

"Yes, Max? What is it?" He seemed to know her, so

he must be reasonably lucid. Surely that meant he was all right? If he was in danger, wouldn't he be rambling and half-conscious?

"Blue eyes. Big sparkling blue eyes. And pink lips. Pink lips ripe for kissing."

Well, maybe he wasn't quite as lucid as she'd thought.

"Hush, Max. Go to sleep now. You need to get well."

She wasn't sure whether he heard her or not, but he sighed and in a moment he had relaxed into sleep. Marietta sat and watched him, resisting the wicked little voice in her head that told her to touch him again.

Touch.

This was the part of her future profession to which she had not given much thought. She had brushed over it, believing that the physical aspects of being a courtesan would just come to her naturally—she *was* Aphrodite's daughter. Surely it couldn't be too difficult, and it wasn't as if she hadn't done *it* before. Still there had been a vague, niggling doubt, deep in her mind, that she may not like being touched or touching in return.

But just now, when she had touched Max, the sensation of exploring a naked man's skin, even if it was in her role as nurse and more accidental than deliberate, had been . . . *exciting*. Was it because it *was* Max? Max, with whom she had no intention of becoming emotionally entangled? Max, who made her feel strangely safe? Possibly. Whatever the reason, Marietta told herself that it was a good thing. A courtesan must enjoy the physical aspect of her relationships, she must feel desire. Max could teach her that—she had a feeling he would be a very good teacher.

Max was still asleep, and when she tentatively touched him again he felt a little cooler. Marietta yawned and sat back down in her chair, trying to find a more comfortable position. She told herself that the doctor would be here soon, and wriggled around so that she could rest her cheek on her hand. That was better . . . In another moment she too was asleep.

Max's head throbbed cruelly. He lay with his eyes shut, desperately trying not to be sick, until slowly, tick by tick of the mantel clock, the nausea began to pass and he could begin to remember. He had gone to Aphrodite's Club, and after being inside had left and walked into the lane. He had closed his eyes for some inexplicable reason. He recalled the damp darkness, the sense that he was not alone, just before he was struck down.

Judging by the brutal pain in his head, his assailant had meant business. It felt personal, but Max supposed that was unlikely. He looked like a rich gentleman, and that was enough for some people to take exception to him.

A flash of image. Max concentrated and in his mind saw big blue eyes peering into his. Marietta Greentree? Yes, she had been here in the night. Now he recalled her hands, cool against his chest, and her voice, a balm for all his aches and pains. Or was it just a dream, after all? Had she really been playing with his foot?

Max opened his eyes.

Marietta Greentree was curled up in an armchair, her red and green skirts spread modestly about her. She was resting her flushed cheek on her folded hand, loose strands of fair hair falling forward over her face. She looked helpless and innocent.

And yet this was Aphrodite's daughter. Max started to shake his head in disbelief, only to stop abruptly when the movement caused a pain to slice through his temples. The throbbing began again. Abominably.

He groaned aloud.

Marietta lifted her head slightly. She peered at him through the tangled strands of her fair hair, as if she was disoriented. Then she pushed it out of her eyes and sat up, stretching and yawning widely. Like a kitten after a refreshing nap, or an innocent with nothing to disturb its conscience. *That* was how he saw Marietta Greentree, Max realized uneasily. Innocent and needing his gentlemanly protection. He was certainly finding it difficult to imagine her as the daughter of an infamous courtesan.

He'd been staring at her for too long. Those big blue eyes were gazing back at him, a growing expression of uneasiness in their depths.

"My head hurts," he said pitifully, and it was the honest truth.

"Poor you," Marietta murmured sympathetically. She laid her hand upon his brow, and there was something so soothing in her touch that it instantly felt better. Or perhaps it was the scent of her skin and the curved swell of her breasts beneath her tight bodice that improved his mood.

"Do you remember what happened?" She was

speaking to him again and he tried to concentrate, but before he had a chance to answer she was doing it for him. "You were attacked in a lane, and one of the errand boys found you. Dobson brought you back here to Aphrodite's Club, and sent for the doctor, who stitched your wound and bandaged it. He promised to call again this morning and see how you are feeling."

She seemed to read his next question in his eyes, so he didn't even bother trying to ask it.

"The doctor thought that moving you might make you more unwell, and it was better for you to stay here overnight."

"So you stayed too?" His voice was husky from disuse.

"Someone had to keep watch over you. I was the obvious choice."

She sounded defensive. Did he make her uncomfortable, or was it their current intimate situation that did that? She had not seemed the type to be easily intimidated, but the way in which she clasped her hands in her lap now, as if she was waiting to be scolded, gave him pause.

Had he somehow given her the impression that he was a monster?

He supposed he had been a little out of sorts during the balloon ascent, and he may have slightly startled her with his behavior downstairs, when he tried to buy her services. Perhaps Marietta Greentree was right to be wary, Max admitted reluctantly. Perhaps he was not always as courteous and polite as his mother had brought him up to be. But his father had always impressed upon him that he was the heir to a dukedom and a certain arrogance was to be expected. Even when the dukedom was no longer his, that arrogance was difficult to shake off—bred into him, he supposed.

"Thank you," he said now, as courteously as he could manage, and closed his eyes.

She was leaning over him, so close that he could hear her breathing. He had surprised her. It was quite a feat to disconcert Marietta Greentree of the clear, fearless gaze and decided opinions. Despite the appalling pain in his head Max found himself struggling to keep his mouth from smiling.

"Are you thirsty again?" she asked anxiously. "Would you prefer water or broth?"

Broth? Good God. "Thank you, but no," he said, with feeling. "All I want is to go home. Ring for a servant to fetch me a cab and I will trouble you no further."

Marietta gave a disbelieving laugh. Dear heavens, he expected her to bundle him into a hansom cab and send him home just because he told her to! What a bossy and abominable man he was.

"I will fetch Dobson," she said in a voice that brooked no argument, and went off to do just that.

Dobson, looking tired and with his red jacket unbuttoned at the throat, was just closing the door on the last of the night's guests. When Marietta explained the problem, he said, "You stay here, miss, and let me deal with Lord Roseby." Then, as he headed upstairs, he called over his shoulder, "Better still, go and get something to eat in the kitchen. That's where everyone else'll be."

Marietta, weary from lack of sleep and cramped from sitting upright all night, thought a hot breakfast sounded most appealing. Now, if she could just find the kitchen . . .

In the end she followed her nose. The kitchen was by far the most comfortable part of Aphrodite's Club that she had seen so far. With its enormous scrubbed-pine table and large range, as well as the shelving full of crockery, and the pots and pans dangling from hooks, it looked as a kitchen should look. The cook, a tubby gentleman with a pince-nez, was modestly accepting congratulations from his feminine admirers. They gathered around him in their bright and flimsy gowns, aprons hastily thrown on to save spills and stains, their mouths bulging with bacon and eggs and toast. The rich smell of coffee only added to the general sense of hominess and well-being.

Eagerly, Marietta moved to join them, but as she drew nearer and her presence was noticed, their lively chatter ceased. Now only the sizzle of the food still cooking on the stove broke the silence.

"Dobson said I should come and have some breakfast," she said with a bright, forced smile that turned a little forlorn at the edges. "It smells delicious."

The plump little cook looked delighted with her compliment, and the women—Marietta guessed they were Aphrodite's protégés—began to tuck in once more. Only one of them, a girl with dark hair and eyes, who seemed a little older than Marietta, held out her hand.

"You must be Aphrodite's daughter," she said, with an accent as soft as Irish rain. "I'm Maeve, how do you do? Come and fill yourself a plate. Henri won't mind, will you Henri? He's Aphrodite's chef and he's been with her since . . . oh, since forever!"

Marietta smiled back, relieved to have found a friend. Maeve handed her a plate and Henri proceeded to load it with food until Marietta cried a laughing halt. Seated among the others, she too tucked in, only then realizing how very hungry she was. When had she last eaten? At lunchtime yesterday, before Vivianna had her son, before she came to tell Aphrodite the good news. Before Max. Was that how she would date things from now on? Before and after Max?

"How is he then?" Maeve said, munching on a slice of toast dripping with butter. "Lord Roseby, I mean," she added, as Marietta swallowed her mouthful.

"He's awake and he wants to go home. Dobson has gone upstairs to talk to him."

"Poor man," Maeve said, and shook her head for emphasis.

"Yes, it was a nasty blow."

"No, no, not the hit to his poor head. I meant him being disinherited by his da like that, and after growing from a child in the belief that he would one day be the Duke of Barwon. How must he feel? I think it's awfully sad."

One of the other women gave an inelegant snort. "Serves him right, I say," she pronounced in a voice that had once been cockney but was learning to be refined. "You can't inherit if you're another man's bastard. Everyone knows that."

"But that's not his fault, is it?" someone else piped up, and this brought forth more cries of agreement or disagreement. Marietta, unable to get a word in, gazed about her wide-eyed and realized that these beautiful women were enjoying themselves. Like rowdy schoolgirls let out of class, they were intent on throwing off the airs and graces they were learning so painfully, along with the good manners and languid smiles to please the gentlemen, and just being themselves. Perhaps here, in Henri's kitchen, was the only place in Aphrodite's Club where they *could* be themselves.

Just then a chilly voice spoke from the doorway. "Are you all still here? Laura, surely you have French lessons? And Donna, you too. And what of you, Maeve, isn't dancing instruction in a few minutes? Ladies, you have much to learn before you can go to bed and sleep. *Allevouz!*"

Cutlery clattered on china, chairs grated as they were pushed back, and the girls scattered. Maeve gave Marietta a grin as she left, but everyone else was too intent on obedience. In a moment the kitchen was empty, apart from Henri, who was conspicuously busy over the stove. Aphrodite came up behind him, almost silent in her silk slippers. "Henri," she said in a voice more weary than it had been a moment before, "why do you encourage them to be bad?"

Henri shot her a mock-innocent look over his pince-nez. "Ah, but they do not need much encouragement, Madame. And besides, it does them good to be bad sometimes—to disobey their maman."

Aphrodite shook her head, her diamond earrings glittering like stars against the black night of her hair. "I am not their maman, Henri, and nor am I an ogre. I am trying to make them what they want to be. Most of them have come from nothing, or worse. They know what it is to be poor and alone, to be desperate, and they do not want to go back to it. I am only trying to make their dreams come true."

Henri smiled at her with gentle affection. "I know that, Madame, but they do not all have your aptitude or strength of character. Sometimes they grow weary and cannot see an end to all that you make them do. It is when they cannot see their destination clearly that the journey becomes too onerous for them."

Marietta glanced between the two of them. Obviously Henri had been with Aphrodite for many years and knew her well, and she respected and liked him, because she did not rebuke him for his comments, even if her expression showed she did not agree.

"They do not have to stay with me," she said coolly.

Henri grimaced, as if to say, Where else would they go?

"I do not run a charitable organization."

Henri clanged his pots and pans. "No, Madame, of course not. You only take in girls who are friendless and without hope and give them a chance at a better life. How could that be charity?"

"Others would say I corrupt them," Aphrodite said frankly. "That they are no longer fit for respectable society once I have had them here."

"Then I think those 'others' should speak with the girls," Henri replied levelly, "and ask them what they think, and whether their lives now are not much better than they would have been otherwise. Some people wear their morals like chains around their necks—they would prefer a girl to die of starvation, or suffer in a bitter home, than live the sort of independent life you can teach her. There is a risk, *oui*, but there is risk in everything we do."

Aphrodite smiled. "You put it very well, *mon ami*."

Henri pushed his pince-nez back up his nose. "Do you think this attack on Lord Roseby is aimed at you, Madame? Does someone wish harm on Aphrodite's Club? Or is it *you* they wish to harm—"

"Henri," Aphrodite said softly, in warning. Her beringed hand came to rest on Marietta's shoulder. "I have come to tell my daughter that Lord Roseby has expressed a wish to go home. The doctor has just examined him and he says it will be safe for him to do so, and right now Dobson is arranging for his coach to come and collect him—I think it will be more comfortable for him to be in familiar surroundings."

"Oh." Marietta glanced from one to the other, her head still reeling from Henri's disclosures. "I am glad he is better."

"You should go with him," Aphrodite said levelly.

Marietta met her eyes, trying to read them, but there was no clue. Perhaps Aphrodite was genuinely concerned for Max's well-being, or perhaps she was giving Marietta the chance to begin practicing on Max.

What would he say when she told him?

He'd say no, of course he would. Well, she would have to find some way to persuade him to say yes.

"Does *he* want me to go with him?" she asked tentatively.

"*Psht!* What Lord Roseby wants is of no importance, *mon petit puce*. You will insist upon it."

Insist upon it. That sounded promising. Maybe she could bully Max into doing as she wished . . . or maybe not.

Max had no idea yet that he was to be the lock she must open to fulfill her goal. Marietta could not help but feel a little weak with dread when she imagined what he would say and do when he did.

Chapter 5

~~⌒⌒~~

When Marietta and Aphrodite reached the vestibule, Max's coach had already arrived and was waiting outside. It was, she thought, a very nice coach for a disinherited duke, with an insignia on the side to show who it had once belonged to, and a large coachman in uniform holding the horses. Just at that moment two burly footmen appeared in the gallery, carrying Lord Roseby between them. Dobson came up the rear, directing the awkward group as they descended the stairs. Max was dressed in the same torn and muddied clothing he had worn last night, his face was white and drawn, and he looked rather sick. But his mouth was set in those arrogant, stubborn lines that Marietta was coming to know so well.

The disinherited duke was clearly set on getting his way, whether it was good for him or not.

"Marietta is going to accompany Lord Roseby," Aphrodite said to Dobson.

"Yes, Madame." The only sign that Dobson was surprised by this revelation was a faint lift of his eyebrows.

Not so Max. There was no mistaking his feelings on the matter. "No, she is not," he said emphatically.

"Yes, I am," Marietta retorted, trying to reign in her impatience. "You look like you're at death's door, Max. What if you were to have a-a relapse on the journey home? You need me there to take care of you, and that is just what I mean to do."

"Take care of me!" But clearly raising his voice hurt his head and he sensibly lowered it. "I don't need help," he said through clenched teeth.

"You do. What are you afraid of? I promise you I have no intention of ravishing you in your carriage."

He laughed, and then groaned, but whether from pain or sheer frustration Marietta didn't know. She pretended it was from the former, and murmured solicitously as she followed them outside to the coach, and helped to make him comfortable inside. There were an array of cushions and bolsters that someone had thoughtfully placed on the seats, and a travel rug, which she tucked around him fussily while he stared at her with haunted eyes.

"For pity's sake," he whimpered, "leave me alone."

"You should have stayed in bed, Max. I did warn you but you wouldn't listen."

He fixed her with a look, his eyes bright through the screen of his dark lashes. Marietta had often heard the saying *if looks could kill*, but she had never really understood its true meaning—until now.

"You may not believe this, Miss Greentree, but knowing you were right does not alleviate my present condition," he said. "Why couldn't one of my servants have accompanied me home? Where is Pomeroy?"

"I don't know where Pomeroy is. Perhaps he was busy."

Max didn't bother to answer that, instead he closed his eyes with grim determination, and kept them shut.

Marietta smiled to herself, and leaned back against the soft squabs as the coach set off. It was very selfish of her, but perhaps Max's injury would work to her advantage. If she could win a promise from him while he was in a weakened state so much the better for her plans.

As they traversed the streets of London, Marietta realized that she had no idea where Max lived. The question had never come up. She opened her mouth to ask him, but he was lying so stiffly opposite her, and was so obviously in pain, that she did not speak after all.

I know hardly anything about him.

The thought gave her pause. Although she felt a strange sense of recognition for Max, a feeling of familiarity, the truth was she and he were near strangers. When she acknowledged it, she felt afraid. Aphrodite had put Max forward as the man to practice upon, and it had seemed a simple task, but now . . . Marietta took a steadying breath, reminding herself that she didn't have to do this. She could change her mind.

Well, couldn't she?

And what then? Live her life in the shadows? Marietta knew she couldn't bear that—it would not be living at all. As a courtesan she would have a full life, and yet be free of the fear of being emotionally hurt again. Her heart would be protected. Safe. The men who would be her companions would give her a chance to enjoy herself in ways that were material and physical, but she would not love them. Max might be a stranger, but he was no more so than the men she must learn to please if she became a courtesan.

Satisfied by her self-persuasion, at least for the moment, Marietta relaxed. Only to be shaken by a sudden crash outside the coach. Their driver shouted and swerved, and the wheels lurched violently. Marietta gripped the leather strap and looked out of the window in time to see an overturned timber cart, with lengths of wood spread across the roadway. Their coach driver must have run over the timber, but he was luckier, or cleverer, than some of those following.

A glance across at Max told her that he would not be impressed by her description of the scene. He had his eyes tight shut and his teeth gritted as agony lanced through the wound in his head. He would have been better off staying at Aphrodite's, but Marietta could sympathize with his need to get home to familiar surroundings.

"Do you want me to—" she began.

"No."

"You don't know what I'm going to say yet," she told him mildly.

"I don't care."

"I was going to ask if you wished to rest your head on my lap. It might be softer, and I could shield you from some of the worst bumps."

Max glared at her, his eyes narrow slits gleaming with bad temper. "You wish me to rest my head on your lap? Would you like to stroke my brow, too?"

"Do you want me to?" Marietta asked, making her eyes wide and innocent.

He snorted, and then groaned as his headache stabbed sheer agony into the echoing vault that was his skull. Although Max had his share of illnesses and accidents—some would say more than his fair share of the latter—such pain was new to him. He'd never suffered from headaches—an innocuous name for what was currently going on in his head. Why on earth had he declined the doctor's offer of a hefty dose of laudanum? What had he been trying to prove? Sheer pigheaded pride and stubbornness he supposed, the same stubborn pride that was preventing him from resting his head on Marietta Greentree's delightful lap.

Without warning the coach rattled over some uneven cobbles, and suddenly his pride dissolved. "Do it then," he said between white lips. "Please."

Looking concerned rather than triumphant, Marietta slipped into the seat beside him, and settled herself carefully among the cushions. She lifted his head, gently, and Max raised himself up with a muttered curse. After a brief, painful period of shuffling about, Max's head was resting on her lap, Marietta was bracing one arm over his shoulders to help steady him, while her other hand lay upon his brow. Her fingers seemed naturally to curl in the threads of his dark hair, as she stroked it back from the bandage.

"How is that, Lord Roseby?" she said sweetly.

Was she teasing him? Mocking his arrogance? Max didn't care. His pain was still excruciating but somehow it didn't matter as much now that Marietta's scent was all around him, and he was enveloped by her soft body. Max sighed as she brushed her fingertips lightly over his skin, almost a caress. Turning his face towards her, he snuggled closer. The swell of her breast was heavy against his cheek. As Marietta held him against the roll and jolt of the coach, he wanted to press even closer. He wanted to . . . to unbutton her bodice and put his lips on her bare skin. To run his tongue over the lush curves of her breasts.

The hot rush of desire surprised him, but at least it helped him to forget his headache.

"Your coach needs new springs," she said in that know-it-all voice he hated.

"Can't afford 'em," he murmured against the stiff cloth of her bodice, and the soft swell of her breast. He had never felt anything quite so tantalizing, being this close and yet knowing that he was unable, incapable, of taking advantage of it.

Take advantage? Max blinked and tried to clear his mind. No, no, *he* didn't take advantage, *he* was a gentleman. Wasn't he? Yes, he was, despite his new scandalous status.

"Oh. So you *can't* afford new springs for your coach, and yet you *can* afford a visit to Aphrodite's? I don't call that sound economics."

He turned his head so that he could look up and see her face properly, and wasn't so distracted by other things. "Is this any of your business, Miss Greentree?"

She fixed him with an intent look. "It may be. Which girl were you going to request at Aphrodite's? Before you saw me, of course."

"Of course."

She sounded smug, and he supposed she had the right to be. He *had* offered to pay for an entire night of her company. What in God's name had possessed him? Some form of madness, that was certain. Well, he was cured of it now, Max told himself, at the same time snuggling in against her. She smelled of roses and woman, and despite her stays, she was incredibly soft . . .

He opened one eye and looked up at her. She appeared to be waiting for something, but when he tried to remember what it was he got caught up in the perfect shape of her face and her pert little nose and those long, curling dark lashes framing her blue eyes.

"Which girl, Max? Have there been so many that you can't remember?" She sounded unhappy with him; now her fingers were tugging at his hair rather than caressing.

Max cleared his throat. "Why . . . ?"

"Was it Maeve?" Marietta asked suddenly, but she was hoping it wasn't. This morning Maeve had seemed like a possible friend, but that didn't mean she wanted Maeve and Max to have been lovers. It made her uncomfortable.

Max fixed her with another one of his slightly unfocused looks, as if he'd misplaced her name. "No," he said at last. "Not Maeve. Anyway, a gentleman isn't supposed to reveal such things."

He said it so pompously that Marietta's fingers itched to yank out the hair she was smoothing. Instead she said, "I'm not asking you to tell secrets, my lord. I'm interested in . . . in whether you have a favorite type of woman. I have heard it said that men have preferences. For instance: dark or fair hair or auburn, blue eyes or brown, tall or short, plump or slender. Tell me, do you have a preference, my lord?"

"No, I don't," he said stubbornly. And then, the frown leaving his face, "You called me 'my lord.' What happened to Max?"

"I decided it was improper. You are a lord, and we are near strangers. I shouldn't be calling you by your first name."

"I'm not a lord, not anymore," Max muttered. He moved restlessly, winced, and then sighed. There was something in that sigh that made Marietta's heart ache for him. Max may be arrogant and bad-tempered, but he was suffering.

His voice was low, so low that she had to bend her head closer to hear him. "I am nothing."

"Oh Max, I'm sure you—"

"*I am nothing.*"

Marietta bit her lip and fell silent. Max, too, was quiet, brooding on his uncertain future. After a moment she looked out of the window and realized they had entered a very elegant square, with a garden and plane trees at its center. The coach drew to a halt on the other side, in front of an austere but elegant Georgian townhouse.

"Where are we?" she asked. "I don't think I know this square."

"Bedford Square," Max said, seemingly glad to change the subject, although he spoke with an effort.

"Bedford . . . ?"

"It isn't fashionable among the aristocracy. My father took the house from the Duke of Bedford for a pittance, when he couldn't get anyone other than lawyers interested in living here. Hoped having a duke in residence would help attract others. It didn't, but at least my father felt he'd got a bargain."

The door to the townhouse opened on the figure of an elderly butler, who hobbled down the four shallow stairs to the street. Behind him a plump woman of the same vintage gathered her skirts and numerous petticoats up above her ankles and picked her way carefully in his wake.

"Daniel!" the butler called, just as the driver jumped down.

Daniel Coachman was a huge man, with wide shoulders and bulging arms, and it didn't take him long to gather Max into those arms and extract him from inside the coach. Another man had joined the little group at the bottom of the stairs, a tall, thin gentleman in a frock coat of an unpleasant green color and plaid pantaloons. He proceeded to direct proceedings, continually urging caution. "Mind now, Daniel," he said in a fussy manner, waving his hands about. "Mind! Is the bed ready, Mrs. Pomeroy?"

Mrs. Pomeroy's round face was flushed. "It is, sir, don't you fret. All nice and warmed up for his lordship here."

"Carry him upstairs then, Daniel. Have you sent for the doctor, Pomeroy?"

The three servants went strangely still, avoiding each others' eyes. "No, sir," Pomeroy answered. "The doctor wouldn't come."

"*Wouldn't come?*" the gentleman's eyes blazed. "What the devil do you mean, he *wouldn't come?*"

"He knows his lordship can't pay him. Sir."

There was more than a hint of animosity in his voice. The gentleman heard it, and his face colored. Suddenly his anger was gone, replaced by discomfort. "Ah, I see. Well, send for him directly and inform him that *I* shall pay him."

"Yes, sir, thank you, sir." The elderly butler looked very relieved.

Daniel Coachman was carrying Max up the steps and into his townhouse, with the elderly Pomeroys tottering in his wake, and that was when Marietta realized she had been overlooked. The gentleman in the green-colored frock coat was last up the steps, calling out more instructions as he went—in a moment he would be gone, too, and she would be left, standing all alone, in the street.

"Excuse me, sir?"

At the sound of her voice the tall, thin stranger stopped and turned. His eyes were the same mahogany brown color as Max's, but far less intimidating. "I'm sorry, you are . . . ?"

"I am Miss Marietta Greentree. I accompanied Ma . . . that is, Lord Roseby, from Aphrodite's Club. He was too ill to travel alone and none of his servants had come to help him."

There was an implied criticism in her words and the gentleman was not slow in understanding her. "As you see, Miss Greentree, the Pomeroys are elderly and would not have been of much use. They were better remaining here, preparing the house. Daniel had to drive the coach, but he is a good lad and could be relied upon to help when needed. As for myself, I have only just arrived or you can be sure I would instantly have offered my services." His tone was polite, but his gaze had grown watchful.

"But, surely, he has other servants?"

"I'm afraid not."

Of course not, Marietta thought. He can't pay them. He's disinherited. This is all he has left—an elderly butler and his wife, and a coachman. He's no longer Lord Roseby—he's a nobody.

The gentleman had ventured back to the street, and now his puzzled gaze slid quickly over her, taking in her emerald green velvet cloak and fair ringlets. Marietta realized that he was trying to decide just what her role was at Aphrodite's Club. Perhaps she did not fit his image of a courtesan-in-the-making, for a moment later he smiled and bowed and introduced himself.

"I am Harold Valland, Miss Greentree—Max's cousin. Pomeroy sent a note to my house this morning, informing me of what had happened. If only I had known last night, I would have hastened at once to his side."

Harold sounded sincere, but was he? Marietta wasn't certain. Perhaps she was predisposed to distrust Harold because he was Max's cousin and the duke had chosen him as the new heir over Max. He did not seem *too* awful.

Marietta smiled. "Lord Roseby has a headache and I think some fever. He will need his doctor to attend him, sir."

"Yes, yes, Pomeroy will go for the man." Then, perhaps realizing that she had been a witness to that scene, Harold looked away. "I don't know how well you are acquainted with my cousin, Miss Greentree—"

"I know a little of his life, Mr. Valland."

"He is a very proud man. One does what one can, but one must tread carefully."

"I imagine one must."

Harold seemed to believe that was explanation

enough. "I should go and see if the Pomeroys have made Max comfortable. Thank you, Miss Greentree, for your kindness to my cousin."

"I must get back. My sister will be worried." Marietta knew a dismissal when she heard one.

Harold was looking up towards the house, obviously keen to get inside and see to Max. "Your sister?" he said vaguely.

"Lady Montegomery."

Harold started, and turned back to her. For a moment his face was blank, and she had an image of his brain, working furiously through a list of the aristocracy currently residing in London. "Do you mean that your sister is the wife of—"

"Lord Montegomery. Yes, Oliver is my brother-in-law."

The penny dropped. He smiled, obviously relieved that she was the sister of a peer, and therefore respectable. "Of course. Of course! Lord Montegomery, of course. But you must come inside and wait, Miss Greentree, while I have a hansom fetched."

Amazing, Marietta thought, what dropping Oliver's name could do. Still, she could hardly hold being a snob against Harold—it was a common enough tendency.

Marietta allowed him to steer her into the entrance hall, where Mrs. Pomeroy was fidgeting about at the bottom of a broad, curving staircase, twisting her hands in her apron. And no wonder. The sounds coming from upstairs were loud and ominous. Just then Max's voice rose in a shout, followed by a terrible, heart-rending groan.

"Oh dear," Marietta said, her eyes wide. "His head hurts him a great deal."

"Poor young sir!" the old woman cried. "I should not have let Daniel take him up to his room, but Pomeroy went off for the doctor and . . ." Her eyes filled with tears. "The truth is, I can't manage the stairs anymore, miss. My legs give out on me."

"Oh dear," Marietta said again. "What a mess you are all in. Perhaps you would allow me to help, Mrs. Pomeroy? I am quite good at helping."

Mrs. Pomeroy's worried face sagged with relief. "Oh, please do, miss. Daniel's a good lad but he's not the brightest star in the sky, if you get my meaning."

"If you're sure you wouldn't mind, Miss Greentree . . . ?" Harold added his own encouragement, and gestured for her to lead the way.

The staircase was grand and beautiful—Marietta could imagine duchesses sweeping down it, in opulent gowns. But Max wouldn't have a duchess; if he did marry she would be a plain *Mrs.*, and Marietta thought she would need to be a very patient and forbearing woman.

The noises were coming from a suite of rooms that obviously belonged to the master of the house. They were decorated in a heavy, dark style she found rather oppressive, and the furniture looked as if it had done service in Henry Tudor's day. The bed in particular. And that was where she found Max.

He had been deposited on the enormous four-poster bed, with its lush canopy and intricately turned posts, and he wasn't happy. A white-faced, stammering Daniel Coachman admitted to lowering him too hastily, and the subsequent jarring had caused his headache to suddenly worsen. Max's face was the color of old parchment, his already reddened eyes were watering with tears of pain and understandable self-pity, and there was a fresh patch of blood staining the bandage around his forehead.

"Do move him carefully!" Marietta cried, seeing the state he was in. "Carefully, further onto the bed! That's it. Best to wait for the doctor before we undress him. No, Daniel, leave his boots. And his trousers! Oh, leave him, do . . ."

"You can go now Daniel," Harold said sternly.

The well-meaning but not too bright Daniel lumbered out. Marietta reached to touch Max's cheek, her fingers gentle, and he shivered as if he were cold. "You poor thing," she whispered.

"Hurts," he managed through gritted teeth.

"I know, I know it does. The doctor will be here in a moment. He will give you laudanum, Max, then you can sleep. I can't understand why you weren't given any before you set out."

Max groaned.

"Max, old boy? It's me." Harold peered out from behind her as if he was uncertain of his welcome.

Max opened slitted eyes. "I know it's *you*, Harold, who else would wear a coat in that vile color?"

"Stiff upper lip, cousin. We'll have you as right as rain in no time."

"Put me back together again," Max managed with a feeble laugh.

"Like Humpty Dumpty?" Harold had caught on. "Yes, that's it, old chap."

Marietta glanced from one to the other, sensing that there was a real bond between the cousins, an almost brotherly warmth and affection that had been born in their childhood and made any betrayal by Harold seem all the more unlikely. Perhaps Harold was as much a victim of the situation as Max, although he stood to gain a great deal more.

Or perhaps he was just a very good actor.

Max's hand was clenching and unclenching on the bedclothes. To stop him Marietta clasped his fingers firmly in her own. Max sighed, as if her touch gave him comfort, and fell quiet. Harold smiled and nodded at her, and went to watch by the window. And they all remained like that until the doctor arrived and gave Max something to make him sleep. Then, finally, Marietta was able to slip away.

"You will let me know how he is?" she asked Harold, as he accompanied her out to the hansom cab.

"Yes, of course, Miss Greentree. Perhaps you will call again and see for yourself? There could be no objection, surely, in visiting the sick?"

"None at all." And if there was, Marietta didn't care. Visiting Max's sickbed sounded like a perfect way to build on their . . . Friendship? Was it a friendship? Or was their relationship too testy, too volatile for such a mellow title?

Harold smiled and bowed over her hand. "I want to thank you for your care of my cousin, Miss Greentree. He, and I, are very grateful."

He was still standing there, watching her with a distinctly speculative gleam in his eyes, as the hansom cab took her away.

All was very quiet at Berkley Square. Vivianna was resting and her son was sleeping. Oliver, too, was taking a nap. Marietta went to her own room to bathe and change, and afterwards she felt more able to face the world. The night she had spent at Aphrodite's seemed like a dream, except that it had been very real.

Did Aphrodite really set her a task to perform, a task involving her asking Max to show her how to kiss? Did Max really get attacked, and by whom? Was Marietta really intending to become involved with Max and his eccentric household? It seemed so, because she was already smiling to herself, imagining their next encounter.

Mr. Jardine was in the hall when she descended the stairs, his blue eyes twinkling up at her. "Miss Marietta! We heard from Aphrodite that you had something of an adventure."

"Did you?"

"How is Lord Roseby?"

"He is uncomfortable, but he's in his own bed now, and his doctor has seen him. I think, once his head stops aching, he will be very much better." Her mouth primmed. "And it wasn't an adventure, Mr. Jardine. It was an act of charity."

"Yes, of course," he agreed, but the twinkle in his eyes was not diminished, and Marietta realized he knew her too well to be fooled by her protest.

"What did Aphrodite say?" she asked him curiously.

"That Lord Roseby had been struck down and, as you were acquainted with him, you had decided to keep an eye on him overnight. It was all very respectable, and so she assured your sister."

"And what did Vivianna say?"

"She expressed some puzzlement as to how you had come to be acquainted with Lord Roseby, but then the baby was brought in and all else was forgotten."

Thanks goodness for the baby! Perhaps, Marietta thought, she wouldn't get a reprimand from Vivianna after all.

"Tell me, my dear, is Lord Roseby the son of the Duke of Barwon?"

Surprised, she met Mr. Jardine's curious gaze. "Yes. At least . . . it's rather a long story. Do you know Max, Mr. Jardine?"

Mr. Jardine gave her a little smile that hinted at much. "I don't know Max, no, but I used to know his father. I was out in the West Indies with him."

"Oh." Suddenly Marietta decided that she very much wanted to confide in Mr. Jardine about Max's dilemma, and to hear what he had to say in return. She trusted him to keep her words to himself, and she knew his observations would be sensible and to the point. "Are you too busy to have a little chat, sir?" she asked him, slipping her hand into the crook of his arm.

He met her gaze and read her in an instant. "No, I'm not too busy," he assured her. "And I would love some tea and cake. I'll send for some of that excellent Pavini cake, shall I? You can come to the library, and help me to eat it."

Marietta laughed. "You understand me very well, Mr. Jardine."

"I should, Miss Marietta. I have known you for most of your life."

When they were settled cozily before the fire, surrounded by Oliver's large collection of books, Marietta explained to Mr. Jardine what she had heard of Max's predicament. It took some time, and they had to pause in the middle of the story to drink their tea and eat their slices of the rich, fruity Pavini cake.

When she was done, Mr. Jardine sat, thoughtfully watching the fire. "I knew Barwon in Jamaica," he said at last. "He was never what I would call a warm man, he was too serious and gruff in his manner. Reserved, except when he spoke of his family. His wife and son were everything to him; he would have moved heaven and earth for them, if he had to. In business he had a reputation for being careful, one might almost say parsimonious, but he had reason to be like that. The family fortunes had been frittered away by his father and it was up to him to restore them. That was why he was in Jamaica, buying up some of the old, rundown plantations and making them profitable again."

"And did he? Restore the family fortunes?"

"Yes, yes, he did. He made a better fist of it than I did, at any rate," he added, with a self-deprecating laugh. "I didn't have the necessary single-mindedness, perhaps."

"You mean that you didn't have the stomach for it?" Marietta suggested less delicately.

Mr. Jardine hesitated, then shook his head. "It was just that sometimes he was less than sympathetic to the people living on those old plantations. I remember one case, the old Creole man had been there for years, struggling to survive. His family declared him mentally unsound, even had doctors sign the papers, and sold the place out from under him. Barwon came in to evict the old man, but he wouldn't go. Maybe he *was* mad, but there was no need for Barwon to destroy him like he did. He brought in a gang of thugs to terrorize him, make his life such a misery that he just gave up and let them take him away. It seemed a cold way to accomplish the business. There were other instances—he replaced plantation workers who had been there for generations, it didn't matter that they had no where else to go. He didn't feel any compassion in that sort of situation— he was simply calculating how much money he could make. I . . . well, I wasn't able to do that."

"He sounds like a monster," she said, with a shudder.

"No, just an able businessman. He seemed to think in straight lines, without the distraction of side issues like moral justice. But in fact he was kind enough when it didn't affect his profits. There was a young Creole girl living wild on the same plantation as the old man, and he took her in. Adopted her, more or less. Yes, he could be very kind, and to those he loved he would do absolutely anything . . . *will* do absolutely anything, but only as long as they are loyal to him. Barwon will not tolerate those who wrong him. I am sure when he learned he was cuckolded and cheated by the woman he adored above all others, and deprived of a son of whom he thought the world, Barwon would strike out violently. I think that explains why he's been on a campaign to destroy his wife's good name and ruin Max. They hurt him, you see, and he needs to hurt them back. It's Barwon's way."

Marietta could not easily forgive how Max had been treated. "I suppose we have to blame his wife," she agreed, "but how can it be his son's fault? Why must he suffer?"

"The laws of inheritance are clear—Harold will get everything and Max will be cut out."

"It's so unfair."

"Cruel, yes, but it *is* fair. If Max is not Barwon's son then he has no right to the title, property or fortune."

"There is something about Harold Valland I do not trust. I wouldn't be surprised if he was far from an innocent bystander."

They were silent a moment.

"Someone," said Marietta, her eyes fixed on the fire, "should do something about it."

Mr. Jardine gave her a sharp look. "Miss Marietta, this is none of your affair. Do not think to meddle."

"Who said anything about meddling?" Marietta said mildly, and sipped her tea.

A tap on the door saved her from further questioning by Mr. Jardine, and when Lil entered the library it was with a request from Vivianna for Marietta to come to her bedchamber.

Relieved, Marietta set down her cup and hurried out, but Lil lingered, exchanging some pleasantries with Lady Greentree's secretary on her current life in London.

"Jacob Coachman's heart is broken, you know that, Lil?" Mr. Jardine teased. "He will never be the same again."

"Oh, go on with you!" cried Lil. "He'll find someone else, you wait and see. Men, they're all the same they are, apart from you, Mr. Jardine," she added earnestly.

But Mr. Jardine did not seem to notice the admiring expression in her eyes or the quickening of her heart. He just smiled at her in his paternal way and told her to be a good girl, although he knew she was, and then went back to whatever it was he had been doing.

With a sigh, Lil left him to it. She had loved him for years, ever since she went to work for Lady Greentree at Greentree Manor. Even though she knew she was unworthy of such a gentleman, she could not help but wish things were different and Mr. Jardine would look at her as a man, and not a father.

Lil had grown up on the streets and through necessity, when she was far too young, had earned her keep by selling her body. Vivianna had found her in that state and "saved" her, and Lil had loved her for it ever since. Vivianna had given Lil the chance at a new life.

Lil was determined to deserve it.

She would never fall back into her old ways, she was far too respectable for that now. Indeed, she studied respectability as others might study music or art, and she was very careful in her every action. But she knew she would never be deserving enough for a wonderful man like Mr. Jardine. Besides, he loved Lady Greentree. It was sad that Lady Greentree still loved her husband, who had died many years ago in India. It was sad that Lady Greentree could not see that there was a man waiting for her, a flesh and blood man, right under her nose.

Lil sighed again, and set off up the stairs after Marietta.

Chapter 6

Max drifted in and out of consciousness, rather like a aeronaught in a gas balloon. The doctor had given him laudanum, and although it helped him to sleep and heal, it was not a peaceful slumber. Once he thought he heard Harold in the room with him, and then, strangely, his father. "Get well, my son," the duke said, and then his breath caught, as though the word had come from his lips unawares and he had realized all over again that Max was no longer his "son" but some stranger's child foisted upon him.

Max and his father had never been close in the demonstrative way Max and his mother were close, but then his father was not the sort of man who could easily express his feelings. However, he had always believed his father loved him, and all the more since his mother had died. The duke had seemed genuinely proud of Max and the man he had become. Now all that was gone. The violent severing of the ties between them caused an ache inside Max's chest very much like the wound in his head, except this one could never heal.

At the age of twenty-nine he had lost both his parents.

He wanted to hate his mother for what she had done, but he could not do that either. The duchess had been a kind, sweet lady. How could Max hate her? And—deep in his heart—how could he believe that she had really conceived him with another man and then married the duke? Deceived and lied and played a part. And yet the duke obviously believed his wife's letter to be the truth, and Max, too, must accept the evidence, however much his heart rebelled against it.

Max tossed and turned in his enormous ducal bed, until eventually his mother's face faded and his thoughts turned instead to a cool palm on his feverish skin, and blue eyes smiling down at him, and a soft lap pillowing his head during that appalling ride home in the coach.

Marietta Greentree.

What was it about the woman that got under his skin, despite his best efforts to keep her out? She was bossy and pert, and he wanted nothing more than to escape her clear, cool gaze and put a stop to her intrusion into his life. He had never asked for her help or her interference, and yet suddenly here she was, inside his world, and he didn't know how to push her out again.

Not exactly sound economics . . .

Her voice echoed in his pounding head, and he smiled wryly at the memory of her reprimand. She had been right—he shouldn't be spending money at

Aphrodite's Club when he couldn't even pay his servants' wages or the tradesmen who called constantly at his door, demanding he settle their accounts. What had he been thinking, to go there? Probably that he was miserable and alone and nothing would ever be the same again. Soon, he knew, he must make a final decision about his future.

Cornwall. That was where his mother's family's house was, where it had stood for generations. Max had only been to Blackwood once, when he was a boy; he barely remembered it, and what he did remember wasn't encouraging. Grim, gray stone and small, dark windows that reflected no light, perched on a precarious cliff above an unfriendly sea. If he sold everything he had left he could then afford to move to Blackwood and live there frugally for forty or so years. Until he died.

Max shuddered in his fever. He would become the hermit of Blackwood House, the last of his line, forgotten except by the gossips who would not let his story die. The Disinherited Duke, that was what they would call him, and shake their heads . . .

What was it Ian Keith had said? Something about this being Max's chance to make a new life for himself, without the shackles of position or privilege. Max admitted that the thought of being cast adrift from his allotted place in the world was not comfortable. Perhaps he was running away to Cornwall, not because he had nowhere else to go and nothing else to do, but because he had not been brought up to be anything *but* a duke. A gentleman did not dirty his hands with actual paid work. A gentleman preferred to keep his hands clean and slowly starve to death.

Maybe Ian was right. Time to put aside the worn

out prejudices, time to think like a man and not a
peer. Max searched his mind for something he could
do, something he was good at, something he might
enjoy. Farming? He could turn the land in Cornwall
into a prosperous concern. He pictured himself toil-
ing with his laborers over the stony ground growing
things like . . . like mangel-wurzels, the sun warm
on his back, the smell of the soil on his hands. But
was it enough to sustain him and those dependent
upon him?

Perhaps Marietta will come and stay with me.

The thought popped out of nowhere. He imagined
Marietta with her fair curls and sparkling eyes tripping through Blackwood's dismal corridors. Marietta, laughing in the candlelight over his pitiful
homegrown meal and sipping the local cider. Marietta, in his bed at night, with the sea crashing below
the cliffs outside his window, and her mouth hot and
eager.

Dear God! What is wrong with me!

Max's eyes sprang open and he glared at poor
Daniel, who had been bathing his face with cool water,
and caused the coachman to start and drop the bowl.

"I-I'm sorry, my lord," Daniel stammered.

Max blinked, and his frown smoothed away. He
was injured and weak, that was what it was. Once his
body recovered he would not need to think of Marietta again—she would be completely and utterly removed from his life. And that was how it should be.
Max knew he was in no position to be thinking about
a woman—any woman. Not when he could barely
look after himself.

"You've done nothing wrong, Daniel," he assured
his anxious servant. "How long have I been in bed?"

"Two days, m'lord. The doctor's been here every day, givin' you somethin' to make you sleep. He'll be back this even, and Mr. Harold and Miss Susannah'll be here, too."

Max wished he could draw his tattered pride about him and send Harold and Susannah away, but he was not a fool and he knew he couldn't manage on his own, not yet. When he was better, when he was able to get out of this wretched bed, then he would begin to set his plans in motion for the move to Cornwall. Besides, it wasn't their fault he wasn't his father's son. He knew how guilty Harold felt about his sudden and unexpected good fortune; he knew how Susannah had suffered over the question of whether or not to reveal the truth, when she found the duchess's incriminating letter. It had been Susannah, the nearest thing Max had to a sister, who had the task of sorting through his mother's papers when she died. Susannah, the duke's adopted daughter, and now Harold's wife. She would make a beautiful Duchess of Barwon, Max told himself, trying to still the ache of loss inside. He was glad, really.

He and Harold and Susannah had been friends from childhood, and they had played rough and tumble games at Valland House, and grown up together, the two boys and Susannah the tomboy. It had been Harold who Susannah wed; Max had always looked upon her as a sister. Perhaps, too, Harold and Susannah had more in common—both had lost their parents at an early age, both were taken in by the duke and duchess, and loved as their own. Although Max could recall Susannah saying to him once, in her soft voice with the Creole accent she had never lost, "I know they love Harold and me, but they love you more, Max."

"The young lady sent a note around this mornin'."

Daniel's voice startled Max back to the present.

"Young lady?" Did he mean Marietta? Max almost groaned aloud, except that Daniel was watching him, his pale eyes wide and guileless, like a dog hopeful of a crumb. He was like a big child, sometimes—he had an innocence of mind that made Max smile. Daniel must come with him to Cornwall. The Pomeroys were too elderly and he would do his best to set them up somewhere—he might even have to swallow his pride and ask Harold to take care of it—but Daniel must be with him.

"I said, sir, that the young lady—"

"And I heard you, Daniel. Very well, what did Miss Greentree have to say in her note?"

"I didn't read it, m'lord. It's here," he picked up the thin envelope. "Do you want me to open it up for you?"

Max nodded in resignation. "Go on then. And read it, if you please. I don't trust my eyesight just now."

Daniel made much of opening the envelope. Inside it was a single sheet of crisp paper, which looked fragile in Daniel's big hands. Pomeroy had taught Daniel to read. "She says: 'I will be callin' upon you at three o'clock this aft'noon.' Then her name, Mary . . . etta Greentrees."

"Marietta Greentree." Max shifted in the bed and found his head did not hurt quite so much. "What is the time now, Daniel?"

"It hasn't long turned one in the afternoon, m'lord. I heard the clock strike."

Then she would be here in two hours. Suddenly Max knew he did not want her to see him like this, lying unwashed and miserable, exactly as she had left him. Damn the woman, what did she want from him? Not that he wasn't grateful to her for sitting with him and caring for him, but she was far too disruptive to what peace of mind he had remaining.

"Fetch me warm water, soap, and a razor, Daniel," Max said in a suddenly decisive voice. "I need to be shaved. And fetch Pomeroy, too," he added. "He has the steadier hands, and I don't want to look like a badly sliced side of beef when Miss Greentree arrives."

"Yes, m'lord." Daniel, clearly relieved to have been spared, went to do his master's bidding.

I'll just tell her that I no longer require her kind interference, Max thought, as he lay waiting for Pomeroy, staring up at the canopy above his bed. *Surely it can't be that difficult? I've dealt with far more dangerous characters than her in my time.*

Then why was he suddenly feeling so shaky? And what was that leap of his heart, at the thought of seeing her again?

There was a lighted lamp on the table by the bottom of the staircase, but it did little to dispel the shadows. Either the house in Bedford Square didn't have gas or . . . maybe the bills hadn't been paid recently. Again Marietta nodded sympathetically, as Mrs. Pomeroy continued to pour out her troubles, but half of her was thinking of other things. For instance, she pictured Max, feverishly tossing and turning in his canopied bed in this big, silent house that no longer belonged to him.

" 'Tisn't right, Miss. Master Max has always been the best of sons and he promised to be the best of dukes, too. Now he's gone and lost everything. Not that I believe for a moment that Her Grace would ever have—" She bit down on her lip, as if she couldn't bear to say it aloud. "Well, I just think it's wrong," she grumbled, as Pomeroy shuffled over to join them.

"Miss Greentree has come to see his lordship," she informed her husband with a worried glance up the stairs. "Is he ready yet for visitors?"

Pomeroy looked particularly spick and span in his butler's uniform of dark blue coat and white knee breeches, a powdered wig set upon his head and gloves upon his hands. "He's all ready and waiting," he informed them grandly. "Miss, if you would follow me . . . ?"

As she followed Pomeroy, Marietta had plenty of time to look about her—he wasn't very quick on the stairs—and notice that the ornate mirror that hung on the landing had been cleaned and polished, and that there was a vase of fresh flowers on the small table beneath it. She admitted she might have been somewhat distracted the other day, but she was sure the flowers weren't there then, and the mirror wasn't polished. In fact at that time the house gave off an air of forlorn neglect; now it was actually sparkling.

Puzzled, she let Pomeroy direct her down a wide corridor towards the archway that led into Max's suite of rooms. More flowers, and a lit candelabra, making a pool of soft light. In the candlelight the furnishings glowed, and there was the unmistakable smell of lemon polish.

It wasn't until she stepped inside Max's bedchamber, and saw him propped up upon his pillows, still bandaged and pale, but freshly shaven, that Marietta realized what had happened. The spit and polish was in *her* honor, because Max and his servants could not bear to think that she should see them at less than their best.

Marietta felt tears sting her eyes and hurriedly blinked them away. It would never do for Max to see how affected she was; any weakness on her part could give him a reason to refuse the offer she was about to put to him.

"Miss Greentree," he said, his voice a little husky but otherwise strong and scrupulously polite. He met Pomeroy's eyes over her head. "Would you bring the tray up now, Pomeroy?"

"Very good, my lord."

Marietta wanted to protest that the stairs were too steep and Pomeroy's legs too old, and she didn't need refreshment anyway, but again she stopped herself. What right had she to refuse their hospitality, for whatever reason, when it obviously meant so much to them?

The door closed behind the butler. The drapes were drawn, and despite the lamp on a chest of drawers, it was gloomy in here. She was tempted to throw back the window coverings and bring in the spring sunshine, but again she stopped herself. The light probably hurt Max's eyes. As she walked toward him, she could see that he was also dressed for the occasion, at least from the waist upwards. He was wearing a clean, pressed white shirt with dark necktie, and, buttoned over the top, a red and purple brocade jacket. His hair was brushed and dampened, to flatten the exuberant curls above his clean bandage, while beneath it his handsome face appeared pale and gaunt.

"You look much better, Lord Roseby," she said, suddenly uncharacteristically shy. She had begun to feel as if she knew Max, but this man seated before her was a stranger—an aristocratic stranger.

"I am on the mend, thank you, Miss Greentree," he answered her in a subdued voice, although his eyes were bright and watchful.

"My brother-in-law was called away on some urgent estate matters, to Derbyshire. My sister required my presence, Lord Roseby, or I would have—"

"Please, Miss Greentree, there is no need to explain yourself to me."

"The doctor—"

"He does not think I am in any great danger, apart from a headache that refuses to go away. But that's to be expected, I suppose, after the crack on the head I received."

"Perhaps you should—"

"Miss Greentree." He sounded chilly, once again a stranger. Surprised and dismayed, Marietta met his eyes and waited. "I know you mean well, and I appreciate your kindness in thinking of me, but I am fit enough now. I am sure you have many far more important matters that require your attention—your . . . your sister, and so on—and that you will be relieved to return to them."

He was giving her her marching orders. In a polite and ducal manner, he was saying that he'd had enough of her. After all she had done for him! Marietta felt something hot and angry catch alight inside her, and knew from the way in which his gaze was suddenly arrested that he saw the reflection of it in her eyes.

"I don't think you quite understand, my lord," she said firmly. "I'm not going anywhere—at least not just yet."

"Miss Greentree, I have nothing to offer that could possibly interest you. And I certainly don't want your pity . . ."

"Goodness me, if you think I care a jot about your appalling situation then you are quite wrong, Max. You can mope about your big empty house feeling sorry for yourself all you like. That is entirely your affair."

Good, she had made him angry. Even as he struggled to control it, she saw it in the tightening of his mouth and the lowering of his eyebrows.

"Then what *do* you want?" he demanded grumpily.

That was more like it—Marietta smiled. "I have a proposition to put to you, Max."

He didn't look happy. "What sort of proposition?" he asked suspiciously.

Marietta had thought about this moment, and she knew that to win Max over she had to appeal to his gentlemanly instincts. The very things that might prevent her from completing the tasks that Aphrodite would set her.

She drew the chair up close beside his bed and sat down on it, ignoring the way he stiffened, and launched into her speech. "I have already told you that my mother is Aphrodite, my *real* mother that is. When I was barely more than a baby I was kidnapped with my two sisters, and taken away from her. I've only been reunited with her for a few short years, but it has been long enough to convince me that I would like to follow in her footsteps. I want to be a courtesan, Lord Roseby."

He didn't say anything, although he turned even paler and his eyes seemed riveted on hers.

"I know this is not the sort of ambition usually expressed by a genteel young lady—but then I am not like other genteel young ladies. I-I am unlikely to make a good marriage, the sort of marriage I once believed I would make. When I was younger I did something very foolish, Max. I fell under the spell of a most unsuitable man and, when my family refused to contemplate marriage, I was persuaded by my beloved to run away to the Scottish border."

"Miss Greentree," he said, and it was a plea for her to stop.

Marietta had no intention of stopping. "Of course he never meant to marry me, and after we halted for the night and he . . . well, ruined me, he left me there. The incident could have been hushed up, that was certainly what my Uncle William Tremaine would have preferred, but by an unfortunate coincidence one of my mother's—that is, Lady Greentree's—disgruntled employees was staying at the same inn, and he recognized me. He took great pleasure in spreading the story about, and soon it was everywhere. I suppose the additional fact that it had recently become known that I was Aphrodite's daughter, made my misfortune lurid enough to capture the imagination of the entire country."

She knew she was flushed with anger and humiliation, but even Max's pitying look wasn't going to stop her now.

"So . . . my reputation was destroyed, and I have

little hope of making the sort of marriage I always believed I would. All the more reason to become a courtesan like my mother."

"Miss Greentree."

"No, let me finish, Max. As a courtesan I can live a free and unfettered life, without any ties and responsibilities except to myself and those men I decide to favor with my . . . eh, gifts. I am not at all conventional, Lord Roseby, and I don't fear the censure of my peers—besides, I mean to take on a new identity to protect my family. I am quite determined in this matter, but I know I cannot do it alone. I need Aphrodite's approval. I need her patronage and her help."

"Miss Greentree—" he croaked desperately.

"I have spoken to her in regard to my wishes and she has agreed to help me, on the condition that I prove to her that I am serious in my desire. And to do that I must first play at being a courtesan with a gentleman who will agree to act as my practice partner. A temporary affair, my mother calls it, to enable me to learn some of the skills I will need, and at the same time refine them upon a willing gentleman. She thinks it is important that we take these precautions, in case I change my mind—I assure you, Max, I won't! But to please my mother the gentleman must be discreet, so that there will be no harm done. Well apart from what has been done already, I suppose. But the world will see me as no different—in their eyes the affair never happened—*that* is the important thing."

She leaned closer, meeting his unblinking gaze with a humorless little smile. "So there you are, Max. I need a discreet gentleman to help me prove to Aphrodite that I have the aptitude to become a courtesan."

"I don't want to hear any more," Max said, and his mouth was hard and straight. "I know what you're going to ask, and the answer is no, no and no."

"Why not? My mother thinks you are just the man for the part. Don't you want to spend the entire night with me, Max?" She gave him her wide-eyed and innocent look.

Max's eyes turned dark but he struggled on. "How can you imagine for a moment that a gentleman would even consider such a preposterous and ridiculous—"

"Please, listen to me," Marietta cut through his outburst, reaching out to rest her hand on his sleeve. "Just listen," she insisted. "Aphrodite suggested that you might be the very man I need because you *are* a gentleman."

He was watching her as one might watch a dangerous serpent—very warily. "So when you say 'practice' you do not mean we would actually . . . ?"

"I would try out my skills on you, such as they are, and you would react. You in turn would teach me from your own experience—which Aphrodite assures me is vast. There may be limits to what we can do, I don't know." She shrugged to show her indifference to the possibility that they may actually lie together in a bed like this. As though her heart was not slamming in her chest like a steam train.

Max knew he was too weak to cope with this now. He knew he shouldn't make any decisions or say anything until he'd had a good night's sleep. He knew all this, and still he was fascinated by her suggestion—fascinated and horrified, all at the same time. A temporary affair, was that what she really wanted? Testing out her skills on him, practicing at being a courtesan like her mother? And he was meant to be her, what, her mentor? Giving her hints on how to . . . to make a man insensible with lust? He swallowed, his imagination working furiously.

It was bizarre. It was . . . tempting. Too tempting, because he wanted her, and a voice in his head was telling him that this was the ideal way in which to have what he wanted.

Marietta Greentree had just offered him the perfect arrangement.

And yet he felt compelled to put up some sort of resistance—for the sake of his upbringing as well as his already complicated life. "Marietta, a gentleman does not, under any circumstances, compromise a lady. And you, despite your parentage, are very much a lady."

Marietta sighed impatiently and shook her head at him as if he was slow-witted. "That is the whole point of choosing *you*. You are too much the gentleman to spread rumors, Max. And what is the use of being a lady if my reputation causes every gentleman who meets me to turn tail and run? You are involved in a scandal yourself, you know what it is like. I have had to suffer that for four years!"

"You will fall in love again and—"

She gave a bitter little laugh that he had not heard from her before. "No, I will not. I have no intention of ever loving a man again so that he can break my heart and destroy my life. I am not a fool, and I learn quickly, and that is one lesson I have learned well."

She meant it. He could see it in her eyes. Behind smiling and beautiful Marietta Greentree was another woman, a somber woman, and she had been broken and she had been hurt. And she had not recovered. Max felt something hot and violent streak through him.

"What is his name?" he demanded.

She stopped, looking puzzled. "His name?"

"The man who did that to you. What is his name, who is he?"

Something else flickered in her eyes—she was disappointed in him, and at first he didn't understand why. "You want to know his name? Is that so you can ask him the details? I assure you, Max, that I have told you the truth. If you have not heard of my plight . . . well, you have only to make inquiries. Some kind soul will be only too pleased to educate you on the finer points of my ruination and disgrace."

He shook his head impatiently. "I'm not interested in that. I want to know his name so that I can break his neck."

She was shocked. The thought that his righteous anger on her behalf was new to her made him even more furious. Had she no brothers or a father to avenge her lost honor? No, clearly not. Marietta Greentree had no Max Valland to ride on his white charger to her rescue, and the injustice of it made his heart ache.

"I don't think that would be a good idea," she said at last, biting her lip to hide a smile. He had pleased her. "I appreciate it, Max, truly, but I want to put all that behind me. I don't know where he is, and nor do I want to. I am looking to the future, to my life as a courtesan. If you want to play the gallant hero, then that is where you can do the most good. Help me to learn about passion and desire."

Passion and desire, dear God . . .

His head had begun to spin. Her fingers, resting lightly on his arm, felt hot and heavy.

"I have no money," he began bleakly.

"Max, it doesn't matter if you have no money. This is a temporary affair where we both take what we want from each other and nobody is the richer or the poorer for it. Don't you understand? We can do what we like, as long as neither of us is hurt."

It sounded like something he had dreamed about when he was a younger man, being given the go-ahead to make love to a beautiful girl without thinking of the consequences. But he was a grown man now, and he knew very well that there were always consequences. Always.

"I suppose I can ask someone else instead," she said mildly, her eyes wide with innocence. "There must be lots of other gentlemen in London who will agree to have an affair with me. Perhaps you could furnish me with a list?"

"No, I bloody can't!" he growled.

"Oh?" Those eyes gazed guilelessly into his. "Then *you* will just have to do it, Max. Come now, it won't be too horrible, I'm sure. We are not at all suited, so there is no fear that we will become attached or anything foolish like that. Courtesans don't become attached, you know, it's bad for business."

She was manipulating him, Max knew it and yet he was too muzzy-headed to think clearly—or so he told himself. In fact his body, weak as it was, was already humming with anticipation. An affair with Marietta Greentree! He hadn't been looking forward to anything so much in years, and to come now, at this time, when his life was at such a low ebb. It was like a gift. He knew he would be a fool to refuse it.

A knock on the door proceeded Daniel and Pomeroy with a tray. Marietta gasped at the sight of it, for as well as a teapot, cups and accompaniments, Mrs. Pomeroy had provided sandwiches, cakes and scones.

"Oh, how wonderful!" she gasped, turning from Pomeroy to Daniel. "Thank you so much, and thank your wife, Pomeroy. I am quite overcome."

Beaming, the two men left the room. Marietta set about pouring two cups of tea and busying herself over the tray, and all the while she could feel Max watching her. He looked so tense she was sure if she touched him he would feel like a fire poker. But that he hadn't refused her outright must mean something, and hope was growing inside her despite all her efforts to be calm.

"You've deliberately caught me at a weak moment, Marietta."

He was frowning at her, but his eyes had a rather endearing expression of confusion.

"Tea?" she asked blithely.

"I cannot imagine what you are thinking to suggest such a thing to me—"

"I am thinking you might be thirsty." Then, when he looked about ready to throttle her, "I'm sorry, Max. But I want to be a courtesan. I want to take control from those who have judged and sentenced me, and live my own life, and I see this as a way to do so. I am not afraid, Max."

He shook his head. The shadows under his eyes had deepened but his voice was strong. "You don't realize what it will mean. You don't understand. Desire gets into your blood, until you crave it. Even if you decide you want to stop you may find you are not able to."

"Well, then, you will have to teach me all about desire and craving it." Marietta munched on a sandwich. "Just pretend to be in thrall with me, and I can weave my . . . my spell on you."

He smiled. Marietta felt that small hope beginning to blossom. *Max had smiled.*

"Your spell," he repeated with heavy disbelief. "I see. Don't say I didn't warn you."

"Then you agree?"

"Yes, I agree. But reluctantly, and only to save you from yourself, or some other man who would not be as scrupulous as me."

He sounded extremely pompous, but she was too happy to care. "Oh, thank you, Max!" She wanted to hug him, but he didn't look like he'd appreciate that, so she handed him a scone instead. He inspected it and then closed his eyes. "I don't think I can eat," he said weakly.

"Well, you will have to try. Mrs. Pomeroy has made an amazing effort and I can't eat it all. What about the tea? Shall I help you with that? It's the least I can do, Max, when you are being so kind and generous as to have an affair with me."

He seemed to think that was amusing, but Marietta didn't ask him why. Instead she came and perched beside him on the bed and raised the cup to his lips.

Max took a sip, but he was watching her, and there was something sardonic now in the lift of his eyebrow. "Is this part of the play-acting?"

"Of course not." Marietta broke off a piece of the scone to pop into his mouth. She glanced at him sideways. "Although it could be, I suppose, but I thought I should wait until you're better. In case you have a relapse, I mean."

He swallowed, laughed, and then groaned when it hurt his head. Marietta set the cup down and smoothed his forehead lightly with her fingertips, as though she would take the headache away. He leaned against her shoulder, and closed his eyes, and he was very big and very heavy and yet somehow she liked the feel of him there. Even when his head dropped lower, so that he rested against her breast, she did not complain but began to stroke his hair. Now that it had dried, the curls were springing up again, and she twined them about her fingers, encouraging them.

"I won't be in London for very much longer," he said at last, sleepily. "This house isn't mine and it's time I faced it."

"But . . . where will you go?"

"Cornwall I think. My mother's house. At least that still belongs to me. I'll live there."

"Max—"

"The house is called Blackwood," he went on, as if he knew she was going to gush sympathy and he didn't want to listen. "It's built of stone and sits on a cliff looking out to the sea, and it has stood there for centuries. I visited when I was a little boy, so I don't remember it well, but I am sure it will suit me in my current straitened circumstances. Perhaps I can do some smuggling, to supplement my income."

Marietta forced a laugh, although she had tears in her eyes again. What was it about Max's bravery in the face of despair that made her want to weep? "Are there still such things as smugglers?" she said.

"I doubt it. But maybe I can start up one of the gangs again. It would give me something to do during the long nights."

This time her laugh was more genuine. He turned his head to look up at her, his dark gaze languorous. *And dangerous.* There was something suddenly so compelling about him, so mesmerizing, that before she knew what she was doing, Marietta had lowered her head and placed her lips against his.

She surprised him, but only for an instant. His lips opened slightly, moved, and then she was in his arms and he was kissing her with a depth and a thoroughness that turned her world topsy-turvy.

Shock held her still briefly, and then she was doing her best to kiss him back. His mouth was warm and she felt the stirring of something low in her belly, a pleasurable ache. He turned his head and nuzzled against her neck, his lips teasing, making her squirm.

Was this the man who had been protesting so vehemently only moments before? She could hardly believe it. Tentatively, not wanting to let a chance pass her by, Marietta stroked his throat, sliding her fingers around to his nape. His skin was warm, just as it had been last night—she remembered now his nakedness and how it had intrigued her.

"Can I take off your shirt?" she asked him impulsively.

Startled, Max pulled away from her, collapsing back on the pillows. For a moment he seemed quite speechless, and Marietta could only think that his head was hurting him again. She checked to see if his wound was bleeding, but it wasn't.

"Is this part of learning to be a courtesan?" he asked her at last.

"Of course," she said, but she knew she had not been thinking of practicing when she first kissed him; she had not been thinking of anything apart from the fact that she wanted to.

"Why do you want to take off my shirt?"

He watched her with a combination of irritation and curiosity, but he didn't seem about to grant her request unless she explained.

"I was with you last night, remember. You had no clothes on and your chest was . . ." She felt her face getting hotter—she would really have to learn how to control her blushes. Aphrodite never blushed. "You and I are very different, physically," she said bluntly. "Although I have been with a man, I cannot say I spent much time *looking* at him. When I am a courtesan I don't want to be surprised when a man takes off his shirt."

He blinked up at her, his eyes dark and warm, his mouth quirking into a smile. *Oh Lord, he is gorgeous,* she found herself thinking. *Not at all as I imagined him that first moment, when I saw him in the balloon. How could I have been so silly as to imagine I didn't like him?*

"You want to see my chest because it's different from yours?" he repeated evenly. "Is that right?"

"Yes, that's right."

He was insane, he supposed, but since Marietta had come into his life he'd lost the will to be his usual cautious self. There seemed to be so little these days to cheer him up—why the hell couldn't he enjoy himself? What English law decreed that he must now be the most miserable man in the land?

He began to shrug himself out of the quilted jacket, ignoring the throb in his temples. She helped him, murmuring so solicitously that he laughed aloud, and then groaned when his head hurt even more. His shirt had to come over his head, and after she had untied his neckcloth, she helped him tug at the sleeves, removing it in one quick movement.

He wondered what she would say, or think, and felt strangely self-conscious for a man who had been naked many times with many women. But she didn't say anything. She simply looked at him, her lips slightly parted, her eyes wide, her expression rapt.

"Max," she murmured. "You're very handsome." She reached out and then stopped, her gaze flickering sideways to meet his. "Can I touch you?"

"Be my guest," he said matter-of-factly. He wondered if she was really going to run her hands over his skin, or whether this was part of a fantasy he had invented in his delirium. In a moment he'd wake up and it would all be a dream.

Her hands closed on his shoulders, her palms soft and warm. He tried not to show any reaction, but he was hot—fever-hot, and the fever was called Marietta. His body reacted despite his present condition, and he quickly checked that the bedcoverings were discreetly placed to hide his erection. No need to educate her quite that much.

She was smoothing her hands up over his upper

arms. Max wasn't vain, but he knew he was a reasonable specimen of a man—an active life had seen to that. She seemed to be fascinated with the dark hair on his chest, and brushed her fingers through it several times, enjoying the coarse feel of it. Her nail scraped his nipple and he winced, but when she apologized she didn't even lift her eyes from what she was doing.

His nipples fascinated her. She touched them again, watching as they hardened, and the heat inside him grew.

"That happens when I'm cold," he said, thinking some sort of explanation was necessary. "Or . . . eh, sexually aroused. It is the same with you."

Now she did look at him, and he could see she was quite amazed.

"I've never noticed," she said. "It isn't something a lady pays attention to, and when I am dressing and undressing I am never completely naked before my maid. Do you mean that my chest would do this too, if you touched me?"

If he touched her? Rubbing his fingers across the tips of her breasts . . . It was almost too much for him to bear in his weakened state.

"Yes," he managed.

For one incredible moment he thought she was going to ask him to do just that, and he knew he couldn't. Not now. He wanted her, and he had said yes to her preposterous plan, but he didn't think it was quite the thing to have her on her back the first day of their temporary affair.

"I'm tired, Marietta," he said quietly.

She was clearly embarrassed. "Oh Max, I'm so sorry. You are ill, of course you are. How . . . thoughtless of me."

"No, not at all," he said, trying to smile but knowing it was more like a grimace. "I enjoyed you touching me."

"Did you?" she smiled in relief. "I enjoyed it too."

"Can you tell Pomeroy to come up?"

Marietta rose at once. "Yes, of course. I'm sorry."

"For what?" He turned and looked up at her, his eyes bright in the lamplight. "Don't—I enjoyed it."

Far too much.

"Good." She looked relieved that she had done nothing wrong.

But Max wanted her to go. He found he didn't know what to say or think or do, and he wanted her to leave him alone so that he could try and understand what was happening to him. So that he could be himself again.

"Goodbye, Max. I'll call on you again soon."

He opened his mouth, but what could he say? No? He had already agreed to her request, and now she was going to make the most of it. Practicing at being a courtesan! When all he wanted to do, right now, headache and all, was to tumble her into his bed and make her his.

God help me.

"Max? Are you all right?"

"Tired," he said, and pretended to fall asleep. Thankfully she took the hint and went away. Alone, he hovered on the verge of sleep. Until he realized he could still smell her scent, just as if she were in the room with him, and jolted awake again, his body hard and wanting her.

"My lord?" It was Pomeroy. "Are you quite well? You have taken off your clothing, sir."

"I was hot."

Pomeroy didn't reply, making a valiant attempt to keep his face from showing any emotion.

"Is she gone?"

"Miss Greentree? She's downstairs, my lord. She insisted on complimenting Mrs. Pomeroy." The old man sounded pleased, so Max bit back the urge to complain. Instead he silently cursed Ian Keith for ever asking him to come up in his balloon when he knew he had troubles enough, because that was when he had first laid eyes on Marietta Greentree. And now it seemed he would never be rid of her.

But more disturbing than that thought—he didn't want to.

Chapter 7

"I'm glad you and his lordship enjoyed my poor efforts, miss."

Marietta smiled at Mrs. Pomeroy's modesty in regard to her excellent tea tray. "I do hope Lord Roseby appreciates you as he should," she said more seriously.

Mrs. Pomeroy gave the long dining table a vigorous rub with her cloth and then admired the shine on the old wood. "He's a good master, and a good man," she said loyally. "I wish—" but tears sprang to her eyes and she shook her head.

"He says he is going to go and live in his mother's house in Cornwall," Marietta said gently.

Mrs. Pomeroy nodded her head sadly. "Aye, he wants to take all his hurt and brood on it. He was always like that, Master Max—kept all his feelings tight inside, locked up like a box. His mother, the dear duchess, could tease him out of his doldrums, but now she's gone, bless her. The duke, he's too much the same. Carved from the same piece of wood, they were . . ."

Her voice trailed off and there was an uncomfortable silence. Around the walls of the dining room the portraits of long-dead Vallands gazed upon them with Max's eyes, as if secretly eavesdropping on the conversation.

"You don't believe it, do you, Mrs. Pomeroy?" Marietta asked softly. "You don't believe the duke isn't Max's father?"

Mrs. Pomeroy hesitated, and then she looked up, directly into Marietta's sympathetic gaze. "No, miss, I don't. I can't. And if you saw them together then you wouldn't believe it neither. It's plain daft to suggest it."

"Then why has Max been disinherited? Why does his father accept this letter as truth?"

"He was angry, I suppose. The duke always flies off the handle when he's angry, and he was inconsolable when he read that letter." Again Mrs. Pomeroy rubbed vigorously at the table surface.

"And now the deed is done," Marietta murmured.

There was a rattle of the knocker on the outside door.

With an exclamation, Mrs. Pomeroy hobbled over to the sash window and peered out. " 'Tis Mr. Harold and Miss Susannah," she declared. "They're around here most days to see his lordship, but that's not surprising. They've always been close, ever since they were children. Miss Susannah was like a daughter to the duke and duchess, for all she'd come from those heathen parts. Jamaica or whatever it's called."

Marietta remembered Mr. Jardine telling her that Barwon had adopted a young Creole girl he had found living wild on one of the old plantations. That must have been Susannah.

She joined Mrs. Pomeroy at the window and peered curiously down to the street. There was Harold, stamping about impatiently, and beside him a tall and slender woman in wide green skirts and a matching feather-decorated bonnet. As if she felt their eyes upon her, she glanced up. An oval face, skin so pale and delicate it was like petals, and dark, tragic eyes. Susannah Valland was certainly beautiful.

Just then a movement on the other side of the square caught her eye. A middle-aged man with broad shoulders and a wide chest packed into a shabby brown coat was standing, watching the Vallands as they entered the house. She noted that his hair was sparse brown, and his face reminded her a little of Dobson's—as if he had been in too many fistfights. Almost as soon as Marietta noticed him, the man glanced up and saw her at the window and hurried away.

The knocker rattled again, and then the door opened. Out in the hall they could hear Pomeroy's important tones, joined by Harold's, and then the voice of Susannah—low and languid with a strangely foreign inflection.

Marietta was tempted to go to the dining room door for another peep at them, but she was not quite brave enough. After all, she shouldn't still be here, gossiping with the servants, and it would be embarrassing for her to be caught—no doubt worse for the servants.

"The duke was here yesterday," Mrs. Pomeroy said quietly, also staring at the door as they listened to the visitors making their way upstairs.

Marietta turned to her in surprise.

Mrs. Pomeroy nodded. "Aye, he came up from Valland House soon as he heard about Master Max's accident. He stood by the bed—Master Max, he was asleep—and he just looked." She sighed. "Pomeroy said the duke forgot he was there, or else he's sure he wouldn't have done it."

"Wouldn't have done what?" Marietta asked softly.

"Called Master Max *my son*," Mrs. Pomeroy whispered.

The dining room door banged open, and they both jumped guiltily. Daniel Coachman grinned at the effect of his entrance, pale eyes sliding from one to the other. "Pomeroy says they all want tea and cake," he announced, "and I'm to fetch it."

Mrs. Pomeroy clicked her tongue. "Do they now," she muttered, setting off to the kitchen. "And Daniel, what have I told you about knocking before you enter a room? You nearly did for me then, you silly boy."

Daniel gave Marietta one more grin, and followed after the housekeeper.

Marietta, left alone in the dining room with the watching portraits, found herself with much to ponder. There was more to Max's misfortune than a husband betrayed by his wife and a son disinherited, far more. Something was wrong—off-kilter. Everyone knew it, felt it, apart from Max that is, but no one was doing anything about it. Marietta felt a stirring inside her, an irresistible urge—apart from the one she had to see his chest again.

Max was helping her by agreeing to be her practice partner; why shouldn't she help him by untangling the mess he was in? It was the least she could do.

* * *

Susannah brushed her cheek against Max's in lieu of a kiss, her liquid dark eyes full of sympathy. As always, he was struck by her beauty. Susannah had been a beautiful child, wide-eyed and silent when his father brought her home to England, and now she was a breathtaking woman. Really, she would be the perfect Duchess of Barwon.

"Max, how are you today?" Harold peered over his wife's shoulder.

"Better," Max allowed.

"The streets just aren't safe no matter who you are," Susannah said, arranging her wide silk skirts about her.

"Max seems to have an angel perpetually watching over him," said Harold.

Susannah reached out and squeezed Max's hand. "I thank God for that," she murmured earnestly.

After a moment Harold cleared his throat. "Has Miss Greentree been back to see you? She seemed like a sweet, caring girl, despite her unfortunate background."

Susannah arched an elegant eyebrow. "Ah, Harold told me about your Miss Greentree."

"She's not mine," Max frowned, when in fact he was already thinking of her in that way. "And her background is hardly her fault, Harold."

Harold pursed his lips, and Max remembered what Marietta had said about her life being ruination and disgrace, and that everyone knew it. Harold would know; Harold knew every scandal. "Tell me," he said shortly.

His cousin leaned forward with a certain amount of relish and proceeded to do just that. "She's the daughter of Aphrodite—the famous courtesan, you know," this aside to Susannah. "There were three daughters and they were taken away when they were very young, a kidnapping or some such thing; it was kept pretty quiet. They were adopted by Lady Greentree in Yorkshire, a respectable woman, one of the Tremaines, she married Edward Greentree, he was in the army in India and died there."

"Get on with it, Harold," Max gritted.

"Anyway, it wasn't until recently that the three sisters were reunited with Aphrodite, which caused an almighty scandal because it turned out that the elder girl, Vivianna, was the daughter of Fraser— very rich, a brewery owner," again for Susannah's benefit. "But Her Majesty was persuaded to give her approval to the girl because Oliver Montegomery was in love with her and wanted to marry her."

"Very romantic," Susannah suggested, her dark brows arched. "What about this other daughter, Max's Miss Greentree? Is she Fraser's daughter, too?"

"Her name is Marietta, and no, she isn't Fraser's daughter. We're not sure who her father is. Still, perhaps her unusual background might have been overlooked because of her relationship to Oliver Montegomery, except that the girl lost her heart to a bounder and ran off with him. They were never married—he abandoned her after the first night— in a public inn, evidently, with no money—and the story came out."

"Oh dear."

"There was yet another scandal in the family, years ago. Helen Tremaine, sister of Lady Greentree and the girls' aunt, ran off with Toby Russell, a fortune hunter and a scallywag. But at least *he* married *her*. Made to, I should think, by Helen's brother the formidable Mr. William Tremaine."

"So poor Marietta has to carry about with her the disgrace of her mother, her aunt, and the bounder who led her to believe he loved her and then left her. I think that is extremely unfair," Susannah said. Then she sighed, "Although I agree that she is completely ineligible. The best she can hope for is to marry some mill manager in the north and retire into obscurity."

"Susannah," Max warned.

"I'm only thinking of you, Max," his sister continued, giving him a sympathetic look.

Max shook his head, then he laughed. "I don't believe Marietta Greentree is looking for a husband, and if she was I don't think she has any intention of marrying me."

"What does she want then?" Harold asked him curiously.

She wants me to teach her about passion and desire.

But he couldn't say that, not even to his cousin and his sister, the two childhood friends whom he trusted above all others. It wouldn't be fair to Marietta—their arrangement was strictly private.

"She feels responsible for me, because she was there at the time it happened."

"In the laneway?" Susannah demanded, wide-eyed, shaken for once from her languor. "This grows worse and worse. What was Miss Greentree doing loitering in a laneway?"

"No, Susannah, not in the laneway, she was at Aphrodite's Club. She was visiting her mother when they carried me in. All I meant to say was that she is being kind."

"Hmm, do you think so?" Harold was watching him with an odd smile playing around his mouth.

Susannah, her beautiful face melancholy, said, "I don't want you taken advantage of. Not when you have so much to bear already. You deserve to be happy, brother. How I wish I had never—"

"Susannah, there is no point in wishing away what is. You know I have never blamed you for what you did."

"It was such a shock," she whispered, her voice trembling. "If it hadn't been such a shock I would have burned it then and there. I had begun to burn it, and then I saw what it said, and I . . . I thought it must be a mistake, and if I showed it to Papa then he would laugh and explain it to me. I pulled it from the fire. You can't imagine how many times I have wished to turn time back, Max, so that I can watch Mama's letter burn to . . . to ashes. If only I had let it burn."

"Susannah, do not upset yourself," Harold said sharply. "What is done is done, and we must move on. I'm sure Max doesn't want you berating yourself like this." He glanced at Max with an appeal.

Susannah was gazing between them with tears in her eyes, working herself up into one of her famous stormy and emotional states. The two men were justifiably wary of that rise in Susannah's voice, the tensing of her shoulders, the flush that appeared on her cheeks. Over the years they had grown used to soothing Susannah.

"I will be all right." Max felt compelled to say it,

even though he knew it was nonsense—sometimes he too wished Susannah had left the letter to burn. But it had the desired effect.

"We'll look after you," his sister promised, resting her head upon his shoulder. "Harold and I won't let anything bad happen to you, Max, I promise."

The spring morning was clear apart from the usual foggy haze that hung over London, the product of its coal fires and factories. Once Marietta and Lil had reached Vauxhall Bridge the air seemed fresher. Below the nine cast-iron arches, the Thames was wide and brown and busy, with lighters and boatmen and the larger barges, all plying their trade.

Lil, who had been hurrying along in Marietta's wake, complaining that Vivianna should not have sent her out when Lil needed to be in Berkley Square to help with the baby, stopped and stared in delight.

"Oh, but this is pretty!"

"There you are then," Marietta said. "Now, do come on, Lil. I want to get to Vauxhall Gardens before dark."

Lil's smile gave way to a frown. "Why couldn't we have taken a hackney, miss? Me feet are killing me."

"That's because you're wearing those half-boots you bought at the warehouse in Regent Street. You know they're too small for you."

Lil tossed her head. "I want to look me best, miss. Nothing wrong in that."

Marietta smiled. "Then stop complaining, Lil, the walk will do you good. I believe you've grown very lazy living here in London. You've forgotten what it's like at Greentree Manor, where you can walk for miles and miles and never see a single soul."

"I was born in London," Lil retorted, and tugged at her gloves, straightening the wrinkles from the fingers.

"Then it must be nice to be home," she said levelly, continuing on over the bridge towards the gardens on the other side. She could see the gleaming pavilions above the trees and her heart lifted—Vauxhall, which had grown a little shabby over the years, had been recently refurbished. "Look," she said, pointing. "Will we stroll down the Grand Walk, Lil? Or perhaps we can lose ourselves in the Dark Walk. At one time that was closed down, you know, the Dark Walk, because that was where so many ladies lost their virtue."

Marietta did not say it aloud but the thought of meeting a mysterious gentleman in one of those isolated avenues, echoing with the sighs and whispers of lovers down the centuries, had always appealed to her.

Lil barely glanced up. Her fair hair was plaited and fastened neatly on her crown, and her small ears were pink, as if, thought Marietta, she scrubbed them clean every morning.

"London wasn't so good to me," Lil said at last, and closed her lips tight, as if she had no intention of saying anything more on the subject.

Marietta did not know a great deal about Lil's past, apart from the fact that Vivianna had found her in York and insisted she be given a home at Greentree Manor, to which Lady Greentree had acceded. Lil had been a fixture there ever since. That she had had an unhappy childhood was perhaps not surprising, and it explained her single-minded determination to adhere to the rules. Marietta sensed that Lil believed that, if she was very, very good and never stepped outside the boundaries, then nothing bad could ever happen to her again.

Perhaps nothing bad would, but in Marietta's opinion such a life must be very rigid and tedious. Surely part of the excitement and pleasure in this world came from taking the occasional risks, even small ones. Lil probably saw this visit to Vauxhall Gardens as overstepping her personal mark.

Marietta saw it as an adventure.

Something large and globular was now visible through the trees in front of them—Marietta recognized Mr. Keith's gas balloon. She laughed as Lil's eyes grew big at the sight of it. "Gawd!" the maid gasped. "Would you look at that, miss! It's one of them balloons."

"Haven't you ever seen a gas balloon before, Lil?"

Lil shook her head, her eyes still firmly fixed on the balloon as it swayed on its moorings. "It don't seem possible," she said, her hands strangling her drawstring bag. "Won't it fall down?"

"Not at all. In fact when the ballast is thrown out it will go much higher."

"How high?"

"Until London seems tiny beneath you."

Lil gave her a suddenly suspicious glance, and Marietta remembered Lil didn't know she had been up in the balloon herself. To distract her, Marietta said, "Why don't you come and meet the aeronaught, Lil? He's a very nice man."

Lil's eyes narrowed even more. "Aeronaught?" she declared with a sniff. "I don't hold with bohemians or eccentrics, miss. And what do *you* know about this aero-person? How do you know his name, Miss Marietta, if you don't mind me asking?"

Marietta gave her a vague smile and hurried ahead. Despite her uncomfortable footwear, Lil caught up with her but by then she was too busy gazing at the rotunda, where a band was currently playing, to ask anymore questions.

Very soon they were entering the area where the balloon was tethered. Lil's steps dragged as they drew closer, and Marietta caught her hand and tugged it impatiently. "Do come on, Lil. I promise it won't bite!"

Reluctantly Lil let herself be pulled forward. "Don't you leave me alone near that thing," she said. "You hear me, miss?"

Marietta laughed. "What a scared little rabbit you are, Lil!" Looking up, she realized that Mr. Keith had seen their approach. He had been busy in the basket, making some adjustments, but now he lifted one long leg over the rim and, with the help of his assistant, jumped down to the ground.

"Miss Greentree!" He greeted her with a smile, before his eyes slid to Lil's prim and upright person. "And a friend, I see."

"This is my . . . this is Lil," Marietta said, surprised and pleased to note the spark of interest in the aeronaught's eyes.

"Are you planning another ascent today? If the wind holds I am hoping to fly right over the top of Buckingham Palace."

"Buckingham Palace?" Lil gasped. "Her Majesty would have you arrested!"

Mr. Keith laughed. "She'd have to catch me first, Miss Lil. Is that short for Lillian, by the way?"

Lil blushed. "That's none of your business," she said grandly, but chose that moment to trip over one of the tethering ropes. Mr. Keith leaped forward to save her, catching her arm and holding her steady. Lil's face turned even redder than before.

"Careful, Lil," Mr. Keith said gently. "I have many silly traps laid here for unwary maidens." His eyes twinkled at her, and Lil could not help but respond with a little smile.

"I've never seen a balloon before," Lil admitted, thawing somewhat.

"Lil was saying on the way here that she could think of nothing more exciting than flying high in the sky," Marietta said innocently.

Lil's mouth opened and shut, but before she could give Marietta the set down she deserved, Mr. Keith interrupted.

"Then please, be my guest. I can take you up on Saturday. Weather permitting, of course. I would like to show you London from the air, Miss Lil."

Lil wriggled, clearly uncomfortable at the thought.

Mr. Keith finally seemed to remember Marietta was there. "Did you say you wished to make another ascent, Miss Marietta? It promises to be a perfect day for ballooning."

"*Another?*" squeaked Lil, with an accusing stare.

Marietta ignored her. "Thank you, no, Mr. Keith. I came because I wanted to speak to you about Lord Roseby."

"Max?"

"I have had the opportunity to speak with him, at length." Well, Marietta spoke and Max listened, but Mr. Keith did not need to know that.

"Dare I hope you've taken a shine to my tragic friend? And on such short acquaintance, Miss Greentree—that does bode well for him. I admit, I hoped at the time the two of you might hit it off."

A matchmaking aeronaught? Marietta wondered if she was as red as Lil, and hoped not. A brief flash of memory filled her head—Max's mouth on hers. Aphrodite had made a kiss from Max her first task— or rather asking Max to show her how. That meant the spontaneous kiss they had exchanged did not fulfill her mother's requirements. She would have to do it properly next time . . .

Marietta smiled. *Next time.*

"Actually, Max and I met again after the ascent," she said. "He was hurt . . . struck down in a lane outside Aphrodite's Club. He is recovering, so please don't grow alarmed, sir."

"Good heavens," Ian Keith muttered under his breath. "I don't like the sound of this. Struck down, you say? Did he tell you that this is but one of many times he has been hurt, or almost hurt, in an accident? When he was a boy he nearly drowned, twice, and there were other things . . . near misses and close calls. Two just last year, before he was disinherited. And now this. It is very strange, *more* than strange. Miss Marietta, I have to say that I find it downright suspicious!"

So many accidents! It could be coincidence, of course, and yet it *did* seem odd. Was Mr. Keith right, was it suspicious? Marietta felt a little tingle inside her, and it was a warning that she knew she should heed. After all, the last time she had felt that tingle was just as she and Gerard Jones were cantering away from Greentree Manor, on their way to the Scottish border.

"Do you really think someone is deliberately trying to hurt him, Mr. Keith?" she asked.

Mr. Keith seemed to realize that in his shock he had spoken hastily, and now—perhaps in deference to Max—he tried to play down his concerns. "I am Max's friend but I know little of the rest of his family. We met years ago, you know, at Valland House, when my balloon came down in the grounds. He was fascinated by the workings of it, and I took him up several times—to his parents' dismay, I might add. The duke was worried his only son might be hurt."

"And now he has hurt him in the worst way possible, by denying Max his heritage."

Mr. Keith looked doubtful. "Struck down, you say? It does sound odd, doesn't it?"

"Suspicious."

Mr. Keith smiled, and glanced sideways at Lil. "Miss Marietta is very determined, isn't she? Do you think Max knows she's taken him up as her cause? I don't know if he'd be happy if he did. Max is a very private person."

"Then you'd best not tell him," Marietta suggested.

"Miss Marietta is headstrong," Lil said, with a sniff. "She an' her sisters all are, the three of them, like bolting horses. I don't try an' rein them in anymore, sir. I just let them run until they're done, and then I give them a piece of my mind."

He laughed, his gray eyes sparkling. "What part of London are you from, Miss Lil? I am a London boy myself."

She looked startled, then wary. "I don' know what you're talking about, Mr. Keith."

"You're a Londoner, I can hear it in your voice."

"I'm from Yorkshire, same as Miss Marietta."

It was ridiculous, thought Marietta. Her accent was indisputable, but clearly Lil was having none of it. She didn't want to discuss her past with Mr. Keith and she wasn't going to—if she said she wasn't from London then nothing he could do or say would make her admit that she was. Marietta caught the aeronaught's eye and gave a slight shrug.

"How did you come to be flying balloons?" she asked instead.

"Sheer luck. I was hired by an aeronaught to help with the maintenance of his balloon, and I showed I'd some skill. He began to teach me, and when he decided to give it away I was in a position to buy the balloon off him. They were using hydrogen gas then, not the coal gas we have today, far more dangerous."

At that moment his balloon jumped on its tether, caught in a swirling breeze. Lil gave a little shriek. "Miss Lil, there is nothing to be afraid of! Here, let me show you," he coaxed her towards the basket, although Marietta could see Lil dragging each step, her already ramrod-straight back like a soldier's rifle at attention.

"No, sir, I don't think I—," Lil was protesting, but Mr. Keith was impervious.

"How will you ever know whether or not you enjoy something if you don't try it?" he told her gently. "Now, come and look at this, Miss Lil. This is a wicker basket and you couldn't wish for anything stronger and more flexible . . ."

On the way home Lil was subdued, a stunned look in her brown eyes. "Do you know, Miss Marietta," she said at last, "I didn't realize such things was possible. That Mr. Keith, he's very clever."

"He is, yes. Despite being a bohemian and an eccentric."

Lil cast her a speaking glance. "And I've not forgotten about you going up in the balloon without telling anyone, miss. Don't you think I have."

"Sometimes I find it kinder not to tell people my plans, Lil—they only worry."

SARA BENNETT

"Yes, despite being a bohemian and an eccentric."
... he ... a speaking glance. "And I've not forgotten ... ... balloon without
telling anyone. ... ... don't think I have."
"Say nothing. ... ... to tell people my
... ... the very ..."

Chapter 8

The following morning, Marietta was busy writing a letter to Lady Greentree, telling her all
that had happened—within reason, of course. Just as
she was sealing the bulky folded pages she became
aware of voices downstairs, and rose to gaze from
her window, which overlooked the green plane trees
of Berkley Square. There was a carriage in the street
outside the Montegomery townhouse, and she recognized it at once as belonging to Aunt Helen and
Toby Russell.

Marietta smoothed her skirts with a grimace. She
loved Aunt Helen dearly—Helen was Amy Greentree's sister—but Toby was an appalling character
and he was only tolerated by the family for Helen's
sake. He had run off with her when Helen was too
young and silly to see him for the fortune hunter he
really was, and William, as the head of the Tremaine
family, had given in to Toby's demands rather than
allow a full-blown scandal. Toby had soon gone

through Helen's money and now they lived in a state of perpetual penury.

Parallels had been drawn between Aunt Helen and Marietta, and she supposed they were justified. They had both been foolish enough to give their hearts to men who were completely unsuitable, and then proceed to run off and ruin themselves. But whereas Helen had ended up being married to her bounder, Marietta had not—and when she looked at Toby, she couldn't help but think she had the better bargain.

By the time Marietta entered the drawing room, Aunt Helen was wiping away her tears as she viewed Vivianna's son in the arms of his nursemaid.

"Now, now, old girl, pull yourself together." Toby shuffled and looked embarrassed. "I thought you were over all that silly nonsense."

Toby had been a handsome man in his youth, but in the last ten years or so his indulgent lifestyle had seen him change. Surreptitiously Marietta eyed his rigid waistline, and decided he must be wearing a corset.

"Such a shame that Amy cannot travel yet," Helen was saying. "She will be longing to see this dear little man. Just think, she is a grandmamma!"

"And she's not the only one," Toby said, with a knowing smirk.

Vivianna shot him a look full of dislike, and there was a little silence. Then Helen straightened and spoke with uncharacteristic boldness.

"Well, as to that, I told William I do not care." Her voice trembled a little, for she was very fond of her brother William and very much influenced by him.

"I told him that I could never look upon Amy's girls as anything other than family, and that I loved them all dearly, and if that made me a fool or . . . or a dupe, then it was just too bad!"

"Oh, Aunt Helen!" Marietta came and gave her aunt a warm hug. "We love you too."

"Good Gad," Toby shuddered at so much open emotion, and went to peer out the window.

"It's just that I rely upon him so," Helen spoke in a little voice. "I do not know what I would do without him. William is so strong, and I have never been very strong."

Marietta exchanged a glance with Vivianna. They both knew that Toby was useless and that Helen did rely on William. In his way, he had watched over Helen. He had even paid some of his sister's outstanding debts when Helen could not do so, and Toby *would* not do so.

"We don't expect you to do anything that will make Uncle William angry with you," Vivianna assured her. "Truly, Aunt Helen, you must not do that. But do you know, it might be a good thing for you, and good for Uncle William, too, if you stand up for yourself occasionally. If you were to say what you really think and feel, rather than saying what you believe will please him most."

"Well, as for that . . . You can ask William yourself, Helen," Toby called out, as he turned from his position by the window with an insufferably smug smile. "He's just arrived."

Helen took a deep shuddering breath. Vivianna and Marietta exchanged looks, before Vivianna went out into the hall to welcome her Uncle William, and

Marietta clasped her aunt's hand and squeezed it, at the same time shooting Toby a speaking glance. He responded with a mocking grin.

William's voice boomed in the hall, and then he was following Vivianna into the room. He took Helen's outstretched hand with a brusque, "Sister," and greeted Marietta as if he would rather she wasn't there. Dutifully the nurse presented Vivianna's son to be admired—William peered at him suspiciously and grunted—and then he sat down in the most comfortable chair in the room.

"I'll have a little milk in my tea, Marietta. And two of those tea cakes," he said, watching critically as Marietta fetched them for him. "It really is too bad," he grumbled. "Despite the fact that Her Majesty the Queen graciously acknowledged Amy's girls three years ago, I still cannot go anywhere without mention being made of the scandal of their birth. I wish it had never come to light. I don't know what any of you were thinking to allow the truth to leak out."

"No one mentions it to me," Vivianna said with only a slight edge to her voice. "And Her Majesty is perfectly comfortable in the company of Oliver and myself. I think you should tell these gossips, whoever they are, to mind their own business, Uncle."

Helen drew in a little gasp of air, clearly far more upset by the exchange than any of the participants. William glared at his eldest niece and informed her in his most pompous voice, "Until you came along there was nothing remotely scandalous about the Tremaine family."

"I find that hard to believe," Toby spoke up.

"Apart from my poor sister's union to yourself, of course," William cut him down.

"More tea cakes, Uncle?" Marietta asked a little desperately, holding out the plate.

He gave her a look, as if he was about to start a category of her own misdeeds, but then his eyes swept greedily over the tea cakes and he changed his mind. "Thank you, Marietta, I will take another one. How is Amy's ankle, by the way? Healing?"

"She hopes to be able to travel south very soon," Marietta replied sweetly. "She asked after you, too, Uncle, in her last letter."

"Did she?" He appeared somewhat mollified. "Well, I am remarkably hale, even though family business runs me ragged."

Marietta, who could just picture her uncle running from townhouse to townhouse, putting out the fires of scandal, tried not to laugh. A glance at Vivianna showed that she too was having difficulty. They were still smiling when a servant opened the door and announced, "Madame Aphrodite, my lady!"

And Aphrodite, as usual dressed all in black apart from her glittering jewelry, entered the drawing room.

The teacup and saucer rattled in William's hand; tea cake crumbs cascaded over his waistcoat. Toby grinned in sheer perverse delight, while Helen moaned in horror. Marietta moved towards the door, determined to protect her mother at all costs, while Vivianna positioned herself before Uncle William.

As for Aphrodite herself, she had stopped dead in the doorway, and her face turned as white as chalk. "*Mon dieu*," she breathed, and it was a prayer.

William finally set his shaking cup down with a clatter, and stood up. "I'm afraid I cannot possibly stay here with this woman," he said, in a voice vibrating with fury and disapproval. "I will call again another time, Vivianna. When you are *alone*."

"Uncle, please, there is no need—" Marietta dove in on her sister's behalf, but no one was listening.

"As for *you*," he said, and suddenly he was looming over Aphrodite, his face mere inches from her own. To her credit Aphrodite did not cringe but stood rigidly still, looking up into his eyes, but Marietta thought she had never seen the courtesan so afraid. William lifted his voice, "I don't want to see you or hear that you've been spreading any more stories about my nieces. I will not have any more scandal. *Do* you understand me?"

Aphrodite said nothing, her eyes fixed on his.

"I am perfectly aware of all your actions," and his tone was softer still. "I have friends who keep me informed."

Still Aphrodite said nothing.

After a moment William made an explosive sound and marched past her, and out of the room. Soon afterwards they heard the outer door close and his vehicle moving away.

Aphrodite took a shaken breath. Vivianna had hurried to her side to hold her hand, and Marietta took the other one. "Come and sit down," she said gently, easing her mother towards the sofa where Helen still sat, apparently frozen.

Vivianna, easily moved to tears since the birth of her son, drew out a lacey handkerchief and mopped at her eyes. "I'm so s-s-sorry, Mama! He was appalling! I have never seen him so horrid."

"I had forgotten . . . but yes, my brother can be

very formidable." Aunt Helen had pressed a hand to her breast, presumably to ease her heart palpitations.

Only Toby appeared to be unmoved by the scene. "Your brother certainly has a temper," he said levelly. "I thought I was the only one who had felt the lash of it, but I see now that I have a rival for the title of Most Likely to Tarnish the Tremaine Family Name."

Aphrodite managed to dredge up a breathless laugh. She lifted her chin and her emerald and diamond earrings glittered. "I do not regard him," she said haughtily. "He does not frighten *me*."

But he did, thought Marietta. Aphrodite was playing at being Joan of Arc, but Uncle William in his part as one of the English lords did frighten her very much indeed. How could he be such a bully!

Aphrodite remained to drink tea and hold her grandchild. Her beautiful, haggard face softened with love when she looked down at him, and Marietta felt a new admiration grow within her for this woman who had lost her own three children and yet somehow survived. By the time Aphrodite left, she seemed more herself again; she gave an impatient shrug when William's behavior was brought up. "*Psht!* Some men are all noise and bluster," she waved a dismissive hand. "It is the only way they can get what they want. I do not regard him."

"I know Mama Greentree has always told us that Uncle William has a temper, but until now I truly did not believe it," Vivianna said, when she and Marietta were alone.

"He was so angry."

"I suppose it was the slur on the family name, or

what he perceives as a slur. And what did he mean about 'friends' who keep him informed?"

Marietta shook her head. "Almost.... I don't know. I was going to say that it was almost as if he had met Aphrodite before. His hatred was personal, didn't you feel it? When he shouted at her, he leaned right over her, into her face, as if he knew her."

"As far as I know they have never met before, and I cannot see Uncle William visiting her club, can you? He is such a prig, such a stickler for all things proper."

"Perhaps that's it, though. Perhaps he has a secret penchant for Aphrodite's and thinks she will tell us all about it, so in his own way he's warning her off."

"You have a vivid imagination, Marietta." Vivianna laughed, and then gave a huge yawn.

Marietta was immediately contrite. "You are tired! Go upstairs and rest. And leave the worrying about Uncle William to me. That is why I am here, isn't it, to take all such trivial domestic concerns off your hands so that you can enjoy your son?"

Vivianna smiled wanly, and her face softened as she looked at her younger sister. "I wish you would look upon your stay here as a holiday, Marietta. You are in need of one, I think. I have always regretted that I was not there when you ran off with that creature Gerard. I could have stopped you."

"I don't think so. I was determined to ruin myself, and I did. And do you know, Vivianna, after he abandoned me I realized I did not love him at all. It was the idea of love that attracted me."

Vivianna sighed. "But you've changed, sister. Before Gerard you were a carefree, generous and fearless girl, and now I see a shadow in your eyes. You are far more cautious, far less likely to open your heart to others. You guard your feelings."

"I was hurt," Marietta said a little stiffly. "I do not want to be hurt again. What is so strange in that?"

"Nothing strange. You are being sensible, of course you are. But I wish . . . I grieve for all you have lost. I think you are not happy, are you, Marietta?"

Marietta smiled, but it was not the spontaneous grin she once had. "I am very happy. Or I will be if you stop talking nonsense and go and rest, Vivianna."

Obediently Vivianna wandered upstairs to Lil, leaving Marietta to deal with Cook and the menus, and anything else that needed attention.

One of those things concerned Max, Lord Roseby. Marietta planned to call on him again this afternoon. A sense of urgency had gripped her since Max had told her he wouldn't be in London for much longer. If Max was leaving for Cornwall then they did not have a great deal of time to conduct their temporary affair, and she still had to complete the first task Aphrodite had set for her.

She must make the most of the moments she and Max had left, to learn all she could from him about desire. Not love, she reminded herself sternly. This was purely about passion and . . . and lust.

Marietta gave a little shiver at the image this conjured up, and the memory of his firm lips on hers, and his warm skin under her fingers. Who would have thought that such a brief liaison could have this effect on her? If she was truthful, then she would admit that ever since she had been compelled to rest her lips on his, she had been thinking about the taste of him, the feel of him, the strength of his arms about her.

If she was honest, then Marietta would have to admit that she was very much looking forward to repeating the experience.

As often as possible.

As Marietta arrived at Bedford Square, a harassed-looking gentleman was leaving. "That was Master Max's man of business," Pomeroy informed her importantly, when she asked. "He sent for him first thing."

Marietta wondered what business Max had that was so urgent it couldn't wait until he was well again. Then the sweet, heavy scent of flowers distracted her, and she realized that once more Mrs. Pomeroy had outdone herself. There was an enormous china bowl of roses on a table in the entrance hall, and Marietta sniffed appreciatively.

"Gorgeous," she gasped, bending over the bouquet to sniff again. "Where did these come from, Pomeroy?"

He beamed at her. "They're from the rose garden at Valland House, miss. Mr. Harold and Miss Susannah kindly asked to have them sent up."

"They're both very fond of your master, aren't they?"

"Oh yes, miss. Mr. Harold and Master Max are like brothers and always have been, and Miss Susannah is like his sister. At least, they were, before—" He broke off, glancing away uncomfortably.

Marietta would have liked to have asked him more, but even she had her limits when it came to gossiping with servants. Besides, Pomeroy would see it as being disloyal and she did not want him to feel he had betrayed Max.

"How is Lord Roseby today?" she asked, as she followed his slow progress up the stairs.

"More like his old self, miss."

Marietta pondered on that as they edged toward the master's suite, wondering if it was entirely good news. Max's old self, in her experience, could be both haughty and arrogant, and may prove difficult to get along with.

At any rate, Max was no longer languishing in his bed. Dressed immaculately in a dark blue coat and tan trousers, he was seated in a small sitting area that overlooked the back of his townhouse, and although his handsome face remained pale and gaunt, he rose to his feet as she entered.

"Miss Greentree."

"Lord Roseby."

Behind them, Pomeroy closed the door.

"I see you are much improved, Max," Marietta declared as she sat down in the chair opposite him, but she noticed that he could not quite hide his relief as he also resumed his seat.

"As you see, hale and hearty."

"And you've had your man of business here?"

He narrowed his eyes. "That's right. I had the matter of my future to discuss, such as it is."

"You seem in good spirits for someone who has nothing to look forward to."

"I told you I was fine, and there was no need to call on me, Marietta."

"Ah, but there is our agreement. I'm certain you haven't forgotten *that*, Max."

Max gave her a long look from beneath his lashes, a look she had difficulty in reading. "No, I haven't forgotten that. I wish I could."

"I hope you don't intend to try and wriggle your way out of it," Marietta said, wagging her finger at him like a governess in charge. "I won't release you from your promise, you know."

"This is utter madness," he answered in an exasperated tone.

"But it is temporary madness, Max," she reminded him. "And I've told you, we're practicing, that's all. In fact I think we should start right now." And with that Marietta leaned forward and placed her hand on his knee.

He went still, eyeing her hand as if it might explode.

"I want you to imagine I am a courtesan, Max. A woman of experience and sophistication whom you have just met . . . and whom you deeply desire."

She had dropped her voice on the final word, giving it what she thought was a sensual overtone. She never expected him to grin at her.

"Max!"

"I'm sorry, but you look nothing like 'a woman of experience and sophistication.' You look like . . . like Marietta Greentree."

"You have to use your imagination," she said, trying not to be irritated by him. "You're just not trying."

He pulled his face back into the haughty frown. "I *am* trying but it is too ridiculous. You have a vivid—"

"No, it isn't. Haven't you ever seen a woman you instantly desired? You are at a ball or a supper dance or some such thing, and you see her across the room. Just one glance—that's enough for you to know that you want her. Everything about her entices you to her side, her elegant dress, the smooth line of her neck, her enigmatic smile. You can't resist. You go to her and persuade her to go home with you, and in the coach you cannot take your eyes off her. Or, maybe you are riding your horse across the moors . . ."

"There are no moors in London."

"Then a park!" she retorted, her eyes bright and eager, caught up in her own fantasy. "You're riding through the park, and you see a girl up ahead, hair flying beneath her hat, riding like the wind. As you draw level you glance sideways at her and see her profile, her figure, and something in you responds. Instantly, immediately. You want her. Hasn't that ever happened to you, Max?"

"No," he said unhelpfully. "As I was going to say when you interrupted, you have a vivid imagination, Marietta, but it has nothing to do with reality. I see a pretty woman across the room at a ball, I may speak to her, yes, and ask her the usual bland, polite questions, but as her chaperone will be seated right beside her, watching her like a hawk, I certainly won't be taking her home in my coach. And then there's the galloping girl. Has the horse bolted on her, and if not . . . I wonder what the hell she's doing out on her own. If she's a lady then she's a fairly rackety one, and if she isn't . . . well, I would probably have a few qualms about whether I should become involved with her or not. The scandal, you know. Or at least, that was a consideration before I became a scandal myself."

Marietta had grown impatient with him long before he had finished his little speech. "You are being far too practical and pragmatic. Don't you have any imagination at all, Max?"

"No, but I'm sure you have enough for both of us."

She sighed and sat back in her chair, glaring at him. "This isn't working," she muttered to herself.

"I told you—"

"I won't give up."

The determination in her voice caused him to make a sound between a laugh and a groan. "You really are unstoppable, aren't you?"

Marietta pretended to consider it. "I don't know. I'm young yet. Perhaps one day something or someone will come along who will be able to stop me. Gerard nearly did. But not you, Max, and not yet. Are you going to cooperate?"

"Have I any choice?" he said darkly.

She smiled, dazzling him. "Not really."

Max wondered once again how he could have fallen into the clutches of Marietta Greentree. There he was, innocently going about his business, and then Miss Blue Eyes appeared upon the scene, and nothing could ever be the same again. He was about to commence an affair with a beautiful blonde who kept him awake at nights. The truth was, he hadn't a chance of resisting her—she just didn't know it yet because she was too innocent.

And there was his problem, really. He had been brought up a gentleman and gentlemen didn't seduce innocents—even innocents whose reputations were in tatters.

Abruptly Marietta stood up and, before he could struggle to his feet, leaned over him, her face very close to his. Curiously he stared back at her, wondering what she would do next and hoping he could bear it with fortitude. After a moment he found himself thinking that her skin was really very fine, like cream, and her eyes were the clearest blue he had ever seen, framed by those curling lashes so much darker than her hair. And her mouth, like a bow with a curl at the edges, always trembling on the verge of a little smile. Oh yes, he found her mouth endlessly fascinating and extremely kissable.

His breathing had quickened—he felt his chest rising and falling. How had that happened? He clenched his hands upon the chair arms to stop himself from reaching out for her, but she had already stepped back, frustration in every line of her.

"I don't know what to do," she wailed. "I'm relying on you, Max, to show me what to do! You promised. I thought a gentleman never broke a promise?"

Somehow he kept his face bland. "You are playing the part of the courtesan, Marietta, surely the seduction is in your hands? *I* am not the one who needs to practice, after all."

She gave him a belligerent stare. "You're enjoying this, aren't you, Max? Frustrating me like this, being a stick in the mud. It's probably what you do best."

He didn't deny it.

She walked around him, her skirts swishing, her pretty vivacious face set in stubborn lines. "Max, I'm relying on you, I really am. At least kiss me—show me how to do it properly. At least do that. You kissed me last time I was here."

"You caught me in a weak moment, Marietta," he said.

"Then pretend this is another one." She came to a halt in front of him, her hands on her hips. "*Please.*"

He wanted to say no. He should say no. But she was so woebegone, and it was so ridiculous, a beautiful young woman begging him to kiss her. Max heard himself say, "If you insist," and then thought that that was even more preposterous.

But it was too late to change his mind.

With a smile of triumph, Marietta leaned in to him and planted her lips firmly on his. And stayed there. It was, he thought, like being held prisoner by an angel fish. Oh God, she didn't even know the basics of kissing a man—hadn't *he* taught her that, the man who had ruined her? Was Max going to have to show her everything?

Kiss her, you want to, don't you! She's asking you to for God's sake, so do it.

Gently, Max lifted his hands and rested them against her shoulders, pushing her back just a little, enough for him to be able to speak. "A kiss is more than just touching lips," he murmured. "You have to caress with your mouth. Feel the other person, nibble and suck and even bite, gently. Like this." And then, like a fool, he proceeded to show her, using his lips against hers in the most delicate, and yet the most intimate, of ways.

Her mouth was soft and uncertain, but definitely not reluctant. He flicked his tongue across the surface of her bottom lip, and then drew it into his mouth. She made a little sound in her throat as if she liked it, and promptly did the same to him. He pressed deeper, his tongue now inside her mouth, not aggressive, but seeking out her own. Tentatively, then with growing confidence, she followed his lead.

How long since he had kissed a woman like this? There had been a time when he thought only of women and the mutual pleasure being with them could bring. He'd earned himself something of a reputation, although that hadn't stopped the matchmaking mamas' pursuit of the Duke of Barwon's only son. But lately . . . sexual pleasure had become little more than a quick tumble, a moment's release from his troubles, and soon forgotten.

This was different. Marietta Greentree was different, and he didn't understand why and he was beginning to think that even if he did, it was too late to fight it.

When at last he broke off their kiss, Marietta's eyes were closed. She was bending over him, with her palms resting heavily against his chest, and her lips parted and flushed from his. "Oh," she breathed, with the flattering air of one who understood everything now.

Max wondered if his head was spinning due to weakness from his wound or from Marietta. His heart, too, had redoubled its efforts to escape from his chest. And yet his voice, when he spoke, was calm and in control, and not showing any of the insanity he knew he had fallen prey to.

"Now you kiss me," he heard himself say in that reasonable voice, and knew it would be the Bedlam for him.

Her lashes lifted and she gazed at him from languid blue eyes. "Do you think I can?"

"It's what courtesans do."

She licked her lips and he almost groaned aloud. And then she tilted her head slightly, to avoid their noses getting in the way, and began to do to him what he had just done to her. He had to hold his arms rigid, to prevent himself from grabbing her and molding that soft, delectable body to his. Marietta might not be an expert but she was keen, and she had a seductive charm that Max had noted from the first. Perhaps she would make a good courtesan, perhaps it *was* her destiny to follow in her mother's footsteps, as she claimed, but there was a resistance to the idea inside him that he couldn't explain, and didn't want to explore.

Marietta felt as if her insides had liquified, turned hot and sweet. She wanted to curl up on Max's knee, and cling to his neck and kiss him forever. Why had no one ever told her that a kiss could be like this? So sensuous and powerful. Not just the prelude to the physical act of connection, but a book all on its own.

Max's tongue slid against hers, and she heard him moan as if he couldn't help it. His hands were now clasped about her waist, tight, and when she would have pressed closer he held her away. Keeping her at a distance. Except for her mouth.

It should have felt detached, but there was something very erotic about that distance between them. Knowing that they were separated by so little, and yet their mouths were fused so hotly. But still she wanted to get closer, to mess up his hair, twist those exuberant curls around her fingers, and then she wanted to undo the buttons of his coat, one by one, and explore. She hadn't forgotten the night he had lain, naked, in bed and she had seen most of him.

There must have been a sound at the door, but Marietta didn't hear it, and she was positive Max didn't either. But the next moment there was a furious clattering, as if a tray of tea cups had been caught in a gale. Shocked, Marietta turned just in time to see Daniel edging back out of the room, his eyes lowered, and then he closed the door with a clunk. There was no doubt he had seen them kissing. One of Max's servants had seen them kissing.

Embarrassing as it was, she didn't care. *I've done it!* she thought. *I've completed my first task . . .* And yet she had been so busy kissing Max, and enjoying it, that she hadn't given a thought to Aphrodite. Becoming a courtesan had been the last thing on her mind.

Had he enjoyed it, too? He was just pretending, was he, playing a part? Huh! She let her lips trail over his jaw, little biting kisses, and then she flicked her tongue against his skin, tasting him.

He shuddered. "Marietta."

And she knew then that he wanted her as much as she wanted him. Whatever he might say, his body wanted hers. For some reason she felt relieved by this knowledge. It gave her a sense of power over him, a sense of immunity from being used and abandoned.

Max sighed and turned his face so that her brow rested against his cheekbone. "I think we have shocked the servants enough for one day," he said in a voice she hardly recognized. "Enough, Marietta."

"Why?" she protested. "He's gone now, and we've only just begun. Kiss me again."

"No." He laughed harshly, and gave her a little push, so that she had no choice but to step backwards. "I can't believe I'm doing this, I must be mad." Then, his eyes looking straight into hers, "I don't want to lose control, Marietta, not yet. And I will, if you keep at me like this."

Marietta stared at him a moment more, feeling extremely hot and bothered. Perhaps he was right. Their affair had just begun and she shouldn't be impatient. Max was for practicing with, and she seemed to be having trouble just now remembering it. In fact it had almost felt as if it was more than that, more than pretend. It had felt as if it was real . . .

Still, better not let him get too complacent.

"I don't know, Max," she said, briskly pulling on her gloves. "Of course you have far more experience than me in these matters, but I feel as if you're in charge and I'm sure it should be the other way around. I am going to be the courtesan, not you."

He shrugged but she thought there was a gleam of triumph in his eyes. Of course, he wanted to be in charge so that he could prevent her from getting the upper hand. It did not help that they were here in his house. That, too, gave him an unfair advantage over her.

Now that Max was recovering from his wound he would leave London. She reminded herself that although she might have accomplished Aphrodite's first task, there was no time to waste if she was to complete them all. And come to that, how many were there, and what would they involve? She definitely needed to see Aphrodite again and as soon as possible.

She turned around, catching him by surprise. He was watching her with a wary look in his brown eyes, as if he thought she might pounce on him and . . . and make love to him. She almost laughed aloud. Well, she wasn't going to do that, not yet, but she was going to ask him some questions he probably wouldn't like very much.

It was time to get Max seriously rattled.

Chapter 9

Max was watching her, new shadows under his eyes, and she almost took pity on him, but then her gaze traveled to the bandage about his head. Was this an accident or a cold-blooded attack? For his sake she needed to find out the truth about the Valland family, and Max had to help her.

Her resolve hardened.

"Mr. Keith told me that you had two accidents only last year. Why do you have so many?"

Max felt his face go slack, and then crease up in the frown he had never learned to hide. His mother had been the same, she had been hopeless at pretending to feel something she did not feel. He had inherited her inability to dissemble and his father's quick temper, a disastrous combination.

"Marietta, this time you have gone too far. My private life is none of your business—"

"Well, it is my business if you're going to get knocked on the head again before we've finished our arrangement," she told him practically. "I'm only thinking of myself, Max."

He wanted to strangle her, but at the same time there was something delightfully artless about her that made him want to laugh out loud . . . and then strangle her. Marietta Greentree was unlike any woman he had ever met before and he was in equal parts enchanted with her, and terrified of what she could mean to his already tangled existence.

"Come, Max, I won't be satisfied until you tell me. What is this about you nearly drowning—twice?"

"I didn't drown, and it was an . . . accident." The word sounded different, almost sinister, and he didn't like it. She had made him think things he preferred not to think.

"Twice?"

"Yes. I went out in my boat and it had a hole in it, but I was a decent swimmer, even though it was winter and the water was bloody cold." He frowned. "The other time Harold and I were diving for coins—it was a game we played—and I became entangled in some reeds. I had a pocket knife and cut myself free. There was no harm done."

"Hmm, and both times you saved yourself." The expression in her eyes was skeptical. "Tell me, what other 'accidents' have you been involved in since you nearly drowned, twice?"

He narrowed his gaze, but answered her calmly enough. "The usual boyhood misadventures, riding accidents, falling from a tree, falling from a window. Don't look so horrified, Marietta, I was like every other boy, never as careful of myself as I should have been. It's natural to be careless of your physical safety when you're young, and my father . . . the duke did not stifle us with too many rules and regulations, as long as we got our lessons done."

"I can't imagine you being reckless, Max."

He looked miffed, and then drew himself up in his Arrogant Heir pose. "Perhaps because you have no brothers of your own, you don't understand boys as well as you think, Marietta."

"Well, *I* was adventurous," Marietta declared. "Francesca and I tramped the moors for hours in all weather. Once we stayed out until it was dark, and waited for the ghostly dog to come. It's a legend, you see, the dog appears to anyone out after dark. It never did turn up."

He smiled. "Did it rain?"

"Buckets. We had the most atrocious colds for weeks afterwards. Mama thought we were going to die."

"Marietta—"

"So you see, I was careless, too, and I didn't have as many accidents as you."

He looked at her strangely. "Perhaps it's different for girls. Although my sister Susannah was always right there with us, trying to keep up. Anyway, when I was sent away to school things changed. There wasn't the freedom any more to do dangerous things, and I had no more accidents. In fact, it wasn't really until last year that I . . . that . . ." He frowned.

Had something odd about the incidents finally struck him, as it had her? Had he never thought about it properly before? Had he never realized that perhaps someone had wanted him dead for a very long time? But whatever uneasy thoughts Max was thinking, he soon rejected them.

"No," he said. "Sheer coincidence. You can turn

any childhood mishap into a crime, if you try hard enough."

"Max," she asked him quietly, "what happened last year?"

"Marietta, it's meaningless."

"Then if it's meaningless you won't mind telling me about it, will you?" She gave him one of her sweetest smiles.

His mouth twitched despite himself, and then he was cross with her, but she knew she had won. "I can see you won't be satisfied until I tell you everything. Very well! Last summer I was shot at while I was out riding at Valland House—our . . . my father's . . . the duke's estate in Surrey." His eyes avoided hers as he made the correction. "The shot missed me, but not by much. I never discovered where it came from, but I believe it was an accident. Why would someone fire on me? Perhaps the shooter took fright when he realized what had almost happened, or else he was ignorant as to what he had done. In any event, we never discovered his identity and it didn't happen again."

"And what of the second accident?"

Max reached up to touch his bandages, grimaced, and took his hand away. "Just before Christmas, I'd come home. I was in the stable—my horse had gone lame and I had made my way down in the night to check on him. Something . . . someone . . . something struck me down. I don't remember much, until a groom found me an hour later. It wasn't very serious, just a knock on the head. There was a piece of wood from the loft. It looked as if it had fallen down and I just happened to be under it. Luckily the horse was quiet that night. He has a bit of a temper and can be tricky."

"You mean you were lucky you weren't trampled to death while you lay in his stall unconscious. You have a lot of lucky moments, Max," Marietta said quietly. "You don't seem to realize it—or maybe you don't want to—but others can see it." She mulled over his words a moment while he sat in stubborn silence. "And these two latest 'accidents' happened *before* your father disinherited you?"

"Yes, shortly before. I was disinherited in January, in the New Year, when we were all gathered together at Valland House. The family come to stay—it's a tradition. No matter how far the Vallands roam they will always return at that time of year. My father instructed everyone to come into the library and there he read my mother's letter out to us. It was . . . distressing, to say the least."

Marietta gasped, her eyes wide. "You mean he read it aloud to the entire family? *All* your relations? Max, that is very cruel! In fact it seems intentionally so. Is the duke a cruel man?"

"It was a cruel moment," Max said grimly. "I suppose he was upset and he just wanted to get it over with."

He was standing up for him—the man who had blasted his lifelong expectations in one brief and shocking moment, and embarrassed and humiliated him at the same time. Marietta looked at Max and wanted to shake him for being so loyal, and she wanted to kiss him for being Max.

"And now this attack outside Aphrodite's Club," she went on mildly. "So many near misses. Aren't you at all suspicious that they may not be accidents after all?"

He frowned. "They're not connected. How could

they be? Why should they be? You're turning something innocent into something sinister without the slightest piece of evidence."

"But think, Max, think. Do you have something that someone else wants?"

"I might have had, once," he admitted grudgingly. "I know what you're doing, Marietta. You're trying to make me believe that Harold wants me dead so that he can inherit. But apart from the complete ridiculousness of such a theory, how can you justify this?" He pointed to the bandage on his head. "Harold already has everything. What's the point of getting rid of me now that he has been named heir? None at all."

"It doesn't make sense, no. Not yet."

"Please, Marietta, just leave it. I don't need you to interfere in my life, and I certainly haven't asked you to. You are one of those women who delight in meddling, aren't you? Well, in this instance, don't!"

"Someone has to look after you, Max," she said, and gave him her wide-eyed look.

"The kissing was easier," he muttered. "At least while your mouth was busy you couldn't ask questions, or inflict your wild theories on me."

"Oh, do you want to practice again?"

He looked at her mouth, and for a moment his eyes darkened, as though he was considering it. And then he rose to his feet, with only a little hesitation. "No," he said bluntly. "No more lessons today. *Goodbye*, Marietta."

Marietta smiled, because no matter how much he was protesting now, she knew he had enjoyed it as much as she. "Very well, goodbye until next time, Max."

The door closed behind her.

Thank God she's gone, Max told himself, and ignored the flash of heat inside him when he remembered his mouth fusing with hers. She had gotten some wild notion into her head and now she would not let it go. And it was wild, he told himself firmly. Harold was his cousin and his best friend; he would never hurt him. Never!

But the damage was done. Marietta Greentree had made him face his doubt, and no matter how he protested against it that sly voice would be forever whispering in his ear.

"I'm just lucky . . . or unlucky," he murmured to himself. "Accident prone, that's all."

Oh yes, very accident prone.

"It means nothing."

Others have noticed. Marietta noticed straight away.

"If someone wanted me dead so that they could claim my inheritance, then why knock me down after I lost everything? It doesn't make sense."

The voice was silent.

Because he was right, Max told himself.

Besides, he had other things to think of. His man of business had made some suggestions about the house in Cornwall, and the possibility of turning the estate into a going concern. None of them had been very optimistic, apart from one idea that appeared workable. There was a mine near Blackwood, long since closed down because the copper had run out at the end of last century. Now many such mines were reopening and being profitably mined for tin. There had been traces of tin found in Blackwood's mine, enough anyway for him to consider reopening it. His mother's little nest egg would be sufficient to repair and reequip the mine, employ some of the local men, and make a new start.

If he lived long enough.

"Blast her," he murmured. Marietta Greentree's insinuations didn't make sense. None of them. Just as his feelings for Marietta herself didn't make sense. She was the most irritating woman, and yet . . . He wanted her. She was already playing upon his desire like a musician upon a harp—she had his strings expertly quivering and humming—and yet she claimed not to know anything about seduction.

It was annoying, Max decided bleakly, looking about him, and very strange when he had just been wishing her gone, but now that she was . . .

The room felt empty without her.

Downstairs, Pomeroy was just divesting a tall, thin gentleman of his top hat and walking stick. Harold Valland looked up as Marietta descended the stairs, his brown eyes so very similar to Max's and yet so very different.

"Miss Greentree! Pomeroy said you were here. How is Max today?"

Marietta smiled as she joined him. "He is much better, sir."

"It is very generous of you to take this interest in my cousin," Harold said, full of sincerity. "Unfortunately since his . . . his troubles, people have been avoiding him. But you are his friend, aren't you, Miss Greentree?"

There was something in his tone she didn't understand. "I-I hope I am his friend," she said carefully. "I have his best interests at heart."

"That is good to hear."

Marietta met his gaze, fixed on her rather piercingly, and decided that now was the time to test Harold's own loyalty to his cousin.

"As Lord Roseby's friend I can't help thinking that it was a cruel thing his father did to him, reading his mother's letter aloud like that."

"So he's told you that?" Surprised, Harold glanced away, but whether because he was embarrassed by his uncle's behavior, or because he didn't want her to see the expression in his eyes, Marietta could not tell. She wished she knew him better; she wished she had Max's faith in him.

"Max tells me many things."

He pondered that for a moment. "The matter is private, but as Max has spoken of it . . . The duke is an intelligent man but sometimes, in times of great distress, his feelings take over. You must understand that he loved his wife and the knowledge of her betrayal almost destroyed him—in my opinion he will never recover from it. When the letter came into his hands he was crazed with pain and anger. The duchess was dead, he could not punish her for her infidelity, but Max was there. I imagine he read the letter aloud to hurt them both, as they had hurt him. Not very logical, but then families often aren't logical in their reactions to each other."

Remembering her own family, Marietta could only agree with him and let it pass. "What I don't understand is how the letter came to light."

Harold grimaced; clearly the memory was not a pleasant one. "You are very curious, Miss Greentree, but still it cannot hurt to speak of it, not when the whole of London knows. The letter was among the duchess's personal papers. My wife had been sorting through them after her death and she came across it. She had placed it on the fire, thinking it of no importance, and then she happened to read some of the words."

"So she retrieved it before it burnt too badly."

Of course she did. She would see at once what such a letter would mean to her and her husband, Marietta thought cynically.

"It distressed her tremendously," Harold went on sharply, reading her thoughts in her silence. "Susannah is very fond of her brother, and she couldn't believe it was true. She thought hard about what she did, believe me, but she decided that it was the duke's right to know the truth about his wife and son, no matter how unpalatable that might be. Lately, Susannah has even speculated that perhaps the duchess wanted her husband to know the truth—why else would she keep a letter so incriminating? Why not destroy it years ago?"

"Yes, I see that. The letter . . . who was it written to?"

"I don't know. I don't even know if it was a letter. It looked more like someone setting down their thoughts. A confession, if you like. That was why she wondered if it had been meant to be found."

Marietta wanted to ask what the letter said, word for word, but she knew that would be going too far. He already thought her insufferably inquisitive, and she did not want him to warn Max against her— Max, who was already incensed with her meddling.

She needed Max, she told herself. He was going to help her achieve her ambitions, and in return she would help him sort out his muddled life. He would be grateful to her, in the end.

"You take a great interest in Max, don't you, Miss Greentree?"

"I suppose I do—"

"It is generous of you to have befriended him," Harold said, still watching her, and again it seemed as if he had read her mind. "He has been very alone lately, and no matter how we try to help him he refuses to allow it."

"I am glad to do what I can," Marietta replied cautiously.

"I'm sure you are." He gave her a little smile, but now it seemed forced and when he spoke next she understood why. "Even though Max is no longer heir to the Dukedom of Barwon, he is my cousin and I am very fond of him. You understand that I would never allow him to be preyed upon by those who mean him ill. Even penniless, Max has rich and powerful relations, and because of that there are some who might believe he is still what is vulgarly called 'a good catch.' "

The words could be read as an affirmation of his commitment to Max, but Marietta knew they were not. They were aimed at her—there had been many such barbs stuck into her since Gerard Jones ruined her, but they still hurt, they hurt a great deal.

"Then it is fortunate I do not mean him ill, and that I am not presently husband-hunting," she said lightly, but her eyes lost their friendly glow. Harold might be Max's friend, but he had just let it be known that he wasn't hers.

"I'm glad to hear that, Miss Greentree," he said affably, but now she wasn't deceived. "I shall hold you to it, you know."

Marietta's smile was wry. "I'm sure you will."

"Perhaps . . . perhaps it would be best if you did not call on him again when I or my wife aren't present."

"Surely that's up to Max?"

His eyes, so like Max's and yet so different, narrowed. "While Max is unwell I am looking out for him, Miss Greentree. In my opinion it is in his best interests not to see you again."

She knew her face was red—she could feel the heat in her cheeks. "Very well, sir," she said quietly. "I will respect your wishes. Good day."

I should not resent what he said, Marietta told herself as she made her way home. Harold was only caring for Max—"looking out for him"—and he could not know Marietta was not an unscrupulous woman out for all she could get. Or maybe it was her curiosity that had caused Harold to warn her off. If he was responsible for Max's accidents, then naturally he would not want her to ask questions, or to prompt Max into asking them.

But either way his words had hurt, and she knew she would find it difficult to shut them out of her mind.

Of course he would not stop her from seeing Max! Not in his home, perhaps, but elsewhere. Max was a grown man with a mind of his own, and as far as Marietta was concerned their arrangement was unchanged.

"You're looking tired, Max."

Harold frowned down at him, and Max laughed. "What are you now, cousin? My nursemaid? As you see, I am an invalid out of bed today, an improvement on being an invalid in bed, I think."

"Yes, and I am wondering why you are out of bed

when the doctor said you were to stay there for the present."

Max gave him a look.

"I'm not impressed," Harold said. "You don't intimidate me, Max, I know you too well."

"Unfortunately. I can see you're dying to say something to me, why don't you say it?"

"I saw Miss Greentree leaving." Harold fiddled with the chain of his pocketwatch, suddenly uncomfortable.

"Yes, she was visiting me," Max replied smoothly, but Harold noticed the faint flush in his cousin's lean cheeks.

There, he was right to warn her off! he told himself. It was clear that the woman was weaving her web around his cousin, drawing him in while he was in a vulnerable state. Harold had made some more inquiries into the Greentree family and the daughters of Aphrodite, and although they were respectable enough on the outside, beneath the surface there were dark rumors of unsavory happenings. Max would be much better off without those kinds of complications when he had so many troubles of his own. But if Max wanted to do something, then Harold admitted that he would have the devil of a job stopping him.

"I hope you're not thinking of behaving foolishly, Max."

Max frowned. "And why would I be? I am not hanging out for a wife, if that's what worries you, cousin. I have far too many problems to want to bring a helpless woman into my life."

Helpless? "I . . . good. Because Marietta Greentree would not do as your wife, even in your present . . . eh, circumstances."

"You are a snob, cousin."

"Maybe, but I know what society will tolerate and what it will not, and Marietta Greentree has too many scandals attached to her. Even the Vallands could not lift her from the mire, Max; she would sink us."

Max gave a bitter laugh. "So what do you suggest? A temporary affair, perhaps?"

Harold pretended to think about it. "I don't see the harm in that, if it's what you want. But don't grow too fond of her, Max. She's not for you."

Max closed his eyes, but whether because he was tired or he just didn't want to discuss the matter any further, Harold didn't know. Still, he felt as if he had said his piece and he was content with that. No need to tell Max that he had barred Marietta Greentree from the house, he thought. His cousin might wonder where she was for a time, but he would soon forget her. Better for the family if he did. Temporary affair indeed!

"Harold, do you think I am accident prone?"

Harold blinked, startled by the change in subject. "Accident prone?"

"Yes, do you think I have had an excessive number of accidents?"

"Well, I've had plenty of my own, if you remember, especially when we were boys. We were always getting into scrapes." Harold laughed, but knew it sounded less than genuine. "I'm sorry, I don't understand what you're getting at."

Max opened his mouth to answer, and then shook his head decisively. "It doesn't matter. I was rambling. How is Susannah?"

Harold smiled and proceeded to tell him, but he had the sense that Max wasn't really listening. And that worried him. Marietta Greentree, the interfering minx, had placed these doubts in Max's mind.

And Harold told himself that would never do.

Chapter 10

The following morning the streets of London were busy, as always, but Marietta, traveling them in Oliver's carriage, hardly noticed. Already she had grown used to the different pace of life here, and although sometimes she caught herself dreaming of the vast stretches of open moorland around Greentree Manor, she did not feel particularly homesick. She missed Mama and Francesca more than she did Yorkshire.

Marietta smiled, remembering the sight of Lil, as she was awaiting the carriage in the entrance hall. The maid had tripped down the stairs wearing a new poplin dress with a single flounce about the hem, and sleeves puffed at the elbows. Lil, with puffed sleeves! And furthermore, her fair hair was dressed in an almost frivolous style, with bunches of beribboned curls above each of her little pink ears.

Aware of her scrutiny, Lil blushed and put her

hands up to fiddle with the curls, or try and hide them.

"Now remind me," Marietta said innocently, slipping an arm about Lil's waist. "It *is* balloon ascent day at Vauxhall Gardens?"

Lil clicked her tongue, blushing furiously. "You are awful, Miss Marietta. It's nothing of the sort, just that I-I was on my way out. For a walk. That's all."

Marietta nodded solemnly. "Of course. I can see you're not dressed up in your best at all, and that you haven't taken special care with your hair."

Lil giggled nervously, casting her a sideways glance. "You're a tease, Miss Marietta."

"I'm sorry for it." Marietta gave her a quick hug. "Don't listen to my nonsense. You have a good time, Lil, and enjoy yourself. You know you deserve it, and if you don't, then you should."

Lil smiled. "I think I do deserve it," she agreed. "I feel quite lightheaded," she added. "Do you think that's a good thing or a bad thing, miss?"

"I think it's a good thing, Lil. Just hang on tight."

Aphrodite's Club seemed almost like home, and when Dobson let her inside, his smile was so welcoming that it warmed her heart.

"Miss Marietta!"

"Good morning, Dobson. Is Aphrodite available?"

"For you, I'm certain of it."

"Marietta?" Aphrodite stood in the sitting room doorway, her eyebrows raised. "Come in here and tell me what it is you wish to see me about today."

It sounded very formal, but then Aphrodite appeared formal. In her black satin dress with black lace overskirt and flounces, her black gloves, and her opulent jewelry, the courtesan was a rather intimidating figure. No doubt she had been up all night and must now be thinking of her bed, but she did not give that impression. Aphrodite had long ago learned the art of hiding her true feelings behind a cool, polite mask.

Perhaps it had been a necessity, to enable her to survive in her chosen profession. If so, Marietta wondered whether she would ever be able to successfully hide her own feelings. She knew that it would be difficult. She was impulsive, too impulsive some would say, and to restrain her vivacious nature would take patience and practice.

"If you have come to ask me a question then you should ask it," her mother interrupted her thoughts. "Surely you are not squeamish, *mon petit puce*? Or shy? None of my daughters are shy."

Marietta smiled. "No, we are not shy. We are all very decided and forthright. I wonder, is that a good thing? I don't know, it seems to get us into all sorts of trouble. And yet I can't imagine living any other way."

Aphrodite seemed pleased with her answer, but she wasn't distracted for long. "Now, then, tell me what it is that is troubling you, Marietta. Not Vivianna and her son, I hope?"

"No, they are both very well," Marietta assured her, putting Aphrodite's fears to rest.

"Then what is the matter? Do not make me guess, *mon petit puce*. I am too old for guessing games."

"Max is the matter."

"Ah, your Lord Roseby. Is he not cooperating?"

"Well, he is, but . . . It is not easy, Madame."

"Of course not. What would be the point of it, if it was easy?" the courtesan replied sternly. "Have you completed the task I set you?"

Marietta smiled broadly. "I have. He kissed me. He gave me a kissing lesson, just as you said."

Aphrodite's dark eyes warmed. "Then I congratulate you, Marietta. You are very talented."

Marietta thought, guiltily, that she was probably not that talented. In fact, not talented at all. Max had done all the work, and she had completely forgotten about her allotted task. It had been sheer good luck that it was accomplished, but she did not intend to tell her mother that.

"Thank you. Madame, there is a problem. Harold Valland does not want me to see Max; he has barred me from visiting him at Bedford Square."

Aphrodite looked furious. She muttered something in French that Marietta had never heard before, and then she said, in a tightly controlled voice, "Does Lord Roseby know this?"

"No. Max would never do something so cruel, and he would not like his cousin acting on his behalf."

"You know this on so short an acquaintance?" Aphrodite asked curiously.

"I-I do. It's as if I have known him always."

Aphrodite nodded thoughtfully, and then took a deep breath. "My advice is don't tell him what his cousin has done," she said. "You don't want to be seen to be telling tales, and Max will discover it for himself soon enough."

"I wasn't going to tell him," she said in a small voice. "It was far too humiliating, Madame. But for the next task we will have to meet somewhere else.

In fact I am sure I would make better progress if I made him step outside the place where he feels comfortable."

Aphrodite nodded. "Very clever, Marietta. You are right, he will always be the master in his own home." She tapped the arm of her chair, the wood carved into a replica of the sphinx. She nodded again, more decisively. "Yes, I have decided upon your next task. It will be an assignation, as if between two strangers. Do not speak with him before you meet, and when you do you must pretend not to know each other. You are two strangers come together and seeking only pleasure. It will be easier then to play your part, will it not? It will be easier for you to take command, *mon petit puce*?"

Marietta's eyes glowed. "Oh, what a marvelous idea! An assignation with a stranger." And especially when the stranger was Max. "I-I like that very much, Madame. Where shall I meet him?"

Aphrodite smiled. "You will meet here, at my club, in one of my private rooms. I will arrange everything—food and drink will be brought to you, and Dobson will be close by if you should need him."

Marietta shook her head and laughed. "I don't think I will need him. Max is a gentleman, and it is very difficult to make him stop behaving like a gentleman. He probably wants me to fail, Aphrodite. I had a great deal of trouble even getting him to kiss me! I had to plead with him. But once he started, well," she smoothed her sleeve cuff, "he was rather good at it, I will admit that. You were right when you said he would know how to kiss."

Aphrodite gave her daughter an amused look. "Indeed. Well, a kiss is a great step forward. You should not slight it, especially when you worked so hard for it. You have done well to get so far with a gentleman like Lord Roseby. And don't despair, I have hopes you will get much further. The harder the task, *mon petit puce*, the sweeter the victory. And it is all to help you, *non*? So that you can decide whether or not you want to be a courtesan, and whether you enjoy having a man kiss you and touch you and . . . and more," she finished, evidently deciding Marietta wasn't ready for too much plain-speaking.

"I do enjoy it," Marietta insisted. "Madame, I *enjoyed* him kissing me."

Aphrodite's lips twitched. "But did *you* enjoy kissing *him*? That is far more important. The courtesan is mistress of the situation, even when the man thinks it is he who is master."

"Yes, I did. Very much indeed. I-I didn't want to stop, but Max pushed me away and told me that was enough practice. I thought that was poor spirited of him, but I believe he was worried he was going to lose control."

"I believe you are probably right," Aphrodite said, straight-faced.

"And I suppose I was taking advantage of him. He is still weak from the attack, although he likes to pretend he is fully recovered."

"Sometimes men need to be taken advantage of. They do not know what is best for them, Marietta."

"I only hope I can complete my tasks before Max leaves London."

"He is leaving?"

"Yes. Now that he has been disinherited he intends to go and live in Cornwall and brood on his future, or lack of one." She rolled her eyes extravagantly.

"You do not feel sympathy for him then?"

"Yes, of course I do. But I don't think he should give up so easily. I wouldn't. And there is something odd about the whole business. Max has had a great many accidents apart from his most recent one, and I don't think they're accidents at all. I think someone is trying to hurt him."

"Marietta." Aphrodite was suddenly alert, the laughter gone from her face. "You must be careful! I do not like the sound of this. If someone is trying to hurt Max, then they may hurt you, too. Perhaps it would be better if we were to forget these tasks altogether. Or find another gentleman."

Marietta realized that once again her tongue had run away with her, and she cried, distraught, "No, oh please, no! I've come this far, and I couldn't start again now. I promise not to put myself in danger. Don't make me stop now, please."

Aphrodite took a moment to choose her words, and uncharacteristically her voice trembled. "Understand this, Marietta. I would never put you in the path of danger again. I have you back now, and I will not risk your life a second time."

Marietta looked up and saw that her mother's eyes were shining with tears. She knew that Aphrodite loved her, of course she did, but to see now how much made her heart melt with joy and gratitude.

"I know, Mama," she whispered. "I won't let anything happen, I promise."

Aphrodite took a deep breath. "I will hold you to that."

Marietta gathered her thoughts. "You have given me my task, the assignation between strangers here at Aphrodite's Club, but what about the rules, Madame? Are there rules this time?"

"The rules, hmm. Yes, very well. The rules are these. You should dress as my protégés do—to be a courtesan, to feel like a courtesan, then you must look like a courtesan. Don't worry, I have some gowns you can try on, and we will find the right one for you. When he arrives, you will greet your Max at the door of the room, and take him to the sofa. There you will make certain he is comfortable, and when the food and drink is brought, you will serve him. You will make him feel as if he is the most special man in the world, Marietta. Nothing should be too much trouble for you, nothing he asks—within the terms of our agreement, of course—should be too difficult. You will provide for his comfort, and give no thought to your own."

"Hmm," Marietta was frowning. "I thought a courtesan would be more . . . forthright. You make it sound like being a slave."

"Ah, but this is only one part of the lesson, *mon petit puce*. Later, then you can make demands on him. For now he must see you as the perfect woman, the one who holds the keys to all his wishes and dreams. That was what I said a moment ago, remember: He must believe he is the master, even while it is you who are really pulling the strings. And you may not believe it, but in my experience most men would like to be waited upon by a beautiful woman."

"Oh, very well." Marietta wasn't happy. Waited upon? No, she wasn't happy at all, but she didn't see how she could refuse. Aphrodite was the one setting the rules, and it was only by abiding by them successfully that she would gain her mother's patronage.

"After he has supped, you can converse with him, but you must talk only of the subjects that interest him. And you must gaze at him as if every word he speaks is a marvel to you."

Marietta felt like yawning. She was beginning to grow bored just listening. "Gaze at him, hmm. I see."

Aphrodite raised her eyebrows at her daughter's tone, but continued on with her list of instructions. "A man likes to believe he is the center of a woman's world, the only thing that she sees in it. Make him believe that."

"I don't—"

"Flirt with him, Marietta," Aphrodite said bluntly. "Can you do that?"

"Oh, yes, yes, of course." She considered it. "Yes, I think I could flirt very well with Max."

"Good."

"Should I kiss him again?"

"Of course."

"And . . . touch him?"

"If you wish to."

Marietta tried not to show her doubts, or her excitement.

"Of course, he may not want you to, remember that. He will not, as you said before, wish to lose control."

No, Max would not want her to take charge of the situation. He would fight her, but she would fight back and . . . Except that she was supposed to be submissive, she reminded herself gloomily.

"If he wishes to touch you then you should allow him to touch your breasts," Aphrodite said matter-of-factly. "If necessary he can touch you as far as your waist."

Marietta had been listening, but her thoughts had taken flight. Max, kissing her, Max touching her, Max holding her in his arms when the balloon landed, his body beneath hers. Unlike the submissive rule, this one appealed to her, this one interested her immensely.

"Yes, Madame, I see," she said at last. "I understand why you worry, but remember, I am ruined. You don't have to be concerned about me losing something I have already lost."

"Perhaps not," Aphrodite said, with a lift of her eyebrows, "but you are still very much an innocent, and there is money to be made in innocence in this business, Marietta. If you have the stomach for it."

Marietta gave her a puzzled look.

"Did you know that an untried girl can sell her virginity? There are even auctions for such things."

She was shocked. Pay for a woman's virginity? Bid to be the first? Surely a woman's virginity was a gift in the woman's keeping? Something to be given when she felt it was the right time and place, and the right man. Not a commodity like a button or a pair of shoes or a carriage horse.

"You are surprised," the courtesan said gently. "But it is so. It happens all the time, Marietta. If you do decide to become a courtesan, then it is something you should know about. It is not such a terrible thing as you might think. Some girls lose their virginity to a stranger in a hayfield, or a boy they admire at a local fair. It is easily lost, more easily than you imagine. Why not make something worthwhile from the transaction?"

"I just . . . I always thought it was a gift, Madame."

"Ah, and I have made it sound like a bunch of turnips on market day? It is a gift, but even gifts can be bought and sold."

Marietta knew she would have to consider what Aphrodite had said, but the concept disturbed her. She had not been brought up to think in such a way—she supposed she had been privileged, far more privileged than the girls here at Aphrodite's Club, and far more privileged than Aphrodite herself.

"Do you still wish to go ahead with the assignation?"

Startled, Marietta met her mother's questioning dark eyes, and then smiled. "Of course. I am looking forward to it!"

"Then we need a time and date. We will say eight in the evening, in four days. I will expect you much earlier, however, so that we can prepare."

"Of course. I'll let Max know."

"No, I will send him the invitation. You are strangers, remember. Do you think he will refuse?"

"He can hardly refuse me, not after he promised to help. And by then he should be well enough to travel the short distance to the club. Especially," Marietta's mouth turned down, "as it doesn't look as if he'll be exerting himself much when he gets here." It would be Marietta who would be doing all the work.

"That is settled then," Aphrodite said, ignoring her daughter's expression, and rising to her feet with a rustle of silk and lace.

It was a dismissal, and obediently Marietta stood up, too. "Thank you, Aphrodite. I will try to . . . that is, I will do as you say."

"Of course you will," Aphrodite agreed. Then she hesitated.

Marietta looked at her expectantly.

"My child, I do not know how to say this . . . You have never asked me about your father, who he is, where he is? Vivianna was eager for such information, but you . . . you do not seem to want to know."

Marietta felt a little chill inside her and knew it for what it was—fear. "I do not need to meet him, Madame," she said quietly. "I am content with you and my sisters. I am sure I would be a disappointment to him."

Aphrodite gave a fierce frown. "That is nonsense! A disappointment, *psht*! You are a daughter to be proud of, and so he will be. I will not have such talk, do you hear me?"

Marietta had never seen her mother so angry. "I did not mean—"

"He is in town."

She stopped, confused. "You mean my father is here, in London?"

Aphrodite nodded. "I have seen him. I can call upon him, if you wish, and ask if he will see you. Of course, it is entirely up to you." She shrugged huffily, and Marietta bit her lip on a smile, but her humor was brief.

Her father. Now a desperate sense of longing had joined the fear. The need to see this man, to look into his eyes and see herself there. It was true she had never asked about him, and she could not say that she had craved this moment, but now that the offer had been made . . . Marietta knew she would not be able to just walk away and forget it.

"Marietta?"

She looked up at her mother, and there was something in the courtesan's gaze, an uncertainty that Marietta had never seen there before. As if she thought Marietta would refuse and throw the offer back in her face. Impulsively, Marietta reached out and hugged her. "Thank you! I would love to meet my father."

And Aphrodite's eyes shone with tears for the second time, as she held her daughter in her arms.

Dobson's big blunt fingers were gently rubbing the muscles in Aphrodite's shoulders, loosening the tension and with it any aches and pains from the long night of making herself agreeable to her guests. It was a talent, to keep smiling even when her body was crying out for rest. Now she closed her eyes and groaned her appreciation. "You have the best of hands, Jemmy. Did I ever tell you so?"

"Frequently, my love, but you can never say it too often."

Aphrodite smiled and bowed her head to give him access to her neck. She thought about her meeting with Marietta earlier, and her smile broadened. The girl had been pleased enough with the new task Aphrodite had set her, but she had been dismayed by the rules. They went so very much against the grain of her character. Aphrodite had almost laughed out loud at the expression on her face. Still, there was no doubt that she would try to accomplish this task, just as she had the previous one. And she would probably manage to do it, too.

Marietta may well be destined to become a courtesan, but Aphrodite doubted it. Her daughters were strong-willed women, yes, who sought to take their own paths through life, but they were also romantics, and romantics followed their own hearts. A courtesan could not afford to be a romantic, to fall in love—as Aphrodite knew to her cost.

Surely it was better Marietta learned her mistake now than suffer heartbreak later on, when she might be trapped into a situation where it was impossible—indeed, dangerous—to follow her heart. Aphrodite had only ever wanted her daughters to be happy, and that had not changed.

Some people, she knew, might consider her advice to Marietta to be morally questionable, but Aphrodite had no time for the borders and boundaries drawn up by a respectable society to which she had never belonged. It was Marietta who mattered to her—her security and her well-being. The fact that she had already been damaged socially made it easier for her to have an affair, to learn beneath the safety of Aphrodite's wing the pitfalls of living life among the *demi monde*. In her opinion the girl should be allowed to enjoy herself with Max Valland, however briefly, if in the process it helped her understand that being a courtesan was not for her. Sharing herself with many men, keeping her heart removed and cold, no, no! The more Aphrodite understood her daughter the more set against the courtesan idea she became, but of course she would not tell Marietta that. She must not risk losing her daughter's confidences.

"You are far away," Jemmy murmured.

"I was thinking of Marietta and Max. Marietta

says that Max has had many accidents, more than is usual for the son of a duke."

But Jemmy was ahead of her. "I thought there was something odd about the way Lord Roseby was knocked down. I've been asking around and there're whispers it was no botched robbery. Someone was paid to do the job on him, and paid well."

"I don't understand. How could Max being dead matter when he is already disinherited?"

Jemmy smiled. "Just because a father is hurt and angry with his son now don't mean he'll stay angry."

"So . . . he might well reverse his decision and restore Max to his position as heir."

"I'd say that's what someone believes."

"And if Max is dead . . ."

"Someone is safe."

"Have you any idea who that someone is?"

"Word is it's probably the cousin, Harold, but no one knows for sure. I'll keep my ears open, if you like."

"Thank you, I would like."

Jemmy's warm lips brushed her nape.

Aphrodite felt herself tingle all over, and it was as if they had not been lovers for these many years. Her body recognized his, readied itself for his, she *was* his, and always had been. It was just that she had not realized it until it was too late. And that was why she would never allow Marietta to make the same mistake—to turn her back on love.

Jemmy kissed her again, and his hand slid inside her chemise, with its narrow band of lace, and cupped her breast. Aphrodite sighed with pleasure, and put aside her own concerns, as she turned into her lover's welcoming arms.

* * *

That night in Berkley Square, Marietta found herself too restless to sleep. Her mind was on the assignation with Max, and although she had told Aphrodite she was not nervous, she was. Excited and nervous, all at the same time. Max would help to teach her to be the best courtesan in London, after her mother that is. One day *she* would wear the fine clothes and the jewelry, to show how many lovers she had had and how successful she had been.

She snuggled down under the covers, trying to imagine what Max would think of her if he were to meet her many years into the future. Would he boast that he was the one who taught her to kiss, or would he listen to Harold and cut her dead? But then again, she reminded herself, Max would be living in Cornwall—it was doubtful she would ever see him once he left London.

The thought unaccountably depressed her, but then she cheered herself up by remembering the assignation at Aphrodite's. Being submissive to Max, serving Max his supper, *flirting* with Max and kissing him, if he'd let her. Never mind, she'd find a way to persuade him. There was a lot that Max could teach her, Marietta thought with a smile, but there was also an awful lot that she could teach him.

And then there was her father. She hardly dared to imagine what he would be like, and whether she would feel a closeness to him. She had spoken to Vivianna earlier tonight, and Vivianna told her about Fraser, and how she felt when she first met him, and how she grew to love him, before the end. Perhaps there was something about sharing the same blood that formed a bond between two people, no matter how you tried to deny it.

Marietta turned over and her eye caught the sober gleam of a leather-bound book, sitting on her bed-side table. Aphrodite's diary. Vivianna had given it to her, telling her that Aphrodite had once presented it to her to read. "She has added to it over the years, but do not expect to find your father's name in there," she said. "I think it will help you to under-stand our mother a little better."

Marietta wriggled up against the pillows, and drawing the candle closer, took the diary into her hands. The tooled leather felt luxurious, almost alive, against her fingers. She let the book fall open, and found herself about a third of the way through it. Aphrodite's neat writing told her that she was living in Paris, on the Boulevard de la Madeleine . . .

> Today the Compte de Rennie offered me his heart and all else he had it in his power to give me, if I would come and live with him at his chateau on the Loire. I should feel wild with joy, but I don't. It is as if the golden gloss has been worn off this life I wanted so much that I was willing to sacrifice anything to achieve it. And beneath the gold there is nothing but base metal.
>
> I left the Seven Dials behind me, and Jemmy, and yet now I think of nothing else. His face is with me when I wake and when I sleep, and I want to go home to him. I want to go home.
>
> I have told the compte that I cannot live with him, that my heart is calling me home. He does

not understand and I hardly understand myself. London. The word is like a spinning top in my head, turning around and around, and I will leave tonight. The servants will pack up the house and follow me. I will not return.

The channel crossing has been rough but I do not care. What is a little mal de mer when I am home again? The journey to London is tedious but I cannot sleep. And then the city bursts upon me and my eyes are stinging with tears as I look upon her beloved face. The crowds and the smells and the sounds, those lovely London sounds, bringing the memories back so powerfully that I can hardly breathe.

I see myself running through those streets, holes in my shoes, my hand in Jemmy's, and I see us clinging together, loving each other, and all the time my face was turned away. My eyes were fixed on the false glitter and I could not see that I already owned the best jewel of all.

And suddenly I ask myself the question that I have not dared to ask before: What if my Jemmy is dead?

Elena is waiting for me at the hotel in St. James's, and her face is so familiar it makes me ache. "It is good to have you back," she says, and I know that she means it. She is a seamstress with her own shop, but it is difficult for her. We talk for a time, and then I say, "I must see the Dials." Her expression tells me that she does not think that it is such a good idea. But I insist, suddenly desperate to see my parents and believ-

ing, somehow, that Jemmy will be there, too. That he will have come back from the war and he will be home, like me. For me.

Reluctantly Elena makes the journey with me. The coach fights its way through the narrow streets, and the raucous voices whose cries are like birdsong to me. So long, it has been so long. And then there is my mother, older, her eyes suspicious of the daughter I have become in my fine clothes. My father will not look at me except for little sideways glances, as though he is ashamed of me.

But I do not care.

"Jemmy?" I ask them, ignoring the ache of regret and the burn of anger. "Have you seen him since I left?"

They look at each other and I know then. I know that Jemmy is dead . . .

The words, when they come, make me strangely lightheaded with relief.

"Young Jemmy's married, 'appened last month. Nice girl, wheelwright's daugh'er."

He is alive. I tell myself that at least he is alive. Does it matter that he belongs to someone else? I tell myself it doesn't, that I am not greedy for miracles, and yet as I ride in my coach back to the hotel, I know that something inside me has broken.

I will go on, I will live my life, but I will never be whole again.

Marietta set aside the diary, and there were tears on her face. Aphrodite had lost her Jemmy, lost her love. It did not sound as if the life of a courtesan was quite what Marietta imagined. Despite all that she had, it had not been enough for Aphrodite—she had still wanted more. She wanted her lost love back again.

Chapter 11

Marietta handed the footman another parcel as she left the milliner's shop in Regent Street. The new plate-glass windows gleamed with the spring sunlight and the reflections of fellow shoppers. She was admiring the tight fit of her new pale green muslin dress with the pink rosebud pattern, and its double skirt with two flounces. Under that skirt she was wearing a new pair of green slippers, tied about her ankles with ribbons. Her feet were aching from the lack of any support offered by the slippers, which were thin and without a heel, but they were very pretty. There was nothing quite like a new outfit to cheer one up, and she had been feeling a little dowdy—Yorkshire was all very nice but it wasn't at the forefront of fashion. In London the styles seem to change every other day, and while Marietta did not consider herself so shallow that she must always have the latest style, she did like to be smart.

Just then a figure paused behind her. A broad chested man in a shabby brown coat and plaid trousers. His eyes, in his rugged pugilist's face, met hers. Marietta was good with faces and she recognized him. It was the man she had seen in Bedford Square when she had visited Max there and stood at the window with Mrs. Pomeroy watching Harold and Susannah arrive. He had seemed as out of place there as he did here, and how odd that she should see him again!

He recognized her, too, she could tell. His mouth tightened and his eyes flared and then he quickly walked on, leaving her wondering whether she should be afraid.

"Miss Greentree!"

Startled, she glanced around expecting to see the same man. Instead there was a large lad in livery sitting upon a coach that looked familiar and gesturing to attract her attention. "Daniel?" she said, unaccountably relieved to see him. "What are you doing here?" Even as she walked towards him she saw that it was indeed Max's coach.

"Master Max wants a word, Miss," Daniel said, clearly proud of himself for tracking her down.

"Does he?" Marietta leaned against the door, and standing on tiptoes, peered inside. "Max? Are you well enough to be out? Your head is barely healed, and the doctor said your brain might swell."

He was looking pale and elegant, and he raised his eyebrows at her comments. "Miss Greentree, perhaps you would be so kind as to allow me to drive you home? Interesting as my private business is to the rest of London, I don't particularly want to discuss it in front of them."

She felt the color in her cheeks. She was being more impulsive than usual, she supposed, but for a moment she had allowed her concern for Max to overcome her good sense and caution. She glanced around and, finding that Vivianna's footman was waiting a little way behind her, she gestured for him to come and open the door and help her inside. "You can ride with Daniel," she told him kindly. "If that is acceptable to his lordship, of course?"

Max ignored her sarcasm, assuring her that it was perfectly acceptable. "We will go by way of Regent's Park," he said for Daniel's benefit, and then settled back in his corner and waited superciliously while Marietta fiddled and wriggled and finally made herself comfortable.

The truth was that her stays were too tight, but she wasn't going to tell Max that. Marietta had never fully accepted her size and shape. The trouble was that her sisters were both tall, and Marietta was short, and although she might be a fashionable hourglass shape, she felt that she was just too curvaceous. With this in mind she had insisted her new dress be made a little smaller, so that to fit into it she must be very tightly laced. At least then, she told herself, she kept her lush curves in check. Sometimes she wondered if she was being a little too self-critical—it might actually be more important to breathe than to look slim—but the recent sight of Susannah Valland's tall, willowy shape had heightened her dissatisfaction with her own.

"Is there a reason you are here, Max?"

"I was going to call upon you," he said in his haughty voice, "but I was informed you were shopping in Regent Street. It was just a matter of elimination as to which establishment you would be patronizing."

"You mean you lurked outside until you saw me."

"If you like, although it is not my habit to lurk anywhere."

"All right, Max. Having found me, what is it you want?"

They bowled along by sunny Regent's Park, with its green vistas and strolling visitors. Marietta peered from the coach window for a glimpse of the zoo and the famous botanic gardens. The sense of being out in the country, though deceptive, was refreshing after the bustle of the shops. Marietta could even bear her stays with fortitude, as she awaited Max's reply.

"Pomeroy said he saw you and Harold conversing. He seemed to think you were upset, Marietta. I want to know what my cousin said."

Marietta met his gaze—he looked ill at ease. For him to come looking for her, she thought, he must have a fairly good idea that whatever his cousin had said wasn't polite. But she wasn't going to be the one to tell him—if he wanted to know, he should ask Harold.

"I really don't wish to discuss it," she said quietly, and looked away. Behind her Max stirred restlessly.

"If you will not tell me what he said, then how can I apologize on his behalf?"

Marietta cast him a sideways glance. "There's no need to apologize. I don't care what Harold thinks or says. My dealings aren't with Harold, they are with you. You haven't changed your mind, have you?"

He shook his head.

Marietta sighed with relief. "Good." She gave him

another look, and found herself remembering his kisses. That feeling had returned, the ache low in her belly, and since it only seemed to occur when she was around him, she considered asking him what it was.

"Max?"

He reached out and took her hand. He wasn't wearing gloves, but she was, and for a moment he rubbed his thumb over her protected palm. Then, as if the thin barrier between them irritated him, he deftly unbuttoned the wrist of her glove and proceeded to tug it off by the fingers.

"Max," she said, with a little giggle. "What are you doing?"

"You're all covered up," he said impatiently. "Look at you! Buttoned to the throat and the wrists, your skirts covering every inch of flesh, and beneath all that there are petticoats and stays and cotton and lace and God knows what. Even your hands, covered."

"Not now, though." He'd freed one of them, and suddenly, with a little frisson, she felt his skin against hers. His fingers were warm, intimate, and she let him entangle them with hers. Perhaps that was *why* women were always covered, she thought, because the touch of skin on skin was so disturbing. So erotic.

He was looking down at her hand, resting now in his, and then he bent his head and kissed her palm. His mouth was hot. She gasped at the sensation. He looked up at her, his dark eyes searching her face, but whatever he saw there gave him no reason to stop. Indeed, Marietta thought, it was more likely to be encouragement.

"I have been thinking about you kissing me," she said, her voice oddly breathless, and not just from the tightness of her stays. "I woke up dreaming of it and I felt . . . I don't know," she glanced at him, and found him watching her with flattering attention. "I felt odd."

"You want us to stop?" he asked quietly.

"No, oh no, I don't want that. I meant that I felt odd in a nice way, a way that made me think of sending you a note to ask you to come and kiss me at once."

"You should have," he said, but he was laughing at her.

"I mean it, Max. And now, with your mouth on my hand, I feel the same sensation. An ache. Almost a longing."

He smiled. "Ah," he said.

"What do you mean, 'Ah'?" she replied irritably. "That isn't an answer. If you know what is wrong with me then say so."

His thumb rubbed back and forth over her palm, then brushed the sensitive skin on the underside of her wrist. He lifted her hand to his mouth again and made a bracelet of little teasing kisses, until she shivered.

"Do you feel it now?" he whispered. He moved in closer, his fingers brushing her cheek, her temple, then down to her lips. His thumb traced the shape of her mouth, and she closed her eyes. "And now?"

"Yes," she breathed. "I . . . I don't remember feeling this with . . . I . . . it's as if I want more, Max. As if, nice though this is, I want something more."

He sighed, and sat back, staring at her with dark eyes that were no longer haughty or smug. "It is a well-known fact, darling Marietta, that the more a woman is kissed and caressed, the more she will want to be kissed and caressed. She begins to crave the sensation. And yes, she wants more. Like any female in the animal kingdom, her body is telling her to mate with the male of her choice."

Marietta glared at him. "So I am no better than the giraffes at the zoo?"

Max smiled. "You asked me to teach you about desire. This is desire."

"I don't believe it." She began to pull her glove back on.

Max leaned forward suddenly and drew down the blind over the coach window. Now it was dim and quiet, and she could hear his breathing close by.

"Max?" She put out her hands toward him.

He captured them with his. Before she could protest he kissed her mouth, his lips caressing, gentle but firm. And kept kissing her, his hands moving to her wrists and then the crook of her elbows. He undid her bonnet, tossing it aside, and reached for the pins that held her hair. It came tumbling down, golden tresses thick and sweet with the scent of her. He ran his fingers through them, his mouth still on hers, his tongue stroking hers with a wantonness that made her head spin.

She felt as if she might swoon. She had heard of women swooning in novels, but never in real life, not from a man's kiss, but Max was coming very close to achieving it.

"Master Max?" It was Daniel's jovial voice up in the driver's seat. "Should we go back to Berkley Square now, sir?"

Max lifted his mouth long enough to call, "Another turn around the park, Daniel," and then dived into the kiss again.

Her body was throbbing. Her breasts felt tender and swollen, and the ache between her legs nearly drove her mad. Because she wanted him. He was right, she wanted to mate with the male of her choice, and the male of her choice was definitely Max Valland.

When he finally stopped, her head fell against his shoulder and he left it there, stroking her hair from her flushed cheek, his chest rising and falling as violently as hers.

"*This* is desire," he said huskily. "What we're feeling now is desire."

Was he right? He must be. And it made sense. If not for desire, why else would women who knew better run off with scoundrels or refuse to leave them or actually marry them? Love and desire, they went hand in hand, one blurring into the other.

He was still very close, his breath warm on her cheek. As if he couldn't help himself, he pressed his lips to her skin, little kisses, capturing the corner of her mouth. With a groan she turned her face, and found his mouth again, opening her lips eagerly to him. This time the kiss was deeper, more passionate, their tongues mating in a way their bodies couldn't. She turned to him and her breasts pressed to his chest, the ache in them intensifying, as his arm wound about her waist and held her there.

As if he understood, he raised his hand and closed it over her, but she could barely feel it through her clothing. Frustrated she made a sound, half sob and half laugh, pushing against him. His fingers squeezed and she felt that, just, and a warm wave of pleasure engulfed her. How would it be if his bare skin was against her bare skin, from neck to toes?

Her head fell back and he kissed her arched throat, his mouth open and hot. "Marietta," he murmured, "we need to think of the consequences. We need to take care."

"Why?" she demanded. "I don't want to take care."

"You may think you have no reputation to lose, but believe me if we are seen like this then there will be an uproar. My family have disowned me—what I do does not matter—but your family will be made to pay."

His words were sobering, but still it was a moment before she could gather the strength to draw away from him.

"My family would suffer if it was known that I intend to become a courtesan. That is why I intend to change my name, to become someone else entirely. It is the best way. Marietta Greentree will disappear and Madame Coeur will appear to take her place."

Max choked. "Is that what you're going to call yourself? I thought the whole point of being a courtesan was not to lose your heart? Maybe you should think again."

Marietta made a face at him. She was smoothing her hair back, bundling it up with one hand, while with the other she searched for the pins that were scattered all over her skirts. "I have thought and that is the best I can come up with."

"Madame Venus? Madame Eros?" Max was watching her.

"I am no Venus," she retorted, shifting in her tight stays.

His eyes narrowed and moved slowly over her. "I don't know about that," he drawled. Then his manner altered, grew serious. "You tell me you are ruined for marriage, Marietta, but it is still possible you could marry well. Your brother-in-law is a wealthy man, is he not?"

Marietta froze, and stared at him wide-eyed. It was the same thought as Vivianna had, for Oliver to buy her a husband. Pick one out for her, as she had just been choosing a pair of gloves! And what sort of man would allow himself to be bought like that? A man with no pride, a man who cared more for his position and fortune than for her. The very idea of it made her shaky and ill.

"I do not want a husband who has been bribed to wed me," she said coldly. "I would despise such a man. Why are you saying this now? It's because you don't want me to be a courtesan, isn't it? You'd prefer I did anything but that; even marry a man who has been bribed to take me."

"Yes," he said, "you're right. I don't want to see you do anything so foolish."

"Why will no one take me seriously!"

Max stared into her eyes, reading what was there, all the passion and wonder that was Marietta Greentree. He had told himself that he could enjoy her without listening to his conscience—he had believed he really could lose himself in a hedonistic whirlpool. That he deserved her. But Max wasn't finding that easy. He kept thinking about Marietta's future, and what would become of her after he had his pleasure, after he had played the mentor to her pupil, and he left for Cornwall and she moved on to some other man.

Max leaned back in his seat, still watching her, feeling angry and frustrated. He must stop her. He must prevent her from destroying herself like this.

But how? He could ask her to be his mistress, he supposed, at least then he could keep her safe. But she would refuse—she had already made it clear she would never align herself to one man again, and besides, Max knew he no longer had the money or position to support her as she proposed. Unless . . . A grim little smile touched his mouth. Unless he imprisoned her in the ropes of desire, binding her to him so fast she could not escape, would not want to escape.

"What?" she demanded crossly. "What have I said now to amuse you?"

Max had no intention of telling her why he was smiling, but he was beginning to think he might have found a way to stop her. It was a drastic measure, certainly, but it could not be worse than the future she intended.

He reached out to flip the blind up, and then thumped on the roof. "We are taking Miss Greentree home, Daniel," he announced loudly. "Berkley Square."

She sighed, and pulled on her bonnet. She looked flushed and hot and adorable. Ever since he had rested his head on her lap and felt her softness and caught her scent, he had been hard. Although he was quite certain it wasn't good for a man to be permanently erect, he knew he had to be patient. Marietta Greentree might believe herself ruined, but she was an innocent in all other ways.

Max was absolutely certain that Marietta wasn't the kind of woman who could live as a courtesan, moving from man to man, and yet keeping her heart intact. She was warm and generous and giving, and it would destroy her. The thought of her broken and despairing, dragged down into the degradation he had witnessed on the streets and in the brothels of London, was too much for him. He must win her over.

Desire. Need. These were things her body was already beginning to crave. Now all he had to do was to make certain that it was Max she desired and Max she needed. He would bait the trap and when she entered, close it upon her.

And Marietta Greentree would be his.

By the time they reached home, Marietta had tidied herself as best she could. Max had been quiet since they left the park, but he rallied when she told him she would no doubt see him in the near future.

"When you are dreaming of kissing me, Marietta, remember . . . I'll be dreaming of kissing you."

She felt quite giddy when she got inside the townhouse, and was glad to get up to her room and loosen her stays. They really were too tight, she thought, taking shallow gulping breaths. Or maybe it was a combination of the stays and Max that made her dizzy and faint.

With a groan she flung herself back upon her bed and closed her eyes, and thought again of his kisses.

Why couldn't it have been Max that night at the inn on the way to the Scottish border? Why couldn't I have fallen in love with Max, and run away with him?

Her eyes sprang open. Instantly she was alert, like a wild animal scenting danger. No, no and no! She would not fall in love again, not with Max, or anybody else. Never again would a man break her heart and make her suffer. Max was well enough, in his way, but he was not a permanent fixture. A free and independent life, that was what Marietta would live, and there was no place in it for Lord Roseby.

Harold gazed down at his sleeping wife. Susannah's brow creased slightly, as if her thoughts disturbed her. He could not help but think she would make the perfect Duchess of Barwon. Max obviously didn't have a clue about such things—he probably believed Marietta Greentree was a suitable duchess. Just as well that he was no longer the heir.

He shifted guiltily, knowing he shouldn't think such things about his cousin. All his life Harold had watched over Max, even now when Max clearly didn't want him around. Perhaps it was time to stop and look to his own future.

Susannah murmured softly, speaking in the language of her childhood. She seemed distracted lately, probably blaming herself for what had happened to Max, feeling guilty for her own good fortune at his expense. Harold told himself that that would pass. Soon she would be too busy in her new role to worry about her brother.

They would go their separate ways.

"Papa!" Susannah gasped in her sleep, but whether she cried for her adopted father or the one left behind in Jamaica Harold didn't know. She never spoke of the past, it was as if she had blotted it from her mind, but he always knew when she was remembering. She vanished into herself. Harold imagined her as a young girl, bare feet and tanned legs, her long dark hair tangled as she ran through the tropical forests, peeping through the shiny leaves and brilliant flowers. Wild. Free to be herself.

His Susannah . . .

* * *

Aphrodite's Club had a deserted air, like a boarding school where all the children have gone home for the holidays. Except that Aphrodite's residents hadn't left—they were resting in their rooms, so that they could sparkle tonight when the guests began to arrive. But at least one of them was up and awaiting Marietta when she rapped on the door.

"Come, they are waiting." Maeve, simply dressed in a white robe, her dark hair fastened at her nape in a smooth chignon, smiled over her shoulder as she led Marietta into a large, private sitting room.

Inside was Elena, Aphrodite's modiste, gowns like resting butterflies scattered about the room, some with matching slippers and accessories. Marietta stared about her at the wealth of beauty, suddenly feeling dowdy in her neat blue wool with the braid trimmings.

Elena cast a critical eye over her and gave a thin smile. "You are very pretty, Miss Marietta," she said in a very refined accent. "Good. That makes my job much easier."

If Marietta had not been reading Aphrodite's diary, she would never have realized that Elena had been brought up in the same Seven Dials streets as her mother. Aphrodite, she knew, had helped the modiste to make a success of her business by wearing her clothing and letting everyone know it.

Elena's smile vanished and she clapped her hands imperiously, causing her assistant to rush forward. Between them they soon stripped Marietta down to her stays and drawers.

Standing about in her undergarments was not a situation she was comfortable with, particularly when the eyes of strangers were upon her. Marietta tried hard to pretend she didn't care, but perhaps she didn't do a very good job of it, because Maeve, sitting in a chair in the corner out of the way, called out sympathetically, "Don't worry, you'll get used to it. We all do."

"I think the China silk," Elena announced, circling Marietta like a shark. "That will display the bosom to best advantage, though it is a little heavy. You should practice lifting your elbows and pushing them back, Miss Marietta. It tightens the breasts." Then again to her assistant, "The waist is nice and trim. Hips are a little plump, but he will like that. Hmm, legs are reasonable . . . maybe a little sturdy and short—"

"Your hair is very pretty," Maeve said quickly. "Do you know, I always wanted to have fair hair."

"Dark hair is the fashion," Marietta reminded her, glaring at Elena. She knew her legs were short—she *was* short! What did the woman want, an ostrich in a dress?

"You should take better care of your skin, Miss Marietta," Elena said in her oh-so-refined voice. "Especially those parts which are hidden under your clothing. *All* of your body should be soft and inviting, not just your face and hands."

"I am sure—"

"And when you bathe, make certain you add plenty of oil to the water. I see some dry patches here, and here."

Marietta decided then that, for some reason, Elena did not like her and wanted her to fail, and she had a good mind to walk out, right now . . . Almost at once her indignation left her. She couldn't walk out, whatever Elena thought of her. She had agreed to do this. She had wanted to do it. She could hardly give up at the first hurdle.

No, she would just have to grit her teeth and put up with the other woman's barbs, and ignore the fact that she was standing before them in very little.

That was when Elena reclaimed her attention with an unapologetic, "Remove your undergarments, Miss Marietta."

Speechlessly, Marietta met her gaze.

Whatever Elena saw in her eyes seemed to amuse her, but not enough to make her actually smile. "The costume we have chosen for you is not worn with undergarments," she explained slowly, as if she was talking to an idiot. And then she crossed her arms over her scrawny chest and waited.

She was no doubt expecting Marietta to refuse, or to walk out—just as she had been planning to do a moment ago. But now that Marietta knew Elena wanted her to fail, she was determined not to. She would put up with the humiliation and the embarrassment, and even the comments about her legs, just to show the modiste that she wasn't a meek, spoiled little girl who could be shattered with a few nasty glances and some unpleasant words. She was Aphrodite's daughter, and that meant something.

It doesn't matter, she told herself. *I must become accustomed to it.* But it wasn't easy and she wasn't comfortable, and she knew her face was a telltale red as Elena's assistant helped her remove her stays. The drawers needed no help, and hurriedly Marietta slipped them down. Naked, she felt more vulnerable than she could remember feeling for years.

"Why do you think we women wear so many

clothes?" Elena asked her, as she turned and gathered one of the butterfly garments up in her arms—a pearl-colored silk. "Because we are afraid of our own bodies. Afraid of the power we have over men. And they are afraid, too. So we hide ourselves away, turn our shape into something it is not, become what we are not."

Surely she is not going to try and cover me with that tiny piece of cloth? Marietta thought, eyeing it uneasily. *Good heavens, she is!*

"A glimpse of ankle beneath petticoats," Elena went on, approaching steadily. "The pale turn of a wrist between glove and sleeve. These things are sensual and exciting, yes, but only because so much of us is covered up. To display a woman as she really is, the bosom unmolded by stays, the waist unpinched, the hips and legs exposed without the wide skirts . . . It is like unveiling a work of art."

The fine silk was eased over Marietta's head—it was a blouse without buttons or hooks. The color was a gleaming pearl, and yet against her skin it took on a more fleshy tone. It was so fine, so thin, it felt like a breath of air against her body. The silk clung to her bosom, and although it was not low cut, indeed the neckline was high, it was more daring than anything she had ever worn.

Elena helped her put on the drawers . . . no, they were really trousers. Wide, silken trousers like someone might wear in a harem. They hung low at her waist, leaving her stomach bare, and rested on the curve of her hips before flaring out over her thighs and calves to her ankles. It was a garment truly shocking to a woman used to five petticoats and stiffened skirts, all designed to hide her shape.

This did nothing to hide her shape. As Elena stepped away, Marietta was left facing herself in the mirror, and she was silenced. Was it really her, barefoot, her body draped in cloth as fine as web? She could see the pale shape of her legs as she moved, and most shocking of all, the dark shadow where the female hair grew between her thighs. With a gasp, she reached down to put her hand over herself, to preserve her modesty, and at the same time realized that the stretch of the cloth over her bosom exposed not only the shape and pale color of her breasts, but also the darker circles of her nipples.

"I cannot possibly wear this," she whispered, appalled. "I may as well be naked!"

Elena put her hands on her hips and met her eyes in the mirror. "And you want to be a courtesan like your mother? I told Madame you would be too prudish. I warned her that she could not expect you to be as brave as she." Her eyes narrowed. "Maeve! Go and fetch Madame and tell her that her daughter refuses to wear the costume I have chosen."

Maeve, with a quick, uncomfortable glance at Marietta, rose reluctantly to her feet.

Marietta knew then that this was a test. If she did not wear the costume, if she did not cooperate, then they would dismiss her hopes and dreams as the meaningless cries of a spoiled child. She could see it in their faces.

"Very well," she said through gritted teeth.

Elena smiled, and gestured to her assistant. The girl picked up what looked like a robe made out of the same fine, pearl-colored silk and handed it reverently to the modiste. Elena carried it forward and held it up for Marietta to slide her arms into the sleeves. This coat, she realized, was made to go over the blouse and trousers. Elena had known that all along. She had simply been waiting to see what Marietta would do.

Evidently she had passed the test.

The coat was just as thin and fine as the rest of the costume, but it prevented anyone from seeing through to her skin—just. As she walked, it drifted out behind her, so that if she wasn't careful the unsecured front opened up, and her body was displayed for whomever was watching.

Would Max be watching? Marietta sighed. It was hardly the sort of covering she was hoping for, but it would have to do. She would just have to move very, very carefully.

"Now," Elena said in a rallying voice. "Your hair!"

Maeve was hovering near the door. "Should I still go and fetch Madame?" she asked tentatively.

Elena frowned. "Of course not, girl. We are managing perfectly well without her."

Maeve flashed Marietta a little smile, and returned to her chair.

The hairdresser preferred to leave Marietta's hair down, with the front and sides drawn back with combs of a similar color to the costume. "No shoes," Elena said, when she tentatively asked about slippers. "We will paint your toenails," she explained, as if there was nothing outlandish in that. When they were done, she looked at herself once more in the mirror, and she was a stranger. Seductive, definitely, submissive, maybe, desirable . . . that was for Max to decide, if she could persuade him to stay in the room with her.

When she told them that, though, Elena smirked

Elena, too. They wanted her to let go of her
ts and restrictions, all the things she had
ed since she was a child, all the rules she had
wed since she was a girl—well, most of the time.
them go and be herself. Except that Marietta was
ing difficulty knowing who that was.

Her gaze slipped past her mother, moving over
m velvet curtains and upholstery, and the pièce
résistance, the four-poster bed swathed in apri-
satin and weighed down with cushions. Feelings
uncertainty swamped her. Could she make Max
forget he was a gentleman who didn't want her to be
courtesan, even for a few moments? And could
e forget she had been brought up a lady and she
as edging dangerously closer to falling in love
ith him?

Aphrodite must have sensed her change of mood.
Maeve." She did not take her eyes off Marietta. "Go
d dress. You are required in the salon."

Maeve left them alone, shooting an encouraging
ile at Marietta as the door closed behind her.

"You have doubts?" Aphrodite spoke quietly.

She shook her head automatically. "No! That is . . .
o not doubt what I want to do, only my ability to
it."

"You do not find Max attractive?"

"Yes, I do." Max was like a storm, ready to pound
into compliance. And she must do everything in
power to stop him.

"You must not underestimate him, Marietta. He is
roper man, do you understand?"

"I-I think so."

"Now, do not fret." Aphrodite rested a cool hand
her shoulder. "You will see. Everything will sort

as if she knew better. It was Maeve who answered,
"He'll be gob-smacked," she said bluntly.

Marietta raised an eyebrow. "Gob-smacked?"

"You'll take his breath away," Elena explained.

Marietta thought about that. "I can't imagine it.
He'll probably give me one of his looks, as if he's the
duke and I'm his slave girl . . . *What* are you doing?"

This last was addressed to Elena's assistant, who
was kneeling at her feet, adjusting the hem of her
trousers.

"Elena says they're too long," the woman said in a
voice very like her mistress. "I'm to take them up an
inch so that the gentleman can get a good look at
your ankles."

Marietta felt like resting her foot on the woman's
chest and giving her a hard push. She controlled herself. If Aphrodite heard she was being difficult then
she might refuse to help her any more and her
dreams would be quashed. So she smiled and nodded and waited passively while they finished. But in
her heart she was dismayed that she had to pretend
to be something other than herself.

"He will be here soon," Maeve called out in warning, as Elena dabbed jasmine scented oil in places
Marietta had never thought of. The time had flown—
when Marietta glanced at the window she realized
that it was growing dark.

"Am I ready?" She looked wildly around at them.
Suddenly, instead of being a cross she had to bear,
this little group of women had become a crutch she
needed. She knew that her near-nakedness under
the thin silken covering was making her feel vulnerable. Safety was in her voluminous skirts and petticoats, with the buttons to her throat, and the sleeves

tight to her wrists. The stays, chemises, drawers, and sometimes, at Greentree Manor, the warm flannel against her skin, had been a form of armor.

Now, she may as well be naked, she decided miserably.

"Miss Marietta?" It was Elena, and her face was no longer unfriendly—there was even a hint of kindness in her eyes. "You can be whatever you want to be. Remember that. The choice is entirely yours."

While Marietta was still trying to work out exactly what she meant, Maeve took her hand and led her toward the door. "It'll be all right, you'll see, Miss Marietta. Now come upstairs. Madame's put you and your gentleman in the Cupid Room." She gave Marietta a conspiratorial wink. "Just wait until you see it."

Chapter 12

The room was beautiful.

Marietta swirled on her bare feet, hea back as she gazed up at the painted ceiling. T had made a blue sky awash with angel swooped and dived, their draperies tangle their limbs, displaying daring amounts o Darting among the angels were cupids, sma creatures with wicked smiles, their bows and aimed downwards, toward the occupants of pid Room.

"It is an homage to love." Aphrodite ha upon them quietly.

Marietta turned to face her, and her mothe at the bedazzled expression on her face.

"I do not think you will find it difficu room, *mon petit puce*, to play at being a c Think of this as your stage; you have only t part."

Perhaps Marietta did understand what s

itself out. Perhaps you are thinking too hard. It is better in these situations if you don't think. Take a deep breath and allow yourself to *feel* instead."

Marietta took a deep breath but nothing happened. "I will try."

"Good. Remember." She held up her finger. "You are strangers. He is no longer Max, he is simply a man you desire."

Her mother had been peering anxiously into her face, a little crease between her brows, and Marietta forced herself to smile as if everything was perfectly all right.

Aphrodite nodded and moved away, running a finger along the edge of a table as she went, checking that her servants were doing their job. "I will leave you to await Lord Roseby—he will be here very soon. Ring twice for the food when you want it sent up. Ring three times if you wish to bring the evening to a halt." She turned and fixed Marietta with a dark, intent look. "You can stop this whole thing whenever you wish, Marietta. No one but you and I will ever know about it. You do realize that?"

Marietta's smile wavered at the corners. "Thank you, I will bear it in mind."

"Then good luck, Marietta." Aphrodite closed the door, leaving her alone at last.

Marietta, arms folded about her exposed midriff, feet bare on the exquisite carpet, wandered the beautiful room like a nymph in a fairytale. She avoided the bed and moved to where there was a painting hanging on the wall. A beautiful woman was lounging upon a grassy bank spiked with flowers, her dark hair flowing about her, her diaphanous gown displaying rather than hiding her charms—rather like Marietta's. Cupid peeped from behind a bush, his pink cheeks bulging with mirth, his bow and arrow raised to pierce the heart of the maiden, or the man who knelt close by her. *He* was fully dressed, of course, his hand hovering above her breast but not quite touching, although from the expression on his face Marietta could tell he was thinking about it. Imagining it. Looking forward to it.

There was an intensity to the painting that held her spellbound. The man reaching out to touch the woman, the woman clearly wanting him to, and cupid ready with his arrow to once more confuse lust with love. Marietta was so intent upon it that she was oblivious to the door opening behind her, and Max stepping into the room.

Lord Roseby is invited to an Anonymous Evening of Pleasure at Aphrodite's Club . . .

The invitation had been lavish with curlicues and written on fine paper. Max wasn't surprised to receive it, but he pretended to deliberate over accepting it. His decision to distract Marietta from her ambition to be a courtesan by binding her to him was a desperate one—he had had time to consider the matter more carefully since their meeting in the coach, and he told himself that he only intended to go through with it if words failed to persuade her.

Tonight was the ideal opportunity to speak with her again. And he wanted to see her; he wanted to save her from herself.

So here he stood, stranded amongst a host of angels and a quiver of cupids. For a moment he thought the room was empty. The bed caught his eye, but he dragged his gaze away and instead inspected the draperies and the sofa with its velvet cushions and the lurid painting on the far wall. A nymph was about to be seduced, or molested, by a soulful courtier—he wasn't certain which, and his wits left him before he had time to decide. Because there was a woman standing in front of the painting.

She was dressed in something pale and transparent that fell in folds about her and still managed to display her curves as if she were naked. Marietta Greentree, with her hair falling in blond waves down her back and gleaming like gold in the subdued lamplight.

Max felt his head spinning and his body hardening. It was something he had come to expect when he was near Marietta, but it wasn't a good sign if he was to keep his mind sharp. He needed to retain some sort of control if he were to use his skills and experience in one final attempt to talk her out of her ridiculous plan.

"Marietta?"

She turned around like a startled angel, the silk floating about her, the edges of the robe she wore flipping back. Her fair curls tumbled about her shoulders and down over her breasts and . . . He realized he could see the pale globes through the paper-thin cloth, just before she pulled the robe back over her, holding it together as if it would somehow protect her.

From what, from him?

The idea gave him pause. He looked at her more carefully, and realized that at the moment she looked as if she was about to bolt from the room. Frightened.

Of him? Or of this whole scenario she had set in motion. Perhaps she was ready to forget about her wild plan, after all, and he wouldn't have to seduce her.

Damn it!

Marietta narrowed those bright blue eyes at him. "Max, you're scowling. And you've taken off your bandage!"

He had, although Mrs. Pomeroy had fixed a small covering over the healing wound on his forehead. In fact, Max had dressed very carefully for this meeting. Black coat and trousers, silk shirt and necktie, his pocketwatch tucked into his waistcoat. Disinherited he may be, but Max had been born and bred to be a duke, and tonight he looked every inch one.

She was eyeing him admiringly, her face open and without guile, as if they were the best of friends. As if there was no need to guard herself with him. He wished she didn't trust him like that, because Max knew that he didn't want to be her friend. How could he be, when he was planning to trick her out of her heart's desire? She would hate him for it if she knew.

He made himself smile as if nothing was wrong. "So, what is the program for this evening, Marietta? Act One, the gentleman arrives. Act Two . . . ?"

"The gentleman is seated and made comfortable. This way, Lord Roseby." She curtseyed and beckoned him towards the fireplace.

Max followed her to the sofa bursting with cushions, trying not to watch the sway of her hips beneath the silken garment that wafted about her like a zephyr. Bloody hell, if he narrowed his eyes he could see the shape of her bottom! No underclothing then.

He sank down onto the overstuffed seat and resisted the urge to mop his brow.

"A drink, my lord?" she asked him sweetly, in a submissive tone completely unlike her usual bossy one.

"Brandy, thank you." A drink might help to strengthen his resolve, and it would give her something to do other than what he feared she planned to do. Keep her busy, he thought, that was the thing.

He watched her as she trotted off to a table full of glass decanters. Her hand hovered uncertainly over one and then another. Finally she lifted a stopper and poured a glass, and carried it carefully back to him, a sycophantic smile plastered on her face.

Max laughed, he couldn't help it. "You look as if you're about to have a tooth pulled, Marietta."

Her smile gave way to a scowl. "Be quiet. I'm meant to be submissive and you're not helping, Max."

"Good," he retorted, and took a sip of the brandy. Only it wasn't brandy, it was sherry, and he nearly spat it out, only just remembering in time that he was a gentleman. He swallowed with a violent shudder, and handed the glass back.

Marietta was watching him in amazement.

"That was sherry," he said.

She frowned, sniffed the liquor remaining in the glass. "It looks the same color as brandy. I don't drink spirits, Max, so how am I supposed to know?"

Max groaned.

"Something to eat then?" she asked him helpfully. "There is a . . . a succulent repast awaiting us."

"Is there indeed?" His gaze slid down over her; he couldn't seem to help it. She was wearing trousers under the robe, transparent silken trousers, like a harem girl, and above that a tight little blouse that didn't quite cover her smooth stomach. There were no petticoats or stays to mold and hide her true shape. All those delightfully opulent curves belonged to Marietta Greentree.

She became aware of his inspection, and pulled the robe together again, eyeing him suspiciously. "They made me wear this," she said. "Do you like it?"

"Do I like it?" he managed, his voice a little hoarse. "Why wouldn't I like it?"

"I don't know. Because it's very daring and you're a gentleman, or so you keep telling me."

"Well I do like it, Marietta. Very much."

"Are you going to kiss me again?" she whispered, her eyes darkening.

"Probably," he admitted. "Yes, I am going to kiss you."

She was staring back at him, and glancing down he realized that her feet were bare, the toenails painted pink. He felt as if the ground rocked beneath him. Somehow he kept himself on the sofa, kept his hands off her . . .

"Aphrodite says that you can touch me, but only from the waist up," she said, and then looked as if she wished she hadn't.

"Not your feet then?" he made a joke of it, but now he was really in trouble. Why in God's name had she told him that? Didn't she know, didn't she understand? But then he looked into Marietta's dazzling blue eyes and knew that that was the thing. She didn't.

Max had a very odd look on his face, Marietta decided. As if he shouldn't be out of his bed yet. Perhaps his wound was bad again, perhaps he had a headache? And then she remembered. This was where he had been attacked—how could she have been so silly as to bring him back to the scene of his pain and suffering? Of course he was upset!

"I'm so sorry, Max," she breathed, coming forward to stand before him. She reached to take his hand in hers, holding it tightly, and rested her other hand against his brow.

His eyes were a little glazed. "Sorry?" he managed. Clearly he was in the throes of remembering the suffering he had undergone.

"I forgot, how could I have forgotten! It was here that you were attacked. I should never have let you come back so soon."

Max blinked, and seemed to regain his senses a little. "Not here. In the laneway," he reminded her.

"Yes, but it's close by. Do you want to go home? Perhaps we should call it off."

"No." He swallowed. He couldn't go through this again. Get it over with, he thought. And then his eyes dropped down and he realized that he could see her breasts, clearly outlined, and the darker rosy circles at their tips, and he closed his eyes and lay back on the sofa.

"Max!" she was fluttering around him like a moth, but he didn't move or make a sound. He couldn't. He kept thinking one thought, and there wasn't room enough for another one in his head. He had permission to touch her from the waist up. He had *permission* . . .

"Max!" She was frantic. In a moment she'd be calling for the servants, for Dobson, and the whole nightmare would begin again.

Max pulled himself together. "I'm all right," he

said. "I . . . perhaps I need some of that succulent repast now, Marietta."

She eyed him uneasily, but he straightened his cuffs and crossed his legs, and even managed a little smile. He didn't look normal, though—he knew his eyes were wild.

"Very well then," she said. "If you're sure. Don't get up, just stay right there. I'll . . . I'll feed you."

He whimpered, and she glanced at him anxiously over her shoulder as she went to ring the bell—as if she expected him to fall over.

"Are you certain you are well enough . . . ?"

He sighed. The truth wasn't always a good thing, but perhaps in this case she deserved to hear it. "Marietta, I am alone in a room with a beautiful girl, and she has hardly any clothes on. No, I am not well. I am trying to stop myself from being extremely ungentlemanlike. *Now* do you understand?"

Marietta opened her mouth, then closed it again. Then she said, "Oh."

"Yes," Max replied grimly. "Oh."

Marietta hurried to ring the bell, but her heart was pounding. Max had been staring at her, his eyes running over her in a way that she found quite disturbing. Of course he wasn't used to seeing her like this, but his gaze was like a touch, and in fact she had begun to imagine how his hands would feel, curling about her waist and then sliding up, to cup the weight of her breasts.

Her heart thumped harder.

She had picked up the glass of sherry, and now she lifted it to her lips and drank the lot. The sweet, strong taste with the burn of the underlying alcohol momentarily took her breath away, and then she choked, pressing her hand to her throat.

He was on his feet and with her in a moment, one hand on her back ready to thump out whatever was choking her. She turned to peer up at him with streaming eyes.

"Marietta? What is it? What—" But then he must have caught the smell of the sherry on her breath, because his expression changed from concern to amazement.

"Marietta?"

She gulped, managed to catch her breath. "Well, you didn't want it, did you?"

He shook his head at her. "Marietta," he said quite gently, "if you need to drink sherry for courage then you should not be doing this. You should not be here. We can stop, right now. Do you hear me?"

She drew back from him, although he did not remove his palm from her back. "You don't understand. I have made up my mind and you can't change it."

"No," he said angrily, "I don't understand. Do you really want strange men doing this to you?" he demanded, pulling her suddenly into his arms.

Marietta landed against his chest with a whoof, and found herself staring up into his dark eyes.

"Doing this?" he demanded, still angry, and bent his head.

And kissed her.

Marietta was surprised, but only for a moment. The feel of his body against her sent a shiver of excitement through her like no other. And she really could feel him this time, almost as if she were naked. The broad strength of his chest and his arms, the narrow power of his hips. His mouth might be hot and desperate, but it was also passionate and needy, and she reached up and wrapped her arms about his neck and held on.

This kiss was different from any of their previous ones. Max's anger and passion were burning bright, and he had forgotten he was a gentleman who needed to retain control—he had forgotten he was the teacher. He kissed her as if he wanted to, as if he wanted her, and he no longer cared why they were doing this.

Her mouth was so sweet, so willing. Max felt as if he were drowning in the touch of her, the taste of her. He felt the swell of her breasts pressed to his chest, so soft and pliable without the hard shell of her stays. Everywhere his hands touched, he felt *her*. The fine curve of her waist, and the outward flare of her hips—whoever had dressed her knew what they were about. In a moment she'd be on the floor with him on top of her, and any chance he had to turn her mind to his way of thinking, to stop them both from doing something irrevocable, would be gone.

For a dangerous second he teetered on the edge, and then somehow he reeled them both back to safer ground.

Max lifted his mouth from hers. He was breathing quickly and so was she, her eyes closed, a hectic flush across her cheeks, her mouth swollen from his kisses. In her silk clothing that was hardly clothing at all, she looked wanton and accessible, but he knew the truth. Despite what she thought, Max knew she was no more cut out to be a courtesan than he.

"Ah Max . . ." she whispered, then swallowed,

and tried again. "Max, would you say that you lost control then? Just a little bit?"

He frowned down at her. "Nonsense. I was fully in control."

She smiled, her pink lips tilting up. "No, you weren't."

It was as if she was pleased that he had almost hoisted her onto the drinks table and plundered her. He wasn't putting her off being a courtesan; he was feeding her delusions.

"Would you say I seduced you just then?" she went on, running a fingertip up his chest to his throat and smoothing the tanned skin.

He laughed angrily. "No, I would not."

Disappointment flickered in her eyes, but the next moment she shrugged. "Oh. Well I think I did, a little. You kissed me then like you meant it, Max."

He swore under his breath, just as there came a polite tap on the door, and Marietta gave him another secretive little smile as she called sweetly, "Come in."

A procession of blank-faced servants carried in several trays of food and arranged the plates upon the table under the window, along with bottles in iced buckets. It was a meal for several, not just two, but he supposed the whole point of Aphrodite's was excess. Excess in eating and drinking, and making love to beautiful and experienced women.

With a brief bow from the one in charge, the servants filed out again and closed the door behind them.

There was a silence, and then Marietta strolled over to the table. "Mmm," she said, bending to take a sample from one of the dishes with her finger. "This looks delicious. I didn't realize I was so hungry. All this looking seductive and being submissive, I suppose."

He grunted. "Submissive! You're hardly that."

She ignored him, and instead slipped her finger between her lips to taste the food. Watching her, Max had a sinking feeling in his stomach. Arrogantly he had believed he was strong enough to do what was necessary tonight—either to talk some sense into her, or trap her with her desire for him. He had no doubt when he set out for Aphrodite's that he was to be the eventual winner in this contest, that he would bend her to his will and she would finally see sense.

Marietta was no courtesan. She was made to be loved by one man, and he was beginning to think that he was that man. But he was being severely tested. What if it was Marietta who bowed him to *her* will, instead of the other way around? What if he ended up following her around like a lovestruck puppy?

What was it about this girl? Despite all the arguments to be made against what he was doing, he knew he would not stop. She had become an obsession. He wanted to save her, but the feelings driving him were deeper than that, darker than that. He knew he had little to offer her—his man of business had made it abundantly clear that his plans to reopen the mining venture on his Cornish property were shaky at best—but his need for her overrode good sense. It was visceral, meshed within him as if it were a part of him. All those years as the next Duke of Barwon, when he had been rich and handsome and fêted, no woman had caused more than a brief flutter of interest in his heart. And now he had found *the* woman in Marietta, but he no longer had anything with which to tempt her; no money and no position, no jewelry or fine things. Only himself, and their growing passion for each other.

Was it enough?

The food really was delicious. There was chicken vol-au-vent and roast pigeons and lobster, as well as a number of other meats, served with a heavily buttered dish of asparagus. There were lemon tarts, an orange soufflé, and ices in special glasses. Marietta saw to it that his plate was kept piled, offering him a taste of this and that, gazing at him expectantly as he sampled each dish and commented upon it, and trying not to argue with him over his choices. He appreciated that she was working very hard at being the perfect hostess, but it was difficult to concentrate on what he was eating when she was flitting backwards and forwards in a costume that fired his imagination. When she began to insist on removing his jacket and shoes he put a stop to it.

"Sit down, Marietta," he said sharply. "You're giving me indigestion."

She sat down, looking dismayed. "I was only trying to make you comfortable," she offered. "A good courtesan would make certain that her gentleman was comfortable."

"No doubt, but as I'm as comfortable as I'm going to be, you can desist."

She was silent for a little while. "You really are ungrateful, Max," she said at last.

Max sighed and swallowed his mouthful.

"I need your help, and you did promise to give it. And it's not as if you have to put yourself out much, is it? You just have to sit there and be pampered. I'm sure there are plenty of other men who would jump at the chance."

"I'm sure they would," he agreed. "But you've chosen me to be your victim, haven't you, and I'm doing my best."

Marietta remembered then, a little guiltily, that Max probably had a great deal on his mind.

"Poor Max," she said, and leaned over to place a gentle kiss on his brow.

He groaned.

"Have I hurt you?" she gasped. "I'm so sorry. Here—"

But as she reached out again he caught her hand and stopped her. There was something in his eyes, something fiery and dangerous that she hadn't seen there before. And that was when she realized how much Max wanted her. She was testing his control without even trying. Marietta would have laughed aloud, if the knowledge had not taken her breath away.

"You're never going to give up, are you?" he growled. "I'm wasting my time trying to talk you out of it."

"I can't give up. I am not fit for marriage and I have no wish to be a spinster aunt to my sisters' children."

"There are other choices."

"Are there? I don't see them. I will not be beaten, Max. I will not fade away just because it would be more comfortable for certain people if I didn't exist. Yes, I made a mistake, a very silly mistake, but I was young and trusting and a man took advantage of that. I broke the rules, but they were not my rules, and I refuse to live my life in penance."

"Marietta—"

Looking into his troubled eyes, Marietta's anger faded and like a clap of thunder she realized what was wrong with this whole scenario. Aphrodite had tried to tell her, and Elena, too, but she hadn't understood. She did now. Max could only see her as Marietta Greentree, and she was looking at him as Max Valland. They had brought along with them all their troubles and all their complications, and that made it impossible to just let go and *feel*.

If they were *strangers*, without any prior knowledge . . .

She jumped up and stood before him, her pretty face intent, her eyes blazing into his. He watched her warily.

"Max," she said quietly, "I think we've gone about this assignation all wrong. We were supposed to be strangers meeting for an evening of pleasure, and instead we've been bickering like an old married couple. I think we should begin afresh. Right now."

"Marietta, do you know what you're saying?"

But she wouldn't let him argue. "No. You don't know my name. I'm not Marietta. I am a girl you've just met, a girl from Aphrodite's, and you've paid for an evening with me, and you are a man I must please."

He said nothing.

"What can I do to please you?" she asked him quietly. "Sir?"

He looked up, his eyes flaring. He swallowed. "Mar—"

"No!"

"There'll be no going back." He sounded serious, final.

"I know. I don't want to go back. My only way out of the mess I am in is to go forward. Now, sir, what can I do to please you?"

His gaze dropped down. "Take off that infernal robe."

She didn't let herself think too much. She let herself feel. Marietta slipped off the robe and allowed it to drop to the floor. And then she stood before him in the trousers and blouse, and tried not to think at all.

His eyes went to her breasts, slowly following the shape of her, returning again and again to the darker circles at their tips. His hand twitched but he closed his fingers, tight.

"Do you desire me?" she whispered.

He gave a breathless laugh.

"Then touch me. I want to know what it is you desire, Ma . . . sir. I want to understand what you're feeling."

But she thought she was understanding perfectly well already. She had understood the other day in the coach, when they drove around the park, twice. The look of hunger on his face, the glitter in his eyes, had made something similar happen inside her. Now her stomach clenched and a warmth washed over her, as if she were caught in a tidal surge and could not, did not want to, escape it.

He reached out and brushed her with his fingertips.

Light as the touch was, it made her shiver. She stared at him, lips parted in astonishment. He smiled wryly, and touched her again, using his thumb to rub against her nipple. She had never realized her own flesh could be so sensitive.

He cupped her breast in his palm, holding it like a gift, and then his arm came about her waist and he drew her forward, between his thighs, and he licked her with his tongue. Marietta's hands clung to his head, pulling him closer. The sensation of his warm mouth against her was exquisite. She made a sound in her throat, like a purr, and he looked at her.

His face was taut with desire, his eyes blazing, and his mouth was smiling. Whatever struggle he had been involved in was over—Max had decided to give himself up completely to what she was offering. For a moment she was confused by his capitulation, but then, still watching her, he ran his hand over her stomach, clearly enjoying the sensation of her bare skin, and she let herself feel again. His fingers brushed up, under the silk blouse, and they were warm and knowledgeable. Her eyes flickered and she swayed.

"Max."

"I'm a stranger, remember," he said, with a certain irony. "I'm teaching you about desire. That's what you want, isn't it, Marietta?"

He was tense, awaiting her answer, and once again, although she did not understand him, she acquiesced. "Yes."

"If you want to stop then you'd better say so. Now."

"I don't want to stop."

His fingers reached the underside of her breast, and then his palm was molding to her full shape, caressing her, gently squeezing her. He met her eyes, as if to gauge her compliance, and then he leaned forward and covered the nipple with his mouth, hot and wet, and sucked at her through the silk.

Her knees crumpled.

He caught her, drawing her down onto his lap, and covered her face in little biting kisses, his hand still stroking her breasts. It was bliss, she thought. Complete and utter bliss . . .

Where was his other hand?

With a shock she realized it was on her knee, heavy and warm and full of intent. She opened her mouth to remind him of the rules, but he swooped down and covered it with his own, and for a time she was lost in the wonder of his kisses.

When she came to herself again, his hand was stroking her belly just above where the top of her trousers met bare skin, his finger dipping beneath the band. She was burning, aching, and it didn't seem to matter whether or not he was touching her in places he wasn't supposed to—her body wanted that finger to move further down. She arched against him with a groan.

"That's the trouble with desire," he murmured in a deep, sensuous voice. "The more you feel it the more you want. Be warned, darling Marietta, once I have you I'll keep having you. Over and over again."

"Just touch me," she whispered. "I want you to touch me."

Obediently he bent to suck at her breast, and her head fell back against his shoulder as if she had had too much wine. Drunk on desire, tipsy on passion. She giggled at the thought, and then gasped as his fingers slid down under the band of her trousers, and trailed through the feminine hair she had been so worried about being visible earlier. Such fears and worries had long since departed—the urgent need for him to touch her overshadowed all.

His fingers had opened her, found the swollen little nub, and Marietta arched against him with a low cry as pleasure spiraled through her. "Max," she cried, in wonder and need.

"Soon," he whispered, and he stroked against her slick skin, pressing further, into the warm heart of her.

She tried to push herself against him, sensing that that was where real pleasure lay, but he murmured reassurance, taking his time, slowly driving her insane. Marietta half lay against him, incoherent with the sensations he was drawing from her body, and for a time he seemed to be content to torment her.

And then he took his fingers away.

She sobbed out his name.

"Soon, darling Marietta," he said, and bent to kiss her, caressing her breasts lightly, making her squirm again as the wave of need rose within her. There had to be an end to this, she thought desperately. There must be a climax to all this pleasure. Why did she not understand it? Why hadn't she realized this before, with Gerard Jones? But she hadn't, he had meant nothing, and it was as if this was her first time.

He turned her in his lap, helping her into a sitting position, so that her bottom rested upon his thighs, and her knees were bent, straddling him, while her bare feet pressed against the sofa on either side of his hips. Despite the silken trousers she felt exposed, vulnerable, open to him. She also felt as if her heart was about to explode with excitement.

Her hair was tumbling all about her—at some stage he had pulled out the combs—and now he caught it up in his hands and drew it back over her shoulders. For a moment he just looked at her, his glittering dark eyes running down over her body.

The blouse was damp, where he'd put his mouth against the silk, and her nipples poked out through the cloth. His eyes rested on the curve of her stomach, and then the area below the trousers that hid nothing of the eager shadows between her legs. He ran his hands up her legs, over her knees and thighs, squeezing her hips with a murmur of approval, and she would have smiled if she had been able to.

Because Marietta realized that she did not feel like herself any more. This was what Elena and Aphrodite had meant. She was free, wild and powerful. Or perhaps she did feel like herself, but it was the self who lived hidden deep inside her—the courtesan.

What would a courtesan do now? she asked herself. Would she draw away and send her man home, still wanting her? Would she promise much but give little? Probably. Marietta frowned. She didn't want to do that. She wanted to go on, not draw back, she wanted to feel what it was like to be Max's woman.

His hips were between her legs, and she could plainly see the heavy bulge inside his trousers. He wanted her as much as she wanted him—he was just better at controlling it—but perhaps she could turn that around.

Marietta reached down and stroked the hot hard length of him through the cloth. Max went very still. The expression in his eyes changed to confusion, and lust, and then he closed them with a sigh. She stroked him again, her fingers searching for the buttons beneath the placket.

"I told you about the man who ruined me," she said, in a husky little voice. "The night he took me to the inn."

The first button popped open.

"I don't even remember it, not properly. I was already having doubts, but I felt trapped. I suppose I hoped it would all work out. While he was doing it, I tried to think of something else. I hardly remember now what he did, and I certainly didn't enjoy it. Not like this, Max."

The second button popped open.

"I don't think it's fair, do you? To be ruined and to not even enjoy the experience?"

The third button popped open. She slid her fingers inside and found him. He filled her hand, heavy and big, swollen with desire for her. For a moment the doubts crowded back in, her fear of love and trust, threatening to destroy all her pleasure, but she forced them away, refusing to listen. This was her time, she deserved it, and she meant to savor it.

Max, his face taut and unsmiling, was gripping her hips, his fingers clenching with each stroke of her fingers on his hard length, but he let her do it. Let her use her hands to examine him, pet him, admire him.

"Are you sure all men have one like this?" she asked, watching him from beneath her lashes.

He laughed, and then arched against the pressure of her hand with a groan. "Rub yourself against me," he said, when he could speak again. "Pleasure yourself."

Puzzled, Marietta thought about that, but he urged her with his hands, and she slid down upon his lap, the silk of her trousers hushing against his thighs, until the length of him prodded hard against her. They both groaned, but then he adjusted her hips, tilting them, and he rubbed over her cleft, making her swollen flesh ache. Pleasure hummed through her, leaving her trembling. She did it again, pushing herself back up with her feet and then sliding, slowly, down onto him. This time it was even better.

Max's hands were still gripping her hips, but now they curved around to cup her bottom, pulling her harder against him as she slid down, using his body to pleasure hers and hers to pleasure his.

Ecstasy was only a heartbeat away. She knew it. Her heart was pounding, her chest was rising and falling as if she couldn't get enough air to breathe. Max groaned, swore, and suddenly he caught the front band of her trousers in one hand and took a firm hold. He looked up, into her eyes, and she knew then what he meant to do and that if he did there'd be no going back. But he waited. For a breath, he waited, to hear her say "No."

Marietta whispered, "Yes."

He ripped. The fine cloth tore, baring her from the navel down, and at once his hands were lifting her, readying her, and he entered her. It was easy, she thought feverishly. So easy. She was wet and ready, and he slid into her, deep, joining to her.

Max moaned, his mouth blind against hers, as he withdrew and thrust again.

"Please," she breathed, pushing down against him and trying to make him hurry. There was an urgency in her she couldn't restrain. But he wouldn't hurry. He drove into her with deep, measured strokes, bringing her a little bit closer to the brink with each one. Her fingers tangled in his hair, tugging the curls impatiently.

He thrust, a slow, deep slide against her most sensitive spot, and she went over the edge and the world exploded about her.

She gasped, wildly crying out his name, feeling him thrusting harder now, driving himself to follow her. Then the warmth of his seed inside her, and he fell back against the sofa, Marietta clasped firmly in his arms.

Chapter 13

There was a long silence. For a time all Marietta could hear was her heartbeat, and Max's close by. Her chest ached with the need to breathe deeply, and her body throbbed with the aftermath of pleasure. But gradually everything returned to normal, the crackling of the fire and the low rattle of a hackney cab outside on the street, and then Max cleared his throat and said, "I apologize."

"For what?" she managed sleepily, wriggling closer against him. Why had no one ever told her desire could be so exhausting?

"You said the waist up. I think you'll find we were working below the waist there."

Marietta giggled into his neck, and then she sighed. "Is it always like this?"

He hesitated. "No," he said at last. "It is rarely like this."

Marietta lifted her head and looked at him shrewdly, her hair tangled about her. "Are you saying that because you don't want me to be a courtesan and do this with other men, or because it's true?"

Max smiled. "Both."

She touched his cheek, her fingers brushing his lips, and something in her heart fluttered. He kissed her fingertips, sucking on the ends of them as he had done once before.

"Are we still strangers or can I call you Marietta?"

"I don't know. If we're strangers then I can stay here in your arms, but if I'm Marietta then I have to start thinking about my future and my past, and—"

"You understand that I won't be able to let you go now."

She smiled. "I don't see how you can possibly keep me. I'm very expensive, you know, and you have no money."

"Sometimes we want the most unsuitable people." His gaze was shuttered from her, far away.

"Max," she whispered, "I'm starting to worry about you."

He laughed and kissed her, slowly, using his lips and tongue to make her forget herself once more. After a little while she felt him against her thigh, hard again, and reached down to stroke the velvet strength of him. His hardness moved in her hand, and Max groaned into her mouth. He had removed her blouse and now he cupped her breast with his palm, enjoying the warm weight of her, and then his other hand was between her thighs, stroking the cleft that still felt swollen and replete from the last time.

"Oh Max . . ."

He was looking at her and there was an expression in his dark eyes she didn't understand. Determination mixed with desire, but something more than that. As if he had come to some hard-fought decision—an epiphany. She reached to caress his wild curls tenderly, her mouth soft and dazed as she kissed his face. She had never felt so happy, and she didn't want it to end, and she certainly didn't want to know what Max was plotting.

"Lie down," he said and, supporting her, he lay her upon the sofa among the cushions. She blinked up at the ceiling where the angels and cupids frolicked, and her fair hair was spread smooth and gleaming about her. Max removed his coat, looking down at her. Then he removed his waistcoat and pulled off his tie, before dragging his shirt over his head.

She caught her breath, reaching out to smooth her palms over his skin, rubbing them back and forth against the dusting of dark hair, exploring his hard stomach.

He stood up and tugged off his footwear and his trousers. And suddenly he was naked, big and gorgeous, looming over her. As he pulled off the remnants of her trousers and tossed them aside, she briefly wondered if her legs were really that short, and then it didn't matter, because he was on top of her and inside her and all around her.

She licked the skin on his shoulder, and then sucked at it. He ducked his head and his mouth was hot and open against her neck. He nuzzled her hair, breathing in the scent. His body moved against her, steady, and she ran her hands over his buttocks, urging him.

"Don't you stop," she said.

"I won't stop. I'll never stop."

The pleasure was building in her again, and she pushed up at him, her bosom flattened to his chest. His fingers reached down between their bodies and plucked at her, and she gasped out his name in dizzy shock. He did it again and lights seemed to burst behind her eyes. Her bones turned to liquid, and the angels above her smiled. But he wasn't finished with her yet. He thrust on, slow, steady, watching her face.

Her eyelids flickered and she looked up at him.

"Come with me to Cornwall," he said.

She couldn't believe it. He must have said something else. While she was trying to decide what to reply, he picked up the rhythm, the hard length of him sliding deeper inside her with each thrust. Amazingly her body began gathering itself up for another leap into ecstasy. She wrapped her legs about his lean hips and pushed back.

He smiled. There were beads of sweat on his face, and he looked pale. This couldn't be good for him, she thought belatedly. He had been ill only a short time ago—he was probably still ill. "Perhaps you should stop now," she panted.

"Not yet."

He lifted his chest higher off her and grasped her thighs in his big hands, lifting her up and opening her wide, and then he came up on his knees above her and drove himself into her with exquisite expertise.

Marietta raised her head and took one look at him slipping in and out of her, and the lights burst inside her head again. She arched up, her voice louder, almost a . . . well, a scream.

He let himself go, driving hard, and crying out as his body released.

Marietta was beyond exhaustion, but it was a nice

feeling. She knew she didn't have a bone left in her body that hadn't turned to water, and she couldn't have raised a finger. Just as well Max was there to lift her in his strong arms and carry her over to the vast apricot satin-swathed bed.

"Poor darling," he whispered, "desire is very fatiguing. And, as you will find out soon enough, very, very addictive."

The bed was feather soft and the coverings were softer and she snuggled in with a sigh. She was almost asleep before she realized he was back again, and although she knew it was Max, dressed in his black coat and white shirt, he seemed like a stranger, this man who had used her so expertly and so well. Someone else entirely.

He bent over her, and kissed her brow, gently. "Marry me and come live with me at Blackwood," he said, and this time she could not be mistaken. Her eyes opened just enough to meet his, and see that he was deadly serious, and then they closed again.

When she woke up much later, Max was gone.

Aphrodite looked up as Max entered the salon. He looked the perfect gentleman, although his hair was a little rumpled, and his necktie slightly askew. He caught her eye and gestured to a private alcove on one side of the room. Frowning, she excused herself from her cluster of guests, and made her way toward him. He took her hand and bowed over it, a wry smile twisting his handsome face and his dark eyes apologetic.

And she knew something had changed.

Her heart turned cold with fear for her child, but

somehow she managed to keep a smile on her face.

"Your daughter says she is ruined, Madame, and that she wants to be a courtesan."

"That is so, my lord."

"I want to marry her."

She closed her eyes and opened them again, but the handsome Lord Roseby was still standing there, his gaze frank and a little amused—as if he mocked himself for his own words.

"I don't think Marietta would agree to that . . . Max," she said bluntly. "May I call you Max?"

"Of course."

"My daughter has sworn off love and marriage. She has her heart set on following in my footsteps." But she was watching him as closely as he was watching her. One would have thought Max Valland had enough problems of his own. It was reckless of him to fix his sights on the daughter of a courtesan who had already disgraced herself once and was threatening to do so again, but Aphrodite wasn't as surprised as she pretended.

"Maybe, but I can change her mind," he said.

"Maybe you can, but all the same I doubt your family will be as eager as you to claim her as their own. I had heard that when your cousin Harold discovered who she was, he barred her from your house."

Ah, he hadn't known that then. She watched the anger come and go in his face, as he put it aside to be dealt with later.

"Madame, I admit I am no great catch as a husband," he began, a bleak little smile on his mouth. "If you had any doubts about my current situation then let me put you straight. I have very little money, I have been disinherited and have lost my lands and titles, and my prospects for regaining them are . . . nil. On the positive side, I have property in Cornwall—my mother's gift to me—and plans to make it pay, I am young and healthy, and I would treat your daughter with the utmost respect. I know this does not sound like much, but surely," he bit his lip, as if he was uncertain how to proceed without causing offense.

Aphrodite, who was fairly certain she already knew what he was going to say, waited.

"Surely it would be far better for Marietta to marry me and live with me in Cornwall, no matter how little we had, than to become a courtesan."

She raised an elegant eyebrow at him. "Are you planning to save her from herself, my lord? I would think you would know better."

He gave an apologetic shrug. "I'm sorry. I mean no disrespect, Madame, but I have come to know Marietta and she is not the sort of woman who could live such a life. It would destroy her."

Aphrodite relented. "It is possible that I agree with you, Max, although if you tell Marietta that I will deny it. My daughter's heart is generous and easily broken, and, yes, I do worry for her. But she is also a woman of strong character and she is determined on her course of action. You may find it difficult to persuade her to accept your proposal, no matter how well meant."

Max frowned, glancing over her head into the salon where a number of eyes were watching them curiously.

"Is that why you are thinking of marrying her? Because you wish to be the hero and ride your charger to her rescue?"

He met her gaze. "At first, yes, I suppose that did cross my mind. I wanted to talk her out of being a courtesan, but she wouldn't listen. She has been too badly hurt to easily trust again. I see now that the only way to make her happy is to teach her that she need not fear to love, that here is a man who will never let her down. If she would marry me and come to Cornwall, I am certain she would not regret it."

"I see." Aphrodite wasn't sure that she did. "Tell me, Max, do you love my daughter? Or do you just want her body?"

Max felt uncomfortable. Aphrodite's eyes were dark and penetrating and he wasn't used to a woman speaking to him so frankly. Apart from Marietta, that is—was this where she had inherited her forthrightness? The truth was he didn't know whether he loved her or not; he had never been in love.

"We are both victims of scandal," he said at last. "We can find solace in each other. We are well suited, I think, and I know we could be happy together. Is that love? Perhaps."

Aphrodite gave a little smile, and kept her counsel.

"I should tell you," Max went on, "that she and I have been intimate in a physical way. We are lovers in every sense of the word and I do not think either of us is capable of halting matters now."

It was as she had feared. The temporary affair was no longer a light-hearted matter; it was a full-blown, passionate amour between two people—a *grandee passion*—and such things were far more difficult to control. It could well end in heartbreak for one, or both, of them. Or it could end in a joyous marriage.

Aphrodite had met Max a number of times, but

she had never looked upon him as a prospective son-in-law. She did so now. Outwardly he was handsome and well made. She knew he was a gentleman, and there had never been any unsavory gossip about him. In short he was as good and honest as it was possible for a duke's son to be—almost too good and honest to be true. It was a pity he had been disinherited . . . Marietta had said something about him being hurt, about there being danger, and Jemmy had been looking into the attack outside the club . . . Aphrodite frowned.

"My daughter thinks you are under threat, that someone has been attempting to harm you, Max. Is that true?"

"Marietta and I do not agree on everything."

"How tedious if you did."

"Madame, I am aware that I am not the ideal husband for your daughter, but I do not mean to idle my life away as if I were still heir to my father's dukedom. I am . . . liberated," he smiled, "and I am not afraid to dirty my hands in good honest work. I believe that if I have a wife and family then I will have all the more reason to strive harder."

"If you were a better catch you probably wouldn't have given Marietta a second glance, my lord. Would the disgraced daughter of a courtesan be on your list of possible wives if you were still in line to inherit?"

"I don't know the answer to that question, how can I?" Ah yes, he was honest. "But I do know that now that I have met Marietta no other woman will do."

Aphrodite was beginning to feel exhausted, but his words were so heartfelt they made her laugh and clap her hands. "Very good, Max! The perfect answer! Tell me, where is my daughter now? Is she waiting out in the hall?"

"I put her to bed, she's asleep."

"Mon dieu!" she hissed. Then, reluctantly, "Very well. I will consider your offer. But it is not I you should be trying to persuade—I am already convinced—it is Marietta. There lies your difficulty."

He looked startled that she was so clearly on his side. "Thank you, Madame. Could I ask one more favor of you? Please don't tell Marietta that you know I wish to marry her. I think, if she is aware you are amenable to the idea, she will feel as if I have conspired against her and want to run as far away from me as she can."

"Yes, yes, all right," Aphrodite answered him impatiently. "I think I know my daughter as well as you, and I will say nothing to her. But be warned, if you hurt her, Max—"

"Believe me, hurting her is the last thing I would ever do."

Again Aphrodite noted his sincerity and then nodded a dismissal. As Max left the salon, she called Dobson over and told him to follow, as an added precaution, to make certain that this time Max was put into a hansom without incident.

"It has been very good for business that his lordship has returned to the club so soon. It would be very bad, however, if he were to be attacked a second time."

As she watched Dobson stroll off, she allowed herself a moment alone with her thoughts.

Marietta, Marietta, what am I to do with you?

Max Valland wished to marry her daughter, but he was penniless and he wanted to take her to Cornwall. It seemed extreme, but as long as Marietta was happy about that it wouldn't matter, although it would be better if she loved him, and he loved her. Having known love herself, Aphrodite wanted her daughter to experience its wonder.

She remembered now the expression in Max's eyes, something hot and familiar. Perhaps he *was* in love with her and just didn't know it yet; he was certainly determined to have his way. But was Marietta as fond of him? She must discover how Marietta felt. A smile played around her mouth—since her daughter had arrived in London, life had certainly become far more interesting.

Marietta was dreaming. She was in the flying carriage pulled by the horses with wings, and they were sailing west, towards Cornwall. Max was beside her, wearing a top hat, and she had a bridal veil. They seemed happy enough, until she noticed there was someone else in the carriage. It was Harold, and just as she recognized him he pulled out a pistol and fired it at Max.

She woke with a start.

Apricot satin hung in folds all about her. When she tried to sit up her body cried out for her to stop, and she gasped. She was aching all over, and there was a tingling, burning sensation between her legs, and she smelled of . . .

Max.

This time she did sit up despite the pain and looked anxiously around the room. The lamp was still burning low, the fire was crackling, the remains of their meal were scattered about, but the room itself was empty. Her eyes crept to the sofa, but apart from some cushions tossed onto the floor and the creased coverings, there was no sign that she and Max had ever reached those dizzy heights of pleasure together. Twice.

Or was it three times?

Max, the gentleman, had loosened the reins on his control with a vengeance—his horse had well and truly bolted. Marietta smiled and lay against the pillows, stretching carefully, letting her mind travel back through the evening.

Well, she knew all about desire now. Max had shown her things that she had only dreamed of—there was no comparison. Aphrodite had not been exaggerating when she said that he was a man of experience . . .

Aphrodite!

Marietta sprang out of bed, and then stopped and caught her breath as the muscles in her thighs cramped. She was sore and sticky, and she made her way to the jug and bowl on the dresser and proceeded to clean herself thoroughly. Her trousers were beyond repair and she couldn't find her blouse, but she still had the robe, and now she slipped it on over her naked body.

She could tell it was very late. How long had she slept? Vivianna knew she was staying with Aphrodite—she had grudgingly agreed to it—so she would not be worried, but Aphrodite would be waiting impatiently to hear how she had got on.

As if her thoughts had conjured her mother, there

was a sharp rap on the door, and before Marietta could utter more than a squeak, it opened.

Aphrodite stepped in and closed the door behind her. For a moment she said nothing, just stared at Marietta standing in the middle of the room in her silk robe. She was wearing her usual black, her hair drawn into a rather severe chignon, but tonight there was a flush to her cheeks and her eyes gleamed with some inner excitement.

Marietta stared back at her uneasily.

"You do not have to say anything, your Max has told me what he has done."

"Oh." She was relieved for only a brief moment. "Well, to be fair, it wasn't just him. Everything . . . somehow we couldn't stop. He did give me the choice, and I didn't want to."

"I see." She rolled her eyes. "Where have I heard that before?" she muttered to herself. "Why do none of my daughters listen to me?"

"Madame?" Marietta whispered.

"It does not matter." Aphrodite waved her hand. "Your Max is not a man to be trifled with, *mon petit puce*, remember that. You should not play him for a fool."

Marietta blinked at her in confusion. "What do you mean, Mama?"

"I mean . . . he seems very able, child. Perhaps I should use him to help some of the other girls. Would you recommend him in his role as mentor, Marietta? I had not thought of such a thing before, but now . . . hmm, the idea is a good one."

A terrible wave of pain rose up inside her; she felt like physically jumping back from the suggestion. Her chest ached and despite her efforts her eyes filled with tears, but her mother was watching her.

"No," she managed to gasp, and cleared her throat. "That is, he is a very good mentor, but I don't think he would ever agree to such a thing."

Aphrodite frowned, looking concerned. "Are you all right, my child? You do not look happy. Come, are you hurt?"

"No, I'm not hurt. Just . . . just . . ." The tears welled up and blinded her.

Aphrodite made a soft sympathetic sound and held out her arms, and after a brief hesitation Marietta ran into them. She snuggled close to her mother, feeling her warmth through the rigid bone of the stays she wore and the scratchy stiffening of the silk dress. None of that seemed to matter, when her mother's arms were holding her and her sweet fragrance was comforting her.

"When a man like Max Valland wants a woman, Marietta, it is hard to resist him. You shouldn't feel guilty or uncomfortable about that."

Marietta snuggled yet closer.

"You have never had the chance to enjoy yourself in that way. Max can open a new world for you, a world of pleasure and sensual treats. I think you should make the most of your time with him, Marietta, because such joys do not happen very often."

Marietta sighed.

"Did you not like what you did together? Was it not pleasurable?"

She hesitated, but she couldn't lie to Aphrodite. "It was wonderful."

"Then if Max agrees I will make him an offer. He should continue to be your mentor and when you are done with him, he can work with some of my other girls. What do you think?" She seemed to be belaboring the point, but Marietta was too emotionally off-balance for it to occur to her. In fact she thought it was an awful idea. The image of Max with other women, doing what they had just done, was so painful and so horrible that she could hardly bear it. And yet it should not affect her like this. He was nothing to her—a casual acquaintance, that was all.

It is almost as if I am in love with him, Marietta thought bleakly.

But she knew she could never fall in love. She could not have her heart broken again. And with Max she suddenly understood it would be so much worse than it had been before. If he were to love her, and make her love him and trust him, and then decide he no longer wanted her—abandon her—then she would be destroyed. Utterly and completely destroyed. There could be no way back from that.

It was a combination of self-preservation and the longing to have a full life that had set her on the path to being a courtesan. She must not be swayed from her goal, not when she was so close to obtaining it. She must not be blinded again by thoughts of love and happiness, only to find them nothing more than a young girl's dreams.

Max was handsome and strong and honest, in fact she had often thought he was too good to be true—all the more reason not to trust her own feelings and senses where he was concerned. Only a fool would make the same mistake a second time.

Aphrodite continued to rock her, but she seemed deep in her own thoughts. "We will talk of this matter again," she murmured at last. "I think that for now you should carry on with your tasks. Max will help you to learn what it is to be a woman who desires a man, *oui*? Just as he has been doing."

"But—" she began, trying not to wail.

"Unless you wish to use another man?" she said innocently, still with that watchful gaze.

Marietta swallowed, feeling sick. Another man in Max's place? Another man kissing her, touching her, smiling down at her as he entered her body. She shook her head decisively.

"Good, then it shall go on as before between you and Max. I think, this time, you will meet in seclusion. A rendezvous between lovers who are not free to love, so the moment is especially piquant, *oui*? Would you like that, Marietta?"

She looked up, her tired eyes amused. "It sounds intriguing, Madame, as you meant it to. Where should we have this secluded rendezvous?"

Aphrodite smiled. "There is a villa in St. John's Wood—it belongs to a prima donna, but she allows it to be used as an introducing house."

Marietta looked confused.

"A prima donna is a kept woman, *mon petit puce*, and an introducing house is a place used by those who wish to remain incognito and yet meet others who are seeking similar entertainments. The villa is popularly known as the Lustful Lady. Max will have heard of it. You will meet him there tomorrow night at eleven o'clock. Do you think you can manage that, Marietta?"

"I am sure I can." The Lustful Lady—what an appalling name! But even that could not stop the sense of anticipation that was already creeping over Marietta. It was as if she was no longer in control of her own desires, and remembering the warnings Max had given her that was certainly a worrying thing.

Marietta pondered whether she should mention to her mother that Max had asked her to marry him and go with him to Cornwall, but decided against it. Aphrodite might not think they should continue, or rightly suggest she find another man with whom she was not in danger of falling in love. And whatever the rights or wrongs of it, whatever the risk to herself, and despite knowing it could lead nowhere, Marietta wanted to continue making love with Max as long as possible—she wanted it desperately.

Max prowled his house in Bedford Square, each footfall sure and certain despite the darkness. The Pomeroys and Daniel were asleep in their quarters and he was all alone. This had been his home since he was a baby and he knew it so well he did not need to see—he could have walked about blindfolded. Soon this house would be gone, handed over to Harold and Susannah, and when his father . . . that is, the Duke of Barwon, was dead, they would have Valland House, too. The life that Max had been so complacent about had been changed irrevocably by his mother's letter, and his father's reading of it at the new year supper. He could still hear the duke's voice, trembling a little at the end, but strong and burning with his righteous anger. It was Max who had weakened and stumbled from the room.

"*. . . the affair was passionate and irresponsible, and a child was conceived. A son. What does a woman do in such a situation? Her lover has abandoned her to her fate and ruin stares her in the face. Even the most honorable of women is tempted to find a way* *out, and if a gentleman then offers for her and she finds that gentleman is in love with her, how can she say no? There are moments when she wishes to tell him the truth, many such moments, but as the days pass and his love deepens, she knows such revelations will destroy the happiness that could be hers. So she pretends the child is his, and he is overjoyed, and when the son is born no one comments upon his appearance. It is accepted that he is his father's son. And he is named Max, and life goes on as if everything is as it should be and not a dreadful lie . . ."*

Max shook the memory from his head and kept walking, his stride growing longer and more determined as he tried to put the memories behind him. There was no point in regretting what was done, that wouldn't change anything. Max had been forcibly ejected from the bosom of the Valland family, and Ian Keith was right, there was a sort of freedom in that. His plan to reopen the mine was beginning to interest him more and more, and the duties and tasks he had been trained to take over on his father's death less and less. He could be whatever he wished to be; his life was a chart upon which he could plot a new course.

Marietta.

He remembered her skin beneath his hands, the warmth of her kisses, her body trembling as he led her with him into sensual paradise. This need for her that was burning inside him was new and disturbing. Stupid, too, because before, when he was heir to the dukedom, thoughts of marriage hadn't interested him. He had believed that he had plenty of time for such mundane matters—of course he knew he would have to marry and produce an heir some day, but he had been in no hurry.

If he had known Marietta then, would he have seen her as the woman he wanted above all others? Was Aphrodite right, would she have been on his carefully chosen list of prospective duchesses? Clearly Harold didn't think so.

For a moment Max grew hot and angry, thinking of his cousin's high-handed interference—but that would keep. He would instruct the Pomeroys to ignore anything Harold had told them, and the next time Harold showed his face here he would deal with him. Harold might have taken everything from him, but he would not take Marietta.

He leaned his head against the cool window and gazed down into the quiet square. Marietta would be awake now in that apricot bed, with the angels and cupids circling above her. He wondered whether she would be thinking of him, and decided she probably was. He had used her well, shown her pleasure that she had never known existed, and she had reveled in it. Still, knowing her as he did, he admitted that Aphrodite was probably right, and she would refuse to go to Cornwall as his wife. She had her stubborn sights set on being a courtesan.

Of course there was more to it than that. Her heart had been badly broken, and with the pain and disgrace that had come afterwards she was naturally wary about having it broken again. He understood that, he respected that.

But Max knew now that he wanted her enough to fight for her. Marietta had stepped into his life with her direct fearless gaze and decided opinions, and he wasn't about to let her out again. He did not know if he loved her, but he wanted her. By God, he wanted her! Every moment he was away from her he wanted her more. It was as if she were a part of him now.

In Cornwall they could be happy, he was certain of it. Children would come, and Marietta would love them, as he would. A quiet life but a happy one—it had its appeal. And the nights, oh yes, the nights . . .

Marietta had begged him to teach her about desire; well, he was going to teach her! He was going to teach her so well that she would never want to be without him.

Chapter 14

$\sim\!\!\sim\!\!\text{CO}\!\!\sim\!\!\sim$

Marietta was pale but determined as she prepared to leave the next morning to return to Berkley Square. Max could believe she would throw all her hopes and dreams away, if he liked, and run off with him to Cornwall, but he was deceiving himself and so he would discover soon enough. She would continue with their temporary affair, but it was just that—temporary.

Aphrodite was standing with her in the vestibule, awaiting the carriage. Marietta glanced at her mother. And that was another thing, Aphrodite was acting peculiarly. Several times she had smiled, a little secretive smile, but when Marietta asked her what she was thinking, her mother shrugged and said it was nothing.

Did Aphrodite know something she didn't, and, if so, what could it be?

"I have something to tell you, *mon petit puce!*" Aphrodite had reclaimed her attention. "I have visited your father and asked him if he wants to meet you, and he says that he does."

Marietta had an odd sense of fracture, as though this moment was not real at all, but a dream. Tears were stinging her eyes. She was going to meet her father. It should not matter to her so much—she had never believed it would—but now that it was happening, it did.

"He has been in seclusion in the country," Aphrodite went on gently, patting her shoulder. "He prefers to live there, away from London. Perhaps you should prepare yourself for a rather melancholy meeting."

"But . . . why has he been in seclusion? Is there something wrong with him?"

"It is a sad story, Marietta. Adam—that is your father's name—had an accident. His legs were damaged when a carriage overturned. Once he was a lively man who enjoyed his life to the full, but now he cannot get about as he did. He is often in pain and he prefers to live a simple life, so that is what he does."

Marietta didn't know what to say. Her father was an invalid. "I-I am very sorry for him then, Madame. Is he . . . has he a wife?"

"Yes, he is married. She is dull." Aphrodite pulled a face. "It means he does not have to exert himself to keep her. Perhaps I am unfair, though, for she seems to be fond of him and he of her. On the few occasions he comes to London she does not accompany him. He is my friend, and she knows that, although she likes to pretend I don't exist."

"But you and he are no longer lovers?"

Aphrodite blinked. "No," she said, and glanced

sideways, to where Dobson was standing by the door. "No, we have not been lovers for many years. But we are fond of each other, and he has been a great help to me in business matters."

Marietta nodded as if it was all clear to her, but she was feeling rather vulnerable. Adam sounded very unlike her and she could not imagine them ever being close after all this time. They may as well be strangers.

"What is his full name?" she said.

"Sir Adam Langley. He is a baronet, and although he is wealthy, he is no Fraser."

Fraser, Vivianna's father, had been very wealthy indeed.

"I wasn't counting on a wealthy father," Marietta said automatically. "Sir Adam Langley," she repeated, and smiled. "I like his name, Mama. I hope I shall like him."

"I hope so, too, Marietta. But there is something more you should know, *mon petit puce*. Your father has other children. Five of them." She said it with a lift of her elegant eyebrows. "So you will never inherit, although . . ." But she shook her head. "Well, I will let him tell you about that."

"Five children?" she whispered uncertainly. "Brothers *and* sisters?"

"*Oui.*"

Marietta felt a stirring of excitement. She would like to meet her half brothers and sisters one day, although it did not sound as if her father's wife would be very likely to welcome her into their family. And truthfully, Marietta could not blame her.

The carriage arrived soon after, and Marietta settled herself for the journey back to her sister's house.

She didn't expect too many awkward questions—fortunately Vivianna's time and attention were taken up with her baby son—although she knew she did not look her best. Max was right, learning about desire was very fatiguing.

A smile tugged at her mouth, and she bit her lip to subdue it. She wanted to hug herself and close her eyes and let the memories fill her head. Her body was still a bit sore this morning but it was a pleasant sort of ache. Now and again she would feel a slight tingle, as if her most sensitive places were remembering Max, too.

Tonight they would meet at the Lustful Lady, and Marietta knew she could hardly wait.

The house in Berkley Square was a shambles. Boxes and trunks were piled up in the hall, and there were servants scurrying about like scolded cats. Her heart beginning to thump with excitement, Marietta made her way into Vivianna's sitting room.

A woman looked up from a comfortable chair by the fireplace, her heavily bandaged foot resting upon a plump cushion on a stool. Fashionably dressed in a velvet traveling gown with fur trimmings, she was middle-aged and attractive, with fair hair and light eyes. At the moment those eyes looked tired and there was a crease of pain between her brows, but both were chased away by joy when she recognized Marietta.

"Mama!" Marietta cried, and in an instant was on her knees at her mother's side, her arms clinging.

Amy Greentree gave a choked laugh, and then she lifted Marietta's face, blinking back tears as she gazed down into it. "Do you know, my dear," she began huskily, "when you were little, if you had done something of which you knew I would disapprove, you always hugged me the tighter when you saw me. So what, Marietta, am I to think now?"

Marietta wondered at herself for being so transparent, but then Lady Greentree always had the knack for seeing straight into her daughters' hearts.

"I am just glad to see you, Mama," she said tearfully, rising to her feet again. "How is your poor ankle? Are you sure you should be traveling so far so soon? I did not think to see you in London for weeks."

Lady Greentree allowed her to change the subject, although the expression in her eyes told Marietta that she *did* know something was amiss and was choosing not to mention it. "My ankle is still a little tender, but I can get about and the traveling was no bother. I simply sat and let others do things for me. Very lazy of me, really."

"Does Mr. Jardine know you are here?"

Amy Greentree's smile was open and without any coyness. "No, he is out, but he is expected back very soon. It will be nice to see him again—do you know, I have missed his sensible conversation."

Marietta experienced her usual frustration. Just a downward sweep of the eyelashes or a flutter of the fingers and she might have been able to hope that her mother felt something more for Mr. Jardine than staid friendship. Yet again it seemed a hopeless case.

"But you have seen Vivianna and your grandson?"

Amy sighed, her eyes growing misty. "Oh, I have indeed. I have been sitting here thinking that I am a very fortunate woman, Marietta. If I had not come upon three lovely little girls on my estate all those years ago I might now have been a lonely and embittered old widow."

"Fortunate? Hmm, I would say you deserve your good fortune, Mama, if that is what it is to put up with three stubborn and difficult females. In fact no one deserves it more."

"I would have to agree with that."

The voice came from behind her, and Marietta turned with a cry of glad surprise. There stood Francesca, tall and slim, her cloud of dark hair barely restrained, her equally dark eyes full of pleasure. Marietta hesitated, thinking: Francesca, here in London?

Francesca laughed. "Yes, it really is me and not a wraith! I could not allow Mama to travel on her own, could I? Besides, I was desperate to see Vivianna's son."

The sisters embraced warmly, they had always had a special closeness, being the two nearest in age. Marietta wished she could tell Francesca everything that had happened to her, but she was wary. Her sister would probably not approve. Of all three girls it was Francesca who most resembled Aphrodite, and yet it was Francesca who most resented being a daughter of the famous courtesan. Was this the chance for mother and youngest daughter to get to know each other a little better?

"I cannot stay long." Francesca immediately dashed her hopes. "I need to return to Greentree Manor as soon as Mama is settled and comfortable."

Amy Greentree gave her youngest daughter a sympathetic look. "Do you already find London too much to bear? I admit, it is very noisy and some of it is very grubby, but Vivianna assures me one becomes accustomed."

"I cannot imagine it," Francesca said bleakly.

She did look paler than usual, Marietta admitted, and there was a wild look in her eyes, a little like a trapped animal. Of them all, Francesca was the one who loved her home in Yorkshire the most. She strode the moors as if she was a part of them, and her vivid, rather melancholy paintings reflected that.

"Well, I for one am very glad to see you, Francesca, and will be very sorry to see you go," Marietta assured her. "In fact I would be extremely hurt if you were to leave before you had stayed at least a fortnight. Or more. There is much to do and see in London, and I want to show it all to you. Wait until you've been up in a balloon—"

She stopped, but too late. Amy was staring at her with narrowed and suspicious eyes. "A balloon, Marietta? I hope you have not partaken of this treat yourself, have you?"

"They are very safe, Mama," she replied sweetly, making her eyes big and innocent, but not actually answering the question.

Francesca choked on laughter, but Amy wasn't impressed.

"Very well, a fortnight," Francesca said, before there was an argument. "But I am only agreeing to it because you have begged me, and you obviously can't manage without me."

"*Psht!*" Marietta replied to that, but she secretly wondered what her sister would think if she were to discover what she was up to with Max. Learning about desire with a disinherited duke. Francesca would be appalled. Or would she? In some ways Francesca was even more unconventional than Vivianna and Marietta.

"What is the matter with Lil?" her sister asked her a little later, as they made their way upstairs. "She was quite strange, not at all her usual dour self. I think she even made a little joke. Of course we were all too surprised to laugh. Has she been ill?"

Marietta cast her a sideways glance. "Sick with love. She has met an aeronaught and spends all her free time flying with him in his balloon."

Francesca was suitably astonished by this. "What of Jacob?" she asked. "I thought it was all arranged that they marry?"

Marietta had always known Lil had no intention of marrying their coachman. She considered herself far too superior, and her sights had been set higher. "Mr. Keith is a very nice man, not at all the conventional sort, and he worships Lil. You will see." She hesitated, and then launched into a subject she dearly wanted to broach with her sister. "Aphrodite has told me the name of my father, Francesca, and I am to meet him. Now that you are here, perhaps—"

Immediately Francesca stiffened, and her dark eyes grew even darker. "I'd rather remain in ignorance, thank you. I am not interested in my father. Or my mother."

"Please, Francesca . . ."

"No, Marietta."

There was no moving her younger sister when she was like this, and Marietta knew it well. With a sigh, she said no more, but she was sorry. Her own need to meet her father was growing stronger. In fact she could hardly wait . . . if only she were not so nervous that he would not like her, or that he had heard about her disgrace and would be disappointed in her.

It was just a pity that Francesca would not share this journey of exploration with her.

Uncle William, Aunt Helen, and Toby had been invited for dinner, and the dining table at Berkley Square was almost festive as the family exchanged memories and stories. Vivianna did her best to smile and enjoy herself, but it was clear Oliver's continued absence was making her unhappy. Marietta herself, though very pleased to see Lady Greentree and Francesca, yet found her thoughts slipping away to Max.

There had been a note sent around to the house this afternoon. Lil had carried it up to Marietta, her head in the clouds as usual. When Marietta took the note and told her so, Lil giggled. *Giggled!* It was unnatural. "Ian . . . I mean, Mr. Keith, is makin' a night flight at Vauxhall Gardens. There's a masque ball, and there'll be fireworks, miss. Mr. Keith's goin' to fly up high with them underneath the basket, and then set them off so as they'll light up the sky over London. It'll be a real spectacle."

Marietta imagined it would be. "You don't think it's a little dangerous to do that, I mean lighting fireworks while you're in a balloon, Lil?"

Lil pursed her lips. "Maybe, but Ian . . . Mr. Keith's a very experienced aeronaught." She had said it so sincerely that Marietta didn't have the heart to smile. "And I'll be with him to help."

"Lil!"

"He's asked me," Lil said sharply, "and I've agreed, so there. No need to get yourself worried on my behalf, Miss Marietta. I like a bit of adventure, I do."

Marietta sank down on the bed when she had gone, still shaken by this example of the new Lil.

The note had crumpled in her hand, and she looked down and began to read. Suddenly all other thoughts went out of her head.

There will be a coach waiting for you by the gardens with my insignia on it. The driver will bring you to me at eleven o'clock as arranged. M.

Her first reaction had been to smile with relief—she had been pondering how she would slip away to the Lustful Lady without getting caught, or needing to request a vehicle to take her.

But thinking of it now, at the dining table among her chattering family, her body tingled.

She would be seeing Max again in only a few hours. What would he say to her, what would he *do* to her?

This time she moaned softly.

"Marietta, are you quite well?" Her mother was staring at her, and Marietta realized with a start that she wasn't the only one.

She forced a laugh. "I'm sorry. I was miles away."

For the rest of the meal she managed to keep her thoughts in the room and not in wistful dreams of being with Max at the Lustful Lady later this evening.

Mr. Jardine, who had been looking ten years younger since Lady Greentree arrived, hurried to help her into the drawing room after dinner. His manner was particularly solicitous as he busied himself making her comfortable in the best chair, and then brought the stool closer, so that she could prop up her injured foot.

Amy Greentree gave a little sigh of relief. "Thank you, Mr. Jardine, you are the best of men."

He smiled down at her, but there was a look on his face . . . Marietta felt her heart ache for him. At that moment she happened to turn, and noticed that Uncle William was standing in the doorway watching them, too. And unlike Marietta his heart wasn't aching, no indeed, but from the tight and painful expression on his face his belly was.

Marietta gritted her teeth, feeling sure they were about to be treated to another of Uncle William's dreadful tirades, but strangely he said nothing. Though when he finally left, his expression was still hard and unsmiling, and there was a look in his eyes when they rested upon Mr. Jardine that boded ill.

Marietta was tempted to warn her mother, but how could she broach the matter without giving away Mr. Jardine's secret love for her? He would never forgive her if she put Amy on her guard with him. Besides, Amy was exhausted from her long journey and soon afterwards retired to bed, so for the moment the opportunity was lost. Francesca, too, had already gone up to bed, and Vivianna had retired to her own rooms.

A glance at the clock as Marietta hurried upstairs to her room showed that it was already a quarter to the hour, and she had barely any time to prepare. She decided to wear the midnight blue velvet and net dress she had worn to dinner, but she quickly brushed her hair and tied it loosely at her back, and tossed her emerald green cloak about her.

Ready at last, Marietta crept down the backstairs and slipped outside.

At first she couldn't see the coach, and then she did—a dark bulky shape against the pale foliage of the garden. Marietta hurried over, wincing as the cobbles bruised the bottoms of her feet in their thin-soled slippers. The still night air was fresh and she filled her lungs and felt alive—more alive than she had been for a very long time.

Had Max changed her, or was it simply that she was taking the first steps along her chosen path at last? But Marietta didn't want to mull over reasons for her happiness; she just wanted to enjoy the moment.

She thought it was Daniel huddled up in the driver's seat, but this man did not turn and greet her and she hesitated, her hand upon the door.

"Lustful Lady?" a gruff voice asked.

"Yes." It was all right then. This was Max's coach—she noted the insignia on the side—only he had not sent Daniel to drive it. Under the circumstances she could understand that.

With a smile, Marietta climbed up inside.

They drove for a little while. Despite being late the streets of London were still busy with other vehicles and people on foot. It was a place that never seemed to sleep, and she huddled into her corner as the gas lamps shone out, keeping the hood of her cloak about her face in case anyone should peer inside and see her.

This was all part of the game, she supposed. A secret rendezvous. A lover with whom she must never be seen in daylight, or recognized with at night. The tingle in her blood was growing stronger, and she peered anxiously from the window, hoping they were nearly there.

Just as the coach drew up.

The driveway to the Lustful Lady was illuminated by flaring torches, while the building itself was an old manor house, set among the trees. A servant in yellow livery hurried to open the door for Marietta, and to direct the coach around to the back of the house. The villa seemed strangely quiet as the servant led Marietta to the front door and gestured that she should enter. His eyes weren't curious—perhaps he saw too many ladies huddled in their cloaks come to meet lonely gentlemen.

"Where do I go?" she asked him anxiously. There was a single lamp inside the door and it hardly penetrated the darkness. Suddenly this did not seem like such an adventure.

"Straight on, ma'am," he said, as if he'd said it a hundred times before. "Stop when you choose to. If the door's open you can join in. If it ain't then don't disturb."

Stop when you choose to? Join in or don't disturb? She didn't understand him, but Marietta had already taken a step forward and the door closed abruptly behind her. For a moment she panicked and was strongly tempted to bang upon it and ask to be released; she wanted nothing more than to go home again to her sister's house and her family, and forget all this nonsense.

Only it wasn't nonsense, was it? This was her life from now on, these were the sorts of places she would frequent, and she'd best get used to it. But the excitement had gone and in its place was doubt and fear and a need for Max to hold her hand.

Once her eyes became accustomed the way forward wasn't as dark as she had thought. There was a hallway, paneled in gloomy wood, that looked as if it were part of an original medieval building, and there ahead of her shone another of the dull lamps. As she set off she became aware of voices, murmurs, and they were close by. Marietta noticed that there was a doorway a little ahead of her and to her side, and remembering what the boy had said she paused and glanced within.

There were people in there, and more than two.

For a moment she blinked, trying to make out what they were doing. Limbs wrapped about limbs, mouths open, like animals rutting . . . And then she understood exactly what they were doing. A face lifted, and a woman's soft voice laughed and called, "Come join us, my lady, the more the merrier!" This was followed by a grunt and a deep groan.

Marietta picked up her skirts and ran down the hallway, her slippers beating time to the thudding of her heart. She had no intention of joining in, she did not want to. She felt so far out of her depth that she was drowning. And she was frightened. More rooms, some doors open and some not. More shadows, more voices, the scent of lust swam sickeningly around her. The Lustful Lady was like no other place she had ever been before, and the ache in Marietta's chest, the fluttering in her stomach, told her that she did not want to be one of these creatures inside the rooms. Never, ever! Indeed, she could not think of anything worse.

There was a staircase at the end of the hallway. She was hesitating, her hand upon the balustrade, when she heard a sound behind her. The scrape of a boot on the wooden floor, the rustle of clothing. With a gasp Marietta turned her head and saw, beyond the lamp's feeble glow, the large shadow of a man. And he was coming towards her.

For some reason she thought of the man in the shabby brown coat she had seen twice before, the man with the rugged face and beady eyes. What if he had been following her about? What if he had followed her here?

With a whimper of panic she began to ascend the stairs, tripping on her skirts and catching at the wooden railing with shaking fingers. She didn't want to look again but she couldn't seem to help it, and when she turned it was to find her worst fears realized. Now the man was much closer, his face a sinister shadow beneath his hat, his cloak flying out behind him as he strode forward. Nearer he came as she tried to escape up the stairs. He reached the bottom of the staircase just as she reached the top, and then she was fleeing down yet another corridor, her blood pounding in her ears, her mind full of the terrible thought that he was going to drag her into one of the rooms.

The doors along this corridor were closed, but there were still sounds to be heard—cries and whispers—an endless spiral of degradation. The images she had seen were all about her, making her head spin, or perhaps that was because her stays were too tight and she could not breathe. Why had she put foolish vanity before good sense? What did it matter now? Marietta gave a little sob of regret.

And then he was upon her. He caught her about the waist, his big chest against her back, his breath hot in her ear, and with a muffled shriek she fought him, pummeling and scratching at his hands, trying to pull away. It must be a trick! Max wasn't coming at all. She was going to be murdered, but first she was going to be—

"Shhh, Marietta." A whisper against her cheek. "Don't be afraid, darling. It's me."

She nearly burst into tears. "Max?" she gasped.

"I couldn't send Daniel with the coach, he's never been able to keep a secret. I drove it myself and then I had to take it around to the stableyard before I could find you. I should have told you instead of trying to pretend I was somebody else. I didn't have the money to pay anyone else and I didn't want you to know. It was vanity and I'm sorry."

"Oh Max! I thought you were . . ."

"I called out to you just now, but you didn't hear and then you ran away."

She looked into his familiar eyes, brown and warm and smiling ruefully at her from the shadows. She had never seen anything more welcome.

"Max, you gave me such a fright—" She clutched his arm with her gloved fingers and her hood slipped back, revealing the gold of her loosened hair. "What is this place?" her voice was shaking, she cast little anxious glances about her. "I don't think I like it."

"This is an introducing house. Men and women come here to rendezvous with others who like the same pleasures," he explained, smoothing a tendril from her face.

"But they aren't couples! Not all of them."

She had amused him, though he was trying hard not to smile at her. Marietta squirmed in his arms, embarrassed by her own naiveté, but he would not let her go.

"Some of these people like to share, and some don't—that's why the doors are open or closed. I suppose it's all a matter of taste. You must remember, Marietta, that places like this are home to many a jaded palate. After years of seeking out every pleasure available, no matter how perverse, I imagine many a gentleman—and lady—needs something different to titillate their senses. I have heard there is even a whipping room . . ."

Marietta felt a curl of nausea in her stomach. She felt no urge to become one of these jaded pleasure-seekers, and yet she had a terrible feeling that many of the women who came here had once been in exactly the same position as herself.

Max reclaimed her attention. "Don't worry, Marietta, I'm not a man who likes to share. I'll keep you safe."

Being here with him did make her feel better, but she wouldn't tell him so. She knew she must learn to be bold, although tonight Marietta didn't feel bold. She felt young and frightened and ridiculously innocent.

"I'm not worried," she said in what she hoped was a breezy and confident voice.

Max's strong arm tightened about her waist, and he led her forward, ignoring the rooms they passed. At the far end of the corridor was a room that was unoccupied, and he turned into it.

Curiously, Marietta glanced about her as he closed the door. A branch of candles had been lit, and the flames wavered in the stir of air. She could see a divan along one wall, and chairs and a table set with a jug of wine and two metal goblets. Everything looked clean enough, and yet there was a secondhand seediness about it she found repellent. How many other couples had stood here, just as they were, contemplating the pleasures of the flesh? What desperate and depraved scenes had these walls witnessed?

Max was standing, watching her, as she took everything in, and his face was somber. She gave him a tentative smile, suddenly so glad that he was here that she ached with it.

"Marietta," Max murmured, and captured her fingers, bringing them up to his lips. She felt his mouth through her glove, and then his warm breath against her wrist as he kissed the only bare skin available to him.

"Your wound," she said. She could see that the doctor's stitches had been removed, leaving a reddened scar that would, she hoped, fade, although Max's wild curls helped to hide it.

"All better," he said, as her fingers lightly brushed his forehead. She stroked his cheek, and he closed his eyes, as if her touch made him as lightheaded as his did her. She stretched up and tenderly kissed the scar on his chin, wondering at herself as she did so.

His eyes flickered open, surprise in their depths.

"We're supposed to be lovers who can only meet in secret," she felt the need to excuse her actions. "I'm just playing my part."

Down the hallway there were a series of noisy shouts and then a woman screamed like a banshee. It might have been bloody murder but Marietta knew it was simply an excess of pleasure. She turned large eyes on Max and bit her lip to stop herself from laughing. Max shook his head and grinned back at her.

There was an uncomfortable moment, as if neither

of them knew what to do or say next, and then Max said, "We are only allowed the room for an hour."

"Oh." The knowledge that their time was so short made her feel awkward, despite all they had done last night. Suddenly Marietta wished herself miles away.

Max wondered what she was thinking. Aphrodite had chosen the Lustful Lady with a purpose. She had wanted Marietta to see what some women were reduced to, were dragged down to, and Max had agreed with her choice because he wanted to observe Marietta's reaction. Just as he had expected, when he had caught up with her Marietta had been both appalled and afraid. He hadn't helped, he supposed, by chasing her like that but she hadn't heard him calling and he'd been afraid she might blunder into one of the occupied rooms.

She must see now that if she continued along the course she was traveling, then she could well be reduced to visiting a place like this on a regular basis. Degradation was something that happened over time, and unless she was very lucky Marietta would get there, eventually. The Lustful Lady was the ultimate destination of many desperate and unhappy people.

But Max was determined that wouldn't happen to Marietta; he meant to fight for her, whether she wanted him to or not.

"Darling Marietta," he whispered, willing for her sake to put aside all his plans to shock her into submission. "We don't have to stay here. We can go somewhere else. Or I can take you home."

"It's not so bad," she said, and took a shaky breath.

"You don't have to stay—"

"But I do," she said in a soft little voice that sounded almost plaintive. "I do have to stay, Max. I have to complete my task so that Aphrodite will help me become a courtesan."

He wanted to argue with her, he wanted to point out to her that many of these women thought they would be wealthy and famous courtesans too. But with a little smile, Marietta wound her arms about his neck, and tugged his face down to hers. Her lips closed on his, eager and warm and wonderful.

And Max asked himself, as he returned her kisses eagerly, just who was seducing whom.

Chapter 15

Desire for Max caught her in its tight grasp, and Marietta could have wept with joy and sorrow. This was a horrible place, but she could bear it because Max was here, and once she had completed her allotted task she need never return.

Not even for a rendezvous with one of your gentlemen?

My gentlemen will not come to places like this!

But the voice only laughed mockingly.

Desperately, to block it out, she kissed Max again, and he responded just as hungrily. Her body tingled, her breasts tightened and her legs trembled—but that didn't matter so much, because his arm came around her waist and held her steady, pressed her hard against him.

His lips trailed down her cheek, down to her throat, and he breathed her in, tasting her skin. Tremors ran through her.

"I've missed you," he said. "I've wanted you all day and you weren't there."

She managed a choked laugh. "I'm here now."

His mouth came back to claim hers, and again he kissed her deeply, until her body began to burn and she could hardly take a breath.

"The divan?" he suggested huskily.

Marietta gave it an uneasy glance, wondering how many dozens of men and women had coupled there.

He seemed to read her mind, and with a low laugh he turned her around, so that her back was to his chest. "Max?" she asked, thrown by his change in tactics. But instead of answering he cupped her breasts, molding their shape with his palms, and she arched into his hands eagerly. His open mouth was hot against the side of her neck, nuzzling into her hair, all the while his fingers caressing her aching flesh against her own clothing.

"Bend over," he murmured, and she felt his pressure on her shoulders, easing her down to the table. Dizzy with the pleasure he was giving her, she did as he said, and then he was hauling up her skirts, what seemed like miles and miles of velvet and net and petticoats, until he finally came to her drawers.

His hands lingered on the thin cotton, cupping her bottom, caressing her hips. And then he reached around her waist and released the ribbon ties, and her drawers fell down to her ankles. The air was cool against her naked thighs and bottom, soothing the heated place between her legs. She felt his fingers against her skin but no longer just a feather-brush of sensation. He was caressing her strongly, and then he gripped her thighs, edging them apart, and she felt his own muscular thigh, pressing between hers, widening her still further.

"Max?" she said on a shaky breath, and then

groaned as he began to stroke her firmly between her thighs, using his thumb to caress that swollen nub, until her legs trembled and shook. She gasped, her gloved hands clenched together in front of her, and jerked her hips, reaching for that pinnacle she could feel was so close.

But he wasn't ready yet.

Max hadn't taken off his breeches, for she could feel the coarse cloth of them against the soft skin of her thighs as he pressed against her. And then she felt the thick and rigid length of him probing her, sliding against her slick and swollen flesh. She went very still, hardly daring to breathe as he sought entry, and found it.

At first he entered her just a little bit, and at this angle she felt her body stretching to accommodate his size. He pressed harder, trapping her between him and the table, driving into her aching flesh until she was gasping and pounding her fists on the table, and begging him, "Please, oh please, do it now!"

His splayed fingers were hot against her belly, tilting her back against his groin, and then he slid his forefinger down between her swollen lips and rubbed against her. Marietta whimpered, and then wriggled against him, urgently trying to get him to hurry up.

He slid into her again, further this time, filling her. His breath was warm against her nape as he bent over her, and murmured in her ear, "Come with me to Blackwood."

Startled from her all-consuming passion, Marietta half turned to gape at him, but almost at once his fingers stroked her again, playing her expertly, and all thought left her. He was thrusting into her more deeply now, and although she tried to push back, to keep up the rhythm, she felt as if she were being buffeted by a sensual storm.

And it felt perfect. It felt right.

Suddenly it was too much and she cried out, her body clenching around him. He stilled, groaned deep in his throat, and thrust one last time, so deep, and collapsed against her.

For a moment all was bliss, and then in another she realized she couldn't catch her breath. She was gasping, the candle-lit room spinning about her, her tight stays preventing her from breathing.

"Max," she choked. "Undo me . . . please . . . can't *breathe* . . ."

He seemed to realize what she wanted, and with a curse, opened the buttons and hooks on her dress with swift, sure hands, roughly pulling apart her bodice, so that he could find the ties of her stays.

"Hurry," she said weakly. She felt like a fish thrown upon the shore, floundering and flapping about uselessly.

He loosened the ties on her stays with quick, practiced fingers, and the pressure upon her lungs eased. She took a grateful gulp of air. And then another. He rubbed her abdomen, gently, keeping her from sinking to the floor, and gradually the room stopped moving and she began to feel herself again.

"Why do you wear these cursed things?" Max demanded, frowning down at her.

"Because I am not the right shape for my clothes," she said, as if he was an idiot.

He blinked at her, then let his eyes slide over her

body, at her breasts spilling out of the open dress, at her lush curves that were already making him hard again. "Wear clothes that fit then," he suggested sensibly.

"If I wore my clothes without a corset then I would look . . . well, I am too plump, Max. The queen has been called fat all her life, and it is the same with me. We are both short, plump women, but she is a queen and at least people do not dare comment to her face. It is different for me. I have always been the short sister, the plump sister—the disgraced sister. The odd one out."

He still didn't look as if he believed what he was hearing. He shook his head, and when he replied he spoke in the reasonable tone one used for people who belonged in Bedlam. "Marietta, you are the most beautiful woman I have ever known. I grant you that you need to be covered, but only because otherwise all men will want you. If you came to Cornwall with me, you would never need to wear clothing—in fact I would insist that you did not."

Her laughter was unrestrained.

"I am serious," he retorted, but his eyes were warm. "I want access to you day or night . . . day *and* night."

"Won't the servants notice?" she asked, but there were tears in her eyes.

"Blackwood is a big house. I'm sure we could find lots of corners to hide away in while we continue our lessons."

She shook her head. "I can't come with you to Blackwood," she said quietly.

"I'm asking you to marry me," he replied a little desperately.

"I know you are. I will never marry. I cannot take the risk. Besides, you're in a vulnerable position right now, you probably don't know what you're saying. You need to think hard about your future, Max, not saddle yourself with a fallen woman like me."

"Don't treat me like an imbecile," he sounded cross. "I know what I want."

"Max, there's no point to this conversation. I have already made up my mind. Don't spoil our time together. Just accept that you must go to Cornwall and I must learn to be a courtesan."

He turned away from her and said nothing, but she could tell by the tension in his shoulders that there was much he was thinking.

"You want me," he said quietly. "That won't go away, Marietta. Believe me, it will only get worse."

She shrugged as if she didn't believe him, but there was a sinking feeling in her stomach. Because he was right, she *did* want him, and it *was* getting worse. But somehow she would have to learn to live with that, she would have to carry on with her life and forget Max. Depression sank over her like a London fog but she refused to acknowledge it. Instead she dredged up the memories of the pain she had suffered after her mistake with Gerard Jones, lingering over her misery and suffering, remembering how she had sworn she would never offer her heart up like a sacrifice again.

Max might seem the perfect choice but could she risk it? And in taking the risk, ruin all hope she might have of becoming a courtesan like her mother? She could end up alone and with no future. And yet . . .

Why is he tempting me like this!

Irritably she began to straighten her clothing, leaving her bodice undone and drawing her cloak around as protection against prying eyes. Her body was still throbbing and aching with the aftershocks of Max's lovemaking, but she could not think of that now. She dared not imagine what it would be like to have him by her side always. What was the point in tormenting herself with romantic endings when her heart would not survive being broken again?

Max was watching her as he rearranged his own clothing with a few sharp tugs and twists of buttons, and she suspected he was plotting her downfall. He held out his arm with an ironic, "Home, my lady?"

She tried a jaunty smile, and although he gave her a brief smile in return, there was something about the set of his lips that increased her suspicion that he had not given up. That he meant to have his way.

She opened her mouth to list again all the reasons it wouldn't, couldn't work, and then changed her mind. Max would just have to accept her decision, and if she stood firm then he would have no option but to give up. It was the "standing firm" part that was beginning to worry her.

Marietta could not sleep. She tossed and turned, remembering Max kissing her, holding her, and the hard strength of his body plundering hers.

I cannot go with him, she told herself.

Why not? If there's a chance of finding the sort of happiness Vivianna has, then surely it's worth the risk?

I promised myself I would never take such a risk again.

Promises can be broken. You're a coward.

Maybe I am, but I cannot give in to him.

But still her body ached and tormented her, and her brain hurt with arguing against itself, until she gave up and lit the candle.

Aphrodite's diary was there on the table, and she picked it up and began to read

I am alone, always alone. I do not want to be alone. Even though I cannot have Jemmy, I can have happiness. Can't I? Am I growing so old that I long for the days I have left behind me? Perhaps I need a family—a family of my own—to love and care for.

F. is a gruff man, but I believe beneath that scratchy exterior there is a real warmth and longing to be loved. We have made a pact. He is without an heir and has no intention of marrying; I am alone and want a child and have no intention of marrying. So we will make a child together, he and I, and he will have his heir and I will have someone of my own to love.

A girl. I will call her Vivianna. F. is not so pleased, he had it in mind that I would give him a braw son, but I am content. We will keep her existence a secret until she is needed. I have been looking for a home in the country, somewhere she will be safe and happy and I can visit her very often. Suddenly my life does not seem so bleak . . .

I have met A. He is sweet and gentle, and he tells me he worships me as the sun worships the moon. I do not quite know how that could be so, but still he makes me smile. I think I could have a child with A., if he is agreeable. We will see.

I saw Jemmy today.

It was as if my heart stopped, and started

again with a cannon's roar. It was Jemmy, I knew him, even though he is older. Now he is a man when I only knew him as a boy.

I was in my carriage, on my way to see A., when suddenly he was there, driving a wagon for a brewery. At first he looked as if his thoughts were weighty indeed, and then someone called out to him from the street, someone he knew, and he laughed. And then I knew him for Jemmy, my beloved Jemmy.

I could not go on to A.. I turned back for my home, and then I wept in my room for times gone and chances lost. Stupid, I know, but that is how I feel these days. A. will understand, he is always so sympathetic.

A. wants a child. He says there is no woman he loves more than me, and if he does not take this opportunity then he never will. And so I think, why not? Vivianna will have a playmate, and maybe this new child will ease the constant ache in my heart.

I have another daughter. A. wants to call her Marietta, after his grandmother, he says. She is beautiful, a delightfully happy child. And yes, she has eased my heart, how could she not? I will think of Jemmy no more; it does no good to grieve for something that cannot be changed.

It was I who left him, and I have no right to want him back again.

Marietta sighed and put the book down. It hardly had the cheering effect she had hoped for. Aphrodite was unhappy, longing for the one man she could not have. But despite that longing she had accepted her lot and made herself content; she had found another reason to live.

The balloon was on the ground, perfectly still—there was not a breath of air as Mr. Keith made preparations for the approaching fireworks evening. Lil watched Ian hurry about, checking this and that, then double-checking. He was working out the logistics of setting off the fireworks. They were to be placed underneath the wicker basket and everything must be just so. If one should go astray and strike the envelope that held the gas . . . well, to put it bluntly, they would fall to earth and die.

"I trust you," Lil had said, when he expressed concern for her. "I wouldn't be 'ere if I didn't, would I?"

Ian smiled. "Thank you, Lil." His smile wavered. "But you don't trust me enough to tell me the truth, do you?"

She looked away, shrugged. "There's nothin' to tell," she said.

Ian sighed. "I know that's not true. I am very fond of you, Lil, and it hurts me that you can't tell me about yourself without worrying that I might somehow think less of you. I couldn't."

It was very sweet of him, thought Lil, but the truth was she was terrified. If she told him that once she had walked the streets—well, huddled miserably in the streets would be a better description, selling her scrawny body to pay her Ma's rent—he would . . . what? She tried to imagine it now. The worst scenario would be if he was so repelled that he never spoke to her again. The second worst would be if he looked upon her with gentle pity, as if she were dying of some dreadful disease. Yes, that *would* be bad.

She couldn't risk it.

For the first time in her life Lil had found a man to love and admire—not a servant like Jacob or a gentleman who loved someone else, like Mr. Jardine. A man who loved *her*! Lil didn't want to take the chance she might lose him.

And yet she was beginning to think that if she didn't she might lose him anyway.

"Max, you must know you can't possibly have anything to do with this girl! She is beyond redemption."

Max cast his cousin so angry a look that Harold was taken aback. Good, it was time someone showed Harold he could not run the world to his liking. If Harold had his way, then everyone with an aristocratic pedigree would be on one side of the fence, and those without one on the other, and as for women like Marietta . . . they would probably be cast into the Thames. Well, if necessary, Max would be quite prepared to join her there!

"I can do what I like, Harold," he said softly. "That's the thing about being disinherited, you see. I no longer have to please my father, or my family. It's quite liberating, actually."

Harold clicked his tongue angrily, but Susannah reached to place a soothing hand upon his arm. "Please, stop it, both of you. Max, you are in a state. This girl has worked her way under your skin and now you cannot think clearly. You are not yourself. Won't you please stop and consider what you're doing?"

"But I am myself," he said with a smile. "That's the whole point. I am more myself than I have ever been."

Harold straightened his sleeves and brushed a speck off his trousers. "Susannah, my love, would you mind leaving Max and I alone for a moment?"

She looked as if she would rather not, but then she gave an irritable sigh and rose elegantly to her feet. "I'll leave you then, shall I? To speak of manly things?"

"Susannah," Harold began.

But she waved a languid hand as she opened the door. "No, never mind. I will amuse myself by asking Mrs. Pomeroy for a list of the townhouse contents, for when we come to live—" She caught Max's glance and gave a helpless shrug. "I'm sorry, but life moves on, Max. We must be practical about these matters. I love you dearly, you know, but I have always been a practical sort of woman."

"I know," he said quietly. "I understand."

She hesitated a moment more, but there was nothing further to say and they both knew it.

"She does her best," Harold said quietly, when the door had shut behind her. "She's feeling a little low, and she's never been strong. Sometimes she remembers the past, when she was a girl in Jamaica, and it upsets her. She dreams of going home. More than you think, Max."

"I thought that was all behind her. She's lived in England most of her life, this is her home now. Her real father died, didn't he?"

"You don't understand, and she doesn't speak of it. Susannah is still a Creole at heart. I have promised myself that one day I will take her back to see the old plantation house where she grew up."

"I thought Father pulled it down. He was never very sentimental about things like that. He never talks about those days, you know. I've asked him and he always avoids the subject. It's as if he feels . . . guilty about it."

Harold shrugged. "Maybe he does, maybe what he did in Jamaica wasn't strictly legal, but he was only thinking of saving Valland House for his family."

"Hardly comfort for Susannah though, was it?"

"She is very fond of you, Max. It's not her fault that this has happened to you."

"I know that, I'm not saying it is!"

Harold cleared his throat. "No need to get niggledy with me, cousin, this isn't my fault either. I'm just trying to talk some sense into you. This girl is completely unsuitable and if you marry her it won't just be your life that is affected. We will all suffer the consequences. Besides, how could you possibly support a wife without help from the family? You can't have it both ways you know, Max; you can't cast yourself off from the family without a backward glance, only to then turn around and beg for an allowance."

"I don't want an allowance." Max was furious, and although he tried to moderate his tone, Harold's eyes widened in mock-alarm.

"Now old chap—"

"I don't want anything from any of you. Can't you understand that? My life is no longer your business, Harold, and I won't have you interfering!"

Harold stood up and his mouth was pinched, as it always was when he was upset. "Very well then, if that's what you want, cousin. I am leaving now because you obviously can't think straight. This girl has turned your brain. God knows what else she's done to you—I don't want to know—but I think you will be very, very sorry. Of course I will have to tell the duke."

Max stared at him in amazement. Was he a child, that his cousin should treat him thus? "Harold," he said quietly, "haven't you realized yet that I don't give a damn who you talk to? Make a speech in Parliament. Take out an advertisement in the *Times*. Please, Harold, be my guest!"

Harold gave him one last glare, and left the room.

Max sank back into his chair, feeling as if he had been wrung dry. Surely his family never used to be so concerned with his private affairs? He could remember several times being involved with women who were clearly unsuitable as permanent mates, and nothing was said.

That's because you never intended to marry them.

Of course not!

Because you weren't in love with them.

No, I wasn't.

But you are in love with Marietta Greentree. Aren't you?

That was when Max knew it to be true. And it was almost a relief; it explained the way he had been feeling lately. He *was* in love with Marietta Greentree. His life would be barren without her. And yet how to convince *her* of that?

He supposed he couldn't blame her for refusing to marry him and go to Cornwall. What had he to offer after all? He was a disinherited pauper, at least compared to what he had been. Marietta was probably better off without him . . .

His eyes flared and he clenched his fists. *Damn it, no!* He wouldn't give in, he would fight for her. She must realize that they were meant for each other. She must!

Outside in Bedford Square, Harold settled his wife into their carriage, fussing about her until she told him to stop.

"Max has upset you," Susannah said quietly. "You are very fond of him, aren't you, Harold?"

"As you are, my dear." Harold sighed and sank back in his seat as they began to move off. "I feel as if I have failed him in some way, as if there was something I should have said or done to resolve this mess."

"Papa was very angry and we cannot blame him for that."

"No, but I thought..." He sighed again, and smiled at his wife. "I thought he would have come around by now and realized that even if Max isn't his son he still loves him like a son. Max doesn't deserve to be treated like this, Susannah."

"Life is cruel," she murmured, staring back at him with big, dark eyes. "Often there are no happy endings. God doesn't give us justice, we have to find if for ourselves."

"But the duke will come around," Harold insisted. "I know he will. I just hope that when he does it won't be too late to save Max from himself."

"Yes, we can only hope it will not be too late."

Amy Greentree stroked Marietta's hair, her long fingers gentle and soothing. She had her foot propped up on a stool and was seated in an armchair in her bedroom, ostensibly resting but in reality enjoying a peaceful moment with her second daughter.

"You have not had an easy time recently, Marietta,

I know that. I wish you had never met that dreadful man."

Marietta glanced upwards at her mother. "Man?" she murmured, thinking, *Max, she knows about Max!*

"That Jones creature. I loathed him the first time I saw him, with his smirk and his bowing and scraping. So false, my dear. But you could not see it, you were blinded by your infatuation." She sighed. "Of course, he was very handsome, and I behaved very stupidly in forbidding you to see him. Vivianna wrote and told me that I should allow him to visit us often, so that you would come to realize what a beast he was. She said that if I forbade you to see him then you would think him all the more fascinating."

Marietta smiled wryly. "I did think he was fascinating. He seemed such a man of the world to me, so clever and witty, and when he stole kisses in the garden I thought him daring."

"And then he was impertinent enough to ask for your hand!" Amy's gray eyes snapped with remembered anger. "I sent him off immediately and told you that you were never to see him again."

Marietta sighed. "He persuaded Francesca to carry a note to me. She has never forgiven him for it. In the note he asked me to elope with him, but in the most romantic terms."

"Ah, romance." Amy smiled. "There is nothing wrong with romance, dear child. Indeed it is something we should all aspire to. But romance sometimes needs to be mixed with a good dash of common sense."

"Anyway I have grown out of that nonsense now," Marietta retorted.

Amy laughed. "Then you are the poorer for it," she teased. "Every man, woman, and child dreams about being loved, Marietta. There is nothing wrong in it."

"He knew just what to say to capture my silly heart," she answered without inflection, "but it was all a game to him, and once he had taken the prize . . ."

"Yes," Amy was sober again. "When I found you gone I was so angry. I sent Mr. Jardine to find him with a horsewhip—"

"A horsewhip!"

Amy smiled. "I have never told you this, Marietta. Mr. Jardine caught up with him a few miles south. The creature had stopped to enjoy a nap under a tree along the road. I don't think he can ever have closed his eyes again without remembering the awakening he had that day!"

Marietta gasped. "Do you mean Mr. Jardine—"

"Yes, dearest, he did." Amy sighed. "But unfortunately that dreadful Rawlings had already spread his poisonous gossip. Impossible to hush it up," she smoothed her daughter's ringlets from her cheek. "Well it is over and done, now."

Marietta giggled at the image of Mr. Jardine with a horsewhip. Her own actions seemed ridiculous to her now, so naïve. Max Valland was more of a man than Gerard Jones would ever be. She wished she had known Max then. If Gerard had never existed, then perhaps she might have considered Max's offer, for if Gerard had never existed then she would never have had her heart broken and her reputation ruined.

It was all very unfair.

"You know that whatever you wish to do, I will support you." Amy was looking down into Marietta's eyes with her own calm gray ones.

Marietta knew then that Amy probably understood her hopes and dreams—understood *her*—better than anyone. Tears welled in her eyes and blurred that beloved face. "I don't seem to know what I want," she said tremulously. "That is the trouble, Mama."

Amy dabbed away her daughter's tears with her lacey handkerchief. "Hush. You are not a child now, Marietta, you are a woman grown. You are intelligent and sensible and there is no need to rush into anything. Take your time, Marietta, and think deeply. You will know what you want when you find it."

Marietta thought she was probably right. The only problem was that she had already seen what she wanted. It was just a pity that she couldn't have him.

Chapter 16

Francesca had insisted that since she was in London she wanted to visit the Tower of London. Marietta, dragging a reluctant Lil after her, plodded behind her sister as best she could, but she had difficulty keeping up with Francesca's longer legs. Francesca was inspired by the grim place, with its cawing ravens and blood-soaked history. Marietta suspected that her sister was already planning to create a bleak little watercolor to commemorate her visit.

Afterwards they did some shopping and set off for home. Marietta found herself yawning, and knew it was Max's fault. She was worn out, she couldn't sleep for tossing and turning and thinking of him, while her body tingled infuriatingly. It would not do, it really wouldn't. Somehow she would have to put a stop to it. But not yet, no, not yet.

Aphrodite had sent a note to tell her that her next task was to attend the masque ball at Vauxhall Gardens, incognito, and meet Max there. It was an event she had always dreamed of attending, and to go with Max seemed like a dream come true. Marietta knew that until the ball was over she would not make any decisions concerning Max.

Back at the townhouse in Berkley Square, she received a shock. Hodge the butler, after directing a servant to take her parcels, informed her in the hushed tones he only used for the most important of visitors, that there was "a distinguished person" asking to speak to her privately.

"A distinguished person? Who is this person, Hodge?" She knew her eyes were big and that Hodge was enjoying being mysterious.

"The Duke of Barwon," he replied quietly. "He's in the best sitting room, with Lord Montegomery."

Marietta stared, wondering if she had heard him correctly, but Hodge wasn't likely to be playing some elaborate joke on her. The *Duke of Barwon?* Why on earth, she thought, her heart skipping a beat, did Max's father want to see her "privately"? And then the second part of Hodge's answer penetrated her muddled brain. "Is Oliver home?" she asked in a hopeful voice.

"Yes, miss, he arrived an hour ago."

Marietta was very relieved that Oliver was there. She had no desire whatsoever to meet with Max's father—if he was anything like Harold then she could only expect hostility from him, especially if Harold had spoken to him about her. In fact that was what it must be about. Harold had discovered she was still seeing Max and he had gone to a higher authority.

Because Max wouldn't have told his father that

he had asked her to marry him, would he? A disgraced nobody from Yorkshire? Surely he would not do anything so impetuous or so silly. Would he? And yet he *had* seemed very determined and Max was the sort of man who was used to having his way . . .

Whatever the head of the Valland family wanted from her, Marietta suspected it was nothing good.

"Marietta?" Francesca had been observing her, curiosity making her dark eyes even more catlike than usual. "Who is the Duke of Barwon, and what can he want with you?"

"I was just asking myself the same thing," she retorted, and smoothed her skirts. "Do I look presentable? Should I go and change into my red and green silk?" Since Max had released her from her stays Marietta had been wary about lacing herself too tightly and had been wearing her older dresses. The sensation of gasping like a fish at the Lustful Lady had cured her of starving herself of air.

Francesca's gaze raked her impatiently—her sister was not interested in fashion. "You look perfectly all right, Marietta." She leaned closer, so that Hodge couldn't hear. "It's about a man, isn't it, 'Etta? I knew it the moment I set eyes on you. You have that *look*."

Marietta blinked in surprise, for once not feigned. "What look?"

"That satisfied look."

She gaped at Francesca, but before she could deny it, they were interrupted.

"Marietta?"

It was Vivianna, standing just outside the door to

the best sitting room. She looked flushed and happy, happier than she had looked in days. That was because Oliver was home, Marietta thought with relief, but her relief soon vanished when she noted the glitter of anger in her sister's hazel eyes.

"Come here and speak with the duke," she said, catching Marietta's arm in ungentle fingers and giving her no time to protest. "I think after what you've been up to it's the least you can do."

The first thing Marietta saw as she entered the room was Oliver, standing by the window, his hands behind his back. He appeared tired, the strain evident in the dark shadows under his eyes, but when he looked at his wife his face lit up. Nearby, and standing in a similar pose, was a tall, thin man who was an older and less handsome version of Max. His dark hair was graying, but was still curly, and his thick brows were drawn down so low that she could hardly see the color of his eyes as he turned them on her.

For a moment he just stared rudely and Marietta stared back, and then Oliver stepped forward and said, "Your Grace, this is my sister-in-law, Miss Marietta Greentree. Marietta, this is His Grace, the Duke of Barwon."

He did not hold out his hand, his expression did not alter from rigid disapproval, and Marietta felt her heart sink even further. But she refused to look away from that critical gaze. She had done nothing wrong, she reminded herself. What was between her and Max was their business and had nothing to do with the duke, or any of the Valland family. They had cast him off, after all.

But the duke did look very much like Max. It was absurd that he would not believe they were father and son.

"My nephew, Harold, tells me, Miss Greentree, that he has asked you to desist from visiting my son at his townhouse in Bedford Square."

Vivianna made a hissing sound, but Marietta forestalled her. "That is correct, Your Grace, he has."

"But you are still seeing my son."

"Not at Bedford Square, however, Your Grace."

"Do you think I am interested in the detail?" he demanded roughly, and turned away, stalking toward the mantel and back again. Marietta watched him with uneasy fascination. He was so like Max it was uncanny.

"Surely," she swallowed. "Your Grace, surely whether or not I meet with your son is no longer any concern of yours. He tells me that he has severed all connection with his family."

"My sister is very forthright," Vivianna stepped in, casting Marietta a warning look, but the duke wasn't listening to her.

"You're quite correct," he said to Marietta. "I have disinherited my son." For a moment he looked lost, as if the enormity of what he had done was about to swallow him up, and then he straightened his already straight back and carried on. "Harold is concerned for my . . . for Max's well-being. He tells me that you have an unsavory reputation, Miss Greentree."

This time it was Oliver who stepped forward, and all the humor had gone from his startling blue eyes. "You overstep yourself, sir."

"I am only repeating what I have been told," the duke said, barely glancing at him. "I would like to hear what your sister has to say on the matter. Max, so Harold tells me, is indifferent to the effect this will have on him and his family. He declares his intention of marrying her whatever her reputation. Ah!" he nodded his head as the shock flared in Marietta's eyes. "You did not know this, did you, girl? Or have you refused him already? You should know better than to refuse a young man in the passionate throes of love—it only makes him more determined."

"Max knows I am not going to marry," she said at last, but her lips felt stiff and her loosened stays suddenly far too tight. "Not him nor anybody else. As you so rightly said, sir, my reputation precludes me from making any sort of respectable marriage. I am content to remain unwed."

He smiled, and the resemblance to Max was even more striking. "I can see why he likes you," he murmured to himself. Then, the glower back, "I will be frank with you, Miss Marietta, as you have been frank with me. My son . . . Max has been disinherited, yes, but even so the title of his wife is one that you can never aspire to."

Marietta wondered why she suddenly felt so very, very angry. Her cheeks flushed and her eyes grew fiery. She had never aspired to be the duchess of anything, and yet she could not bear that this man was refusing to allow her to imagine herself in that role, however unlikely it might be.

"You have destroyed his life and now you think you can tell him what he can and can't do? You underestimate your son, sir. He will not forgive you for your treatment of him, and he will certainly not follow your orders. Why should he? Max is his own man now."

The duke's expression darkened; if possible his brows came down even lower. "You know nothing of my son. You should remember, Miss Greentree, to whom you are speaking."

Marietta knew to whom she was speaking, and she didn't like him one bit. Mr. Jardine had told her that Barwon was a cold man who saw life's twists and turns as straight lines, who did not allow the morality of a situation to prevent him from ploughing ahead through the feelings of others. Now he wanted to control Max's life even though he no longer recognized him as his son. Max would never stand for that.

"Max is a grown man, sir, and you can't—"

Barwon drew himself up taller so that he could stare down at her. Despite herself Marietta was intimidated, but she did not step back.

"Do not test my patience, Miss Greentree, by presuming to tell me what I can and can't do! Only my wife has ever been able to order me and . . ." He seemed to remember then that his wife was lost to him by more than death, that she had hurt him beyond bearing, and his face twisted as he fought the pain. But evidently it was too much for him. His Grace, the Duke of Barwon, walked out of the room.

With a speaking look at his wife, Oliver followed. Marietta could feel Vivianna's eyes on her, like little daggers in her back. She took a breath and turned to face her sister. What she saw frightened her. Vivianna had always protected her and looked after her. She loved Vivianna, and knew Vivianna loved her, but there was no love in her face now—just a hard, angry dislike.

"How could you?" she whispered. "You have put Oliver in an untenable position. What do you think you are doing, meeting Max Valland incognito? Do you think this is a game? The scandal last time was bad enough, but now you mean to embroil us in another one! I will never forgive you for this, Marietta. Never!"

Tears fell from her eyes and she fled from the room.

Marietta stood, shocked. She knew her own face was white, because when Oliver came back into the room he walked straight over to her, took her in his arms, and held her. She didn't cry, although she felt like it.

"I didn't mean to harm you or Vivianna," she said in a little voice. "I would never do that, Oliver."

"I know, 'Etta. Vivianna knows it too, she's just upset."

"She hates me."

"The baby tires her, and with me being away . . . She's worried about you—she thinks she's failed you and her mother by neglecting you. You slipped beneath her watchful eye and she's berating herself for that. Forgive her, Marietta."

But Marietta wondered whether Vivianna would forgive *her*, especially when she learned her wayward sister had no intention of changing her mind. Hard to ask forgiveness and not alter one's behavior one jot.

"What do you plan to do about Max Valland?" Oliver said softly, and held her away, his handsome face somber as he gazed down at her. "Has he asked you to marry you?"

"Yes, he's asked me. And he's asked me to go to

Cornwall with him," she admitted, "but I've told him no. He knows I can't, he knows I have other plans and that I won't let my heart be broken again."

Oliver shook his head at her. "But 'Etta," he said gently, "you can't guard your heart. It's impossible. And if you do . . . well, you will never be properly alive if you don't love. I know you've been hurt but you can't go into hiding because of it. Your heart will shrivel and die if you don't give it a chance to love again."

"You just heard what Max's father said," she wailed. "He won't let me marry Max anyway, I'm not good enough, so I'm right to refuse. I'm right to protect myself from being wounded all over again."

Marietta turned and fled, following Vivianna up the stairs and slamming her door.

Max looked at his father and said nothing. The duke had arrived half an hour ago, and Max had kept him waiting while he finished the letter he was writing to the estate manager in Cornwall, explaining that he would be arriving in the not-too-distant future to take up permanent residence. That done, he had joined his father in the upstairs drawing room, where Pomeroy had served a tray of his wife's excellent tea and scones.

"Come to see if I have vacated the townhouse yet?" he asked, sitting down, as if they had not been estranged for months.

The duke cast him a droll look, and sipped his tea. "As a matter of fact I have just been to see your . . . Miss Greentree."

Max wondered if he looked as angry as he felt.

Perhaps he did, because his father stopped sipping and set his cup down as if he feared it might end up in his lap.

"You're interfering in my private business, sir."

"You are my son."

"I am not your son, you've made that abundantly clear."

Barwon cleared his throat, and suddenly he looked old and tired—a different man from the bitter and blindly furious one Max remembered. He asked himself what his father was doing here, prodding at the wounds. Was it possible . . . could it be that he was having regrets? If so it was too late and this was madness, painful madness, and it wasn't doing either of them any good.

"I . . . I want to make you an allowance, Max. Of course Harold and Susannah must have the lion's share of the estate, that's only just, but I want you to remain a part of the family. I am going to formally adopt you as my son. There will be some legal details to sort out, but . . . well, soon everything will be settled, and . . . You'll be my son again."

He was smiling, looking pleased with himself, as if he thought that was all that needed to be said. It was unbelievable! Max was speechless and shaking with hurt and anger. Worse still, the duke seemed to take his silence for compliance, and reached out to grasp Max's arm.

Max jerked back as if from a striking snake. Slowly, stiffly, he rose to his feet, looking every bit as formidable as the duke.

"I will not take anything from *you*, sir. I will not have anything of *yours*. Please leave."

Barwon appeared shaken. "You don't understand," he said, and his voice had lost all its former arrogant certainty. "When I read your mother's letter it was as if I had sustained a fatal wound. When she died, at least I could mourn her, but then I lost her again and this time I could only hate."

"That wasn't my fault," Max said quietly.

"No," the duke nodded his head slowly, like an old man. He *looked* like an old man, the lines scouring his cheeks, his shoulders bent. "No, it wasn't your fault, Max. When it happened I couldn't think clearly. I wanted to hit out at someone and there was only you left. I-I lost my temper."

"Do you expect me to forgive you?"

"I regret deeply what has been done! I want to make amends, Max. Let me make amends."

Max looked at him bleakly. Where did he begin to explain that the relationship between them could never be the same again, no matter how much money the duke threw at him? Couldn't his father see that? Was he so deluded that he did not realize that it would never be what it was?

"Have you told Harold and Susannah about this plan of yours?"

"It has nothing to do with Harold or Susannah, but I will inform them. I wanted to talk to you first, Max. Besides, Harold will do as he's told."

Max looked at him with dislike. "I see."

"I want to put all this unpleasantness behind us."

At that moment Max felt his anger soar to new levels. He did not think he had ever been this furious before in life, but neither had he felt so free to express it. Being disinherited was more liberating than he could have imagined.

"Do you know, father, I don't care what you want.

I don't even care about Valland House. I'm quite content with mother's house in Cornwall. I'm looking forward to it—I have plans for the old mine. You'd probably scoff at them as paltry, and I would have agreed with you, once. But I don't have to think about the estate any more. I don't have to remember I'm a duke's son and I must behave accordingly, that I have duties and responsibilities, and my life is structured around them. I am simply Max Valland and I am free to do whatever I want to. So I'm going to Cornwall to live . . . with Marietta if she'll have me." He paused, and now his voice dripped ice. "And if you've hurt her, Father, I won't be responsible for my actions."

"For God's sake, Max! Right now you probably don't believe you're worthy of a respectable woman, but stop and think! When I've sorted matters out you'll be able to have your pick again and—" The duke's voice rose and took on a desperate note. "Max! Max, come back!"

But Max had walked out. He could hear his father's voice behind him, one moment angry and the next pleading, but he didn't listen. He walked downstairs and out the front door, ignoring the twittering of Mrs. Pomeroy and Pomeroy's anxious questions. He walked along Bedford Square and into Bloomsbury Street and he kept walking. And for the first time in his life he didn't give a damn if he never saw the Valland townhouse, or his father, again.

Francesca was patting her sister's back, murmuring comforting noises. The door opened and she looked up, her voice anxious as she said, "She won't stop crying." The bed shifted beneath the weight of another person, and Vivianna's gentle hand smoothed aside Marietta's tangled hair so that she could see her flushed, damp cheek and swollen eyes.

"Marietta," she whispered, "my dear. I am so sorry. I don't know what came over me. I do not care if you insult the duke, insult him all you like. I do not care if you insult the whole of London society and poke your tongue out at the queen . . . Well, perhaps not the queen," she added cautiously. "But the rest of them don't matter a jot to me. You are what is important and I think, for a moment there, I forgot that. Forgive me or I will never be able to bear it."

Marietta turned her face and saw that Vivianna was crying too. With a wail she flung herself into her sister's arms, and found that Francesca had joined her.

"We need to be together," Vivianna said, trying to catch her breath on little sobs. "We need to stay together. We've always survived by staying together, and if we don't . . . if one of us should be hurt again, then we will all be hurt."

"All for one," Francesca said in a muffled voice.

Marietta giggled. "And one for all?" she asked, sniffling.

Vivianna nodded seriously. "Exactly."

There was a tap on the door, and Lil stuck her head around it, eyes widening at the sight of the three sisters with their tear-streaked faces. "Sorry to interrupt, my lady, but there's a gentleman downstairs to see Miss Marietta, and he don't look very happy."

Marietta covered her face. "Not the duke again."

Lil shook her head. "Not this time, miss. This time it's his son."

Max, here? Marietta sat up. "I . . . I'm in no state. I can't face him. Not after what his father said."

"Do you love this man?" Francesca asked her seriously. "This Max? I've never seen you like this before, Marietta. Never. I think you must feel something for him."

Marietta looked bleak. "I don't know what I feel. I count the moments until I see him again, and I miss him when I'm not with him, and I dream about him at night when I'm asleep."

Vivianna sighed elaborately. "Oh dear."

"Is *that* love? But what does it matter if I *do* love him? I can't marry him—I've told him so—and I'm afraid," her voice trembled. "Remember what it was like when I was left at that inn and I had to find my own way home . . . I had no money and the wood carter gave me a ride on his wagon, and then Mr. Jardine came and when I-I called out to him he didn't even recognize me. His face." The hot tears ran down her cheeks. "The shock on his face. I felt utterly destroyed. I can't let myself fall so low again, I just can't!"

Vivianna patted her back comfortingly, but her voice was firm. "Marietta, why do you imagine Lord Roseby would ask you to marry him unless he meant it? He is an aristocrat, despite his damaged reputation, a gentleman with connections and class. Frankly he is not the sort to ask you to marry him unless he sincerely wanted you to be his wife. If you love him, Marietta, then you should think very seriously about accepting."

Marietta swallowed nervously. "My heart—"

"Oh bother your heart," Francesca interrupted. "Really, I think you worry too much about getting it broken. You can't go about with it wrapped in tissue paper like a family heirloom, Marietta. Take it out, dust it off and give it another try."

"But how can I face him alone? Perhaps his father has spoken to him and persuaded him to withdraw his offer? What if I say y-yes and he's changed his mind!"

Vivianna hugged her. "We'll all go," she said firmly. "Francesca, too. If he has anything to say to you, dear sister, then he can say it to all of us."

Marietta laughed shakily, but Lil rolled her eyes. "You'd better hurry then," she said dryly. "He looked like the sort of gentleman who'd only wait so long before he came storming up here after you."

When she opened the door, the first thing Marietta thought was that Lil was right. Max looked capable of anything. His face was taut and pale, the healing scar standing out dramatically on his temple, and his dark hair blown into wild curls by the wind. He must have walked here from Bedford Square—she did not put it past him. But it was his eyes that caught and held her attention.

They were burning with raw emotion.

"Max?"

"Marietta." Relief softened his expression briefly, until he saw the other two women behind her. Vivianna and Francesca edged into the room and stood silent and watchful.

"My sisters." She answered his unspoken question. "Lady Montegomery and Miss Francesca Greentree."

Max bowed politely, and she smiled to think that he was so much the gentleman that even in circumstances like these he must do the right thing.

"Can we speak alone?" he asked.

"I . . . no, if you have anything to say I think it should be said before my sisters. Your father has already called here today."

Max sighed. "My father, yes, I see. He has never had any common sense when it comes to dealing with other people's emotions. He thinks it is enough to say sorry." He shook off his melancholy. "I do not ask you to forgive what he said to you, only to consider it in the light of his misguided affection for me."

"He needn't worry," Marietta said stiffly. "I won't marry you, Max. You're quite safe from my unsavory reputation."

Max groaned and looked as if he'd like to tear his hair out.

"Marietta, I don't care about your reputation! We can be happy together. This other nonsense . . . I can't bear to think of you throwing yourself away like this."

"I'm not throwing myself away," she said quickly. "I'm protecting my heart, Max."

"I love you."

There was a tense silence. Francesca caught her breath, and Marietta could imagine what she was thinking—Max as the perfect Byronic hero. Vivianna said, softly, "Lord Roseby, do you know what you are proposing?"

Max's eyes did not leave Marietta. "I want to marry you. I love you." He lifted his arms. "What else can I say?"

Tears were stinging her eyes but she held them in. She had the terrible urge to tell him she loved him, too, and throw herself against him. As she teetered on the edge of the precipice, she remembered Oliver and Vivianna's words, about happiness not being something she should lightly throw away. She had made a bad choice last time, and she had suffered for it, but that did not necessarily mean she would make a bad choice this time. And Max didn't feel like a mistake; he felt completely and utterly right.

Perhaps the time had come to trust her heart once more.

Tentatively Marietta took a step forward, and it was easier than she had imagined. So she took another. Max was watching her, holding himself still, waiting to see what she would do. When she reached him he still didn't move, and now it was as if he was afraid of frightening her away.

She reached up and touched his cheek, the most tender of caresses.

"Yes, Max," she said. Just for a moment it was as if she was falling to earth with a crash, but then the sensation changed and she was floating with happiness.

Max smiled his gorgeous smile. "Marietta," he breathed, and drew her into his arms in front of her sisters as if he had forgotten they were there. Or perhaps he didn't care. "You'll never regret it," he murmured in her ear.

"I hope *you* never regret it," she said in a little voice. "I'm glad you're not going to be a duke, Max, because if you were we would never have met, and I could never have married you." And then she gasped as he held her tighter.

As if he would never let her go.

Vivianna cleared her throat. "Lord Roseby, I think you should release my sister now."

He looked at her, his eyes dazed.

"So that we can congratulate you!" Vivianna added, and came forward with her hands out, her face beaming. Francesca, not far behind, was laughing and saying that when she came to London she never expected to see Marietta agree to be a wife.

By the time he had been welcomed into the Greentree family by Marietta's two sisters, and then by Lady Greentree, who arrived back from visiting Aunt Helen, and Mr. Jardine, who appeared to be more of a family friend than an employee, Max was exhausted. Oliver drew him aside for a glass of brandy, and to tell him quietly that Marietta was a dear girl and he was very fond of her. Which, Max supposed, meant that if he ever did anything to hurt her he'd be in for it.

"Cornwall will be a long way from her sisters," Max said, watching the three women laughing and talking, already making plans for the wedding.

Oliver shrugged. "She can always visit them, and they can visit her. If she is happy she won't notice so much."

"Yes." Max smiled.

Just then Marietta caught his eye and her face lit up. She did love him; he could see it. He was happy, truly happy, and if he hadn't mentioned to her his father's plans to reinstate him in the bosom of the Valland family, then it was because he had refused the offer.

Refused it irrevocably!

Besides, if she thought for one moment that he might be a peer again, then she wouldn't marry him. And Max knew he couldn't bear to lose her now she was finally his.

Chapter 17

A. is an astute businessman—unusual in a gentleman. We spoke of a dream I have had for some years, of setting up an exclusive club in London, where men like himself can come and be entertained by the most beautiful and the most accomplished women.

We have decided the club will be known as Aphrodite's, and A. has spoken to his banker. Together we can run it, and I trust him to be my friend, even when the passion between us cools. He is the sort of man who will never betray me.

There is something I have not told him yet, I didn't know how to. But I am carrying his child. I hope he will be pleased.

Another daughter. I am so happy. My little family seems complete, and although her father and I are no longer lovers, we are close friends

and business partners. Aphrodite's Club pros-
pers. It seems that we are all the rage.

I woke up this morning and realized that I was
happy. I have my girls and I have a new gentle-
man to tell me he worships me. Although I no
longer believe such declarations so blithely, still it
is very nice to be told one is beautiful and desir-
able. So, I am happy, and even the thought of
Jemmy and what might have been cannot cloud
my horizon.

Perhaps my life has reached calm seas at last.

The room was shaded, as if its occupant could not
bear the sight of the bright sunny spring day. Marietta saw him, a dark shape slumped in his chair.

Aphrodite touched her daughter's hand, and
when Marietta glanced at her, nodded towards him.
"He is in pain. The traveling is not easy for him. But
he wants to meet you, Marietta, very much. You must
be kind to him, and patient, *oui*?"

Marietta nodded and approached her father. She
was glad now that she had read the diary last night.
To know even that small piece of her father's past,
and that he had a long-standing business relationship with her mother. He had helped her to start
Aphrodite's Club, shared in the costs, but allowed
her to run it as she wished. Aphrodite trusted him so
completely that even when they were no longer in
love she still thought of him as her friend, and asked
his opinion on business matters.

He was watching her, his head resting on his hand,
his eyes following every step. His legs, withered and
useless, were covered by a woolen shawl despite the

warm room. Marietta tried to smile but her lips were trembling. This was her father, she told herself, and she was to know him at last.

"Marietta," he said, and she saw then that his eyes were blue, like hers, and his hair fair, though graying at the temples. "I am sorry you should see me like this, daughter. The journey to London was painful for me and I am not yet fit for company."

"I am sorry to hear about your . . . troubles."

He held out his hands and she saw that his fingers were long and elegant and he wore a jeweled ring on one of them. "Sit down with me, Marietta, and let me see you properly."

She sat down on the sofa and felt her chin lifted, her features scrutinized as he turned her face to one side and then the other. Then he sighed. "What is it?" she whispered, wondering if he was disappointed in her. The possibility hurt her.

"You are so beautiful, daughter," he said. "You have the look of my mother. She was a pocket Venus, too. A small whirlwind who my father adored. I will always remember her now when I look upon you."

Aphrodite came forward and, smiling tenderly, bent to kiss his cheek, and Marietta realized anew how fond they were of each other. "My poor Adam," she said gently. "I do not like to see you like this, *mon ami*. Should we go and leave you to rest?"

"No, no," he murmured. "I want to gaze upon our beautiful daughter, Aphrodite."

Aphrodite turned her smile on Marietta. "She is lovely, certainly."

"And what are you going to do with all that beauty, child?" Adam asked. "You are twenty-one and still unwed, your mother tells me. I cannot believe the men of England are so blind. Perhaps you are waiting for the perfect man, eh? Well, believe me, you will never find him."

Marietta glanced at her mother. She had not yet told Aphrodite about Max's proposal. She had wanted to wait until they were together, her parents and herself, before giving them the good news.

"I *have* found the perfect man, sir. His name is Max Valland and he has asked me to marry him, and I have said I will."

Aphrodite gave a little gasp. "Marietta! You naughty girl, you kept this secret from me."

Marietta tried to read her eyes. "Are you glad?" she whispered. "I am sorry I will not be following in your footsteps, Mama, but I . . . I do not think I would make a very good courtesan."

Adam's eyes had been fixed on their faces, and now he laughed. The laugh turned into a spluttering cough, and Aphrodite fetched him a glass of cordial and held it to his lips. He drank, coughed again, and managed to regain control of himself.

"She reminds me of you, my dear Madame," he said at last, his voice husky from exertion. "Beware of following your heart, Marietta. It can lead you into places you would rather not be. Isn't that so?" This last was to Aphrodite, who pulled a mocking face at him.

"Life is for living," she retorted. "I may have made mistakes, Adam, but at least I have lived."

He nodded, all humor gone from his face. "You are right. Make certain that this Max treats you well, daughter, or he will have me to answer to."

"He is a duke's son," Marietta said. "At least he was . . ."

"I don't care," Adam retorted. "You're too good for him."

Marietta was delighted. This was the first time since she had met Max that anyone had said such a thing, and it warmed her heart.

Aphrodite took both their hands in hers. "I am very happy," she said. "I did not think it was right for you to be a courtesan, Marietta, and Max . . . He is a gentleman, and I can see he loves you very much. Please, be happy."

Adam squeezed her fingers. "Perhaps Marietta, you will come and visit me in the country? I have a house in Somerset, and there I live a simple life. Do not laugh, but I even work in the garden with my hands, potting plants and watering them."

"I would very much like to come and visit you at your house in Somerset," Marietta said firmly.

"Good, good." He patted her hand and smiled, and it was as if he could not think of anything else to say. He exchanged a meaningful look with Aphrodite.

She turned to Marietta. "I have something important to tell you, *mon petit puce*. Aphrodite's Club belongs jointly to me and Adam, and we agreed many years ago that as our child, it should be yours when the time comes. We want you to be the owner of Aphrodite's Club, Marietta. What do you think of that?"

They were both watching her intently.

Marietta did not know what to say. Her eyes filled with tears. "Oh," she whispered.

"It is a business," Adam said quickly. "You should think of it like that, my dear daughter."

"It is a house of pleasure first and a business second," Aphrodite retorted.

Marietta smiled to hear them bickering.

"Are you shocked?" Aphrodite asked her gently, her watchful eyes serious. "Do you wish to say no?"

"We will understand," Adam murmured.

Marietta didn't know whether to laugh or cry. Aphrodite's Club would be hers! In a way, she would fulfill her dream of following in her mother's footsteps, and she would have Max, too.

"I would be proud to be the owner of Aphrodite's! Thank you both so much."

Adam nodded, pleased, and Aphrodite sighed. "Then I am glad, too, Marietta. But let us hope that day is far off, *oui*? Now," she stood up, "your father is tired. We will leave you to rest, Adam. Perhaps Marietta can come again before you return to Somerset?"

"Of course, I would like that. It has been too long."

Marietta hugged him tightly, and then they left him. Aphrodite peered at Marietta a moment, and then curled an arm about her waist. "Do not fret, *mon petit puce*. It is sad that such a thing has happened to him but he is fortunate in other ways. You should not pity him."

"I don't pity him," Marietta said thoughtfully. "I just wish he was able to walk again, for his sake, not mine."

"I had planned another task for you, remember? You were to meet your Max at the masque ball at Vauxhall Gardens. Do you still wish to go ahead with this?"

"Oh yes, thank you!" It would be a celebration of their happiness, a triumph for love.

"It will be your last assignation, *mon petit puce*. I have decided that you will be wearing a golden mask and a red cloak with fur at the hem, and Max will be wearing a black cloak and a silver mask. You will meet him at the rotunda and he will take you with him through the Dark Walk. Very romantic. There, that should please you! My engagement gift to you."

It *did* please her. "And what are the rules this time?" she asked curiously.

Aphrodite laughed. "Why have rules? You could not obey them last time, so I will not bother with them this time. You can set your own rules, Marietta. Be happy; there, that is my rule for you this time—you must simply be happy."

I will be happy, Marietta told herself. And yet . . . Now there was a new doubt to ruffle her calm seas. What would Max think of her one day owning Aphrodite's Club? He might say he cared nothing for her reputation and her scandalous parentage, but could he also turn a blind eye to her being the proprietor of a bordello?

I won't tell him. After all, it won't be for years and years and years.

And yet in not telling him Marietta felt as if she was already betraying him.

Max smiled when he received the note from Aphrodite, congratulating him on his coming nuptials and informing him of his rendezvous with Marietta at Vauxhall Gardens.

He would miss the intrigue and excitement of such meetings, but the thought of being married to her brought a warmth to his heart that he had never felt before. There would still be passion and desire, but there would also be trust and love, and the joy of spending his life with the woman he wanted above all others.

"Max?"

Startled he turned, the note fluttering from his fingers. Harold stood inside the room, watching him, his mouth pinched and unhappy.

"I have heard that you are to be adopted by the duke."

"I have declined, cousin," Max said cautiously.

Harold shrugged, as if he didn't believe it. "I am glad for you, of course I am, but I cannot help but wonder whether he means to restore you to your previous position. Susannah thinks he will. Where does that leave us, Max? I feel as if I am in limbo."

"I have no intention of accepting—"

But Harold waved his hand impatiently. "You say that now, but in time you will weaken. He will work on you and you will agree. Marietta Greentree will work on you, too. What woman in her position would not want to be a duchess!"

Max felt anger tighten his muscles and sinews, but he held it in check, reminding himself that his cousin was upset. This was his father's fault, once again he had ploughed ahead through other people's emotions, his eyes fixed only on his desired goal. He moved to the drinks tray, to pour some brandy for them both. "Sit down, Harold, and we can talk."

"It isn't for me, you understand," Harold didn't seem to hear him. "I am thinking of Susannah."

He turned and found that Harold had retrieved the note and was reading it. Max felt his cheeks color at the intrusion into his private life, but Harold didn't even seem to notice what he was reading. He set the note down and took the drink Max held out to him.

"Marietta and I are getting married, and we will

live at Blackwood. I have decided to reopen the old mine. It will give employment to the villagers and perhaps put some cash in my pockets. You probably think it very strange, Harold, but I don't need Valland House or anything else that I used to think of as mine. There is freedom in being without, and besides, I will soon have the brightest jewel of all."

"I wish," Harold began, but whatever it was he wished for he changed his mind about sharing it. Instead he swallowed his brandy and said, "Am I invited to the wedding, Max? I promise to be on my best behavior."

Max fixed him with a stern look. "I'll think about it."

Harold smiled, and shook his hand. "Good luck, cousin," he said, "and I do mean that."

Max stared thoughtfully after him. Harold was not himself, but then who could blame him after what the duke had done to them both? He wondered if his cousin was right, would he weaken and allow his father to reinstate him as the heir? And if he did, would that mean losing Marietta? She had made her feelings plain on becoming a duchess—she thought her reputation cancelled out such a future. If it came to a choice between being heir to a dukedom and Marietta's husband, Max knew which of the two he preferred. He was in no doubt at all.

In the library at Berkley Square, William Tremaine was giving Mr. Jardine one of his infamous glares.

"I've seen the way you ogle my sister, Jardine. Don't think I'm blind or a fool, for I am neither."

Mr. Jardine felt his face burning. "You are wrong, Mr. Tremaine. I have no intention—"

"Yes, well, save your explanations. I don't want to

hear them. In fact I think it would be best if you offered your resignation forthwith."

"Certainly not!"

William's blue eyes narrowed dangerously. "You're disobeying me?"

"I am not employed by you, I am employed by your sister. Of course if *she* were to ask me to resign, that would be a different matter, but until then I will continue on as I am."

"Setting your sights at her! I know what you're up to. You think you'll retire on her money and in the comfort of her home. Well, I won't have it, do you hear! I won't—"

"William!"

Before William could finish his sentence, another voice spoke from the doorway. It was Amy Greentree, leaning on her walking stick, her cheeks pink with anger, her eyes glittering very much like her brother's.

"How dare you speak to Mr. Jardine in that manner! And how dare you infer that he would in any way try to harm me or . . . or insinuate himself into my private life. He is a gentleman and a dear friend as well as my secretary. I am furious with you. You have no right to speak to him like that!"

William blew out his cheeks. "I have every right. I am the head of the family and—"

"That has nothing to do with it. I-I am grateful for your concern," she said, clearly not grateful at all, "but I have never sought your advice."

He dismissed that with a wave of his hand. "You are a woman, Amy, and you need a man to correct you when you make mistakes. As your brother, it is my right to—"

"I am a mature woman, William. A widow with three grown-up daughters. I do not need anyone to correct my mistakes."

"You do not know the world as I do, sister. There are men in it, marauders, who would worm their way into your affections simply for what they could pillage."

Amy was breathing fast, her hand clenched upon the walking cane, and when she replied her voice was deceptively quiet. "Be warned, William, if you persist in interfering in my life then I will cut you from it."

He stared at her a moment as if he could not believe what he had heard. "I am the head of the family, Amy. I will have no scandal and this man is—"

But she stopped him. "I will not hear Mr. Jardine slandered by you. Go home, William, and mind your own business. You are not wanted here today."

He opened his mouth, closed it again, and then with an angry huff, stood up and left the room.

Amy took a deep breath, and then another. She was trembling. "I don't know how I could have been burdened with such an insufferable brother. I do apologize."

Mr. Jardine approached her carefully, as if William's words had made him extra sensitive about his behavior around her. "It is not your fault, Amy. Do you think I would pay any attention to a windbag like that? You know me better, I hope?"

Amy laughed, tears of anger and upset drying from her eyes. "Yes, I do. At least I hope I do."

"Then put it from your mind, as I shall."

"I wish I could," she sighed. "I wish I could understand what has him in such a state. He is always difficult, but lately he has been worse."

"At least you can be sure when you return to Yorkshire that he will be unlikely to make the journey to see you."

"Yes, I am safe from him there."

She looked at him a moment, blinked, and then looked away. Her face paled slightly. "I-I will leave you to your work, Mr. Jardine."

He bowed, and then stood, listening to her faltering steps fading in the hall. Had she seen something in his face? Had she suddenly realized that William was right, and that his feelings for her were much warmer than a secretary's should be for his employer? Strangely he almost hoped that she had—at least then the truth about his love for her would be out in the open between them.

For so long he had been content to love her in silence. He was a hopeless case, he supposed, but what was the alternative? The thought of upsetting a sweet creature like Amy Greentree with inappropriate advances appalled him.

But she was right about William. For whatever reason he had been diabolical of late—perhaps the three girls had put him in a state, they seemed to be always attracting scandal or gossip. Had he heard the latest about Marietta and Barwon's son? Maybe that was it. Whatever had put a flea in William's ear, Mr. Jardine was looking forward to getting home to Greentree Manor and some sense of normality.

And then a glimpse of Amy's face a moment ago flashed into his mind—her eyes not quite meeting his—and he wondered if things could ever be the same again.

* * *

Amy Greentree stood alone in the entrance hall. For some reason she felt disoriented, as though she were on the verge of some momentous decision. Although her anger for William still lingered it had been swallowed up by something else. Something she realized she should have seen a long time ago.

Mr. Jardine loved her.

But she loved Edward . . . *still* loved Edward, even though he had been dead now for a great many years. Losing your husband did not mean you stopped loving him. And yet at this moment she longed to feel a man's arms about her, to rest her head upon a masculine chest, to be treasured and protected and loved.

Mr. Jardine loved her and she was very fond of him. She had not realized until a moment ago, when William was threatening him, just how fond of her secretary she was. Just how much she would miss him if he went away. Her life would be quite . . . empty.

Amy Greentree felt as if she had been asleep for a very long time, and now she was about to wake up.

"David?"

Startled, he stood up, knocking his pen and papers to the floor. Amy had returned, and she had called him by his first name, something she never normally did. As she came toward him he noted that her face was pale but determined, and this time her gaze was fixed on his.

"Amy?"

She placed her hand carefully upon his shoulder, and looked deep into his eyes. Mr. Jardine didn't move—he couldn't. He wondered what she would see there in his eyes—love for her, certainly, and all the years of devotion and loyalty he had given to her. But would she see the promises he longed to make to her, and the life he wished to have with her?

Amy smiled, and she was so beautiful he blinked. And then she leaned forward and touched her lips to his, the lightest of kisses.

"This is for being you, David," she whispered.

The door closed gently behind her.

David Jardine collapsed back into his chair like a man who has looked through the gates of paradise.

Chapter 18

Marietta reached up to make sure that her gold mask was secure. The smiling disguise covered the upper half of her face and it was surprising how difficult it was to tell her identity once she had it on. Her red cloak with the fur hem swirled every time she moved, while underneath the cloak was a dress of the same vibrant red. The color made her skin seem almost translucent, while her hair gleamed like gold and her eyes blazed like sapphires. Aphrodite had fondly told her she looked like a princess—Marietta had dressed at the club—but she did not think she resembled anything so insipid as a princess. She was more like a pagan goddess; an idol to be worshipped.

She smiled. Already the tingle in her blood was growing warmer, anticipation made her body alert and her heart beat faster. Her senses responded to the clothing she was wearing—the softness of the velvet and fur, the silken luxury of her stockings, the tight push of her stays beneath her bosom. The neckline of her red gown was low, almost indecently so. Marietta had never worn anything so daring in public and she wondered what Max would think.

She glanced over her shoulder. Aphrodite had sent Dobson with her to Vauxhall Gardens, and she saw him now, waiting a few paces behind her until she found Max safely. Her mother was being very cautious tonight, but Marietta was glad of it. Dobson looked dangerous and tough, standing amidst the crowd with his arms folded.

Was Dobson the Jemmy her mother spoke of in her diary? The man she had loved and lost? Marietta did not know how the two of them had been reunited— the latter part of her mother's story was yet to be told. At first she had not thought Dobson particularly remarkable, but as she came to know him and witness her mother's affection for him, Marietta had revised her opinion. Behind his gray eyes lurked humor and a sharp intelligence, and, whenever he looked at Aphrodite, a flood of warm affection. Hmm, and desire. He loved her, and she loved him.

As if he had read her thoughts, Dobson winked at her, and spoiled the tough image he had been conveying. Marietta smiled beneath her mask as she turned to scan the crowd for her own lover.

There were colored lanterns everywhere; they hung from the trees and swung from poles. A man on stilts blew fire into the air, and a woman shrieked with more excitement than fear. The private boxes were for those who preferred to sit and eat their thin slices of cold ham, enjoying the ambience while they studied the endless stream of humanity that wandered past them down the tree-lined avenues. Marietta smiled at one particularly loud group, the women shrieking with laughter as a gentleman drank champagne from a slipper. She knew that those who came to Vauxhall Gardens were a mixture of genteel and far-from-genteel, rich and poor, good and bad. The proprietors had attempted to ensure the safety of their patrons by increasing the number of lanterns in the walks, and employing men to patrol the area in search of pick-pockets and to break up affrays, but no one could change Vauxhall.

It was rowdy and exciting and a little bit danger-ous, and Marietta loved it.

The band in the rotunda finished their piece and were duly applauded, and as the sound died away, a voice spoke behind her.

"My lady."

Marietta turned. A tall, broad-shouldered man in a black cloak and a silver mask was standing there. Her gaze dropped to the small scar on his chin, and then rose to his mouth. Oh yes, she knew that mouth very well.

"Sir," her voice was throaty, "you are late."

"I have been watching you ever since you arrived, enjoying the scenery."

His head dipped and he stepped closer, until their bodies were almost touching. A lock of his hair brushed hers, and his fingers closed around her arm. "You are so beautiful, Marietta," he murmured.

She smiled. Tonight she felt beautiful, because Max loved her and all was right with the world.

The band in the rotunda struck up again, and now a woman was singing, her voice wobbling a little on the high notes. Max grimaced as if his senses had been assaulted and Marietta laughed.

"Perhaps we should stroll in Dark Walk?" he suggested, his eyes narrowing behind the mask. "It will be quieter there and you might find it instructional."

"Instructional?" Marietta breathed, her imagination taking flight.

"In an educational sense. I know a great deal about the Dark Walk, my lady. I can show you the secret arbors and the bowers where ladies have been ravished by gentlemen throughout the centuries."

His voice had dropped a notch and Marietta felt it brush over her, exciting her. But she had a part to play, and she assumed a cautious pose as she replied, "I have heard that gentlewomen should not venture into the Dark Walk. That it might be injurious to their reputations."

"What about gentlewomen who are engaged to be married? Surely they are beyond censure?"

"Only if they are in love."

Max slid his arm about her waist and gazed down into her eyes. "And are you in love?"

"Oh yes." Marietta stood on tiptoe and kissed his lips, a brief butterfly kiss. "Very much."

Max groaned at the brevity of the kiss. The vocalist hit another high note and he began to lead her out of the crush, toward one of the tree-lined avenues. "If this is our last rendezvous I want it to be one we'll both remember," he said. "And I want to go somewhere quiet so that I can see if what you're wearing under that cloak is as heart-stopping as I think it is."

She pretended his words hadn't affected her. "I don't know if I should allow you to *touch* me, Max."

He stopped by a hedge that shielded them from passersby and took her in his arms. And he kissed her, deeply and thoroughly. "You were saying," he said at last.

Marietta took a moment to answer and when she did she had abandoned her play-acting. "Will we be happy in Cornwall?" she whispered, with her head resting against his chest.

He bent and kissed her hair, his hands smoothing her back and shoulders. "Do you doubt it, my darling?"

"No, not really, only sometimes. I'm not used to being happy like this, Max. I'm not used to thinking about a future with you in it."

Perhaps some of her lingering doubts did sound in her voice, because Max removed his mask so that she could see his face properly. His dark hair had been slicked back from his forehead, and he looked different, handsome certainly, but also more like an aristocratic stranger. This was Max Valland, Lord Roseby, the Duke of Barwon's son, and Marietta did not doubt it for a moment.

Her heart gave a little skip of trepidation.

Max took her hands in his, his fingers strong and warm and comforting. She looked down and they were Max's fingers, Max's hands; they had held her and stroked her and made love to her. These were the hands she would hold as she made her vows on her wedding day, and that their children would grasp as they took their first steps.

"Darling Marietta, I want you to know that I will never leave you. We will go to Cornwall and I promise you I will do everything in my power to ensure that you are happy. With you at my side, Marietta, I feel as if I can be anything, do anything. I feel complete."

It was a wonderful speech, the sort of speech she

used to dream about as a girl. And yet, as Marietta gazed into his eyes, she found herself wondering what he would think when she explained to him about Aphrodite's Club. She knew she must be a coward, but she was afraid to tell him that one day his future wife would be the proud owner of a bordello.

Vauxhall Gardens was so like a fairytale tonight, Marietta could not bear for reality to creep in.

"Come with me." His breath was warm in her ear as he drew her along the gravel paths, further and further away from the crowds. The shadows were thick here, despite the lanterns, and the trees and shrubs loomed about them. It was isolated, and that was its charm, but after what had happened to him Marietta pondered whether it was entirely safe for Max to be here.

"Should we go back?"

He leered like a stage villain. "Why, are you frightened I'll ravish you?"

Marietta gave a husky laugh. "Not frightened, Max. I'm looking forward to being ravished tonight."

Max brushed his fingers down the opening of her cloak, parting it and holding it aside so that he could see the dress beneath. Her bosom, pushed up and prominently displayed, threatened to spill over the gold braided neckline. The waist was pinched in, displaying her hourglass shape to perfection, while the skirts were snug to her hips and fell in smooth folds to the ground. The dress was fashioned to appear medieval, and Marietta wore no petticoats so that Max could see the shape of her legs. Without the cloak it would be considered indecent.

"Oh yes," he murmured approvingly.

His slid his fingers over her white skin so lightly

she might not have felt them, except that her body had become so completely sensitized to his. She trembled, her lips parting and her eyes fluttering closed. His mouth made warm, wet circles on her breasts, and then he had found the hooks that held everything together and began to undo them. The neckline sagged and her bosom spilled out into his hands.

"Max," she gasped, "I need you. I need you now, Max."

He covered her with his palms, preserving her modesty, his thighs brushing hers through their clothing. "I love the way you always tell me what you feel for me," he murmured, kissing her throat, his mouth warm and seductive.

"I'm not straitlaced or conventional," she said, trying to concentrate on what he was saying while his hands were stroking her breasts, making her flesh quiver and ache.

"And I thank God for it," he said. He was drawing her along a winding path that left the main walk, into the trees, the scent of earth and foliage all about them. There was an arbor, overgrown and secret, and Max led her inside.

Marietta wound her arms about his neck, her breasts pressed to his chest in a manner designed to tease. "Do you?" she whispered. There was a devil inside her, urging her on, and she heard herself saying, "What if I did something outrageous, Max? What if I became the proprietor of a club like Aphrodite's? Would you thank God then?"

He laughed. He thought she was joking. He didn't take her seriously at all.

Just then the fireworks began to rain brilliantly

from the sky. The arbor reflected the colors, red and blue and gold, bright as day one moment and dark again the next. Marietta had jumped when the first volley went off, but Max wrapped her in his arms, safe, and he bent to cover her mouth was his. Tasting her, caressing her, promising her everything.

Marietta kissed him back, the ache in her body building as she pressed against him. And yet even as desire spun out of control, the little devil in her head was still there, spoiling the moment for her, gleefully listing all the terrors she had thought vanquished: Being left, being abandoned, her heart being broken.

Would Max leave her when he understood Aphrodite's would one day be hers, or would he insist that she refuse her parents' gift? Marietta wondered how she could bear to scorn what they had offered her with such love in their hearts. And was a man who insisted she do such a thing to preserve his own reputation really worth having anyway?

Max had stopped kissing her.

"What is it?" he asked, a new sharp note in his voice. "Marietta?"

She opened her mouth but nothing came out.

Max set her away, and even in the shadows she saw how his brows had drawn down over his eyes as he stared at her. Gently he reached around to the back of her head and undid the ties, finally removing her golden mask.

Marietta felt as if he had stripped her naked—and this time it was not a pleasant sensation.

Something was wrong. Max could see it in her eyes, read it in her face, sense it while he was kissing her. One moment she was his, completely and utterly in tune to him, and the next he had lost her.

"What is it?" he demanded, worried. "Marietta, what's the matter?"

She stared back at him like a rabbit would a fox. The expression in her eyes frightened him—he felt as if there were a hollow opening up inside him—and he wanted to shake her until she widened her gaze in that mock-innocent way and laughed and admitted it was nothing, and that she was just playing with him again . . .

"Max, I have something to tell you." Her voice was quiet and a little tremulous. It was the voice that belonged to the girl who had spoken about her past; the somber girl who had been abandoned and hurt, and who had never recovered.

She is going to tell me she can't marry me, he thought bleakly. *Can't or won't. And everything I have been hoping for and planning for will be gone.* His sense of despair was so great it was beyond imagining, because Max knew that without Marietta Greentree his life would cease to be.

More fireworks thundered overhead, their beauty truly spectacular, but Max didn't see them. His gaze was fixed on Marietta's face, and he was waiting for her to speak.

That was the reason he didn't notice the man in the shabby brown coat, walking along the narrow path that passed by the entrance to the arbor. He couldn't hear him, either, the fireworks were too loud.

"Tell me then," Max said, sounding cold and distant, as if he was already alone.

But Marietta's gaze had shifted past him and widened. A splash of green in the sky turned her face a sickly color, and then her fingers dug hard into his arms. "You!" she gasped, just as Max began to turn.

The man standing behind them wasn't very tall, but he was broad, with the sturdiness of someone who had worked physically hard all his life. His clothes were cheap and well worn, and his face was misshapen and rather frightening, as though he had once been a fighter. All of this Max saw in a moment, before he realized the man was holding a pistol.

Marietta screamed, clutching at Max's arm as he tried to push her away, out of the line of fire. The man raised the barrel.

"Move aside," he snarled. "I don't want to kill you too, lady."

"You've been following me," she said, her voice shaking violently. "I've seen you before."

"Not you," the man retorted impatiently. "*Him!* I was waitin' my chance, and now I've found it. Now get out o' me way so I can earn me money."

"No, I won't let you . . ." She clung on to Max, despite his efforts to unfasten her fingers from his clothing and push her to safety. She was shaking with terror, but she wouldn't be moved. The man with the pistol growled again for her to get out of the way.

"No!" she screamed, the sound shredding the night. "Don't hurt him, don't hurt Max, please! Oh please!"

Max could see the man's frustration was making him even more unpredictable. The pistol was waving dangerously as he took a step forward and then a step back. In a moment he would shoot, and it was

Marietta who would be hit. And Max could not allow that to happen.

He struggled with her, lifting her bodily, and this time he wrenched her hands free, holding them as he shoved her aside. She stumbled, cried out, and sank to the ground.

The man lifted the gun, his face grim and determined, and prepared to fire. "I'll make it clean, sir. Don't worry, you won't feel nothin'."

"I wouldn't do that if I were you, Slipper."

Dobson's voice was soft with menace as he stepped out of the shadows on the other side of the path. He was holding a pistol of his own, and this one was aimed at Slipper's back.

"Bloody hell," Slipper moaned, twisting around to see who it was. "Is that you, Jemmy?"

"Drop your weapon or I'll have to fire, and I'm not as good a shot as you."

Slipper dropped the pistol, eyeing Dobson cautiously.

"I didn't think you hurt women," Dobson said. "Your mam wouldn't like to hear you've been mistreating ladies, Slipper."

Slipper sighed. "Why won't nothin' go right for me anymore? Since I took up with the duchess there's been nothin' but trouble for me."

Marietta picked herself up, feeling dizzy, as if she might faint. The fireworks were still exploding in the sky but they seemed inappropriate now, an distraction from the important business of the night. Max was standing a little way from her, staring at the man Dobson had called Slipper, and his face and body were rigid.

"Duchess?" he whispered. "What duchess?"

Slipper shifted his feet, his ugly face turning from Max to Dobson, as if he didn't trust either of them. "I call her that," he explained, "because she looks like a duchess, not because she is one."

There was only one woman Max thought looked like the perfect duchess.

Slipper eyed him slyly. "You wanna know who she is, right? If I tell you, will you let me go?"

Dobson laughed. "Still the same old Slipper. Tell us anyway."

Slipper hesitated, but after Dobson had another little talk with him, he told them.

Dobson squeezed Marietta's arm gently as they stepped from the hansom. "Are you all right, miss?"

"I think so. I'm worried about Max."

"Max is tougher than any of us, don't worry about him."

But she couldn't help it.

Dobson had explained that Slipper had been one of his sparring partners when they both spent some time bare-knuckle fighting. It was useful sometimes, he said, having grown up in Seven Dials; it meant he knew just about every villain in London, and just about every villain's mother. Slipper's mother was a fire-breather and he was more afraid of her than any policeman. It had been fear of his mother that Dobson had used to convince Slipper to finally tell them who had paid him to kill Max.

Marietta glanced at Max now, but his expression revealed nothing to her. Since he had heard the name he had been silent, holding his emotions inside, preparing for the confrontation.

The house they had come to was not as grand as his own. Lights blazed from the windows and the sound of a piano drifted from one of the upper rooms. Max walked up the steps and knocked, loudly. Marietta followed more slowly, dreading the next few moments. They had argued in the hansom—Max had wanted her to go home and wait for him, but she had refused, and after a short, tense battle he had given in. She needed to be with him, to support him or simply to watch over him. Marietta had almost lost him tonight and she was caught between elation that he was alive and unharmed, and dread of what might have happened. What might still happen.

Max strode past the servant who opened the door. "Mr. and Mrs. Valland are not receiving visitors," the man began, his gaze sliding to Marietta and Dobson. "Sir, I'm sorry but you—"

Max ignored him and climbed the stairs with barely a pause, heading toward the sound of the piano. Dobson took Marietta's arm and they followed in his wake. By the time they reached him, Max had already flung open the door, sending it crashing back against the wall.

That was when Marietta realized how angry he was—Max had the Valland temper after all.

"Max!" It was Harold, staggering to his feet. He had been half asleep in front of the fire and he looked bewildered, his hair on end, his shirt sleeves rolled up.

Max said nothing. He looked at Harold as if he had never seen him before, and then he turned his head toward the piano. Susannah was seated there, her hands still resting on the keys, but her face was blank, as though she was seeing a ghost.

"Yes, it's Max," he said quietly, grief meshing with the anger in his voice. "I'm sorry to disappoint you."

"Disappoint us?" Harold echoed, puzzled, coming forward. He saw Marietta then, and behind her Dobson, and his expression grew even more confused. "What is this about, Max? What are you doing here? And why have you brought these people—"

"Susannah can tell you what it's about. Why don't you ask Susannah?" Max moved toward his sister, his eyes never leaving her.

Marietta had expected to hate Susannah, to be so angry she wanted to strike out at her and hurt her as she had hurt Max. But now . . . she was confused. Susannah was picking out some notes on the piano, trying to recapture the tune she had been playing a moment ago.

"Harold likes to be played to in the evening," she said, as if to excuse herself, as if Max regularly forced his way into her house.

"Susannah—"

"We did not have a piano in Jamaica, so I could not play there. We were poor and my father could not afford to have me educated as he would have wished. We had our land and our house and our past glories, that was all. When I came to England I learned to play. I learned to become a lady, a cold and polite lady. Did you know, it is not considered proper to have feelings in England? You must suppress them, you must pretend to be indifferent, and sometimes if you pretend long enough then you begin to feel as if you are dead."

Anger glittered a moment in her eyes and was gone again. Suppressed. She smiled at Max.

"I'm glad *you're* not dead," she said.

Marietta felt it then, the tragic air that enfolded Susannah. The silent suffering in the line of her mouth and the set of her shoulders. Susannah was in pain, but whether it was justified or not, real or illusion, Marietta could not tell.

"Max," she murmured a warning.

But Max was beyond understanding such subtleties. "You're glad I'm not dead?" he shouted, his voice so full of anger and betrayal that it made Marietta wince. "Then why did you pay Slipper to kill me! Do you hate me so much? What have I ever done to you, Susannah? You're my *sister* . . ."

"You don't understand, Max," she said, and sighed. Her face was beautiful but it was also gaunt, as though her life was being eaten away from the inside. "This has nothing to do with my love for you or yours for me. This is to do with justice. Papa took me away from my father and our home. He took everything, so that he could use the money to save Valland House and rebuild his fortune. My father had nothing, but he had me, and then the duke stole me too. So my father took his own life. Where was the justice in that, Max? Papa . . . the duke said he was sorry, afterwards, and I know he felt guilty when he looked at me. I always remind him, you see, of the kind of man he really is."

"But that's in the past," Harold began.

She turned on him, her dark eyes blazing. "I have never forgotten! It is always with me, always!"

"Susannah?" Harold was staring at her, his mouth working. "Why are you speaking like this? Max, why is she saying these things?"

"It's all right, Harold." At once the anger was gone and her smile gentle. "I want to explain. I want Max to know why."

"Know what?" Harold whispered, but now there was dread in his face, as if he was beginning to realize they were entering a place from which there could be no return.

"That the reason I tried to take him away from Papa was because Papa had taken me away from my father and my home. What he did was wrong, and he needs to be punished for it. If I take Max from Papa, then he will understand. Then he will suffer."

"You tried to kill me," Max said bluntly.

"Of course," she replied. "At first it was just a thought in my head, an impulse. The day I threw the coins into the lake for you and Harold to dive in and fetch, that was when I thought, what if I throw Max's closer to the reeds? What if he gets tangled in them and drowns? No one could blame me for that, and I would have given my father what he wants from me. Justice. But you swim too well, Max. So then I made the hole in the boat when I knew you were going out in it, but that didn't work either. There were other times, other accidents, but I didn't really plan them. They just seemed to happen. I didn't want you dead, you know, Max. This isn't about you, you can see that, can't you? You understand, don't you Max?"

Harold made a sound and turned away, and Marietta saw that he was crying like a little child.

"Last year you tried to shoot me? Was that you, Susannah?" Max's voice had taken on an emotionless quality, as if he was sleepwalking.

"Yes, I was always a good shot, but for some reason I missed or you moved, I forget. There was a timber that I pushed onto you from the stable loft. I saw it hit and you fell and . . . After that I . . . I didn't try again. I felt sick afterwards. And anyway, Mama died. I was looking through her papers and I suddenly thought: What if there was a letter confessing that Max wasn't Papa's son? It just happened, and I pretended to find it and . . . I was as surprised as anyone when I was believed. Papa was so angry, and I was glad, because I could see that both of you understood then how it had been for me. How my poor father felt when he lost me. You can understand now what it means to be wrenched away from where you belong."

"You *wrote* the letter?" Max shook his head. "I don't believe—"

"Of course I did. I used to do your lessons for you and Harold, didn't I, when we were children? So that you two could sneak off fishing or whatever it was you boys did. I was always very skilled at copying handwriting, Max, and I knew Mama's as well as I knew my own. Have you forgotten?"

He said nothing; there seemed to be nothing to say. He felt as if the earth was shaking beneath his feet and in a moment it would collapse and take him with it. Susannah was so reasonable, her tone was calm and persuasive, and her words even made a terrible sort of sense. But Max felt chilled to the bone by her.

"When he read the letter, Papa disinherited you and sent you away just as I'd hoped he would, but I knew that it wouldn't last. Papa loves you, Max. He loves you more than me, and more than Harold. He loves you best of all. He would never let you remain an outcast. His temper got the better of him for a while, but now it has cooled he will eventually recant."

"So you hired Slipper?" Marietta had forgotten

Dobson was there, but he came forward now. "You got him to attack Lord Roseby in the lane outside Aphrodite's Club, and tonight you paid him to shoot him at Vauxhall Gardens."

"That's right." Susannah gave him a smile. "I hired Slipper. I couldn't bring myself to try again, not after the last time. So I found a man who would do it for me, and Slipper was very fond of me. He called me his duchess. Vauxhall Gardens seemed like a good idea, and Harold saw a letter inviting you there, Max, and he told me. And I told Slipper."

She nodded at her own cleverness.

"Max." It was Harold, recovered now, although his face was still flushed and stained with tears. There was a desperate light in his eyes. "Please, don't listen to her. She's not well, you know that. She hasn't been well for years."

"My dear Harold, you must not say that. Apologize." With a reproving frown, Susannah held out her hand to him. Harold hesitated, and then reached to take it with shaking fingers. He bent and pressed his lips to her skin, squeezing his eyes shut, as if he would hide from the truth.

"Sometimes it is necessary to take matters into one's own hands," Susannah said. "Make one's own justice. The dead demand it."

Such cold-bloodedness was breathtaking.

Harold gave a sob and shook his head. Marietta knew that Harold could not have known the truth about his wife; he had been so besotted with her that he had believed she could do no wrong. Poor Harold was just as much a victim of this as Max.

"Well," Susannah stood up and smoothed her skirts. "This is very nice, but I wish to retire."

She smiled vaguely and drifted toward the door. No one stopped her, Dobson even stepped aside to let her pass, and they listened to her footsteps fading into silence.

"All those years," Max said bleakly, shaking his head in disbelief. He looked at his cousin. "How could you not know, Harold?"

"I didn't know," he insisted. "There were times when she was low, when she stayed in her room, but Susannah has always had her moods. You know that. We always took great care not to upset her. I did not think it was anything more than melancholy. I didn't realize it was . . ."

Madness.

Harold's voice took on a new urgency. "Max, let me take her home to Jamaica. I'll buy a house for us and she can live there quietly. I can find a doctor. I can . . . Please, do this for me. For all the years we have been friends."

Max turned and read the same misery and shock in Harold's eyes as he knew must be in his own. It was easy to convict someone in hindsight, and how could he blame Harold for failing to see something he had not seen himself?

"Don't let her go to court," Harold whispered. "The scandal. It would kill her, and destroy us. Max?"

"Yes," he said, "do as you think best."

Harold stretched out his hand and after a moment Max took it. Their fingers gripped hard.

"Do you think she really wanted me dead?" Max asked as if he couldn't help it.

Harold hesitated. "She tried so many times and failed. I wonder if she really meant it to happen. She was such a good shot, Max, and yet she missed you that day."

"Yes," Max seemed to take comfort from that.

"What does it matter anyway?" Harold went on, his voice shaking. "We'll be gone and the duke will make you his heir again. You will be Duke of Barwon and live at Valland House. It's your destiny and it seems that no matter how you wriggle like a worm on a hook, you can't escape it."

And with a grim smile, Harold followed after his wife.

Max sat down on the piano seat as if his legs could no longer hold him. He felt sick. How could he have thought he knew Susannah so well? She had been a stranger to him. Had he failed her when she first came to England? Perhaps if he had paid more attention to her, got her to talk about her past . . . But the duke hadn't wanted that. He had warned Max and Harold not to remind the girl of sad memories, and they had obeyed him.

"Max?"

The voice was familiar, but for a moment he was so lost he couldn't place it.

"Max, it's me," it went on gently. "It's Marietta."

He turned to look at her. "Marietta," he said. He rubbed a hand over his face. "I suppose you're going to tell me you can't marry me now."

She stepped back from him, startled, her eyes as blue as the ocean. He wanted to lose himself in them, find the love and peace he knew was there, but he held back.

"It's ironic, isn't it? My father will want to reinstate me as the heir to the dukedom of Barwon, and all that goes with it—I'll be one of the richest men in England—and you don't want me."

He was not himself, Marietta could see that. She did not blame him for being angry and hurt after what he had just witnessed; he must be wondering if he could trust anyone ever again. But Max had nearly died tonight; Marietta had nearly lost him forever. That tended to put things like soiled reputations and scandals into perspective.

"I want to marry you, Max. I love you. I can be a duchess if you want me to be, in fact I think I would make an extremely good duchess."

Was that a smile in his eyes? But it was gone as quickly as it came. He looked bruised. "But there's more, isn't there?" he asked bleakly.

"Yes, there's more. I was about to explain to you at Vauxhall Gardens, when we were interrupted by Slipper."

"Marietta," he groaned, "will you just tell me."

"Aphrodite and my father plan to leave me the club. Not now, of course, but later on, when Aphrodite can no longer run it. They've said they want me to have it and, Max, I think I would like that very much. But I can see you may not approve of your wife being the owner of a place like that, and I'll understand if—"

Max frowned. "What nonsense is this?"

Marietta was trembling.

He stood up. And then he said, loudly, so there could be no mistake, "I love you. If I have to be a duke, then the least you can do is make it bearable by being my duchess. And as for the club, I don't give a damn. Do what you like. Open half a dozen."

He meant it; he really didn't care about anything except having Marietta as his wife.

She began to cry, and then she clung to his neck and kissed him, and he kissed her back.

"I thought he was going to shoot you," she sobbed. "I thought I would lose you, Max, oh Max, I love you so."

"I thought I was going to lose you," he retorted hoarsely. "Don't ever play the heroine again."

And then they just held each other, finding comfort in their love, and grateful that despite all of the bad things that had happened they still had each other. And that was the best thing of all.

Epilogue

One year later in Cornwall . . .

Blackwood wasn't as grim as Max had threatened, although it was certainly no Valland House. Marietta found its isolation rather exciting, especially at night, like now, with the sky ablaze with stars and the sea breaking gently against the sand. They had been married for ten months and every day was wonderful, but it was no easy matter being the wife of a man in Max's position. She had duties to perform and tasks to oversee, and hundreds of underlings who looked to her for guidance.

Exhausting.

Which was why it was so nice to be here, at Blackwood, alone together. Well, almost.

Marietta grimaced as she picked her way down the cliff path that led to the cove and its white sand. Max had been very diligent, checking over the details of the running of the old mine he had reopened.

The people in the village had applauded him, actually cheered and clapped as their coach passed through, on the way to the house. Marietta had not realized until then how much the mine meant to them, and how desperate they were for the employment Max had given them.

He was a hero.

But even heroes need to enjoy themselves, and Marietta had something she wanted to tell him, so she'd left a note on his desk, where he could not help but see it.

The duke had reinstated Max as his heir and publicly apologized. Max had not forgiven him yet, not completely, but Marietta had seen signs of him weakening. Whatever the duke had done in the past, he was Max's father after all, and despite herself, she had felt almost sorry for him. Sensing it Barwon had begun to turn to her more and more—they dealt quite well together these days. But Max had warned her not to take sides against her husband, and proceeded to show her what she would be missing if she did. Very pleasurably.

Harold and Susannah were gone, although there were letters. Max had insisted that the duke return Susannah's property to her, and although it was far too late and far too little, at least it went some small way to balancing the ledger. Susannah seemed not to remember what she had done and why, and Harold spent his days making her happy. Marietta wanted to be angry, and she was, for Max's sake, but she pitied them, too. At least, she told herself, they had each other.

Lady Greentree and Mr. Jardine were very coy of

late, but Marietta was beginning to believe they might find their happy ending. As for Lil and Ian Keith . . . matters had cooled between them. Lil would not discuss it, but Marietta hoped that whatever impediment lay between them would eventually be resolved.

Love conquered all. Didn't it?

The night was warm, and a salty breeze stirred the sea. It was calm, hardly any waves at all, and Marietta smiled as she reached the sand at last. She glanced back then and saw him following, his dark shadow against the moon. She begun to remove her robe as she walked, letting it fall to the sand. The air was cool against her skin.

She heard his steps quicken, drawing closer.

"Marietta?" he sounded as if he needed to swallow.

"You've been neglecting me," she said gently, walking naked toward the waves, her golden hair rippling down her back and brushing the curve of her bottom and thighs.

He cursed, and when she glanced over her shoulder, saw that he was hastily removing his own clothing. With a smile she began to wade into the water, shivering a little.

His arms came around her, his hands cupping her breasts, his mouth hot against her cheek. "My darling courtesan," he murmured. "Have I really been neglecting you, Madame Coeur?"

"A little. I just wanted you to myself for an hour or two. It's impossible at Valland House, and even in London there's always something to do or someone to see."

"Ah, the hectic life of a budding duchess."

He turned her in his arms, letting the waves wash over their legs, content for a moment to hold her naked body against his.

"Are you sorry you married me after all?" he asked her at last.

Marietta reached up to kiss his mouth, her hands stroking the hard flesh of his chest, and smiled into his eyes. "No, never. Every moment is wonderful."

Max grinned back at her. "My scandalous wife."

"Very scandalous," she whispered.

He dipped his head to kiss her breasts, eagerly, his hands sliding down her back to cup her bottom and lift her, so that when he bent his knees slightly, and parted her thighs, he could enter her and be where he longed to be.

Marietta gasped and arched her throat, gazing up at the night sky. The stars shone down on them, their reflection dancing in the wash of the waves. The pleasure built as gently, peaking and then slipping away to leave them basking in its glow.

When they were dressed again, Max carried her in his arms across the sand, back toward the house on the cliff.

"I have something to tell you," Marietta said, nuzzling against his throat, enjoying the scent of him.

"You're not opening a bordello?"

She smiled against his skin. "No, I'm having your baby."

He stopped and looked down into her eyes, and the joy and elation in his face brought her to tears. And then he began to walk again, his arms tightening about her, as if she was the most precious thing in the world.

Great stories, hot heroes, and a whole lot of seduction are coming this November from

Avon Romance...

This Rake of Mine by Elizabeth Boyle

An Avon Romantic Treasure

Miranda wants nothing to do with the scoundrel who caused her ruin years ago, but the students of Miss Emery's Establishment for the Education of Genteel Young Ladies, where she is a teacher, are all atwitter at the attraction that crackles between them. So the girls come up with a plan to get them together, and Miranda and Jack don't stand a chance . . .

The Boy Next Door by Meg Cabot

An Avon Contemporary Romance

Melissa Fuller is bored by her life. But then all sorts of strange things start happening when the lady next door is a victim of a suspicious robbery/attempted homicide. This young woman is determined to unmask the criminal. And most interesting of all is the man who comes to "house sit" while his aunt is in the hospital. Could she have found a boyfriend next door?

Keeping Kate by Sarah Gabriel

An Avon Romance

When Captain Alec Fraser takes custody of a beautiful lady spy, the handsome Highland officer must discover information that only she knows—and refuses to reveal. With secrets of his own to protect, Alec never expects the stunning, stubborn girl to cause him so much trouble—nor does he expect to open his closed heart ever again.

Gypsy Lover by Edith Layton

An Avon Romance

As the poor relation to a wealthy family, Meg Shaw is obliged to be a governess companion to their daughter. But when her charge runs away, she embarks on a search of her own to find the missing heiress and clear her good name. Little does she expect that her path will cross Daffyd Reynard, a wealthy and dashing gentleman with the wild spirit—and heart—of a gypsy . . .

REL 1005

Avon Romances
the best in exceptional authors and unforgettable novels!

as if she knew better. It was Maeve who answered, "He'll be gob-smacked," she said bluntly.

Marietta raised an eyebrow. "Gob-smacked?"

"You'll take his breath away," Elena explained.

Marietta thought about that. "I can't imagine it. He'll probably give me one of his looks, as if he's the duke and I'm his slave girl . . . *What* are you doing?"

This last was addressed to Elena's assistant, who was kneeling at her feet, adjusting the hem of her trousers.

"Elena says they're too long," the woman said in a voice very like her mistress. "I'm to take them up an inch so that the gentleman can get a good look at your ankles."

Marietta felt like resting her foot on the woman's chest and giving her a hard push. She controlled herself. If Aphrodite heard she was being difficult then she might refuse to help her any more and her dreams would be quashed. So she smiled and nodded and waited passively while they finished. But in her heart she was dismayed that she had to pretend to be something other than herself.

"He will be here soon," Maeve called out in warning, as Elena dabbed jasmine scented oil in places Marietta had never thought of. The time had flown— when Marietta glanced at the window she realized that it was growing dark.

"Am I ready?" She looked wildly around at them. Suddenly, instead of being a cross she had to bear, this little group of women had become a crutch she needed. She knew that her near-nakedness under the thin silken covering was making her feel vulnerable. Safety was in her voluminous skirts and petticoats, with the buttons to her throat, and the sleeves tight to her wrists. The stays, chemises, drawers, and sometimes, at Greentree Manor, the warm flannel against her skin, had been a form of armor.

Now, she may as well be naked, she decided miserably.

"Miss Marietta?" It was Elena, and her face was no longer unfriendly—there was even a hint of kindness in her eyes. "You can be whatever you want to be. Remember that. The choice is entirely yours."

While Marietta was still trying to work out exactly what she meant, Maeve took her hand and led her toward the door. "It'll be all right, you'll see, Miss Marietta. Now come upstairs. Madame's put you and your gentleman in the Cupid Room." She gave Marietta a conspiratorial wink. "Just wait until you see it."

Chapter 12

The room was beautiful.

Marietta swirled on her bare feet, head tilted back as she gazed up at the painted ceiling. The artist had made a blue sky awash with angels; they swooped and dived, their draperies tangled about their limbs, displaying daring amounts of flesh. Darting among the angels were cupids, small round creatures with wicked smiles, their bows and arrows aimed downwards, toward the occupants of the Cupid Room.

"It is an homage to love." Aphrodite had come upon them quietly.

Marietta turned to face her, and her mother smiled at the bedazzled expression on her face.

"I do not think you will find it difficult in this room, *mon petit puce*, to play at being a courtesan. Think of this as your stage; you have only to act your part."

Perhaps Marietta did understand what she meant,

and Elena, too. They wanted her to let go of her doubts and restrictions, all the things she had learned since she was a child, all the rules she had followed since she was a girl—well, most of the time. Let them go and be herself. Except that Marietta was having difficulty knowing who that was.

Her gaze slipped past her mother, moving over plum velvet curtains and upholstery, and the pièce de résistance, the four-poster bed swathed in apricot satin and weighed down with cushions. Feelings of uncertainty swamped her. Could she make Max forget he was a gentleman who didn't want her to be a courtesan, even for a few moments? And could she forget she had been brought up a lady and she was edging dangerously closer to falling in love with him?

Aphrodite must have sensed her change of mood. "Maeve." She did not take her eyes off Marietta. "Go and dress. You are required in the salon."

Maeve left them alone, shooting an encouraging smile at Marietta as the door closed behind her.

"You have doubts?" Aphrodite spoke quietly.

She shook her head automatically. "No! That is . . . I do not doubt what I want to do, only my ability to do it."

"You do not find Max attractive?"

"Yes, I do." Max was like a storm, ready to pound her into compliance. And she must do everything in her power to stop him.

"You must not underestimate him, Marietta. He is a proper man, do you understand?"

"I-I think so."

"Now, do not fret." Aphrodite rested a cool hand on her shoulder. "You will see. Everything will sort